THE AFTER WAR

BRANDON ZENNER

Library of Congress Control Number: 2017909598

ISBN-13: 978-0692907627
ISBN-10: 0692907629

Dedicated to Bernard 'Opa' Zenner,
A true artist in every definition.

Also dedicated to my best friend and running partner, Wyatt.
Our countless miles together helped clear my mind and sort out the more difficult chapters.
Yes … Wyatt is my dog.

Part I

To Alice

Chapter 1
Brian and Steve

Brian Rhodes cracked open the solid steel trapdoor of the bunker, using his shoulder to carry its weight as he stepped up to the next rung of the ladder. A rush of warm, dusty air sucked down the entry chute, pulled in like a vacuum from the plank-board shed built to conceal the shelter door and the two men who had been hiding below ground. Brian kept his pistol at eye level as the metal door creaked, and a horizontal slit of light—real sunlight—hit his eyes for the first time in over two years.

Adrenaline and fear pumped in his chest, distracting him from that first breath of fresh air. The loose wooden floor of the shed lifted as the trapdoor opened and fell off to the side, disturbing the settled dust that covered everything in that tiny room. Particle clouds rose, the motes illuminated in the strips of sunlight shining through the slats of the wooden walls. Brian stifled back a sneeze.

At the bottom of the landing, Brian's cousin Steven Driscoll stared upward, gripping the sides of the ladder.

"What's up there, Bri—"

Brian hushed him with a shake of his open palm and continued up the ladder until he was standing outside. Carefully, he rested the heavy trapdoor against the far wall of the shed.

Brian looked down the entry chute to Steven at the bottom. He knew that five minutes ago, the only thought going through Steven's mind had been the complete and utter fear of facing whatever unknown nature of humanity might remain outside that bunker door. Now his cousin looked panicked as the filtered light reflected the sheen of sweat on his forehead, his body tensed, as if the all-encompassing blackness in that room was squeezing him toward the exit. Steven's eyes darted over his shoulder in the direction of the one piece of equipment they had not shut down entirely—the walk-in freezer. The red, glowing light from the switch illuminated the far wall. Steven seemed frozen, transfixed.

Not the time to be thinking about what's in there, Brian thought.

Steven shuddered and turned to the ladder. He was halfway up when Brian hissed down to him.

"The gear, Steve. Pass the gear."

Steven jumped to the landing and hefted the first, and then the second military-issue backpack up the passageway to Brian's waiting hands. The large backpacks barely fit through the narrow opening with all the detachable pouches filled to the brim and the secondary detachable scout backpacks stuffed with the essentials.

The blackness of the bunker crept over Steven's hands as he shoved the packs through the circular opening, briefly cutting off the sunlight from the outside. Brian saw that look in his cousin's shadowy eyes, as if the darkness was seeping into his body and being filtered into his lungs from the air he breathed.

Brian was still heaving the second dark green backpack from the opening as Steven hurried to the mouth of the ladder, his broad shoulders and chest pinched momentarily at the narrow, circular entrance before pulling himself free.

Steven's eyes were darting about the walls of the shed like those of a caged animal. For a moment, they were both silent, listening to the wind outside and the occasional chatter of birds far overhead. They pressed their faces to the cracks between the plank walls, blinking their eyes at the outside world, but all they could see were slivers of the vast fields beyond.

"All right then," Brian whispered. "You keep lookout. I'll cover the hatch."

Steven swallowed and nodded.

Brian closed the metal door and turned the circular locking handle on the top. He grabbed a rusted length of chain hanging on the far wall among other rusted tools, wrapped it through the handle and an eye-loop bolt, and padlocked it shut. He placed the floorboards back in position, covering the stenciled diagram of an octopus that was etched into the top of the hatch door. A hammer and box of nails sat on the workbench where he had left them all that time ago.

A silky sheen of dust had settled over the handle, and when Brian brought the hammer down, the noise made Steven jolt. He turned to Brian. "Can't you do that any quieter?"

Brian didn't look up. His cousin was dumber than the box of nails rattling beside him as he hammered away. "What you seeing out there?"

"Ain't nothing to see." Steven turned back to the slat in the wall, and Brian continued hammering until the floorboards were secure.

When he'd hammered the last nail, Brian stood and dusted off his knees. "Give me a hand here." He walked to the end of the workbench and took hold of the far corner. Steven grabbed the other end, and they carried the cumbersome piece of furniture over the hollow floorboards. Not that they had any desire to ever go back down into that underground room, but the sanctity of that place had to remain a secret … just in case. Plenty of food and water still remained in the storage room, and for all they knew, the outside world was nothing more than a burnt-out shell—the rivers dry, the soil infertile, and humanity wiped from the pages of existence like wet ink smeared over by a thumb.

They hoped and prayed that that was not the case. Not entirely, at least.

"You ready?" Brian asked.

"Hell, no."

They grabbed their packs and hefted them over their shoulders, feeling the weight pull at them. Steven had his Winchester shotgun—passed down from his father—attached to the webbing of his pack, and Brian had his scoped hunting rifle attached to the webbing on his own pack. Both of these weapons had wooden stocks and were the only weapons in their inventory that were not jet-black and designed for warfare. They each carried identical assault rifles on tactical shoulder slings, and each also holstered a pistol. Spare magazines and ammunition for these weapons were stuffed in pouches and attached to their belts and gear. Most of their equipment was military issue and had never been fired.

Only moments ago, as they readied themselves to depart the bunker, they had traded in their well-worn jeans and flannel shirts for olive-drab jumpsuits, shin-high black boots, elbow and kneepads, and tactical vests. Brian thought the seams on Steven's jumpsuit were going to bust as he watched his cousin wrest it over his burly chest, his bear-paw hands fumbling with the zipper. Brian's own jumpsuit felt snug, but he was nowhere near his cousin in stature.

They were late leaving the bunker. The date on the calendar came and went. Brian had crossed it off with the big black marker and then both men just stood and stared at it.

"We gotta get moving," Brian had said.

Steven nodded, and then added, "We ain't ready."

As time passed, it had become obvious they would never be truly ready to leave their lavish bunker. Despite spending two years underground and feeling on the verge of insanity, their bunker had carpeting and fluorescent lighting, separate bedrooms with real beds, and a TV with a video game system. The kitchen and living room were at the very center of the bunker in a domed room with cylindrical arms reaching out in separate directions—like the octopus logo on the trapdoor—to the various bedrooms, generator area, and storage.

As far as underground shelters went, theirs was indeed luxurious. All the same, Brian and Steven had not seen the light of day for more than a fraction of a second—that one time they *had* to open the hatch door. It was time to come out of hibernation to face the road ahead, and complete the task they had promised their Uncle Al they would take care of.

They crouched by the shed door, assault rifles armed and ready. They were clean in their new army jumpsuits, freshly shaven with rough-looking red faces, their hair trimmed short. Steven's dark-blond hair was already plastered to his forehead with sweat.

Brian turned the handle of the door and pushed. The flimsy plywood bent in the middle, stuck at the bottom.

"It's the vines there," Steven said, pointing to the weeds protruding through the wooden slats. It took several shoves, along with a few hacks with Brian's combat knife, until the door swung open.

The rush of air that hit their faces was laden with a southern dampness, smelling of wildflowers and the live oak trees covered in dangling moss that grew all over the property. Brian looked to the sky for the sun he so longed to see and feel, but the expansive heavens were overcast with rolling gray clouds.

They stood in the middle of a vast plain. In the distance was Steven's house, where Brian had lived with his cousin for many years. An old plantation home, it had been passed down from generation to generation, until it was handed over to Steven. The luster and charm it once radiated was lost after the death of Steven's parents, when he took up residence and failed to maintain the responsibilities of homeownership.

The house looked dark and cold on the horizon, a whispery building lost among the weeds and gray sky.

Brian turned to see the longing in Steven's eyes. "I know what you're thinking," he said. "We ain't going."

Steven stared at the house—his house. The large picture window facing the valley was gone. Even from his distance, Brian could see the gentle inward and outward flutter of a large black tarp, perhaps a garbage bag, constructed to cover the window opening. There was a mound of something on the back porch that looked charred. This was not how they had left it.

Steven had that look that Brian knew so well. He was seeing red, but fear and uncertainty kept his anger from boiling over. Maybe all that time spent in solitude had given Steven the ability to control his anger, quell the tide of rage that so easily overtook him. Brian wasn't so sure. How many fights had Brian pulled Steven away from throughout their lives, only moments before his cousin killed the other person? Brian couldn't even guess. Once Steven would calm down, he'd go on to explain, "I just see red. All I see is red, and I can't—I don't think."

If he makes a charge for the house, Brian thought, *I can't stop him.*

Steven spat in the windswept grass. "I know we ain't going. I don't wanna go."

"Let's get on then."

Brian patted his breast pocket, a final check for the folded weatherproof map. The route east was marked with a permanent felt-tipped marker. It was the route Uncle Al had traced for them over two years ago. Steven had a similar map folded in the breast pocket of his tactical vest, and he took it out and looked it over. Brian doubted his cousin could discern much from the lines and colors—he had once got lost walking to a bar one town over.

The two men stood up from their crouching position in the tall grass, turned from their old house, and began their trek into the unknown.

Chapter 2
Simon Kalispell

Simon's qi was all out of whack.

It was time to go. It was time to leave the cabin.

But the fear of leaving the safety and security of the wilderness was a difficult obstacle to overcome. Although, due to recent events, the safety and security of the cabin was not as assuring as it once had been. The perimeter had been breached, and Simon was now *sure* that he was not the last person left alive in the world. Two years of absolute seclusion, deep in the woods of British Columbia, had made young Simon Kalispell believe all sorts of things.

He paced back and forth between the cabin and the van, his eyes darting this way and that, looking for things he might have forgotten to pack. He had been doing this, pacing back and forth, for over an hour, and the van was as packed as it was going to get.

"Winston! Winston, where the hell are you?" He clapped his hands and whistled. "Winston, you idiot. Come on, boy!" Then he remembered he'd put his dog in the passenger seat of the van ten minutes ago. He turned to see the half-Shepherd mix peeking his head through the window at hearing his name.

"Oh, right," Simon said.

They stared at each other for a minute. Winston was panting against the window, his brown eyes wide and his tongue drooping over the side of his mouth. When Winston realized Simon didn't actually need anything, he went back to lying down on the passenger seat, leaving the window foggy and smeared.

"Okay, okay … what else do I need?" Simon began pacing again, pawing at his scraggly beard with jittering fingers, and then stopped mid-step. He closed his eyes and took a deep breath.

Christ, I'm all out of whack.

He took another deep breath and began repeating his mantra:

I am the wind. I am the rock. I am the tree, and my roots grow deep …

He repeated this to himself over and over, feeling the grass under his feet, the brisk breeze through his beard and long hair. He wanted desperately to go down to the stream, take his clothing off, sit under the moss-covered pine tree—the one with the depression at the base that fit his body so well—and breathe and focus. It had been ages since he'd felt this sort of anxiety, this fear and panic, and it felt awful. He did not want to get into that van and turn the key. He did not want to leave the glory of nature behind and face the certain horrible realities of the world.

But he had to leave. Especially after last night.

The woods had told him it was time to go.

He had to listen.

Simon took two long and slow breaths, feeling the cool air touch his nostrils as he inhaled. His lungs expanded down to the pit of his stomach, and he held his breath to absorb every molecule of fresh oxygen. Then he exhaled in a whisper, feeling the warm air pass over his lips to be released back into the endless supply of flowing air all around.

He opened his eyes, walked toward the van, and opened the door for Winston. "Come on, stupid. Out. Let's go."

Winston, with his right ear raised and the left one floppy, looked at Simon with a cocked and furrowed expression that seemed to say, "What? I was sleeping." But the old dog lumbered out of the car as instructed, and stretched his back while yawning. Simon scratched the patch of dark fur next to his ear, and then Winston lumbered off to his usual sunny spot on the grass.

Simon watched him sniff the ground and walk in circles until he settled and twisted into a ball. His big brown eyes closed, and Simon noticed that Winston's fur had lightened over the past few months. His coat was mostly brown, with a lighter patch on his belly, and a few patches of black fur in random spots. Lately, the fur around his mouth and face had become riddled with white and gray.

"We'll leave in an hour. I promise," he called to Winston, who didn't stir.

Simon walked into the woods. He followed the stream until he arrived at his spot—his pine tree—and extended his hand to touch the rough bark, feeling the patches of soft fleshy moss against his palm. He swung his M1A scoped rifle from his shoulder, rested it against the tree, and then unbuckled his belt and coiled his holstered pistol on the ground. Then he removed his flannel jacket and T-shirt, and stood as steady as the trees all around, his body as skinny and hard as a thin birch. Plummets of steam escaped with his breath as he watched the water flow down the narrow stream. He stood tall, hands by his side, palms out, letting the wind from above the water cleanse every inch of his body, rejuvenate his skin, and renew his resolve.

Breathing in, I see the wave come in. Breathing out, I see the wave go out. Breathing in, I see the never-coming-in and the never-going-out of the water as a whole.

A moment passed as he contemplated this mantra, which he'd spent countless hours pondering, and then he bent to the stream. He dipped his hands into the frigid water and splashed handfuls of it over his face and beard. Despite the cold, Simon could feel the coming of spring in the air and water, and that made him all the more reluctant to leave.

Two winters alone, stuck in the cabin—once for almost two weeks straight, trapped inside by the snow—was maddening. He had faith in his ability to hunt and gather edible plants, but it was foolish to believe he could master nature. Controlling the environment was out of his hands.

This last winter was long and harsh, with the snow coming down in an endless supply. When the snow finally broke, and Simon tunneled his way out the bedroom window to the top of the snowdrift that almost entombed the entire cabin, his stockpile of food had been largely diminished. The fresh meat and jerky were down to the last few meals, and there were only a few bags of grain left, along with several boxes of emergency rations.

He caught and killed a small marmot with a snare trap the second day out, skinned and cleaned it, and roasted it whole. He fed Winston the scraps, and the dog devoured the flesh and bones entirely. Winston had been living off a scoop a day of fire-dried vegetable kibble left over from the previous year's harvest, before the winter overtook the garden. The dog's desire for meat had been ravenous.

The cold water on Simon's face reminded him that he was in the present moment, and that it was not wise to stress over what may come in the future, or what might have already passed, no matter how painful or uncertain those thoughts may be. Future events will happen as they unfold, and the past cannot be accounted for.

His reflection in the water stared back at him, distorted with the light rippling. Simon unsheathed his Buck knife and tested the blade against his thumb. It was sharp enough to shave. He grabbed the tuft of his beard in his fist, and gently, without yanking, cut a handful away, dropping the scraggly hair in the water where it drifted out of sight.

When he had gotten his beard as short as possible with the knife, he used a pair of nail scissors to cut the hair down to his skin. He repeated the process with the hair on his head, methodically, until it was as neat as he could make it. When he finished, he washed his face, and the coldness of the water on his vulnerable skin was shocking. Even the air from the slight breeze made his cheeks and neck tingle and sting. His reflection over the moving water looked different. Younger, maybe, although he still looked much older than his mid-twenties. His reflection reminded him of his youth, and that living in the wilderness had a way of making his years on the earth irrelevant.

The face looking back at him was a face he barely recognized.

It was hard to remember what he had been like before fleeing to the woods. He was soft back then, well fed. Living in the wild had reshaped him, made him lean and strong with a sinewy strength.

He leaned his back against the tree and sat with folded legs. He focused on his breathing, but the sensation of the breeze hitting his newly shaven face felt funny, and it was hard to stop touching his tender cheeks. Laughter was hard to suppress, his mind and body fighting the meditation.

This went on for some time until Simon realized that the laughter itself was the meditation he needed. A weight had been lifted off his chest without him even realizing it, and his mind had shed some of the clutter that fear and uncertainty had poisoned it with. He put on his shirt, jacket, and holster, shouldered his rifle, and started toward the van.

"Winston! Come here, dummy. Come on, boy."

Winston poked his head up from his coiled position, stood and stretched his back, and then lumbered toward the van. Simon opened the door, and

Winston jumped in the passenger seat. Simon cracked the window and decided to take one last tour of the cabin just to be sure nothing was left behind. Again, just to be sure—although he was positive nothing was.

The axe was no longer stuck in the large chopping log, which meant it was packed. *Check.* He opened the door to the cabin and looked at the barren living room and kitchen. He already missed the magnificent cast-iron stove in the living room, which kept the cabin warm during the most frigid of nights. As he walked past, he let his fingers glide over the cold metal. How many nights had he warmed his hands before the radiant heat of the thick metal sides?

The first thing Simon had done when he arrived at the cabin over two seasons ago was drag the mattress out of the bedroom and into the living room, across from the cast-iron stove. There was no sense wasting wood to heat both rooms, especially in the dead of winter when trekking outside was dangerous and difficult. Before the winters hit, Simon filled the majority of the bedroom with chopped wood, from floor to ceiling. The remainder of the bedroom he used for food storage, since the room remained significantly colder than the rest of the cabin.

He had pried up several floorboards and dug out the earth below until the hole was large enough to fit the small refrigerator on its back with the doors swinging upward. The cold emanating from the ground did a good job keeping the interior chilled, and animals and insects could not get inside.

During the winter months, he gathered snow from outside the window and packed it around the edges of the refrigerator. The meat inside would freeze and remain fresh for as long as he replenished the snow.

Simon checked the spare room, opened the refrigerator door, checked the pantries in the kitchen, slid open the drawers, but found nothing that he needed.

He removed the stack of photographs he had tucked in the breast pocket of his shirt, and flipped from one to the other. His free hand slowly contracted into a fist, and his heartbeat quickened. He tucked the pictures back in his pocket, buttoned the flap, and walked out of the cabin.

This is it. It's time to go.

The small moving van was the kind used by contractors and construction workers. Words on the side said, *Kalispell Sports*, but the letters were painted over and could only be seen up close.

Simon slid the side door open and took quick inventory. All the food and perishables, including the few boxes of canned goods and meal replacement bars—mostly expired—were all raised several inches off the floor of the van by improvised risers that Simon had made out of logs, sticks, and some bricks he found in a pile behind the cabin. He touched the carpeted floor. It felt dry.

Two fifty-five-gallon steel-drum barrels were tied against the sidewall. The bottom of one barrel was corroded and rusted to the point of near bursting with a fragile bump the size of a golf ball sticking out from the side.

Simon had removed the tarp covering the van several weeks ago when the snow had finally melted, and when he slid the side door open, the pungent vapors of gasoline flooded his nostrils. The smell was so appalling that he gagged and covered his nose with his shirt. Three of the four barrels had corroded, and two of them had cracked at the base, causing gasoline to dribble out during the winter months. Nearly a hundred gallons of fuel had soaked through the carpet and trickled out to the ground.

Seeing the empty barrels frightened Simon to his core.

The reality that he might be stuck in the deep woods of British Columbia, almost three thousand miles from home, without any fuel, scared him more than anything he had yet witnessed. It was the deciding factor on whether or not it was time to go. Seeing the human tracks, only a few hours fresh and just a half-mile outside of camp, was frightening enough. And actually *seeing* people pass in the woods just a week later had been horrifying. Awful-looking people, draped in ragged cloaks, and so rancid that Simon could smell their caked-on gore from where he hid high in a tree. The thought of being truly stranded, with such loathsome wanderers coming about, gave him nightmares.

He rechecked the two remaining barrels. A blanket was folded in a square and duct-taped to the side of the corroded bottom of one of them. It was the best he could do, and he hoped to God that the barrel would hold long enough for him to use the remaining fuel, or transfer it to another barrel. But even if the barrel did hold, two drums of fuel would not be enough to get him home. He would have to do the one thing that he had planned specifically *not* to do—scavenge. But even if he did find fuel, there was a real chance that the gasoline would be spoiled. His own barrels were past expiration, and despite them containing large quantities of stabilizers and the barrels secured airtight—until the recent leak—the fuel could stop powering the engine at any moment.

Simon couldn't let his mind wander to such thoughts. His fuel was still burning, and he would have to take his chances with anything he could find on the road.

The back of the van was packed and secure to the best of Simon's ability. He slid the door closed and went to the driver's side. Winston lifted his head as he entered, and Simon could hear his tail wagging against the seat.

"Good boy, Winston." He scratched the dog behind the ears, and Winston panted and licked at his hand. "I hope you're ready, because I'm not."

Simon dug the keys from the small backpack he kept on the floor below Winston. The backpack was loaded with just enough supplies to survive if he ever had to make a run for it. He called it his "get the hell out of Dodge" bag. He put the key in the ignition. The engine rattled and revved, and after a moment, sputtered to life. Simon watched through the rearview mirror as clouds of dark blue smoke rose from the muffler. To keep the battery charged, Simon made sure to start up the van every few weeks to a month, and never did the engine disappoint. It was a good van.

He continued staring at the rearview mirror, lost in a trance. The smoke rose and dissipated in the air, flooding his memory with visions from when he had first entered that van, departing from home into the unknown: the smoke rising from the brick-lined driveway in that early morning, the frost beginning to melt as it twinkled over the windshield, his father holding his mother in her robe and slippers as she cried into his shoulder. The sun was barely up … and Simon had driven away.

Winston barked, and Simon came back to reality. Five minutes had passed. Simon took a deep breath, feeling the rattling of the motor through the steering wheel, and he shifted into drive.

"Hope you peed before, because you're not getting another chance for a while."

Winston wrinkled his nose and sat up in the seat to stick his panting face out the window. Soon, the van was lurching over the overgrown dirt driveway that would take them to the highway.

Simon had scouted the path earlier that day, cutting back overgrown branches and moving a few large rocks that he did not remember being there when he first arrived. But still, the road was rough, and every bounce made his heart skip a beat. He paid close attention to the damaged barrel in the back, smelling the air for the pungent odor of fresh gasoline, and listening for the sounds of trickling fluid.

The van crawled into the woods. Simon's gaze was drawn to the reflection of the cabin in the side mirror as it became obscured from sight behind trees and brush, until the structure he had called home for the past two years disappeared. It was just as before, only this time, his mother and father were not standing behind him, watching him leave. This time they would be waiting for him to arrive—he knew it in his heart. They just had to be.

With the cabin out of sight, all that remained was the road ahead. When he came to the highway that intersected the long dirt driveway, Simon put the van in park and climbed out. He removed the branches used to cover the entrance and peered out over the sweeping interstate, listening to the wind.

The roadway stretched on for miles in either direction, up and around large and small hills, seemingly endless. Nothing stirred. No movement at all. Sticks, leaves, and branches littered the pavement, and Simon thought it was possible that the road had not been traveled upon since he'd first arrived.

Back in the van, he checked the rounds in his rifle, and then did the same for his Colt .45. He laid the rifle and pistol on the console between the two seats.

Then he put the van in drive, moved forward several feet, and stepped out of the van again to replace the branches covering the entrance to the dirt driveway. He looked back one last time before returning to the idling van.

"This is it, boy—now or never." He looked at Winston. "How about some music before jumping in, hmm?"

On his drive there, Simon was glad to have found an old company cell phone with a collection of music on it, since he had forgotten to bring music himself. The music was classical, which Simon didn't mind. It reminded him of his father. The blaring of horns and the sharp keys of pianos were constantly bellowing through the closed door of his dad's office in the mansion he'd grown up in overlooking the Ridgeline River.

The phone's digital display read *Beethoven: Sonatas & Concertos*. Violin Sonata No. 5 came through the speakers. Simon pushed *Next* until he heard the shrill, telltale violin introduction to Beethoven's Violin Sonata No. 9. He closed his eyes and took in the music like a plant absorbing the sun.

"All right, Winston. Let's go."

The van inched to the edge of the highway, and Simon looked both ways once more. Still, he saw nothing. He realized he had turned on his blinker out of habit, and flicked it off.

"No need for that, Winston," he said and turned left on the highway, traveling eastbound. His hands were trembling on the wheel.

The road before him was long and straight, and thick on either side with rolling hills covered with tall, lush, green pine trees, cedars, junipers, hemlocks, spruce, and firs.

Simon's vision was bright with fear, and his whole body began shaking and sweating as he drove back into the world.

Chapter 3
Nelson

Brian and Steven's path was not the route marked on their map; nevertheless, the men found themselves walking in the woods parallel to Pearl Street, close now to the center of Nelson. The tops of buildings filled the horizon, jutting over the thicket of trees. It was at that moment that Brian and Steven came upon the first corpse they would witness along their journey. Neither man saw it at first, hidden before them in the knee-high grass, until Steven nearly trod upon it.

"Hellfire!" Steven shouted, stumbling back and whipping his rifle around. "Christ almighty."

Brian's grip on his assault rifle tightened, his finger trembling over the trigger. Both men pointed their guns at the shriveled brown corpse as if it might jump forth from its earthen grave.

Ain't this some divination of hell, Brian thought.

But the body did not stir. It did not budge from the soil that had laid claim to its flesh long ago. The hollow eye sockets in the desiccated face stared blankly up from the wall of tall grass; its mouth was stretched wide by the taut flesh dried tight over the skull. Pockets of exposed bone shone white from holes in the leathery skin.

Brian lowered his gun. "It's okay, Steve. He's dead." He looked around. "There's no one here."

Steven lowered his rifle, wiping his palms on his thighs and brushing the sweat from his eyes.

"I said he's dead, Steve—"

"I reckon he's dead, Brian. I *see* he's dead."

"Come on now. We're right at town."

They sidestepped around the corpse and then walked until it was well behind them. If the body was someone they had once known, it was now impossible to determine who that person might have been.

"That won't be the last of them," Brian said. "You better get your head on straight."

Steven opened his mouth to speak, but then shut it again.

They stepped onto the road as the first house emerged from the woods. They walked past it, taking careful notice of the blank windows—as black as the eye sockets of the corpse—and scanned for any sign of movement, like the fluttering of drapes, or the partially covered face of a person peering out from the darkness with a shotgun clenched tight in their hands. Anything.

But there was no movement.

"Think anyone's left?" Steven said, with a crack in his voice.

Brian shrugged. "I know as much as you do."

The yards around the homes, and Pearl Street itself, were spotted with litter and debris of every kind blowing in the gentle breeze. Overgrown tree roots buckled sections of the sidewalk and emerged from cracks in the pavement. They passed the police station bordering the center of town. The cruisers were vacant in the parking lot, and the building was cold and silent.

Nelson was nothing more than a strip of businesses on either side of Pearl Street, which stretched on about a block in length, and began and ended in total wilderness. The men had lived and worked in Nelson their entire lives. Their family had once owned a plantation nearby many, many years ago— back when the community had a name for itself in the farming industry. Nelson was once a picturesque town.

Now, the plantations around Nelson were little more than dilapidated mansions surrounded by overgrown fields, much the same as Steven's home. Nelson served as a reminder of days long gone. Brian's chest felt heavy as they walked the streets, his footfalls cutting through the layer of dust that covered everything, casting the whole town in a drab hue.

The businesses they passed were boarded up with posted signs that read, *Closed. No Trespassing.* and *Take What You Will. Be Safe.*

A few drops of rain began to fall, leaving dark spots on the pavement.

"There's nobody here," Steven said.

Brian didn't answer.

"They're all dead. You reckon they're all dead, Brian?"

"I *reckon* I don't know."

They passed Nelson Pharmacy, Clark's Clothing Supply, and the office of Dr. Morgan Forester, their lifelong physician, whose walls were covered in the same Norman Rockwell paintings that the interior so closely resembled. They sidestepped several piles of broken glass left on the sidewalk before some of the businesses, until they found themselves standing in front of Hendricks Bar and Grill. The front window was boarded up, and a sign was nailed to the front, scrawled in familiar handwriting, *Retired. Be Safe and God Bless.*

The sign was unmistakable, written by the meticulous and fragile hand of Nancy Hendricks. Brian had insisted she nail it up before they all turned their backs on Nelson and went their separate ways.

The glass panel on the door was shattered, and the frame hung open on its hinges. Beyond the broken glass was nothing but pure darkness. The small thirteen-stool bar and four-table restaurant was invisible as they peered inside. Steven stepped forward.

"Don't, Steve." Brian shook his head. "Just don't."

"We gotta go in, Brian. We can't leave without knowing."

"There's nothing to know. They're not in there. You're fixin' yourself for disappointment."

"Maybe they left a note?"

"There's no note."

They stood motionless for some time. The building was more than just a bar to them, and it was more than just a job they had once worked. It was the bar owned and operated by their beloved Nancy and Ben Hendricks. The elderly couple had practically been family—practically parents—to Brian and Steven.

Brian found his flashlight and aimed the beam of light through the gloom. They looked at the weathered sign above the building, each man lost in thought. Years of their lives had been spent working behind the worn wooden bar and sweating over the grill in the back. But mostly, Brian was lost in reflection over Nancy and Ben.

He saw the old man's denture-filled smile, and the way his upper back had begun to curve as his years progressed. He saw the clear, loving eyes of Nancy. Nancy with her small, fragile hands—the same hands that had painted the sign on the front window with precise and delicate lettering. Those tiny hands held more power over Brian and Steven than a bar full of brawling ironworkers. A slight touch of her warm fingers on Steven's shoulder could snap him out of his "seeing red" moments. A gentle rub on Brian's arm after a long day at the bar put his mind at rest.

Steven shook his head. "They should have come down with us. We should've forced them."

"It was their choice. They didn't want to live their remaining years underground. We did all we could."

"We should have forced them. And Stanley too. He should have come down with us."

"Steve," Brian said, "you gotta get Stanley out of your head. We've been over this a million times. He couldn't abandon the town back then, he was the deputy."

"He was our best friend. We could have saved him, we could have done more."

"He was a cop. He was needed. Come on now, we can't keep talking this over. It was their decision, all of them."

"I'm going to Nancy and Ben's house." Steven started marching down the sidewalk, going north on Pearl Street.

"Steve, wait. You know what you're gonna find if you go there. Don't do this to yourself. We gotta get on. There's nothing left for us in Nelson. This ain't our home any more. Just think of Bethany; she's been looking at the calendar same as us, she knows we're late. She's panicking for sure."

Steven stopped in his tracks, gazing down the road.

Brian continued, "Remember what Uncle Al said? We have to keep course; we can't be led astray; we can't get off-kilter."

Steven's Uncle Al had laid out a very careful plot of direction for them and warned against burning through what little resources they had. Side trips were an unnecessary danger. Uncle Al, or rather, Lieutenant General Albert Driscoll, had done everything in his power to secure the safety of the two men, along with Steven's sister, Bethany, who lived in Aurora, well over half the distance between Nelson and their destination on the East Coast. Far, far away.

Uncle Al went to great lengths to build them the underground bunker using government funds—quite illegally. But when the cousins asked him about it, he said, in his faded southern accent, "It doesn't matter, boys. In a few months' time, money won't mean a thing. Neither will the United States Government, for that matter. Might as well spend what you got now while you still can and while there are still supplies left to buy. Soon, you'll be hard-up to find even one bottle of water."

Those words had made Brian and Steven quiet.

Everyone knew that war was inevitable and that it was going to involve the bulk of the world, but Uncle Al was privy to information that was kept hidden from the majority of the population. He knew about *the disease*.

Brian and Steven could only imagine the chaos that must have gone on in the big cities like Chicago and New York, where there were far too many people and nowhere for them to hide. Brian had been to New York once, and it was hard to fathom *anyone* leaving that mess of a city in a time of crisis, unless they got out early—way, way early.

So, Uncle Al gave Brian and Steven clear objectives. "You stay in that bunker, come hell or high water, and you don't open the door for nobody. When you get to the date marked on your calendar, you leave. You get Bethany and her husband George, and you boys bring them here." He pointed to an area circled on the map. "I'll be waiting for you. I know how strong you boys are, but you'll have to muster all of your strength. Do not veer from the plan. Do not stray from the marked path. Stay strong, and keep your minds sharp."

Steven stood now on Pearl Street, lost in thought. Then he turned around and marched past Brian on the sidewalk. "I don't want to go to their house anyway. Let's get on."

Brian stood where he was. "Okay. But you were heading in the right direction. We can pick up the trail north of Nelson."

Steven turned back around without missing a step. He glanced crosswise at Brian as he passed.

Brian looked over his shoulder at the bar. They were leaving Nelson, probably forever. Brain had been outside of town several times, but the trips were short, and he always knew he would be returning. The farthest he'd ever gotten was New York that one time, and to Florida and South Carolina making deliveries back when he worked at old Frank Meyer's farm. But he had always returned. He couldn't imagine what his cousin was thinking. The man had only ever ventured to the few neighboring towns, and never any farther.

Brian wanted to tell Steven to take one last look, but he remained quiet. He faced forward, and the men took to the woods as they exited the town.

As if in congruence with Brian's thoughts, Steven shook his head and said, "I don't want to remember Nelson like this."

Brian took a shallow breath. "I don't either."

Chapter 4
Beyond the Broken Glass

The road drove straight and true for miles, then up and over rolling hills and mountains, snaking left and right in large fluid curves. Thick greenery blanketed the earth in every direction, making it easy to feel small and insignificant among the vastness of nature.

Yet it was the immensity that made Simon feel that he was part of something bigger, something important.

He drove fast when he could, slowing at times to pass fallen tree branches, but there were none so large that he had to stop completely. Little human litter was evident—soda cans, clothing, candy bar wrappers—and that made Simon happy. Perhaps he would catch a few nights of peaceful sleep before entering the towns and populated cities, the thought of which caused the fear inside him to spread like dark clouds in a storm.

It was necessary to take deep breaths often and focus his energy on anything positive to combat the darkness. Simon envisioned each breath filling his lungs with clean, white air, and his exhaled breath pushing black smog out through his nostrils. As he focused on his breathing, Simon let his eyes catch trees along the far horizon, or spots of color belonging to flowers on the side of the road, and follow them until they passed by in a blur. The goal was to have his mind stay in a state of perpetual vacancy, yet remain sharp and vigilant—a task he found difficult under the circumstances. His mind longed for the stream by the cabin and the tree that fit his body so well in the crook of its roots. But even these thoughts he tried to push from his mind. Longing for the past only brought about despair.

Simon approached an intersection along the long road, leading to a highway that would bring him southwest into Montana. He approached the intersection with care, remembering the small ranger station he had passed on his way up. The building was tucked to the side of the four-way stop, surrounded by trees and brush. Easy to overlook. He could see the structure now as he crept forward, slower and slower, until he stopped altogether in the middle of the road and looked to his side. A tan building no larger than the one bedroom in his cabin sat nearly swallowed by the overgrowth.

He clicked the stereo off.

There was a pickup truck parked in the gravel lot, and if Simon was correct, that same truck had been parked in that same spot when he passed two years ago. The truck was painted the identical drab, tan color as the office, and both the office and the truck had a logo painted on the side: a white oval with a green border and green lettering. It said *BC PARKS*, with the outline of a crest resembling mountains.

"Well, Winston, we have to start somewhere."

Simon looked all around him and in the side mirrors of the van, but nothing stirred. He turned into the gravel lot before the station and stopped in front of the building to peer at the one and only window facing the road. It was black as night.

"All right, Winston," he said, and let out a breath. "I'll be back. Stay here, boy."

Simon opened the door, grabbed the small backpack from the front seat, holstered the .45, and held the rifle in his hands. He checked the chamber and clicked the safety off. After a deep breath, he began walking toward the station, leaving the car door ajar.

Maybe there's a large gas can in there, and I won't have to stop anywhere else, he thought. *And maybe it will be full of gasoline ...*

Fat chance.

He stepped forward on his toes, the gravel underfoot crunching, making his eardrums vibrate. The gravel and the rumble of the van's engine seemed to be the only two noises in the thicket of wilderness, and they were both terribly loud.

The two wooden steps leading to the front door creaked, and Simon's heart began to race.

There's nothing in there. Go back to the van.

I have to check. I'd rather find a barrel now than have to stop later.

You're not going to find anything now. And you're not going to find anything later …

Simon shook the voices out of his head. Negativity was racing through his veins, and he knew the best thing to do was to realize that fear and apprehension are both outward experiences, and it was entirely possible for his mind to remain peaceful even under the most grueling of circumstances.

My mind is an island. My mind is an island. My mind is an island.

Simon put his face against the window, cupping his hands to block out the sun. The faint outline of a chair was all he could make out. He walked to the door, gripped the handle, and gritted his teeth.

Maybe there's a gas barrel.

And maybe there's a monster ready to tear my fucking head off.

My mind is an island. My mind—

He took a deep breath, turned the handle, and opened the door. Light poured in, so that he could see the entire room. It was vacant. A desk with a phone occupied most of the dusty space, along with three chairs, a sad-looking couch, and a filing cabinet. On one wall hung a stock photograph of a mountain from Glacier National Park, with snow capping the peak and the skies a vibrant blue.

Simon went to the desk and searched each drawer, but all he found were the usual assortment of office supplies. He opened the filing cabinet and flipped through the folders and files on the various trees and wildlife, along with bundles of maps of local roads and trails. He picked up the phone from the cradle, but he knew what to expect. The line was dead.

He left the station, passing Winston, who had lumbered away from the van despite his command to stay. The old dog was relieving himself in the bushes, so Simon didn't mind his disobedience. Winston trotted alongside Simon as he approached the pickup truck.

"There was nothing in the office, buddy."

Winston's tongue bounced out of his mouth, and he looked up adoringly at Simon with big dark eyes. Simon bent and ruffled his head. The dog panted, trying to lick Simon's moving hand.

"That's my good boy, that's my buddy, that's my bud-bud." Simon had an overwhelming longing in his chest to stop everything he was doing and hug his dog tight, let Winston lick his face with abandon. But he kept walking.

Simon peered into the truck, cupping his hands around his eyes.

"Well, would you look at that?" Simon pointed to a mounted gun rack above the seats.

He tried the handle, but it was locked. A few feet away in the gravel yard, Simon found a grapefruit-sized rock.

"Watch out, boy." Winston looked at him with a cocked expression. Simon gave a brief high-pitched whistle and motioned Winston back with his hand. Winston trotted away. Simon steadied the rock in his palm and then he threw it straight through the driver's side window, shattering the glass.

"Ha! Winston, look at what we have here."

He reached in and unlocked the door, looking at a rather clean and well-preserved Winchester twelve-gauge shotgun left attached to the gun rack mounted above the front seats. Simon brushed his fingers over the sleek wood and cold metal, removing it from the rack.

"I can't believe someone just left this here. I can't believe nobody else found it." He cocked back the forend, and the mechanisms all slid like they were supposed to, but there were no shells in the ejection port or chamber. He pressed his finger into the springy entrance of the magazine loading port, but it too was empty.

It then dawned on him that the station itself had been left unlocked, and the truck left out front all alone with a gun mounted inside, clearly visible. It was possible that whoever owned this truck had departed in a different car, and expected to return. It was also possible that the ranger went into the woods and never came back. Either way, the office door should have been locked, and the gun should not have been left in the truck. More importantly, it meant that no one else had come this way in a very long time.

He searched the inside of the truck, but there were no shotgun shells or anything else of use. He flipped the dials and tried the switches on the radio receiver, but it was dead. No lights came on when he flipped the power switch, and no noise came through the speaker when he hit the button on the microphone. He put the microphone down. Who would be listening on the other end? No one.

Back at the van, he put the shotgun on the seat, and grabbed the red five-gallon gas container and plastic tubing.

He siphoned what he could from the truck's tank and took everything back to the van, making two trips to deposit the almost eight gallons of fuel. Winston was in a bush on the edge of the yard, his wrinkled nose pressed deep in the soil.

"Winston! Winston, come on boy!" Simon gave a high-pitched whistle. Winston came running over to the van and jumped to the front seat. Simon got in the driver's side, started the engine, and then paused.

In the far distance, he could hear birds, loud and squawking. The noise cut through the roar of the engine. He put the van in drive, made a wide turn, and was back on the road.

***

Towns along the interstate were few and far between, just dots on a map lost in a sea of green. But Simon could not dodge civilization forever, and he neared the first small town after driving for only a few minutes south toward Montana.

Desolation and carnage preceded the center of the township by several miles, giving evidence to the state of the world. Cars littered the side of the highway, driven straight into the grassy shoulders and abandoned—many with their engine hoods open, and some with the doors left ajar.

The first corpse Simon witnessed sat slumped in the driver's seat of an abandoned Cadillac, left in a cluster of vehicles involved in a collision.

The van came within inches of the automobile as he navigated through the wreckage. Simon could have reached out and touched the leathery face of the corpse as he passed and thought he could even smell the staleness of its dried flesh in the air, thought he could taste it in the back of his throat. The corpse's mouth was agape, the skin stretched tight over the cheekbones. Eyeglasses slid halfway down its face, no longer supported by ears or a nose. The eyes that stared back at him were dark voids. The head of a second body was crammed between the glove box and the splintered windshield, with wisps of long hair still clinging to cracks in the dirty glass.

A cold chill spiked at the base of Simon's skull, like a frozen nail whacked into his nerve column. He gripped the handle of the Colt .45.

Behind the collision, he saw another wrecked car on the side of the road, wrapped around the base of a large tree. That car was a blackened shell of corroded and twisted metal from a long-extinguished fire. The tree was scarred and black, yet patches of healthy bark had started to reclaim the injury. The tree was still alive, but the same could not be said for the driver, who appeared nothing more than smoldered coal and powder. It looked as though a slight gust of wind could dissipate the body into dust.

He drove fast through that nameless town. The few stores and hotels were all boarded up, with nothing disturbed or trampled upon.

At the end of the town, which was only a mile or so long, Simon came upon a gas station. A large wooden board tied to the front of the pump said, *NO GAS* in large painted letters. Cars were lined up before the pump and left where they had run out of fuel. A one-car service station with an attached office was behind the pumps. The glass window in the front was shattered, and the sunlight reflected a million dancing sparkles of light upon the splinters on the sidewalk.

Simon sat in the van with the engine idling. Shadows beyond the broken window played tricks in his mind, and he thought for a moment that he saw a dash of movement. His hands trembled.

"Not this one, Winston. Not this one."

Chapter 5
Dreadful Wind and Rain

It began to drizzle as Brian and Steven neared the perimeter of Nelson. As they crossed the town border, the light rain turned into a steady stream that poured from the sky. The wind carried cold air, thick with precipitation that pierced through the men's clothing. They donned their olive-drab rain ponchos and continued marching onward.

The two remained vigilant and quiet, mindful to spot litter, old campfires, clearings made in the brush, or any recently trampled soil. There were no other people in sight—no signs at all that humanity might still remain. But the woods around Nelson, near the Smoky Mountains, were thick, and few people lived in these parts or knew how to travel the paths. Towns and cities would be another story.

Brian looked up through breaks in the canopy of branches overhead. Somewhere high above, the sun was reclining against the hills, yet the sky remained an endless gray canvas of rolling clouds.

"We should set up camp," he muttered.

"I reckon so."

They found a gap in the overgrowth and strung up their camouflage tarp, tying the ends to trees and staking them into the ground to form a tent. They dug a shallow hole, maybe a foot deep in the soil, and poked a second exhaust tunnel into the side of the pit with a stick. Steven placed kindling and tinder at the bottom as Brian collected a few dry twigs. They set fire to the wood, not letting the flame rise above the floor of the earth, and went about opening two cans of chili.

"Don't take the top completely off," Brian said.

Steven kept his eyes on the can. "How many times we done this? I know what I'm doing."

"Yeah, and how many times you cut the whole damn top off? You won't be able to fish your can out of the fire if the top's not attached and bent. Don't get yourself riled."

"You done got me riled."

Brian looked to the fire.

Steven held a compact military can opener, small enough to fit on a key chain. It was made out of two flimsy pieces of metal on a hinge—one with a hook to catch the rim of the can, and the other with a blade to pierce through the top. The thing was far too small for his hand, and he fumbled with it on the lid, dropping it twice.

"Fucking thing's too small," Steven said, his cheeks reddening. Brian didn't respond. His can was already over the fire.

The top of Steven's can was now punctured in several places, and every time he got the opener going, it slipped again. Sauce was running out from the top and over his fingers. He steadied himself and began twisting and turning the small opener over and over, cutting away. The metal can buckled in the middle, and chili jumped from the opening and splattered over Steven's poncho, speckling his face.

"F—Fuck! Fucking thing! I can't get a grip—"

"Quiet down, for Christ sake. Give it here."

Steven sat on the ground with the can in one hand and the opener in the other, liquid dripping between his fingers.

"Here, take it. Damn thing's too small," Steven said. "It's broke."

"It ain't broke."

"It's broke." He licked the sauce off his fingers and wiped his face.

Brian opened the can, bending the top back to form a hook.

"Here." He passed the can back to his cousin, who placed it over the small flame. He held the opener in his palm. "You want this back?"

"You keep it."

They waited until the liquid was bubbling and producing a constant flow of steam before fishing the cans out with their knives and placing them down on large rocks to cool. It was quiet, with the infrequent patter of rain falling on the tarp.

"Long walk today," Brian said. "How are your legs feeling?"

"They're fine." Steven took a spoonful of chili to his lips, blowing away the plumes of steam. Brian wanted to tell him to wait, that the chili was still too hot, but his cousin was not in a particularly chatty mood. Steven nibbled a bit off the edge of the spoon, then instantly spit it back out. "Jesus, that's hot. God damn."

The sun was low as they finished dinner, and with the last few rays of light, Brian went to his bag, then came back to the small fire with his hand behind his back.

"Here," he said. "I was going to wait till tomorrow, but it'll be better today." He swung his hand around, revealing a Twinkie with a cigarette stuck in the middle. "Happy birthday, brother." He handed his cousin the Twinkie.

Steven chuckled. "Shit, I nearly forgot it was my birthday."

Brian knew he was lying. "Well, I didn't forget. Thirty-one tomorrow. Now, I'm not gonna sing to you, so you go on and eat that cake and smoke that cigarette."

"Ha!" Steven tore the Twinkie in two, offering Brian the smaller half.

"I got the other one here. That one's all yours."

They ate the Twinkies, which were unbelievably good. Sweets, cakes, and the like were not the sort of thing the men had stocked in the shelter. The few desserts they did have, they saved for birthdays and holidays. The same went for the cigarettes. Neither of them had smoked back before the bunker, only occasionally when they were drinking. However, after a few weeks underground with only three cartons of cigarettes between them, they wished to God that they had brought more.

They grew to understand smoking. Huddled around the radio, back when there was still news coming in, sipping at a bottle of bourbon, they would listen to the gore reported over the waves and feverishly chain-smoke cigarettes. They had to stop at the last four packs and ration them out over the course of their seclusion, on holidays and the like. It was the only thing to do those first weeks until the airwaves turned to static and never came back to life. They were now down to the last six remaining cigarettes.

Brian lit one for himself.

"Thank you, Brian," Steven said, as he leaned back on one elbow and closed his eyes.

Brian exhaled a deep cloud of smoke. "Happy birthday, Steve."

"You remember the last time we had a cake? A real cake?"

"Yeah." Brian paused. "Yeah, I reckon I do."

"Nancy made it for your birthday."

"I remember. That was the night we had that talk with them."

Steven shook his head and sat up. "I don't get it. I don't know what they were thinking. They should have listened to us; we should have forced them—"

"No, Steve, it was their own choice. We couldn't have made them do anything they didn't want to do. Forget it now. Let's just enjoy our smokes."

"Yeah, it's just—"

"There's nothin' you can do about it."

"I know. You're right."

They smoked their cigarettes, flicked the butts into the fire, and covered the fire with dirt when the flames had burned low. Steven tossed the empty chili cans far away from their camp and wiped the splattered juices off his poncho with wet leaves.

They unfolded a second tarp on the ground beneath the one strung to the trees and unrolled their sleeping bags. Careful not to drag dirt onto their blankets, they unlaced their mud-caked boots and removed their bulletproof vests before retreating for the night.

The men fell into fitful sleep, waking often at the slightest noise. Their rifles lay by their sides, armed and ready.

***

The morning fog hugged the earth like a wet cotton blanket, startling Steven as he woke, thinking momentarily the fog was smoke creeping over the campsite. The precipitation increased as the day went on, beating at the misty clouds to clear the air in long intervals. By afternoon, the men were soaked as they entered the wasteland that was Stephenson Acre, and proceeded into the heart of the town. A flash of movement ahead halted them in their steps, and the men dropped to their knees behind a dilapidated brick wall.

Steven stared, transfixed, then whispered, "That's a big son of a bitch."

"Shh!" Brian turned sharply to face him with a finger over his lips. Steven turned back, sliding his binoculars from beneath his poncho, and Brian did the same.

The marked path cut through this town, yet they could have gone around it—and maybe they should have. But it would be impossible to avoid towns altogether. Soon, the farther northeast they walked, the less wilderness there would be, and their trek would become almost entirely urban.

Their eyes fixed on a filthy home, which stood out like a rotten tooth in a mouth full of broken teeth. The decrepit beige-brick building was a rectangular two-story structure, a bit taller than the surrounding homes.

From where they crouched, they could see several neon orange signs strung up in the windows, which read *PRIVATE PROPERTY* and *NO TRESPASSING*. Those signs might have been there for years, or maybe they were hung more recently by the group of large black men and the two sickly white men who were idling about the porch steps.

The men had a fire burning in a steel barrel with a makeshift grate stretched over the top. Thick, greasy smoke curled up from an unrecognizable lump of meat smoldering over the flames. The largest of the men used a knife to flip the mass over, and a billow of smoke puffed and twisted into the air.

The large man was wearing a black sleeveless T-shirt despite the coolness of the day, with his massive shoulders extending far out from the armholes, his skin nearly as dark as his shirt. An AK-47 was strapped over his shoulder, and a machete was attached to his belt. The man was talking to the others, who all looked feral, filthy, and wore an assortment of military fatigues and ragged jeans.

As the horde stood about the fire, they picked at the smoldering meat, tearing into the flesh with their hands, and tossing something—bones, perhaps—over their shoulders with reckless abandon. They sucked the juice off their fingertips like hot wings.

Like baby hands, Steven thought. *It looks like they're eating baby hands.*

His mind conjured up horrid images, some real and some imaginary— close-ups of rotten and broken teeth, gnawing and chewing. Blackened, seared flesh torn from the bone. He shook his head, but the images remained. "Let's get the fuck out of here," he whispered.

Brian nodded.

They retraced their steps, crouching low until they were around the corner of a burnt shell of a building and out of sight from the gathering. Corpses were scattered about, looking much the same as the first one they had encountered—brown leathery skin pulled taut over semi-exposed bones, bodies twisted in awful and unnatural positions. Loose strips of decomposed clothing matted over skeletons, melding into the soil.

They passed a corpse in the front yard of a house, a nice house that had probably had a nice lawn and a garden, possibly maintained by that same body that now lay in the knee-high grass. There was another corpse lying on the side of the road, facedown in the crook between the pavement and the curb. Another was sprawled halfway in the doorway of the next home, its legs sticking outward toward them.

Steven saw these bodies and realized that at some point in time, people—whoever was left alive—had given up on burying the dead, and cadavers were left to rot wherever they fell. Bodies scattered the streets and lawns, parks and sidewalks. They littered the earth, mixed with the blown-about roof shingles, tree branches, trash cans, crumpled soda bottles, and all manner of waste that society had discarded.

We're garbage …

The men moved fast out of Stephenson Acre, with their rifles at the ready, cautious of the pockmarked terrain, until they were back in the safety of the woods. Soon their pace slowed.

"What do you think they was eatin' back there?" Steven asked.

"I don't know."

There was a pause as they stepped over a fallen tree, and Brian stopped to check his map and compass.

"You think that's people they're eatin'?"

"I said I don't know. I doubt it. Of course not. Probably birds, mice, or something. It won't do your head any good thinking that way. They're gone now. Let's move on."

They started walking, and the rain that had turned and sullied the air into a patchy mist all morning now began falling in droplets again. Thick clouds of steam rose from the lush mountains in such waves that Steven again thought it might be smoke he was seeing.

The men tightened the drawstrings around the hoods of their ponchos and continued walking in the thickening mud.

Chapter 6
The Huntsman

The security of driving in the van was not as comforting as Simon thought it would be. His senses were dulled with the outside world passing in blazing speeds.

Out in the woods he had been able to hear, see, and even smell the environment all around him. It had been the scurrying of squirrels and the sudden flight of birds that alerted him to the presence of the wanderers who had come lurching out of the woods about a mile or so outside of camp.

Nature acts like concentric rings of disturbance in a pond. When a pebble is thrown in still water, the circles start in the middle and work their way out. The wanderers that day had startled a deer, which in turn startled a rabbit, which then startled a squirrel, which startled a bird, which startled Simon, who startled the ants and spiders in the tree that he scrambled to climb.

In the wilderness, Simon's senses were sharp. The threat of an incoming person would be seen or heard long before that person would see or hear him. That much Simon was sure of. He had tested his abilities many times. He had hunted the primitive way, the way his teacher, Marcus Warden, had taught him. Having tested his ability to stalk and hunt deer, Simon had no doubt that he could evade people out in the wild. The senses of a deer are much keener than those of a human.

Soon after reaching the cabin, Simon had prepared for his first hunt alone, by fasting for twenty-four hours so the scent of food would not emanate from his body. He then spent two hours in the sweat lodge he'd constructed out on the bank of the stream. The frame was built out of large saplings bent to form the rounded top, and a tarp was used for the skin and then covered with large tree branches so that it looked like little more than a slight hill. It was just tall enough for Simon to crawl in and sit. The fire—or hot rocks and water—was directly in the center.

After the sweat, Simon swam in the stream, removing the impurities from his body and making his human scent clean, pure. He used this time to meditate on his life and the impermanence of all things.

Just as the water flows in the river, ever changing, Simon thought, *so do all things—the cells in my body, my positive and negative thoughts and emotions, my life, the life of the animal I am about to take. The only moment in time that is real is this moment, and even that has now become the past. All things, all dharma, they all die and are reborn, just like time. Each passing second is gone forever, and each second in the future is not yet born.*

With clarity of mind, Simon left the water and constructed a fire along the shore. He used a tree branch to beat at the flames, creating thickets of smoke to waft and encompass his body and soak into the pores of his naked skin.

He dressed in shorts and nothing more. When the fire cooled, he removed charcoals from the cinder and rubbed the blackness over his body. He then covered much of his skin with mud from the stream bank and added a few strands of grass and plants to his hair and beard. In the end, he looked just like the brush and trees that were all around. An untrained person would find him difficult to spot, if not for the whiteness of his eyes.

Then Simon left for the hunt, going to the deer runs that snaked all along the stream bank.

He walked with meticulous steps, his foot touching the earth on the ball behind his toes, then slowly dropping from the outside of the foot in, touching down to the heel. The wooden spear he carried was sharpened to a razor point and hardened by fire, and a length of rope was wrapped around his midsection.

The scouting process was long and deliberate. He looked for new tracks, fresh tracks. He needed to find a set that looked slightly off from the others— a small or hurt deer, one that was alone and weaker than the rest. It was difficult to comprehend preying on a weak and unfortunate animal, but he himself was a weak and unfortunate animal—much weaker and more vulnerable than the trained animals of that wilderness. Taking a life was a matter of survival. If Simon did not kill the weak animal himself, the wolves would, or the changing of the seasons from fall to winter.

The scouting process was long, the time lost to Simon in his state of focus, but he found the tracks he was looking for. They were small, and one of the deer's hooves left shallow, off-center prints. The edges of the dirt where the hoof sunk in were still moist to the touch, and Simon followed the tracks for hours. He crawled around thickets of bramble and thorny vines until he came within sight of a small deer, barely visible in the distance.

His heart thumped loud in his chest, awakening him momentarily from his focused state. At this point he was barely human. He was an animal in the wild, and typical human thoughts were not processing as they normally would. His mind had never been as crystal clear as it was at that moment.

A purely instinctual thought process was replacing the calculated and constructed methodology that he typically relied on. A grace he did not know he possessed overtook his motions as he moved from rock to rock, and tree to tree. His body and mind were working faster than he knew possible despite his movements being agile and determined.

When Simon neared the edge of the field, he stopped with his chest pressed against the rough side of an oak. He stood there, just watching the small deer graze for quite some time—hours, maybe. Time had no relevance. It grazed in the field, going from tree to tree, and then walked to a small stream to drink before returning to the field. The animal had a routine, and Simon was learning it.

As the animal grazed, Simon moved in the bush, so slow and so steady that not a twig broke under his bare feet and not a leaf crunched. He moved with the breeze, only when the wind ruffled his surroundings. He made his way behind a wall of land, carved out of the earth by the stream's running water. The deer's path went down a sharp decline from the top of the ridge to the water, and the grass there looked trodden. Simon's shoulder edged close to the decline, just hidden from view from the top of the ridge where the deer was grazing in the field beyond.

The noise of the flowing stream made it hard for Simon to hear the coming of the animal, and he was sweating so profusely that he was afraid that the deer would smell him. But he did not stir; he did not falter. He stayed like stone, his back pressed to the dirt wall, the spear gripped tight in both hands, cocked back and ready to lunge. Every muscle and sinew in his body was rigid, taut and strained, and his mind was clear and moving with incredible speed, carried on the wind and running water.

The deer did not smell him or sense his presence.

It approached, lazily down the earthen ramp, unaware of the danger that lurked behind the bend.

Simon saw the wet nose first and then the side of its head. In a twitch, he sprang forward and plunged the spear deep into the animal's neck.

The animal bucked wild, knocking Simon into the stream, before falling to its side, writhing. In an instant, Simon's animalistic senses evaporated, and he was human again.

His heart was an exploded grenade.

Splashing in the water to get back to his feet, Simon stared in awe at what he had done. He jumped to the dying animal, saw the dark eyes stare up at him as the life within them faded and disappeared. The deer snorted, and then it stopped moving.

Teardrops fell from Simon's eyes onto its fur.

He cried and howled and cursed himself. He cursed the world, cursed humanity, and cursed the fact that he was hungry—so hungry. He tried to remind himself that every piece of meat he'd ever eaten represented an animal that had died in a similar way—a worse way, a tortured and inhumane way, in a slaughterhouse. But at that moment, he did not care. He had not been responsible for those deaths. This death he was. His own hands were stained in its blood, and he had now witnessed death firsthand.

He rose to his feet and constructed a sled out of a few sturdy branches tied together with the rope he had coiled around his torso. Slowly, he carted the animal back to the cabin.

Negativity welled inside him. He could not even look at the dead animal. He did not want to eat the meat, tan the skin with the animal's brain to use for warmth. He did not want to use the bones for glue and tools.

Simon had killed the defenseless creature, and in doing so he felt he had taken a step over the line separating humanity from monsters.

Back at camp, it was getting dark. He heaved the carcass on top of the sturdy butchering table not far from the cabin and went to the stream to wash away the blood, the soot, the mud, and his sins. Tears welled in his eyes as he lowered himself in the ice-cold water, letting the flowing stream and the moonlight wash over him.

As time passed, something happened. A twinge of that animalistic instinct came back, a vast and distant memory of the wildness he was a part of—which all of humanity was a part of, or once had been. Life comes, and it goes. Even his own. The impermanence of all things was everywhere he looked, all around him, in everything that could be seen and touched, and even the things that could not.

At that moment, and forever after, he was no longer the same person he had been before arriving at the cabin. He was no longer the same person he had been only hours previous. Simon Kalispell was the bear, the wolf, and the tiger. He was a predator—a wild animal living in the wilderness, in wild times.

Simon's mind stilled, clean and sharp again, as the waist-deep water flowed around him.

The sky was clear with a million stars, and his body glistened in the thick moonlight as he stood dripping from the water. He prayed in his own way for the sanctity of the animal and his gratitude for the life it had given so that he may live to see another day. Hunger stung at his belly. His stomach was a pit, an empty void. He would eat with relish, like the wild animal that he was.

To this day, after Simon's first primitive hunt, he had accepted death and survival in an entirely new light. It was now something he was a part of, and not just observing.

He was no longer in a survival class, able to go home whenever he wished. Survival was now imperative above everything else. He had to survive. He had promised his mother and father that he would. He'd promised that he would return home, return to them. The wild had made him strong, his abilities extreme. Simon was no longer the boy who had entered the woods; he was a man forever changed by nature.

Chapter 7

Waterlogged

Mud, mud, and more mud. The ground underfoot was loose, and Brian's and Steven's boots sank at times to their ankles and made a *thoop* sound when pulled back out. They had given up wearing the kneepads and elbow pads, as they only made walking more difficult, and somewhere along their journey they'd left them behind. Their tactical vests were worthless under their ponchos, so those too were removed and packed away in their rucksacks.

But Brian and Steven continued on.

The day grew into evening, and the rain was now pouring from the heavens, coming down in sheets to batter the earth and to make the bark on the trees soft. Their entire bodies felt as damp as a frog's skin despite the thick ponchos that covered them down to their ankles.

"Careful here," Brain called to Steven over the roar of thunder, pointing to a rock jutting out of the mud. "It's just pissing down, ain't it?"

Their throats were sore and harsh against the cold wind, and the men took to long periods of silence with their eyes cast to the ground, carefully traversing the muddy earth and feeling the rain beat against the tops of their hoods.

Brian looked to a large fallen tree that lay across their path. The rooted side jutted out of a steep grade, and the leafy top had fallen in a thicket of climbing vines that seemed to go on indefinitely. They walked to the side of the great oak and Brian reached to take hold of the grooves of the bark. His hand slipped, but Steven hoisted him up until he steadied himself on all fours at the top of the fallen side. Brian reached down from the top and extended his hand to Steven.

There was a branch on the opposite side, halfway between their perch and the forest floor. Brian stepped carefully onto the branch and then down to the earth, where his boots were sucked deep into the mud.

Steven steadied himself on top and then stepped down to follow. But as he did, the spongy bark under his foot broke free, and he fell forward. His leg caught the branch on his ankle, and he fell face first into the mud. He caught himself on his left knee and elbow, his body weight pushing them deep into the earth. The large rucksack he wore rode up on the straps, hitting his head and smashing his face deeper into the muck.

"Jesus! You okay?" Brian rushed over to help his cousin.

He grabbed Steven's arm around the bicep and pulled. Steven shot up on his knees, yanking his arm free from Brian's grip. Dirt was plastered to his face.

"Fuck!" Steven screamed. "Jesus, fucking, FUCK!" He spit dark grime from his lips.

He strained to get to his feet, but his knees were still suctioned to the ground, and he fell backward, his back hitting the branch that had tripped him.

Brian saw Steven's eyes—his gaze piercing, his teeth clenched, the filth washing down his cheeks—and said nothing.

"Fuck!" Steven screamed again, and he beat at the earth on either side of him with clenched fists. He used the branch to pull himself up, and when his knee suctioned free from the mud, Brian saw blood trail out from a rip in his pants.

"You okay?"

Steven did not answer.

Thunder crashed in the sky, and the rain fell over their faces in waves.

"You cut your knee? Let me take a look."

Still, Steven did not answer. Brian saw anger and frustration in his eyes, but it was transforming to something else. It was the same look he used to get when they were younger, and Steven was teased and taunted at school because the other students thought he was stupid, or because of the slight lisp and stutter he got when he was angry and could not form words into sentences quick enough. The look always came after the anger, and after the epic beating he would impart on whoever had teased him. It was the look of sadness and the acceptance of reality.

"I'm fine," Steven mumbled. "Le-let's get out of here." His eyes were thick and watery.

Brian felt a spike of cold enter his body from a gust of wind. The dire and instinctual need to be warm and comfortable was overwhelming. Life in the bunker was glorious in comparison to the outside world. There was ping-pong in the bunker, and a weight bench, and enough food to last them both almost another year. Brian knew that the last place on earth Steven Driscoll wanted to be at that moment was where he was—cold, hurt, tired, and miserable.

"Let's take five," Brian said.

Up a ways, they found a large pine tree with swooping branches around its wide base. They parted the branches and crawled into the open, nest-like cavity. They both had to sit slumped over, but there was plenty of space for the two men to lie out, and the inside was relatively dry. The boughs of the tree did a good job shielding away the wind and rain.

The ground was littered with dry pine needles and smelled deeply of the very tree they were using for cover. Steven peeled up his soaked and ripped pant leg, and when he moved his foot, mud pushed out from the top of his boot. A laceration about one inch in length trailed blood from above his kneecap.

"You're lucky," Brian said. "It's not bad."

"*You're* lucky, 'cause it ain't happened to you."

Brian shot his cousin a quick look that implied, *Stop being a pussy.*

"It don't hurt," Steven said.

"No, but it's bleedin' plenty."

Brian pulled a first-aid kit from his pack and rolled Steven's pant leg up higher over his knee. He poured clean water over the wound and then squirted the area with iodine.

Steven's face reddened and his hands clenched the pine needles blanketing the ground.

"Hellfire!" he said through clenched teeth.

"Thought it didn't hurt?"

"Don't be an ass."

Brian covered the wound with gauze and wrapped waterproof tape around the joint. "That should keep it clean. We'll change the bandage later. If you start feeling sick, or if it gets puffy and infected, you start taking antibiotics right away. We don't got much, but you can't wait until a fever sets in."

Steven looked off.

They dug a shallow hole and started a tiny fire with handfuls of the dry pine needles and a few low-hanging dead branches they snapped off from the tree. It was dangerous and stupid to start a fire under a tree, where it was dry with a layer of tinder covering the ground and branches not so far overhead, but the last thing they were concerned about was setting fire to the tree. If the fire got out of control they would just leave. Simple as that. Let it burn. Let the dead world burn to the ground.

The tiny flame did marvelous things for their demeanor. The heat on their puckered fingers brought their hands back to life and sent warmth to their hearts.

It had grown dark outside the safety of the thick branches, and the men unrolled their sleeping bags, curling themselves around the base of the tree. They slept better than they had since leaving the bunker. At first light, Brian started another small fire as they readied themselves, taking turns to pass their battered fingers before the warmth.

Once the fire burned out, Brian said, "We should get on."

The cousins emerged from the dry shelter, their bodies aching, and continued on their path. About a mile into their journey they came upon a circular arraignment of rocks on the ground. The sides of the stones were blackened, and the coals in the center were so absorbed with water that they turned to mush as Brian touched them.

"A few days old," Brian said. "Maybe less."

Steven looked over his shoulders then continued walking out of the clearing. Brian stood and followed.

Chapter 8
Crossroad

Simon forced himself to drive up the dirt driveway in front of the gas station and park next to the service garage. A sign hung from the pump: *No Gas*.

With his rifle in hand, he got out of the van. The desolate interior of the building could be seen through the plate-glass front, and the door had been left ajar. Simon nudged it open and entered.

The shelves on the far wall were empty, and a soda machine sat cold in the corner like something dead, its door agape and its interior void of cans. Scattered papers littered the ground, blown about from an old wooden desk. Simon went to the door behind the register to inspect the one-car garage, but found nothing useful in the various tool cabinets and chests. The important things—oil, wiper fluid, lighter fluid—were nowhere to be seen.

Back outside, he walked across the dusty yard to the pumps. He tried the handles, but as he expected, nothing came out. The smell of vapors was faint.

On the side of the building was a shiny metal trash can, dented from tumbling about in the wind. Simon picked it up and shook out some debris. It was fairly clean inside. There were no visible cuts, holes, or rust, and Simon guessed that it could hold about twenty gallons of gasoline. He put the can in the back of the van, then walked to the passenger side to let Winston out. Winston stretched, sniffed the ground, and then lumbered to the corner of the building to pee. Simon followed and peed alongside him, and when they were done, he found a thick stick in the grass.

"You want this, buddy? You want this?" He held the stick in the air, just out of Winston's reach. The dog's tail went wild, and he panted, the corners of his mouth curling like a smile.

"Go get it!" Simon threw the stick far in the grass field, and Winston took off like a bullet.

***

The border crossing at Scobey was nearly as desolate as when Simon had driven through two years earlier. A number of abandoned cars and trucks lined the entrance leading into British Columbia, but none blocked the lanes traveling into Montana.

The van crept along as he passed the service station window. The same window where, two years ago, he had handed across his passport, along with a bag containing ten thousand dollars, to a guard named Stephen Parks—a man his father had made previous arrangements with. The window was now pitch-black.

Simon thought about stopping to inspect the inside of the building, but decided against it. A few shells for the twelve-gauge would be nice, but the likelihood of finding any was slim. Park offices and police stations were prime targets for looters, and Simon was late to the game. Plus, the shells weren't necessary; he had plenty of ammo for his rifle, and he was a damn good shot with it.

The land ahead of the guard post, in Montana, was just as large and vast as the land he was leaving. Fields and valleys stretched on for miles in every direction.

Simon drove on.

As the sky began to darken he turned off the main highway and drove down a dirt road that looked to go on forever in an endless straight line across the boundless range. When the highway was safely out of view, he parked behind a cluster of trees and made camp for the night.

Dinner consisted of cold jerky, and Winston ate from the kibble of dried meat and vegetables. Simon gathered wood and started a small fire close to the van, placing a flat rock at the edge of the coals to be used as a skillet. The light from the flames made him feel uneasy, exposed. However, the warmth the fire provided was overwhelmingly pleasant. The nights turned cold fast, with winter still in the air. He could see the breath escape from his mouth and evaporate with the smoke and flames.

Winston curled up on a blanket beside him, and Simon put another blanket on top of the old dog, tucking it around his neck. He sat on a log with a deer hide draped over his shoulders and opened a bag of flour made from wheat he'd gathered near his cabin and ground with a mortar and pestle. He mixed a scoop of the flour with a few splashes of water and stirred it until a thick dough formed. Then he began rolling small balls of the batter in his hands, and squashing them between his palms to form patties. The patties sizzled on the flat rock, and within a minute they were scorched and ready to flip. He made a dozen or so of the little cakes, plenty for a few days ahead.

As he ate one of the small, flaky flatbreads, he pondered whether he should sleep in the van as he had originally intended. There was enough room to lay out in his sleeping bag, tucked between the wall and a pallet of goods. But the interior was still pungent with gasoline, and he didn't like the isolated feeling. His awareness of the outside world would be cut off.

So he decided to sleep on the ground under the sky.

As cold as it was, he was warm and toasty inside his two-person sleeping bag. Winston came in to join him, and he stuffed the sides and bottom with blankets and animal furs. The fire died down to a crackle. The sky above was a brilliant array of stars, like the flecking of a million dots of paint on a canvas—only entirely more brilliant and awe-inspiring. Several shooting stars streaked across the sky before Simon closed his eyes.

***

"Gory, gory, what a hell of a way to die! Gory, gory, what a hell of a way to die! Gory, gory, what a hell of a way to die! He ain't gonna jump no more!" Simon was singing to Winston and tapping the steering wheel. Winston stared at him with a cocked expression, occasionally barking and wagging his tail.

"That's it, Winston! Sing along! *Gory, gory* ..."

Despite Simon's constant fear, he saw no signs of life at all. The small towns were few and far between, and avoiding the larger cities had been easy so far. It was simple enough to keep in good spirits and try to ignore—if only temporarily—the situation that he and all of humanity were currently enduring.

However, on the outskirts of a town named Sherrie, the battered road sign reading *Population 750*, Simon drove past several mounds in the earth, each maybe seven feet tall and twenty feet wide. A backhoe sat cold beside a heap of dirt that had been dug up and piled to the side. Whoever started this work had never finished. As Simon approached, it became apparent that the first mound was not dirt at all, but badly decomposed human bodies, piled from head to toe. Skeleton and sinew.

Simon stopped singing.

He drove straight past Sherrie, trying not to look anywhere but the road ahead. In the next town, he witnessed another large stack of bodies, this one in the middle of the town square and burned nearly through by a funerary blaze. Then came more. Some graves complete, others not so much. Piles upon piles of corpses had been left in great heaps, or buried in large holes with clusters of crudely constructed crosses sticking out from the mounds. Many were left in blackened pyres, barely recognizable as having once been something human. Simon wondered how many hundreds—thousands—of mass graves existed off in the fields, far from the roads, never to be seen.

Then he imagined the cities. What did they do with all the corpses where land was scarce? Were whole parks dug up? Did they incinerate the bodies in fires, stacked as tall as buildings? Or were they just left where they fell? Probably all three. He shook the thought out of his head.

As he passed through the towns, he stopped and inspected four additional gas stations with no luck, but he was able to siphon a few gallons of gasoline here and there from a number of abandoned vehicles. At a small stream, he filled the metal trash can with water, and it proved to be watertight. He filled it with siphoned gasoline from the corroded drum, found a lid that roughly fit, and duct-taped the hell out of it. The thought of taking inventory of the fuel was frightening. He knew he needed a lot more, and there was a strong chance that any gasoline he'd find would be spoiled. But all he could do was continue onward and keep searching.

The highway drove straight and true in a southeastern direction, when he passed a sign on the side of the road that read, *Welcome to the Town of Rochelle, Population 220*.

The town was the same as the others—a strip of dismal buildings, boarded up, wiped clean, burned down. Everything gray with dust. Dead.

At the far end of town, about a half mile away from the last building, came the gas station. *CRAIGS,* the sign said, and of course, another sign on the pump read *No Gas*. The front was a flat dirt lot, with tufts of wild sagebrush dotting the terrain. Dust billowed in the wind. A thicket of trees behind the building edged a small section of woods, with wild pinegrass taking advantage of the moist forest floor.

Simon parked in the trees behind the building and left the door open for Winston, who was sleeping, as he gathered his pack and rifle. He walked to the front of the garage. The building was wiped clean, the racks barren of anything other than aged litter.

In the garage, Simon looked from the tool chest to the shelves on the far wall, and something caught his eye. It shone on the floor, under the lowest shelf. He reached under and grabbed a pile of crushed, silver candy wrappers. He dropped them back to the ground and wiped the chocolate from his hand on the oil-spotted cement floor. Bending over, he noticed a rolled bundle of blankets tucked in the back of the shelf. He pulled them out. They were torn and ragged, but not entirely useless. He left the blankets where they were and continued inspecting. There was an assortment of tools back there: an old camping stove—the fuel spent—articles of clothes, and a few jackets in acceptable condition. Then Simon found a small, red gas canister. He swished the fluid inside, watching where it hit against the walls of the container. There was just under a gallon. Farther down the shelf was an assortment of books, a few tattered magazines, and several well-thumbed-through comics, dirty from greasy fingers.

He took the container, along with the books, and left.

The wind was sweeping small clouds of grit from the packed-earth lot as Simon crossed to the gas pumps. The day was warm in the sun, and a layer of sweat was forming under his shirt.

He took the nozzle from the cradle and sniffed. The same stale gasoline fumes as at previous stations stung his nostrils. He put the hose back in the cradle and began walking off when he noticed the lids on the ground where the gasoline was stored in underground tanks. The thought of checking the tanks had never occurred to him, probably because the other station had been lined with cars and trucks, and the lids were never visible. But if there was gasoline down there, and it wasn't coming out of the pump, how would he get it out?

With a rope and bucket, he answered.

The metal covers in the ground were smaller than a regular manhole opening and nearly coated with packed dirt. He placed the books and gas container on the ground and stuck his fingers in the pry-bar holes, but the metal was heavy and there was little room for his fingers to grasp. The rifle slid off his shoulder as he bent to his knees, so he rested it on the ground. Reaching back, he removed his knife from the sheath and slid the blade into the groove, working it back and forth so the embedded dirt broke away. He pressed and pried, and the blade buckled. The knife flew out of his hand, cutting across his pointer and middle finger.

"Son of a bitch!" he shouted.

Then he heard it. A high-pitched voice traveled over the windswept ground.

"D-don't m-m-move, mister," the voice said.

Simon stopped moving. He could feel his blood pumping from the wound.

Chapter 9
A Town on the Horizon

Brian and Steven sat huddled in the crevice of a mountain, barely large enough to shield them from the onslaught of rain. From their vantage point, they had a clear line of sight to the valley bellow, and to the distant range of mountains that encircled the valley.

"Thii-tthhiss is sooome sh-sh-shit," Brian said, his whole body rattling in the wind.

The nonstop crackling of lightning diffused through the expansive evening sky like spiderwebs in the clouds. At times the lightning spread out from behind the mountain range, as if the bolts were rising up from the earth; other times, the lightning came straight down in gigantic columns to the floor below. The thunder that followed bellowed over the valley as if the men were camped in the side of a drum.

It was cold against the damp rock, a cold that crept into their bodies through their spines. A cold that emanated from deep within the mountain, from the core of the rock itself. A thick mist wafted in, covering their bodies and making blankets pointless to use.

If they slept at all—curled up like gargoyles, with their knees tucked into their chests under their ponchos—it was brief. When the sky turned pale, with the sun emerging somewhere behind the clouds, the rain slowed to a light shower, and the lightning stopped altogether. Brian and Steven were happy to stand and stretch their frozen limbs and step out from their rocky crevice. As groggy, miserable, and sore as they were, the storm they had witnessed that night would remain burned in their memories for the rest of their lives, as the most awesome and terrifying display of nature they would ever behold.

Steven stopped short, looking down to the basin far below. "Brian. Brian." He pointed down. "Something's stirring. Look."

Brian squinted. The blanket of trees in the valley moved together in the wind. "I don't see nothing."

"There, by that big rock."

Brian studied the terrain. "Horses."

Steven turned sharply to Brian. "There riders down there?"

"Look wild to me. This was all farmland; probably nothing to it. Come on, let's get on."

The storm had made a mess of the terrain, with fallen trees and flowing floodwater crisscrossing their path. Carefully, they proceeded down the treacherous mountain.

When they reached the bottom, the land leveled out.

Steven coughed, and then snorted mucus back into his throat. "I feel like shit," he said.

"So do I."

"I can't feel my toes."

"I haven't felt mine in days."

They were both sniffling, and Brian's head felt as swollen as the saturated earth beneath their feet.

Steven spat. "I think I'm getting sick."

"I reckon we're both sick."

Brian led the walk, and he sped up when the terrain cleared.

"Should we be taking some medicine?" Steven asked.

"I don't know."

"What? I can't hear you. Slow down."

"I said," Brian stopped dead in his tracks, turning to face his cousin, "I don't *fucking* know. I ain't a doctor. If you want to take some medicine, you go on and take it. You don't need my permission."

"No shit, I don't need your permission. I never asked nothin' from you."

"Good." Brian turned and continued walking. "Then if there's nothing else, let's get the hell out of this shit-valley and this piss-rain."

They didn't speak again for a while.

Brian stole glances of his cousin, whose face looked cold and numb. Steven appeared lost in angry thought, and Brian could only guess the words stirring inside that massive head of his. *No shit, I ain't asking your damn permission. You ain't the boss of me.*

Brian was lost in thought as well, but he was saying to himself, *All we need is fire. Just one night with fire. Please, God almighty, let this rain stop for a few hours. All this water ain't natural.*

With each step they took, the gear on their packs became heavier and heavier, and they were stopping to rest more often. Brian knew he was losing weight fast; he had tightened his belt two holes since leaving the bunker. Steven's face looked thinner, but it was hard to tell if he'd lost any weight with him wearing a poncho all day and night. The last time they built a fire— just a small fire before the rain drove them to cover—they'd removed their shoes and peeled back their wet socks like banana skins. They let their bloody and blistered feet dry near the flames before bandaging them up. That was two days ago, and neither of them had removed their boots since.

"Hey, look at that," Steven said.

"Look at what?"

"That." He pointed to an old, half-disintegrated car tire buried in the mud. "And that over there." A ragged plastic bag was blowing, stuck in the branches of a bush, with a mess of decomposing garbage nearby. "We must be nearing a town. Even more trash up ahead."

"Looks like it," Brian said. He took the map out of his breast pocket, hunching over to shield it from the rain. The laminating film was peeling along the edges, and the paper beneath was wet and puffy. He traced his finger over the paper, leaving a trail of dirty water. "Okay," Brian said. "We should be right … here." He pressed his finger to a spot on the map.

Steven leaned in. "Where?"

"Right here." Brian looked at the land ahead, which rose in degree like a ramp. "There should be a town just over this hill." He looked back to the map, squinting. "Odyssey."

They walked up the earthen trail to where the hill overlooked the town below. They lay on their stomachs under a low-lying tree, looking through their binoculars at the town of Odyssey in the distance. It was a valley town, nestled inside a circling mountain range. From their vantage point they couldn't see much, just a section of buildings before it swept lower into the unseen valley below.

"You see anything?" Steven asked.

Brian scanned back and forth, pausing at each house. "Not a damn thing."

They lay still for a while, not speaking. Neither of them wanted to say it first, but they were both thinking the same thought—they wanted to sleep in a house for the night. Maybe two nights. It went against everything Uncle Al had told them about avoiding cities and towns, and sleeping in parks when civilization could not be avoided. But they were cold and tired and in desperate need of warmth and shelter. They had bandages to change and needed to tend to their feet. And a hot meal would do wonders for their morale.

Brian asked Steven, "What do you think?"

"About what?"

"It'll be dark soon. You want to head on, or find a place here for the night?"

Steven didn't answer.

Brian took Steven's silence as an agreement. He'd noticed that his cousin had been walking funny the past few days. Steven's injured leg was stiff, and he grimaced when climbing over rocks and fallen trees. Brian had asked him several times if he'd been changing the bandage or checking for infection, and Steven would say, "I'm fine," and leave it at that. But being that the only times they'd spent away from each other had been when relieving themselves, Brian knew that Steven had not changed the bandage since it was first applied. His wound was most likely infected and bound to get putrid. Staying indoors for a night was a necessity.

"Let's find a house on the border."

Steven remained quiet, but he stood when Brian got to his feet and he readied his rifle on his shoulder as they began to make their way down the hill. There was a trail still visible going from the edge of the dense woods, and they stuck just outside of the pathway as they entered Odyssey. They passed the first few homes set far out from the rest of town on large parcels of land. When they arrived at the back of a house set on a city block, they walked with their backs to the wall, their feet treading through the knee-high grass. Brian cut across the yard to the next house, using a fence for cover.

Steven scrambled after him and whispered once they were up against the wall. "What's wrong with the houses we passed?"

"Look." Brian pointed to a house set higher than the others on a small hill, just a few buildings away. "We could see the whole town from there, overlooking the valley. It's safer."

"Fuck the rest of the town. Let's just go in this one."

Brian shook his head. "It's right there, Steve."

Brian didn't wait for a response. He ran to the next property, gun up and at the ready. Steven followed, covering the sides. They went from house to house, looking for any sign of movement, but there was nothing to be seen. All Brian heard was the sound of the rain; all he saw was the movement of the grass in the wind.

They neared the house on the hill with its roof taller than the rest. It was a two-story cottage with a small yard surrounded by a white picket fence. The yard was cluttered with garden gnomes, birdbaths, and little signs with phrases like *Home Is Where the Heart Is*.

A crack of thunder made them both jump. Brian looked up into the sky. There were no storm clouds.

They looked at each other and dropped to their knees. The sound hadn't come from the sky. It came from the unseen valley below.

Chapter 10
Two Years Prior: Meet the Kalispells

The sky was a light shade of blue with the coming of morning, and a much younger Simon Kalispell was the only student awake to enjoy it.

He crouched over the ashen campfire, with the circle of sleeping students around him. A small degree of warmth could still be felt against his fingers as he turned the larger chunks of cinder over, emitting faint wisps of smoke. He blew gently and the cinders began to glow. After a light scraping with his knife and a few long and methodical blows of air, smoke began to steadily rise, and bright orange embers radiated. He crumbled a handful of dried straw and leaves in his palm, held them to a glowing ember, and blew into the spark. The bundle of dry tinder fumed, and then came to life with a burst of flame.

Simon added another handful of dried straw, leaves, and birch bark, then placed a few pieces of kindling meticulously over the dancing flames. Once those pieces caught, he added larger pieces, until the fire was burning unaided.

The other six campers were still asleep, or pretending to be asleep so they could stay curled up in their sleeping bags as long as they could. Despite the cool morning, it was shaping up to be a nice spring day, with a brilliant blue sky and only a few white and puffy clouds in sight.

This was the last week of the Advanced Scouting and Tracking class. From here on in, they would no longer be sleeping in sleeping bags at night, or using matches and lighters, or any other conveniences readily found in the outside world. They would be sleeping under debris huts for shelter—small dwelling made out of branches and leaves that were surprisingly warm and protected against the elements—and eating only what they could scavenge or kill.

Simon added a few more sticks to the fire, then stood to look around the campsite. Where was Marcus Warden? This was the first morning that the instructor was not present as the students awoke.

Maybe Marcus was checking the figure-four traps, the snares, and the deadfalls for breakfast? That would be unusual; the students always checked the traps and reset them if need be. It was part of the training. Maybe he'd gone off in the woods to relieve himself?

Simon heard a few of the students rustling about in their sleeping bags and turned to see Frank Peters and Terry Litz sitting up and stretching. They stood and joined Simon by the fire, everyone nodding to each other. As a general rule, there was no talking until the sun was fully up or all the students were awake. The mornings were a spiritual time, and quiet solitude was important.

Terry—or, "The Owl," on account of him spotting a magnificent screech owl their first night of class—was filling three cups with water. He passed over a small pine branch so that they could each make a cup of pine-needle tea. Simon was tearing off a cluster of needles when he heard a noise.

It was distant, an engine of some sort. As the sound grew louder, he could see a vehicle far off in the trees. The other students were now unzipping their sleeping bags and sitting up to face the direction of the disturbance.

No one moved as the birds all about them screeched and sang, and the movement of squirrels and small animals scuttled about in flashes. The car, which they could now see was a Jeep, approached the camp as close as it could before the thicket of trees became too dense. The vehicle came to a stop with the engine idling. The passenger and back doors opened, and two men approached. One was Marcus Warden, only he was wearing a shirt and sneakers—which he never wore in the wild—and his shoulder-length hair was pulled back and looked combed. The other man with Marcus was a ranger, in full uniform and wide-rimmed hat.

Marcus stepped into camp. "Good morning," he said.

The group nodded, and everyone repeated, "Good morning."

His face was blank as he addressed his students, and his eyes were cast to the ground. "I'm very sorry to wake you all." He looked at Simon, who was sitting before the fire. "Simon, can you please come with me for a moment?"

***

Simon remained speechless for the entire ride to the base camp of Marcus Warden's Wilderness Survival School. It was a good school with a great reputation. It taught everyone from park rangers to police, military, and special ops. Simon couldn't believe he was being pulled out of class. And this was the last class—just one more week until graduation.

He expected to see her there, at the school, but she was nowhere to be seen. For the first time since arriving, he put on his shoes and laced them up. His toes felt cramped and his feet were not fully stable on the ground. He said goodbye to Marcus, and they shook hands.

"You're a good student, Simon. I'm sorry we have to cut this short."

"I'm sorry, too."

"You've learned a lot. Just remember to always be aware of your surroundings and listen to your inner voice. Never doubt yourself or your abilities." He pointed to Simon's chest. "Somewhere deep inside, you'll always find the answers that you seek."

"Thank you, Mr. Warden."

"Marcus."

"Marcus."

They parted, and another ranger drove Simon out of the woods to a park station a few miles away.

Simon took his gear from the trunk, thanked the ranger, and walked past the station to the only car parked in the vacant lot.

And there she was, standing beside the limousine.

Simon walked up. "Hello, Mother. It's good to see you."

"Yes, Simon. You look … well."

He knew that he looked filthy. His hands and nails were dark with grime, and his hair was wild.

"I promise I bathed," he said. "Yesterday."

"In a pond?" Her forehead was raised, as if the tightness of her ponytail was pulling her head back.

"Actually, it was a stream. Are you going to tell me what this is all ab—"

She sighed and reached forward to hug him. It took him by surprise, and he didn't hug her back for a moment. She smelled like lilacs, the same as she always smelled since before he could remember. Floral. The animal fur around the neck of her coat tickled his nostrils, and he thought he was going to sneeze.

She said, "I'm sorry you had to leave camp early."

They parted.

"Class, Mother. I was in a class. Not camp."

"Yes, that's what I meant."

"What's the emergency?"

"Let's get in the car. It's freezing out here. Aren't you cold?" She reached out, pulling the collar of Simon's flannel jacket closed, and began buttoning the top button when Simon pulled away. "I'm fine."

She opened the door and Simon got in, tossing his duffel bag on the floor. She sat opposite him, and the car began to move.

"How was class?"

"Good. It *was* good. Just one more week, Mom. Just one more week, and I would have graduated."

"Yes, well …"

Simon doubted she knew how many classes he had already taken, or how long he was gone for. Ever since he'd had that talk with his parents, they had been giving him the cold shoulder. So what if he didn't want to go to college at Princeton or Stanford like his asshole brother Marty? So what if he dropped out of college right before it started, and told his father—who sat across from him behind that huge, pretentious mahogany desk—that he did not want to follow in the family business? Managing the chain of sporting goods stores, buying and selling properties worldwide, and doing whatever it was that the family business did, was not in his deck of cards. His father heard him out and took it well, until Simon told him his true ambition.

"A *park ranger*?" His father had leaned over his desk. "You want to become a park ranger?" He loosened his tie. His father understood numbers and letters, not sticks and stones.

"Y-yes. I think I do."

"You want to give up on the family, turn your back on the business your great-grandfather began when he was just a boy your age, to do what … walk around in the woods? Your great-grandfather started this business so that his family, including you, wouldn't be forced to do exactly that. He started this business so that none of us would ever have to worry about having a roof over our heads or a hot meal in our stomachs. And you want to show him your gratitude by becoming a park ranger?"

"It's more than that, it's …"

But he couldn't explain. He couldn't express the raw happiness he received when he was out in the woods. He couldn't tell his father that every day when he came home from school, he would go over to Alice Springs Park to stalk animals, identify edible plants, and sit upon the twisted roots of his favorite old tree. Like sitting on a throne, he overlooked the Alice Reservoir in deep meditation.

That tree was how it all started. When Simon first saw it bathed in sunlight like it had emerged from some spiritual world, when he stepped out on the steep perch of branches with the water twenty feet below and the pale green leaves nearly transparent against the bright sky, he felt a connection with the earth that he could never put into words. He touched the side of the bark, felt compelled to remove his shoes and feel the roughness on the bottom of his feet.

Sunlight filtered in from overhead, touching his face with warmth. When he looked out over the reservoir, the water shimmered with a million sparkles of reflected light. The realization hit him like a jolt—he was a part of something bigger. A deep happiness that he had never felt before overtook him—a high of sorts. A floating sensation tingled in his body, and a calming that was almost unreal soothed his mind. It was a brief taste of nirvana, and he wanted more.

Now, if he told his father any of this, the man's head would have exploded, ruining the crisp collar of his suit.

But, in the end, it was Simon's choice. His father paid for the classes Simon wanted to take, but he muttered to himself when signing the checks and never once asked how things were going. "Hippie shit," Simon once heard him say from behind his office door. And when his mother asked him about the classes, she never really listened for a response.

It was best not to talk about it.

"Is that Santo in the bag?" Simon asked his mother.

"Yes, it is." His mother unzipped the snazzy-looking pet carrier on the seat beside her, and the prized Pomeranian, Santo—named after the island of Santorini where Simon's parents owned a house—leapt out. The dog commenced its yipping and jumping all around the cabin of the limousine.

"Hey, Santo. Come here, boy." Simon patted his knees, but the little dog was not paying attention. Santo went to the closed window and smeared his tiny nose all over the glass.

"No, Santo," his mother scolded. "Now we'll have to get the car cleaned."

She scooted Santo back into his stylish little carrier and zipped it up. Santo's beady black eyes stared out through the netting.

"All right, Mother, now can we talk about why you took me out of class?"

"I didn't, Simon. Someone from the school called last night. A Steven, I think … or maybe Justin? Whoever it was, he said the class was cancelled. Everyone is being sent home. I believe I was just the first to arrive."

"What? That's bullshit! Why wouldn't they tell us? Are we at least getting our credit? Do I have to take the class all over again?" The car came to a stop, and Simon could see a curved line of traffic out the window.

"I don't know. I didn't ask."

Simon was listening, but his attention was stolen outside. Up ahead, he thought he could see a Humvee. Then the cars inched forward, and from around the bend a massive tank came into view. There were men in army fatigues standing about.

"What the hell is going on?"

"It's a checkpoint, Simon." She lifted her bag and rummaged through it. "Here, I brought your passport. It's in here somewhere."

"A checkpoint? Why?"

"Because we're at war. While you've been off gallivanting in the woods, the rest of the world has been getting ready to destroy itself." Her hand fumbled about in her purse. "Here's your passport." She handed it across the seat. "I'm sorry, Simon. I didn't mean to snap at you. It's been … a tough couple of weeks."

"We're at war?"

"It's …" She looked down and shook her head. "Any day now, any hour."

"Turn the news on. Jesus, I thought it was all just a bunch of political bullshit."

"You can listen to the news when you get home. I have a headache. Things are going to be … bad."

He turned his gaze from the window to face his mother. She was just as lean and regal as ever, but the lines on her face had deepened, and he could see the bags under her eyes through her makeup.

"Talk to your father when we get home. He'll tell you everything."

***

The limo made the familiar twists and turns up scenic Ridgeline Road, and Simon took in the mansions and age-old carriage houses, mostly hidden at the end of long driveways. The town's proximity to New York, and the excellent fishing from the Ridgeline River, gave the area immediate affluence after being settled. That affluence had grown over the years, and was evident in the size of the manors that now dotted the shore.

Fishing in the river was not as prominent as it once had been, as the water had been polluted over the many years due to its nearness to New York. Now the river was little more than a playground for the rich. Many of the homeowners had yachts tied to private docks in their own backyards, and jet skies were everywhere, crisscrossing the river during the summer months. Simon had once gone on a yachting trip with a neighboring friend, his friend's father steering the boat. It was only a short distance until the river fed into the ocean, and the sailing beyond was limitless.

The limousine slowed and turned to the gated entrance of the family's estate. The driver leaned out and typed a code into the sentry box, and the mechanical hinges on the gate began to open without so much as a squeak.

They drove down the winding driveway, past rows of buttonwood trees with mulched bases and flowering plants artistically arranged around the bottoms. They passed another swerve in the driveway, and Simon's house came into view—a massive structure, designed to imitate European or Southern grandeur. The facade of the house was mostly stone, partially covered with ivy and with several circular turret windows and intricate craftsmanship around the wood-shingled roof.

The limousine swung around the paved brick roundabout with the three-tiered fountain in the center and came to a stop before the house entrance. Two large moving trucks were parked just ahead of them. A dozen or so men were coming and going from the front door, carrying boxes and large pieces of furniture draped with white canvas sheets.

Simon scratched his jaw. "We're moving?"

"Just putting a few things in storage," his mother replied. "Just to be safe."

The driver got out and opened the car door. His mother stepped out, followed by Simon carrying his duffel bag.

"Master Simon," Anthony, the driver said. "Welcome home. Please, let me take your bag." He reached out.

"No, no, Anthony. Please. I got it. It's good to see you." Simon reached out and shook Anthony's waiting hand.

"Thank you, sir."

"Anthony, it's Simon."

"Yes, Master Simon."

"Just Simon."

Simon followed his mother up the steps to the front door. They stopped beside the two-story columns to let several men carrying a couch pass by, and then they entered. There was activity all about. The moving crew and maids were coming and going. The entryway was already cleared out—the benches were gone, the Persian rug was rolled up, and all the paintings and artwork had been removed, leaving rectangular outlines on the walls.

"Your father should be home soon. Why don't you go upstairs and freshen up?"

Simon nodded, and went to the semicircular staircase. The activity in the house made him quicken his pace as he walked up the stairs and down the east wing toward his bedroom. The door was cracked open.

They better not have packed up my stuff.

He pushed the door open, expecting to see a vacant room, but it was still fully furnished. Winston was sleeping on his bed. The dog's eyes darted open when Simon entered, and his tail went wild, thumping against the mattress, his mouth open and panting.

"Winston!"

The dog flew off the bed, and Simon dropped his bag and fell onto his back, wrestling with Winston and ruffling his head. He scratched at the dark spot by his ear. Winston bucked his head and panted, stepping back to stretch in a play-bow. He then leaped back to assault Simon with his drooping tongue.

"I missed you so much, buddy. I missed you so much."

Simon closed his eyes and mouth as Winston's tongue went wild over his face with the crazed love that only a dog can provide.

After a few minutes, Simon sat on the ground with Winston, who was now tired and content.

"You're a good boy, aren't you, buddy?"

The dog panted, looking up with his dark eyes.

After another minute on the ground, scratching Winston's head, Simon looked across the room to the door to his private bathroom. After all that time in the woods, a hot shower sounded unbelievable.

***

From his bedroom window, Simon watched his father's car pull up. The back door of the limousine opened and his father hurried to the front steps with his cell phone in one hand, his briefcase in the other.

Simon wanted to run downstairs to talk to him, but he knew the best way to ensure his father's attention was to give him a few minutes to settle into his office.

Simon stepped away from the window and looked over the rows of books on the bookshelf, and the various knickknacks and trophies mixed in. He picked up a football trophy—the entire team had received the same one—and felt the alloy-metal statue of a football player running in mid-stride, ball in the crook between his elbow and chest. The trophy looked silly to him now, and thinking back to when he was twelve and adored the thing made him feel stupid. If he was going to be staying home, he would have to redo his room. Get rid of the clutter and the childish mementoes.

Simon put the trophy back on the dresser and headed toward the door, taking a deep breath.

It's now or never.

He walked to the stairway, went downstairs, and continued past the kitchen to his father's office at the far end of the house. It was surprising to see the door open, and Simon could hear the television as he approached.

He hesitated at the doorway. His father was leaning against his desk, watching the news from the television in the built-in mahogany shelving. The sleeves of his father's shirt were rolled up, and his jacket was off.

Simon knocked on the doorframe and his dad flinched.

"Simon. There you are." He picked up the remote and hit the mute button.

"Hello, Father."

"Come here; come in."

Simon put his hand out to shake, but his father did something surprising—he gave him a hug. And not just a quick hug, but a long and powerful one. When they parted, his dad said, "Sit, sit. Take a seat." He went around the desk to his own seat. "How are you? How was the class?"

"I'm good, I'm fine. And the class was going well."

"You look skinny. Strong. Those classes are getting you in shape, huh?"

Simon nodded. Why did his father care? He'd certainly had no interest before.

His dad took a deep breath. "All right, let's cut to the chase … I have something here for you." He opened a side drawer, pulled out an envelope, and handed it across the desk.

The envelope, addressed to Simon, was cut open along the top. He was about to protest at his parents opening his mail, but then decided against it. Two pieces of paper were folded inside, one smaller than the other. He read the heading on the larger paper: *ORDER TO REPORT FOR PHYSICAL EXAMINATION.* The smaller paper listed his name and personal information: birthday, height, weight.

"It's a draft card, Simon," his father said. "I didn't mean to open it. It was a mistake. I saw an envelope from the government, and I didn't look at whom it was addressed to. I'm sorry."

"A draft card?" Simon started reading the fine print. Indeed it was a draft card, and an order to report for physical examination. "I've been drafted?"

"Everyone's been drafted."

"Oh … God." The letter felt heavy in his hands. "I-I'm going to be sent to war? We're at war? Oh Christ …"

"Not yet, but it's only a matter of time. Just look at the news." He pointed to the TV, but Simon remained examining the letter.

His father spoke, "There might be … another option for you. We've been discussing alternatives." His dad leaned forward, resting his elbows on the desk. His tie was so loose around his collar that the top of his white T-shirt was visible.

"I don't see how anything would make a difference." Simon's voice wavered, and he swallowed back a lump in his throat.

Not in front of Dad, God damn it!

"I've heard some things … things about this war. It's not going to be pleasant. You remember Tom Byrnes, right?"

Simon nodded. There was a picture of Tom Byrnes on the built-in shelving, next to his father's various awards and trophies—trophies not unlike those in Simon's room, only these were made of solid metal and glass and actually meant something.

The picture of Tom Byrnes had been taken when Simon was a boy. His father had taken him fishing along with Tom and Tom's son, who was about the same age as Simon. They were all holding their day's catches and looking silly in full fishing gear, standing on some boat, somewhere beautiful.

Simon couldn't remember the details. He had been young then. The name of Tom Byrnes's son eluded him, although he remembered the boy arguing with Simon over who got to hold the largest fish for the picture. Simon knew that Tom Byrnes was a highly decorated military man, as well as an alleged CIA affiliate. *Allegedly.*

His father went on, "I talked to Tom recently. He's scared. He called me two nights ago in a panic, and we had a long talk. FEMA is not only preparing for wide-scale nuclear devastation in almost every major US city, they've just dispatched emergency teams to be stationed in towns bordering potential strike zones, ready to go in with hazmat suits. There's something like ten million body bags for New York alone, and that's not even for the city. According to Tom … the cities have been written off. The body bags are for the surrounding areas where bodies might be found." He stopped to let that fact sink in and then continued. "Our own missiles are on standby. It's going to be … just horrific."

He closed his eyes and rubbed the bridge of his nose, shaking his head. "Just look at what they did to Boston and Chicago." His dad pointed again to the silent news, where every scene seemed to display something burning, someone protesting, people dead. "And if that's not bad enough, Tom told me that something else is coming. It's already here, but the reporters are blocked from covering it. The government doesn't want the public to panic, because they are powerless to do anything to stop it. Some sort of disease, a plague, but Tom wouldn't give me the details. It's already struck Africa, the Middle East, Europe—and it's here, in the US. He's scared. And if he's scared, we should be terrified. He only told me because … because we have to leave. There is still a chance to get out of here. He said we have to drop everything and go far away from the East Coast. Right away."

"Why-why won't they allow the news to cover it?"

"Just think of the chaos news like that would create. There's nothing that can be done. It's here, Simon. It's too late."

They became quiet, and Simon didn't know what to say. The gravity of their situation was hard to comprehend. "Where … but what … where will we go?"

A voice spoke up from behind him, and Simon turned to see his mother standing at the doorway. "Do you remember Uncle Timothy's cabin?" she asked. "You've been up there before, when you were younger."

Simon remembered his deceased uncle's cabin fondly. Only the men had gone for hunting trips—his father, Uncle Tim, his brother Marty, and sometimes a few cousins. They fished, hunted, and started huge bonfires. He loved those trips, just the guys out in the woods, shooting guns, splitting wood, wearing knives on their belts. Being men. His dad even let him drink a beer a few times and sip some whiskey, even though the last time he was up there he had only been eleven. After his uncle passed away, and the cabin went to his father, they never returned.

"We're going to Uncle Timothy's cabin?"

"Not exactly. Your father and I can't leave yet." She walked into the room and sat in the chair beside him. "Marty's in Paris. He was meeting with investors about opening a third store in France, outside of the city. He can't … they've grounded all international flights." She looked at the floor.

"Is he safe?"

"Yes, he's safe. But he won't be able to leave France. Not for a while. He's heading now for our vacation house in Bouches-du-Rhône, where he'll have to weather things out. It's safe there, secluded."

His father cut in, "I tried sending the private jet, but even that's not allowed outside of US airspace. France and all of Europe are on lockdown. Soon, we will be too. Only domestic flights are flying. A curfew has been put in effect for many of the cities: Chicago, Boston, and I think Los Angeles. The looting has been terrible there. New York will be next."

"So, we have to leave now?"

"Yes, Simon." He cleared his throat. "*You* are leaving immediately. You're not going to war." His father pointed to the draft papers still in Simon's hand. With all the news his father had been telling him, it was easy to forget at least for a moment this additional circumstance. "This war will only bring quick death to all who participate, I assure you that."

"And … you guys are leaving when?"

His mother and father exchanged glances, and Simon knew something was up.

"We're not going to the cabin," his mother said. "We still have a lot to do here at the house before we leave, and by then it will be difficult to drive all the way to British Columbia."

"Yeah, but, didn't you say," he gestured at his dad, "that we all have to leave right now? All of us. That the entire East Coast is in danger? Where are you guys going to go?"

"Simon," his dad said, "we'll be leaving only a few days after you. I promise. The cabin is the safest place for you to go. It's in the middle of the woods. No one will find you. As for us, I'm in the process of buying property in North Carolina, outside of Asheville. That's where your mother and I will be going."

"Then that's where I'm going too."

"No, you're not. Your uncle's cabin is safer. End of discussion. We're not trying to get rid of you, Simon. You have to understand, it would be arduous on us—your mother and I—to live in the woods. The water and electricity have been turned off, and we know nothing about living off the land. But you do. The cabin outside of Asheville is a good second choice."

"I can take care of you. I can fish and hunt. There's a stream with fresh water. We'll be fine."

"No, Simon. We wouldn't be fine. Not your mother and I. And it will be easier on you to care for yourself. Plus, like I said, it will be a few more days until we can leave, and by then, crossing into Canada may not be an option. I've entrusted someone to buy the property down south, but I don't have the location yet. I'm sorry, but this is the way it has to be done. We don't have the luxury of time. We'll all meet back here, in *this* house, when things have calmed down. Tom said it could take about two years for the virus to die out."

"Two years!" The prospect of living off the land for two years was a challenging one that both intrigued and terrified him. But to do it alone? "Why that long?"

"Because that's what Tom Byrnes told me."

They were silent.

His mother leaned forward, taking his hand in hers. "You have to realize how hard this is for us. Your brother is trapped in France, and we're sending you off to live in a cabin alone." She blinked as tears rolled down her face, smearing her makeup. "Please understand that we gave this much thought, and we wouldn't be doing this if it wasn't the best possible solution, for all of us. Do you understand, Simon?"

"Is the house down south safe?"

"Yes," his father said. "It's in the woods; that much I know, and it has an underground bomb shelter. I'm having it fully stocked with supplies and enough gasoline to keep a generator running indefinitely. We'll be safe there."

"I still think we should all go north ... but ... I understand. I'll do whatever is best for the family."

"We'll be okay, Simon." His mother hugged him, and her lilac perfume smelled strong.

His dad sighed. "Let's take a break from talking about this for a while, what do you say? There's a lot to do before you go, but tonight let's have a nice dinner, together."

***

Simon woke before dawn, kicked Winston off the bed, got dressed, and crept downstairs while the house was still silent and dark.

He walked into the kitchen to make a cup of tea and was startled to see Emma, the household maid, already up. She was perched on a stool breathing in the vapors of a cup of coffee.

"Emma, have you been awake for long?"

"Simon," the elderly lady said. "Just got up. I thought you were home. Come here, my boy." Emma had lived and worked in the house since Simon was born and had raised him just as much as his own parents, if not sometimes more. She crossed the kitchen in her nightgown and robe to embrace Simon in her thick arms. The curlers in her hair scratched his nose. "Oh, my my, you've gotten so big," she said. "And skinny, too." Her loving hands started grabbing and poking him around the ribcage.

"I'm okay, Emma." He squirmed out of her grip. "I didn't see you yesterday when I got in."

"I was out of town visiting my brother, Lord have mercy on him, and got home late. You're not eating enough. Sit, let me fix you something."

"I'm fine, Emma. Thanks, but I have to get going. I have a lot to do today." He wanted to get to the warehouse before it opened.

"I know you're busy, and that's why you need some breakfast."

"I … maybe just some juice."

She heated the cast-iron skillet over the fire and began removing eggs and bacon wrapped in brown parchment paper from the refrigerator. She fluttered her hand at Simon. "You go on and get yourself some juice. I'm making breakfast."

It was impossible to refuse this lady who had waited outside of school for him almost every day of his life, watched every baseball, soccer, and football game he'd ever played, wrapped his little cuts and scraped knees in bandages, and put ice on his bruises.

Simon sat and they ate together. The food was delicious; he was glad that he had stayed. He missed Emma. His father told him the night before that Emma would be moving with them down south, and that made him happy. But at the moment, he did not feel like discussing such things with her. Emma asked him about his class, and he told her all about it.

"You always liked it out in parks and such," she recounted, sipping her coffee. "I would take you to Alice Springs almost every day when you were young, and you would run and play and dirty your clothes like a young boy should. Used to make your momma so mad, me bringing you home with your knees all covered in grass stains. I would always tell her, 'It does a boy good.'"

Simon smiled.

They sat and talked and ate, and when Simon was finished, he stood with his empty plate in hand.

"That was great, Emma. Thank you so much."

"Nonsense. You're too skinny, boy. Sit; I'll make you some more."

"No, really, I have to go. I have to."

She had probably missed him more than his own mother and father—a thought that made him wince. But he missed her too, and making him breakfast was a way for Emma to slow down time and tell him all the stories about himself growing up that Simon had already heard. "I'll be back for lunch. I promise."

After five minutes, Simon escaped from her and left the house. The sun was just rising, and the morning frost was melting in wet sheets across the pavement.

Simon arrived at the warehouse around seven. The town of Mumford was almost entirely commercial. UPS and FedEx had warehouses the sizes of football fields nearby. His family's warehouse, one of the many owned by Kalispell Sports, was not nearly as large, but it was big enough.

The parking lot was empty, and the ports for the commercial trucks were still closed. No one was expected in for another hour. Simon drove to the side, by the large double doors used by the staff, and noticed two pickup trucks parked with their tailgates down. He parked and killed the engine.

He walked past the trucks on the way to the door and noticed they were half-full with boxes and supplies—dehydrated meals, bottled water, rifles, ammunition, and wool blankets. Just as he was about to grab the door handle to the warehouse, it swung open and he came face to face with a tall, skinny black man carrying a box. The man was middle-aged, the ends of his wiry hair gray, and his back bent from years of hard work.

"Oh, Jesus Christ," the man said. "You nearly scared me to kingdom come. Simon, is that you? Hot damn, son, you've grown tall."

"Hey, John. How's it going?"

"Good, my boy. Here, let me put this down." He put the box in the trunk of the van and turned to Simon. "I've been waiting for you."

"I got held up."

Simon knew his father was letting many of the employees take whatever they needed before the looters took the rest.

"That ain't the car you're taking, is it?" He pointed to Simon's sedan. "Won't fit much in there."

"No, I'll need a van."

"Keys are in the office. Go to the lot out back and take your pick. You need me to show you around?"

"I'm good, I think. I'll find you if I need help."

"All right then, son."

Simon took a dozen keys from the rack and went to the lot. He decided on a midsized, construction-type moving van with low miles and a good service report. The lettering on the side that read *Kalispell Sports* would have to be painted over, to avoid any unwanted attention on the road. But other than that, the van was nice. Practically new.

He drove the van to the entrance and entered the warehouse. Pallets upon pallets were stacked up high, towering to the ceiling. He stuck mostly to emergency ration bars with long expiration dates and high calorie counts, along with plenty of water, although he didn't go overboard since there was a stream near the cabin. The rest of the space he crammed with blankets, a folding shovel, an axe, a saw, water filters, and various survival supplies. Room was left for the gasoline barrels that his father was having filled.

Simon drove the van home, parked it in the garage, and walked to the house. The courtyard was bustling with activity; two new moving trucks were parked outside.

He entered and walked past the commotion to his father's office in the back. The door was open and his father was sitting with his back to him, looking out the window at the Ridgeline River in the distance over the ample backyard.

Simon knocked, snapping his father out of his reverie.

"Oh, Simon, you're back."

His father was not wearing a tie. He looked strange, incomplete.

"I'm all packed."

"Good. That's good."

The television was showing images of whole armies marching in demonstration, cell-phone clips of men firing machine guns, rockets, and flamethrowers, towns and cities exploding into smoke and ruin, but the volume was off. Classical music, Brahms perhaps, whispered from the stereo.

His dad sighed. "All right. I have a few things to show you." He stood and grabbed a set of keys from the desk drawer. "Follow me."

His dad led him through a door on the side of the room, which opened to a long hallway extending to the kitchen at the far end. Along the hallway was a bathroom, a stairway leading upstairs, and a door to the greenhouse and the outside beyond. It was sort of a secret tunnel so his dad could work, eat, and go upstairs without bumping into any staff or guests.

Simon followed his father down the hallway, and they stopped before the door to the greenhouse. "In here." His dad opened the door. A rush of muggy air hit them, along with the smell of dirt and earth. The greenhouse was just as Simon remembered, a large, almost two-story room, comprised of glass walls and a glass ceiling. Benches were set in rows, where the landscapers grew the flowers and plants for the yard. They were covered in bright and cheerful-looking sprouts. To the left was a little shed made out of cinderblocks where the tools and spare planters were stored.

His dad led Simon to the shed, opened the door, and grabbed the end of a planting table inside.

"Give me a hand," he said. Simon grabbed the other end and they moved it over several feet.

His father started clearing the ground in the center of the shed.

"What are we doing?" Simon asked.

"You'll see."

When the ground was clear, his father said, "Do you remember this house when we first moved in? It's a bit different now."

Simon nodded. "I think so. A little."

His father took two crowbars from the tools hanging on the wall and handed one to Simon. "Start with this one." He pointed to a large paver-stone on the ground, about twelve-inch by twelve-inch. His dad fit the edge of the crowbar in the crevice between the two and began prying at the stone. "You going to help or what?"

Simon helped him remove the stone, which was at least two inches thick and heavy, then began prying up more.

"Do you remember after we bought this house, when we made the expansion for the office and this greenhouse?"

"A little."

"Do you remember what the demo team found?"

Simon tried to recall.

"They found a hole underground. A room. You were young then. Does any of this ring a bell?"

"Yeah, I think so. I remember you talking about it. A room for hiding slaves or something, right?"

"That's right. The house originally on this property was built well before the Civil War. Whoever lived here must have been a sympathizer for the slaves, because he built a room to hide them while they were on the move. The room was covered up and forgotten about until we started construction. The town sent a member of the historical society to inspect it and they verified that it *was* indeed used to hide slaves."

"I thought you had the room filled in?"

"That's what I told you."

They continued moving the pavers, piling them to the side, until a rectangular metal door became exposed.

"Wow. This is cool."

"Yeah, it is. I had some work done to the room—made it longer, had this door installed, and put in new stairs. Some of the walls are original. I'll show you."

There was a padlock on the handle, and his dad entered a code, removed the lock, and swung the door open to rest on its hinges. A dark and foreboding staircase presented itself, extending down into the earth.

"There's a light switch and flashlights at the bottom." His dad led the way, and Simon followed. They descended into the darkness where the temperature dropped and the air smelled stale.

At the bottom, his dad hit the switch and exposed lightbulbs hanging on cords from the ceiling illuminated the room. It was large and cavernous, expanding back maybe twenty or thirty feet, but the ceiling loomed only a few inches above their heads. Metal shelves lined the walls on either side, stocked with boxes and supplies, some draped with canvas sheets.

"This, Simon, is what I call the emergency room."

"Yup, this is definitely cool."

"It won't work as a bunker. There's little air supply when the door is shut, and there is no toilet. I wasn't thinking of that when I had the work done. It was only meant to keep things hidden."

His dad took him from shelf to shelf, showing him the various rations of food and water, the drums of gasoline, and the generator. At the far end were three tall metal safes, the tops just shy of the ceiling. His dad entered a code into each lock, and the doors swung open.

"And this is where we keep our real valuables, not the stuff the moving crews are taking to storage."

He pulled back a cloth from the first safe to reveal stacks upon stacks of cash piled to the top. It was more money than Simon had ever seen. In the next safe were boxes filled with gold and silver bars, property deeds, gems, and stocks and bonds. After a quick tour, they moved to the third safe. "This is where we keep the good stuff." He showed Simon paintings wrapped in white cloth and tied with twine, his mother's and grandmother's jewelry, and photo albums of the family.

"The temperature down here is not ideal for our good paintings, the Picassos and van Gogh. Those are in a temperature-controlled storage, but these are still worth a pretty penny."

His father delicately removed a few paintings and set them aside. He then reached back into the dark recesses of the safe and pulled out an old cigar box. "This is for you, Simon. Don't tell your mother."

He handed Simon the box. Simon was surprised at the weight of it. He opened the lid, and there was something inside wrapped in a grease-stained cloth. His dad took the box as Simon unwrapped a perfectly preserved, and quite beautiful, Colt .45, military issue, with a spare magazine.

"This has been in the family since World War II. It has been handed down from generation to generation, and now I pass it on to you. I'll show you how to take it apart and keep it clean. It still works just like the day it was made."

Simon felt the weight and cold metal in his palm. The family owned several hunting rifles and shotguns, but his mother would not allow handguns. Absolutely not, no way, positively no.

"She knows I have it, your mom, but she doesn't know I'm giving it to you. It will serve you better than it will serve me. Pick out a rifle or two as well, and take plenty of ammunition. More than you think you'll need. And then take more."

"Thank you. I mean, really, thank you."

"You're welcome. Now put it away; let's get out of here. My allergies go crazy down here." Simon's allergies were getting bad too, but he hadn't noticed until his father brought it up.

Simon picked a rifle and began loading a duffel bag with ammunition from the floor-to-ceiling shelving. When he was done, his dad took two more duffel bags from a shelf and went over to the first safe. He counted several stacks of cash and put them inside. "Give this to the guard at the border. He'll be expecting you. His name is Stephen Parks." He handed Simon the two duffel bags. "The other one's for you. It's more than enough to cover any expenses you may encounter. Buy more ammunition when you get out west. That won't be enough." He pointed to the duffel bag strapped over Simon's shoulder, then turned to close and lock the safes.

They moved toward the staircase.

"There's one more thing I want to show you." He grabbed a flashlight and brought Simon to a wall on the side of the room where a space was clear of shelving. The beam of light cast upon it. "See that?"

Simon squinted. There was something scratched into the wall. "Is that … does it say … is that a name?"

"It says Sue. And next to it are carvings, as crude as they are." Simon looked at the images scraped into the wall by a rock or a piece of sharp metal. They looked like the hand of a child had carved them. The name Sue was clear, and the wavy outline of two people standing, holding hands. There were more scratches, but they were undecipherable. Another name, incomplete, with only the letter M legible.

"They were carved by the slaves who hid down here," his father said. "It's remarkable."

Simon stared, transfixed. "Yes ... it is."

***

Simon woke up before dawn and tiptoed downstairs to the kitchen. Emma was nowhere to be seen, and Simon was glad. He wanted his departure to be as pain-free as possible. The lights were still off in the kitchen as he entered, and when he flipped them on, he was startled to see his mother sitting at the far table. The smell of coffee was thick.

"Good morning," she said.

"Mom, I didn't know you were awake."

"It's nice to watch the sunrise over the river." She turned toward the window behind the kitchen table, which looked out over the backyard and the river beyond. The sun was starting to produce a gentle red glow on the horizon.

With a barely audible sigh, she said, "Sit. I made you coffee."

"Thanks." He sat, and they quietly sipped their coffee. She stroked the top of his hand and smiled, and then she said, "I'm so proud of you."

And Simon almost lost it.

She continued, "We never meant to be so hard on you; we only wanted what was best for your future. And although we don't always show it, we're both very proud of the man you've become. I know how good you've been doing at the classes. I've talked to Marcus Warden several times, and he's assured me of your abilities in the wild. The best in class, he said, and he meant it." Simon wanted to ask her when she had talked to Mr. Warden, but he didn't.

She leaned around the table and hugged him, and his face sank deep into the softness of her robe. She smelled of sleep and a slight hint of lavender and lilacs, very faint. Something in that smell registered deep within him, beyond remembrance, to the infantile stores of childhood memories, when his mother woke up in the middle of the night to cradle him. He buried his face on her shoulder and felt the wetness of her tears as she hushed him gently, brushing back his hair.

This was why he'd woken up early—to avoid this, for everyone. He had written notes, ready to be left on the counter. One for his parents, and one for Emma.

He heard the faint squeak of the front door opening, as far off as it was, and they parted. "Wh-who's that?" Simon looked toward the entryway.

"That's your father. He went to get the van ready. Come, let's get going."

His father was also wearing a robe and slippers with a white V-neck T-shirt and pajama bottoms underneath. They met at the door and moved outside, his mother taking a seat on the steps of the porch, hugging her legs to her chest against the cold morning air, the cup of coffee placed beside her producing thick plumes of steam. His dad walked Simon to the van.

"It's all ready," he said. "Just letting the defrosters melt the dew."

The sun was turning the sky pale blue, and the ice would all be melted soon enough. "I had to make some extra room in the back," his dad said.

"For what?"

"Dog food. Winston's going with you. I packed a few bags, but you'll have to pick up more on your way. Get as much as you can—and then get more."

Simon looked at the passenger side window and tapped his fingernail against it. Winston's head sprung up, panting against the frosty window, ecstatic to see him. Simon smiled, and after a moment Winston lay back down.

They were quiet. Then his dad spoke, but his voice cracked, high-pitched and awkward. "That's it," he said, palms open, and then they hugged. His mother came over and hugged him again, her tears hot against his cheek. His father's face was red and swollen, and his hair was matted with sleep. He said, "Let Simon go, honey. He has to go."

"I'll be back," Simon said. "I'll meet you guys here, I promise."

His mother nodded, her eyes glassy. His father said, "I know you will, son."

Simon got in the van. He ruffled Winston's head and let the dog barrage him with licks until he settled down. The frozen dew was mostly evaporated from the windshield and clearing fast.

He put the van in drive.

Simon turned around the fountain and started down the long driveway. He watched his parents in the rearview mirror. His father was pulling his mother in tight, and her hands were covering her face as she cried into her palms. He watched them grow smaller as his mother now buried her face in his father's shoulder, and his father reached out to wave. As he drove around a bend, they disappeared from view. At the end of the driveway, the gate swung open and Simon turned right. Half a block later, tears were streaming down his face, hot as firewater.

Chapter 11

Odyssey

The clamor in the valley echoed loud.

Steven said, "What's that—" but Brian hushed him. A rumbling noise was now unmistakable, growing louder … and then something else. Steven's eyes grew wide, staring at Brian. There were muffled voices in the distance—many voices, some laughing, others obscure.

Brian stood and motioned forward. They sprinted to the waist-high fence in front of the house, swung the gate back, and ran to the door. They paused. Brian held the handle and took a deep breath.

They exchanged glances, nodded, and then stormed into the house. Brian led, crouching lower than Steven, who swept his rifle to the left and right. They entered the living room and could see straight back into the small kitchen. Many of the cabinets and drawers had been left open and cleared of anything other than mouse droppings. The counters and side tables held little ceramic knickknacks and family pictures, all placed on top of yellowed doilies. Everything was covered with dust. Some pictures had fallen to the ground with the broken glass scattered about.

An ashtray sat on the coffee table, overflowing with cigarette butts, several of which had been extinguished on the table itself. Beside the ashtray were two half-bottles of brown liquor. Brian and Steven swept the bottom floor and proceeded to the stairway, passing a pile of garbage—empty soup cans, crumpled cigarette packs, broken bottles.

The stair treads groaned with each step as they went upstairs. The hallway at the top led to bedrooms at both ends and a bathroom directly across from the staircase. The bathroom was empty, and they proceeded to the far bedroom. The simple room had a bed in the center, a TV on a dresser, and two nightstands on either side of the bed. The windows were open and the wind billowed the once white curtains. A four-poster bed occupied the bulk of the room, and under a soiled knit blanket lay the form of a person.

"Oh, Jesus Christ," Steven said.

They approached the body. Brian was shaking and sweating, his finger vibrating over the trigger of his rifle. He stepped close and extended his hand to move the blanket away, but Steven reached forward and grabbed his wrist. Brian looked at him; he was shaking his head and was as white as paper. Brian looked back at the body. The form was small and shallow, and the bedding around the body was stained yellow. Bones.

They left the bedroom and ran to the room at the other end of the hallway, which faced the direction of the valley. The room had been in the process of being painted before the owner perished, and all the furniture was draped with canvas cloths. Paint cans and rollers were set on plastic sheets, dry and brittle.

They crouched behind the double window and Brian found his binoculars under his poncho. His fingers trembled on the focusing wheel.

"Dear mother of God …"

A procession was heading down the main street of town. Two columns of savages marched in near unison. But these men were no soldiers. They were ragged and filthy, and carried with them a wide assortment of weaponry—rifles, machine guns, pistols. Many held sledgehammers, machetes, various swords, and large and small pry-bars, some the size of walking sticks. These improvised weapons were scoured at the ends to reveal the steel of which they were made, gleaming like silver, and were muddied with earth and gore. The men looked as if they had marched out of some dismal pit of hell that had vomited them forth, seeming to defile the earth of which they trod. They wore a vast array of military clothing of no particular origin and had adorned themselves and their weapons with torn pieces of red cloth, like flags, along with garnished trophies of war—what looked like dried, brown human ears and tanned hides. They cast about them a red and brown hue, as if they wore these shades as part of a collective uniform.

Pickup trucks rumbled along with the procession, their flatbeds full and covered with sheets. Long ropes trailed from the bumpers, extending to latch around the necks of several pink, naked human beings, both male and female, all with their hands and wrists bound. A body dragged along the ground, bumping over the pavement, lifeless and ground raw. The naked humans who were still alive were prodded forward by whips and crudely made spears with strips of red material tied under the points, so that they blew in the wind like macabre flags of the damned.

Brian removed his hunting rifle from his backpack, unsnapped the covers on the scope, and leaned it on the windowsill.

At the head of the cavalcade rode a man on horseback. His face was too distant to see clearly, yet he loomed large over his pale stallion. The sidewalks on either side of the horrid procession were lined with corpses. Bodies hung from the streetlights and electric poles, some by their necks, others by one or both feet. Others were impaled on fence posts. Some were burned to blackened crisps, and others had been crucified. Some were so badly decomposed that only a torso or limb remained attached to the implements of their demise.

Then Brian heard laughter. Close. Not from the procession in the street.

The two men ducked below the window. The front door creaked open and then shut, and they heard muffled voices of two people talking downstairs. Brian's heart was thumping so loud that he was afraid whoever was downstairs would hear it.

Chapter 12

The Gas Station

"D-don't m-m-move, mister!"

Simon did not move.

He stared down at the manhole cover, his vision bright and pulsing with his heartbeat. Droplets of blood emerged from between his clenched fingers and trailed down his injured hand.

The rifle was on the ground next to him. His pistol was in its holster.

"Don't reach for that gun," the voice said. "P-put your ha-hands on top of your head." The voice was squeaky, and Simon could detect shakiness in the stutter. Slowly, he looked up. It was only a boy, maybe ten. His blond hair was wild, knotted, and plastered to his forehead with filth. The clothes he wore were made for an adult. The boy's military jacket went almost to his knees, and the cuffs around his ankles and wrists were baggy and loose.

"Don't t-t-try nothing. I-I'll shoot!"

"Okay," Simon said, putting his hands in the air, letting the blood flow from the open wound to trickle down his forearm. "Okay. My hands are up. Let's take it easy." These were the first words Simon had spoken to another human being in over two years.

In the wild, he'd often worried that it would be difficult to communicate effectively with other people after being alone for so long. He often spoke to Winston in a plethora of random noises and sounds, clicks, and whistles. But now, he spoke without realizing it. "I didn't know anyone was here."

The comic books, you idiot. The gasoline, the blankets ... the chocolate on the wrapper was still wet ...

"S-s-stop talking!" The boy shouted. Simon scanned behind the kid, back to the garage, but couldn't see anyone else around.

The boy balanced the rifle in his tiny hands, yet he held it firm, despite the rifle being nearly as long as he was tall. It was a wood grain, bolt-action hunting rifle without a scope. The boy fidgeted from one foot to the other, and his eyes were huge and glassy. Even from this distance, Simon could see the vividness in his gaze.

"Hey," Simon said. "You hungry? I bet you're hungry. I'm hungry, too. Why don't I make us both some—"

"I said, I said shut the hell up!" the boy yelled. "I k-k-know what m-men like you do to kids like me. I ain't stupid. My momma told me all about you."

"I don't want to do anything to you. I swear it. What do you think … where's your mother?"

The boy was shouting. "She t-told me you—"

A thunderous crack cut off the boy's words as the rifle bucked in his hands.

Simon's body jerked, and he bit his lip so hard that he tasted blood. The bullet hit the dust out of sight.

The boy jumped back, almost dropping the rifle. The look on his face changed from surprise to panic.

"Jesus!" Simon roared.

They stared at each other in wide-eyed silence.

Whether the boy had meant to fire the gun or not made no difference now, because the bullet-fire put the kid in a panic, and he began fumbling with the bolt to re-chamber a round.

"Wa-wait! Just wait a second!" Simon shouted.

The chamber sprung open, and the shell casing spiraled to the dirt. The boy made a sobbing sound, as if his own life and death hung in the balance.

"Don't-don't do that! Hey, kid! Hey! Stop what you're—"

The boy chambered a round, slammed the bolt shut. Someone had taught this kid how to handle a firearm.

"Damn it, boy!"

The kid shouldered the gun and eyed down the barrel. Simon dove to his side, grabbed the wooden stock of his M1A rifle from the ground and swung it up. In one fluid motion, Simon aimed and fired, and at the same moment, the boy pulled the trigger of his own rifle. The gun buckled in Simon's hand,

and the events transpired in a blur of speed, and yet felt so slow that each millisecond was frozen in time.

The boy's bullet made a *plunk* sound on the manhole cover by Simon's knee, ricocheting off somewhere unseen. Simon saw the boy fly backward. The rifle he was holding flew out of his hands, and a puff of red mist and stuffing from his jacket lingered in the air. The kid hit the ground and blood began pooling around him. He gurgled once, and then stopped moving.

For a moment that might have been an eternity, nothing happened. Then Simon jumped to his feet, grabbed his scout backpack, and ran to the edge of the gas station. He ran to where the van was parked in the woods, and stopped short in his tracks.

The driver side door of the van was open, like he'd left it. However, the door to the trunk was also open. And he had not left it that way.

"Shit," he muttered through clenched teeth, and swung behind a tree. "Winston!" he shouted, and instantly the dog sprinted to him from the front seat of the van, his ears pinned back, frightened from the sound of the gunshots. "Winston, Winston!" he kept shouting, until the trembling dog was behind him.

From where Simon stood, he could see the side of the van. He leveled the rifle, leaning against a tree to help balance his shaking hands, and aimed at the back door.

He yelled, "Who the fuck is there!"

There was no reply, but he saw a glimpse of movement, a tiny sway of the door, and heard feet scamper off into the woods behind the van.

There was a moment of silence, and Simon tried to regain his composure, focus, and the awareness that he could usually tap into. But his mind was reeling.

He breathed. *In and out, and in and out …*

Some clarity returned and he listened for the faintest sound, watched for the slightest disturbance in the woods.

Then a shot rang out. A wild shot, but Simon flinched all the same. He saw the ruffle of leaves from a bush beside an elm tree. Simon steadied his aim, breathed, and fired a round into the thick side of the elm. Bark and splinters erupted in an outward explosion. Simon paused, breathed again, and squeezed off another round—slightly to the left, closer to the bush. He paused, breathed, steadied his aim, and then …

"Don't shoot, mister," a young voice squealed, crying. A girl's voice. "Please."

There was another voice. "P-put down your gun!" Another boy.

Simon answered, "I don't think so."

There was no reply, only the sound of tears from both the girl and the boy.

"You ... you kill Billy?" the girl asked.

"I ... was that Billy at the pumps?"

There was no answer, but Simon knew that it was. "I ... he's probably ... he might be dead. I don't know. Where are your parents? Where's an adult?"

The girl was sobbing. "Mitch, Billy's dead ... Billy's dead!"

"Shut up!" The boy's voice was wavy.

Tears were welling up in Simon's eyes, but he remained vigilant. These children—these wild children—had shot at him, three times now, and would kill him without a moment's hesitation.

"I said, *where the hell are your parents*? Answer me, or so help me God!"

"They ain't here," the boy said.

"Are they coming back?"

"No."

"Are they dead?"

"Yes."

"Are you alone? Are there more of you?"

There was no answer. Simon figured they knew better than to admit if they were alone. But the kids could be lying all the same. Maybe the adults were out on a hunt and would be back at any moment.

"All right," Simon said, "this is what we're going to do. First, you're going to throw that gun of yours on the ground. Next, I'm leaving in that van. When I'm gone, you can pick up your gun. I don't want it; you can keep it. Is that clear?"

There was no reply.

"I asked, *did I make myself clear?*" Simon chambered a fresh round in his rifle so they could hear the clicking sound that it produced. He picked up the expelled bullet.

"Do it, Mitch! Listen to the man."

Simon readied himself to fire another warning shot, then a small black pistol flew out from the brush and landed in the grass.

Without hesitation Simon ran forward, his rifle aimed the entire time, and motioning for Winston to run ahead to the van. He put the keys in the ignition, threw the gear in drive, and stepped on the gas pedal, kicking up a cloud of dirt.

He swung to the road, eyeing the boy he had shot. The kid had not moved, and a cloud of dust swirled over his body.

Simon hightailed it down the deserted road. A half mile out, he screamed loud and began punching the steering wheel.

"Winston! Why didn't you bark; why didn't you warn me! Why didn't you bark, Winston! Why didn't you bark?"

He kept punching the steering wheel, tears rolling down his face. "Winston, why didn't you bark? Why didn't you bark?"

A mile farther and Simon came to an abrupt halt in the middle of the road. He hunched over the steering wheel.

Winston lay curled on the floor of the passenger side, his ears pinned back, and he stared up at Simon with his big brown eyes. Simon held his own face in his hands, and Winston slowly stepped up on the seat, nudging his wet nose close to Simon, and began licking at his face. Simon held Winston's head. "I'm sorry, boy. I'm sorry."

A moment later, Simon got out of the van. The back door was still open. The first thing he did was inspect the gas barrels. They looked to be holding up. Luckily most of his supplies were tied down, but he took a quick mental inventory. If anything had been lost, it wasn't much. A box of survival energy bars was ripped open, as if an animal had torn through the packaging, and the silver wrappers were blown about the cabin. The two kids had eaten enough bars to supply a grown man with sufficient calories for a week. Simon threw the empty box out the door and re-strapped the food that the kids had begun to ravage.

Simon had no doubt that the boy, Billy, was only there to stall him while his friends raided the supplies. Only the kids were so hungry that they started eating rather than emptying the truck. Or maybe they thought they had all the time in the world because Billy was supposed to kill him. Either way, it didn't matter now. He was alive, and that boy was dead—most likely dead. Simon sat in the trunk of the van, quieting his mind, and deciding his next move.

A few minutes passed, and Simon was in the driver's seat, putting the van in reverse, and turning back toward the children.

He sped past the gas station, and saw the two small kids dragging Billy's rag-doll body away. When they saw the van, they dropped the boy and ran back toward the woods.

Simon made another U-turn farther down the road and then sped to pass again. He veered close to the dirt lot and slowed just enough to toss a duffel bag out the window where it bounced over the ground, kicking up a dusty trail. The duffel bag was stuffed with energy bars, basic medical supplies, a thick wool blanket, and a few emergency pouches of water that hopefully didn't burst.

Simon continued down the road, looking back through the mirror as the gas station grew smaller and smaller until it vanished altogether.

He had managed to stay hidden from the war and the savagery for two years as it soured and destroyed humanity, but now, after leaving the cocoon of the cabin and entering society for only a short period of time, he had been forced to become a part of the brutality that had ravaged mankind.

Chapter 13

Demons in the Night

Steven sat with his back pressed to the wall under the window, his rifle aimed at the doorway. He had a clear line of sight straight down the hallway to the bedroom at the far end.

He leaned into Brian's ear and whispered, "We need to get the fuck out of here."

Brian's eyes shot large, and he hushed Steven quiet.

Muffled voices rose from the rooms below, laughing at times. The smell of cigarette smoke came creeping through the floorboards. From somewhere in the valley, shots rang out, and a bolt of fear stabbed at Steven's heart. A warm fluid spread down his thighs and under his legs and butt, and he realized too late that he had pissed himself.

Oh Jesus Christ …

The urge to cry was nearly overwhelming.

They did not move as the room faded to dark with the night, and it became difficult to see down the hallway. Steven could just make out the form of the bed in the far room and could occasionally see the movement of curtains blowing in the wind.

The voices grew louder, raucous.

"They're drunk," Brian whispered.

"Let's get the hell out of here."

"We can't. We don't know if there're more outside, and it's too dark to see anything."

"What are we gonna do? I ain't staying the night."

"We don't have a choice. When they leave tomorrow, so will we."

"No Brian, we can't—"

"We got to stay."

There were many noises outside, farther down in the valley, and Brian and Steven took turns sneaking glances out the window. The bouncing glow of a raging bonfire chased away shadows from behind a cluster of buildings, just out of view. Occasionally, a gunshot rang out, and crazed laughter was frequent. They even heard the sound of a guitar being played. There were screams—deep, guttural and human—slaughterhouse sounds, which made Brian and Steven cringe.

The urine around Steven's legs was now cold, damp and awful. He doubted Brian noticed, as wet and filthy as they both already were in their long ponchos, but he still burned with shame. *Get yourself together, Steven, for Christ's sake. Get yourself together. You're tougher than this. You're Albert Driscoll's nephew. You don't piss yourself. Pull yourself together. You're the strongest man in this town.*

He remembered his old summer job with Brian over at Frank Meyer's farm when they were just teenagers, moving rocks from Frank's fields and piling them in mounds nearby. Brian would later go on to making produce deliveries, but Steven stayed out in the fields doing the heavy work. No other man could carry the weight that he burdened on his shoulders. Nobody.

He thought about the various bar fights he'd been in over the years, and how he'd never been afraid, never been bested. People liked to test themselves on the largest man in the room. Most of the time the fights were nothing more than a blur. He wouldn't know the outcome until the fight was over and Brian was holding him back from killing the other person. His mind would snap back to reality, and a bloody heap would lay before him.

Steven called those experiences his *seeing red* moments. His peripherals would throb in red, until it enveloped his entire vision. Usually, he blacked out completely. And when that happened, God help whoever was standing in his way.

The voices downstairs quieted as the night became black, then stopped altogether. Brian tapped him on the shoulder and whispered, "Want me to take first watch? You can get some shut-eye."

Steven nodded, but it was too dark for Brian to see.

After a moment Brian asked, "You there?"

"I'm here."

"That good?"

"It's good."

They pulled the canvas drop cloths from the ground and used them as blankets. Steven turned away from his cousin and closed his eyes. For hours he lay there, but sleep never came. Images of the horrid procession in the valley were fresh in his mind. The reality that some of those wretched men were sleeping below him caused his heart to race. Occasionally, his mind would come to the brink of dreams, in a state of total exhaustion, only to snap back to a panicked vigilance. The tiniest creaking of branches outside or the flapping of loose roof shingles in the wind set his mind in a whirl.

He thought back to earlier that day when Brian asked if he wanted to find a house for the night. As badly as he had wanted to sleep under a roof, the thought of all the corpses, all the dark and foreboding windows, had made words impossible to form. At the time, he was envisioning men eating children's fingers like buffalo wings, throwing the tiny bones over their shoulders. No, he did not want to go into town. No, he did not want to risk his life to sleep under a roof. But Brian never waited for him to respond. If Brian had waited, they wouldn't be in this mess. Steven played out the conversation in his mind. He saw himself telling Brian that they should bypass Odyssey, that it wasn't safe.

I would have saved our lives.

Time passed, and he did not turn from his side; curled up in the fetal position with gritted teeth. Every manner of wicked thought raced through his mind. The bunker was a luxury compared with the outside world.

The feeling of a hand on his shoulder made him jerk, and he realized that it was Brian waking him up for his shift.

Did I sleep at all? Oh, Jesus Christ, I'm so tired.

He sat up in the darkness and Brian rolled over to shut his eyes. They did not speak.

Steven stared, blinking down the black hallway, rubbing his swollen eyes. His eyesight was well adjusted to the darkness, and some shapes could be made out, like the outline of doorframes.

It was very quiet …

… and in a rush, the thoughts racing inside Steven's head went from dark to pitch-black.

The corpse is there, at the far end of the hallway, Stevie. Can you see it? Can you smell it? Can you taste it in the air?

Steven shook the voice out of his head and started rubbing his temples. He was unbelievably fatigued. Popping and snapping noises seemed to be going off in his mind, and the rushing of blood made the arteries in his temples feel like an overwatered dam on the verge of catastrophe.

The last thing he wanted to do was look down the hallway into the blackness. There were noises outside, things in the wind, crunching and crackling.

They're coming to get you, Stevie. They're right outside the window. They're right beneath you. They're going to eat you, slowly, for days, so you don't … spoil. Tell me, Stevie, did Stanley Jacobs … spoil? Or did you keep him … fresssh?

Steven gulped, and shut his eyes tight. Images flashed in his mind, so vivid they might have been real. Nancy. Benjamin. The conversation he and Brian had with Uncle Al, sitting at the table with hands crossed.

"You do right by them," Uncle Al had said. *"They raised you lads, and now it's your turn to care for them. They're old, and it's not right for them to live out their remaining years in this hell-storm that's brewing."*

I failed you … I failed them.

"You make them go down in the bunker, come hell or high water. Ben and Nancy, they're old now. They probably won't make it two years underground. But you make them comfortable, and when they pass…

… that's,

for when they die down there …

… what the walk-in freezer is for …"

Steven shot his eyes open, chasing the memories away. Every muscle in his body contracted. His forehead swelled as if his head was going to pop clean off his neck. He wanted to wake Brian. He wanted to reach out and shake Brian's shoulder. In the darkness, he reached his hand out, could see the outline of Brian's body … but he stopped.

Go on, wake him up. Wake up Brian so he can protect his little Stevie. Wake up Master Brian so he can protect his sidekick. You can't take care of yourself. You're incapable. Look at yourself, sitting in your own piss. Wake Brian up so he can take care of you, like he's been doing your entire life. He never wanted to stay in Nelson, you know. He stayed because of you, because you're pathetic, because you're—

There was movement in the hallway.

Wait ... was there?

Was it in the bedroom?

... Or was it nothing at all?

Steven clutched his rifle.

It's the corpse on the bed, Stevie. It's awake and dancing around and around. Can you taste the death that it brings? Can you smell the pungent odor of the earth dying, crumbling to its core? The skeleton is dancing, Stevie. It's dancing around and around, and Nancy and Ben are there too, dancing and dancing. Stanley is with them, but Stanley can't join in the dance. You know why, don't you, Stevie? You know why Stanley can't dance. Because Stanley is ... fresssh. You remember me, don't you, Stevie? You know who I am. I was with you in the bunker. You remember my voice.

Steven's head was between his knees, his palms gripping his ears, his eyes closed tight. He tried to speak against the voice in his mind, but every word he spoke was lost.

The voices in my head are my own, he told himself. *It's only fear talking, just like last time.*

But his logic was indecipherable.

Then the voice bellowed, reverberating the walls, shaking the floorboards.

LISTEN TO ME!

Steven looked up.

The corpse in the bedroom down the hall was awake, throwing back the soiled sheets from its withered bones and crawling on all fours down the hallway, closer and closer, blurry in the darkness. And with that, all manner of demons awoke in the night. They crawled through the doorway like a swarm of ants from an anthill, over the walls and ceiling, covering every square inch, and getting closer and closer, bones clicking and cracking. The corpse was almost to their doorway, dragging along the ground, its bones rattling, closer and closer, its long pointy fingers reaching out, clawing at Steven's toes—touching the blanket ...

***

Brian awoke in sunlight. Sleep was tough, but total exhaustion had forced him to close his eyes. He might have slept longer if the voices downstairs hadn't woken him.

Sitting upright, he pushed the drop-cloth sheet off his legs. Steven was awake, sitting up straight, his back like a board. He was staring wide-eyed down the hallway, as if in a trance. The voices downstairs were grumbly, unclear ... then Brian heard the unmistakable sound of stair treads creaking.

Neither he nor Steven moved as the sound grew louder.

A man entered the hallway from the staircase, clear as day. He was wearing pants, but no shoes, and a greasy T-shirt that was no longer white. The man walked straight across the hallway to the bathroom on the other side without so much as a glance in their direction.

Brian and Steven looked at each other in panic, then got to their feet. They hurried to either side of the doorway, their shoulders only inches from the corners. Brian heard the man pissing in the toilet. *The fucking plumbing still works?*

The man yelled to the other man downstairs, "Don't burn the bread!"

"I ain't burned nothing." The voice of the other man was gruff. Brian could smell food in the air, maybe beans and something charred, burning.

The man in the bathroom said, "Hmmm," as he pissed, and mumbled, "Shit, my head's throbbing." Then there was silence. It seemed to last many minutes. Brian and Steven looked at each other across the doorway. They held their rifles to their chests, and Brian unsnapped the button securing his knife in the sheath.

The man downstairs yelled, "What the fuck you doing up there? Breakfast is ready!" A sigh came from the bathroom, and the man answered, "Yeah, yeah." They heard the sound of his feet shuffle across the hallway floor. The floorboards creaked as he approached the stairway ... then the noise ceased. Brian's heart seemed to skip a beat.

"Why'd you leave a rifle up here?" the man asked.

Brian and Steven both turned to see Brian's scoped rifle leaning against the window frame. Their backpacks were there too, and so were the ruffled canvas cloths they'd used as blankets.

Brian's heart was now hammering in his ears. He looked across the doorway at his cousin, and saw the look in Steven's eyes ... red was coming

… red was here. Yet, there was something more, something crazed lurking in the dark circles around his eyes.

The man downstairs said, "What? I didn't leave nothing up there. C'mon, the beans is ready."

The man in the hallway did not answer back, but he also did not move from where he stood.

Please go downstairs, please go downstairs, please go downstairs …

Then the floorboards started squeaking directly toward their room.

"I'm looking right at a goddamned rifle, and it ain't mine." He was getting close, his feet shuffling audibly.

And then he walked clear into the room.

"And you left a backpack by the wind—" Steven reached out and grabbed the filthy man around the neck with one hand, his other hand going over the man's mouth. The man was yanked out of the doorframe in a flash, his head squeezed into Steven's chest. The man's feet were off the ground, wriggling, and then Steven threw him face-first against the hardwood floor.

"Jeees—"

Brian could not finish the sentence before Steven was running. Brian grabbed the closest backpack and ran after his cousin, who was already at the stairway. He looked briefly at the man on the ground, not moving, blood pooling.

At the bottom of the staircase, Brian saw Steven run toward the other man, who was scrambling to stand from a small circular table with two plates of steaming beans upon it. He stared slack-jawed at Steven, scratching at a holster on his belt. Steven did not stop moving as he swung his giant fist straight into the man's face, producing an awful crunch. The man was thrown backward, his head bouncing over the ground, the table falling over in a crash.

In seconds, Steven was outside, Brian on his heels. He had never seen his cousin run so fast.

Brian wanted to yell, "Steve, wait!" But he didn't. They were running like the wind in the direction from which they had entered Odyssey the previous day. Brian did not dare look back. He was certain bullets would come flying over his head at any given moment—but he did not look back, and he did not hear any gunshots.

***

93

Off in the woods, a man named Mark Haines sat with his back against a big tree next to a fast-moving stream. He was rubbing the morning from his eyes while fixing the rubber waders around his knees. It was his and Ned Patterson's job to check the fish traps first thing every morning.

Mark Haines stood, stretching tall while yawning into the sky. He strode into the stream, cursing at the cold morning water. The hangover raging inside his head made every step an ordeal. The last place on Earth he wanted to be at that moment was out in the ice-cold water. But he had a job to do. A ways off, Ned checked the western trap. Mark looked out for him, but didn't see any movement other than the rushing water.

He should be done about now.

Mark was halfway across the stream when he heard something. Leaves crackling. "Ned, that you? Anything in the trap?" Ned didn't answer. The man scratched his white beard. "Ned, where you at?"

Behind the tree he had just left, a beast of a man wearing a dark poncho charged out from the brush. The man came crashing down the small incline, pummeling into the water, and coming straight at Mark. The man's mouth was foaming, and his eyes were a dreadful stare.

It ain't human.

"F-fuck!" Mark Haines dropped his wicker fish basket into the water, where the fast current carried it away. He stepped back, but his ankle caught on something and he fell into the frigid water.

In a flash, Mark jumped back to his feet, looking at the bank where his rifle sat leaning against a tree. He began to draw his pistol, screaming, "Ne-NED! NED!"

Mark did not have time to raise his revolver before the beast was upon him. His large arms wrapped around Mark's head, squashing his face into his chest. Mark's feet rose into the air, thrashing about over the water. The man squeezed with all his might and jerked his body to the side, snapping Mark's neck and dropping him in the water at the same time. The movement was fluid, graceful. A perfect symphony of violence.

The current swept the floating Mark Haines away, and Steven lumbered on, crossing the stream to the bank on the other side.

From the northwest end of the stream, the man named Ned Patterson came crashing through the water. When he saw Steven, he stopped short.

"Shit!" He raised his rifle. Ned had Steven dead in his sights.

A shot rang out.

But Steven did not fall. Ned Patterson flew backward. He never saw Brian Rhodes standing on the opposite bank, his rifle aimed squarely at him.

Brian lowered his gun. "Holy hell," he spoke through labored breaths. "Christ in heaven." Ned's body swept past Brian, facedown in the stream as the rapids carried him away.

Brian Rhodes sprinted into the water and continued after Steven.

Chapter 14
Ejército Mexicano

Sleep was difficult. Freeze frames of the boy at the gas station flashed through Simon's mind. The small body flying, a cloud of red mist and jacket fibers suspended in the air. He heard the boy's squeaky voice and replayed their conversation, changing words, trying to make things right.

But there was no way to make things right.

Shortly after speeding away from the gas station, Simon stopped the van and stumbled outside to vomit. He vomited again when he made camp that night, and in the morning, he felt weak, his mind lost and his body in pain.

Winston might have sensed something, because he stayed at Simon's side the entire first night. Even the next day as they drove on, Winston repeatedly tried to walk across the seats to sit on Simon's lap.

Simon scratched the spot on his head. "I'm so sorry I yelled at you, boy. I'm so, so, sorry." His emotions were uncontrollable. On two occasions, Simon stopped to try and meditate, but it was impossible.

As the drive went on, he was reminded of a teaching he had once read. From where, or what book, he could not remember. It taught that emotions, negative or positive—but with a strong emphasis on the negative—were products of the mind and not of the outward world. They were two separate things. Therefore, when an event occurs in the outside world, which would be described as *negative*, it does not mean that the mental state needs to be negative as well. Inner peace and clarity of mind: these things are possible, even during the worst circumstances. Even death.

But what about the killing of a child?

It went against everything Simon had studied. Killing, murder, death, violence—these things were not permitted. Buddhists do not eat meat because killing an animal is an act of violence. Not that Simon considered himself a Buddhist. He accepted killing and eating animals because he did it for survival, but he understood and accepted the principle.

A teacher at one of his classes—not Marcus Warden, but a female instructor named Mica—had told him that even flowers scream out in pain when they are picked from the stems; it's only that we can't hear their voices. Simon focused on these thoughts, these teachings; he needed something, anything, to put his mind at ease.

So he tried to dissociate himself from the act. He rationalized it as an outward event, and although it happened, he could maintain that the present moment was positive in his current space and time, and he did not have to maintain a negative mindset. Yet, he was the one who had pulled the trigger. This was not an event he witnessed—it was a result of his actions.

Was it better to be dead?

Should he have let the boy kill him to maintain the zero-tolerance-for-violence law? He went over the conversation by the gas pump again and again, trying to change the words, trying to change the outcome.

However, all of these events were now in the past. He could not change his words or actions. He needed to stay in the moment—the here and now. Staying focused was imperative, if not for himself, then for the fate of the next young boy he might encounter.

This thought gave him some peace. He knew and accepted that killing the boy was an act of violence, and it would haunt him forever. Reality had to be accepted, the past left behind, and the future must unfold as it will.

Out in a field, behind a group of trees, Simon stopped and ate lunch. He tossed a stick around with Winston. If he himself could not be happy, at least he could get Winston in a good mood; and seeing Winston run around with his floppy tongue bouncing always brightened his spirits.

He ate from a bag of boiled chestnuts and thought about what the boy had said to him, "I k-k-know what m-men like you do to kids like me." *I know what men like you do.* What did men like Simon do to kids like him? He was not sure he wanted to know. Simon sealed the bag of chestnuts, put some water in a bowl for Winston—who lapped it up in haste—and packed the van.

"Come on, idiot, get in." Winston looked up, licking the dripping water off his lips. Simon laughed. "Your face is soaked."

***

The roads became more congested with abandoned vehicles the farther east Simon drove. He had to veer off the shoulder for long stretches at a time and slow to a crawl over rocks and ruts. Unfortunately, he knew it would only get worse farther east. The traffic on the opposite side of the highway, heading westward, was double in volume. Those were the people fleeing the coast.

In the town of Crawford, Simon witnessed large-scale devastation, unprecedented by anything he had yet seen.

The business district was easy to bypass, but he could see from the passing streets that the city center was reduced to rubble. The skeleton of a helicopter sat black and scorched, sticking out from the top of a tall building. The fire that consumed it had left nothing but twisted metal. Army vehicles—nothing more than shells—were everywhere. Bodies littered the land, many left where they fell, others in charred heaps, indecipherable from the wreckage and carnage of that blackened land.

Outside of Crawford, the road stayed flat and straight for many miles, leading to a range of mountains far on the horizon.

Simon traveled on, reaching the hairpin curves in the road leading over the mountains. When he reached the highest point, he could see the interstate and valley on the opposite side. The sun was full and bright, and the valley below twinkled in the light like a sky full of stars. Simon stopped the van and grabbed his binoculars.

"Holy hell," he said, scanning the area for miles around. The road itself went straight and then veered to the right, where he could see the glimmer of a city far in the distance. To the left, scattered over the valley like a thousand fallen raindrops, were the remains of fighter planes and drones stretching as far as the eye could see. What nationality the planes belonged to, Simon did not know. It looked like a scrapyard. Debris lay scattered across the landscape, and dark craters pockmarked the land where aircraft fell from the sky.

He got back in the van and drove on.

Once in the valley, the land was too flat to see much of the devastation that was all around, and the road stayed straight and true. The abundance of vehicles increased as he neared the town, and the going was tough and slow. He had to veer off the road for long stretches, with the van bouncing on its springs. The gas barrels in the back were always on his mind, and with every bump, he listened for the sound of leaking fluid.

He drove on the sidewalk as he entered the town, past rows of abandoned vehicles. Buildings were taller here and closer together. This town—whatever its name may be—was the closest thing to a true city that Simon had yet seen.

There was just enough clearance for the van to drive through the cluster of vehicles, and Simon wished that he had a motorcycle, or one of those smart cars. He would have to consider trading out the van soon. There were plenty of vehicles all around, left everywhere; he could take whatever he wanted.

The path between cars brought him back to the pavement, crammed in the middle of the two lanes. The road turned to the right, circling around a large open park with a tall statue in the middle—an ancient-looking man standing atop pillars, covered in vines. The buildings circling the park had a Southern or European look to them with cast-iron balconies and dark-shingled roofs. They were all boarded up, deserted—dead. Grass in the park was wild, grown taller than the benches. There were few bodies on the ground, but the cars were full of them—like a citywide mausoleum.

Driving through the park itself would have been easier, but it was impossible to get over. Simon approached a narrow gap between two sedans that left little room for him to pass. As he inched between them, he heard the squeal of the cars' bumpers rubbing up against either side of the van.

Then Simon heard a loud *pop,* and the steering wheel jolted.

His heart was filled with dread. "Shit," he said. "Shit, shit." He smacked the steering wheel with his palm. "Damn it! Winston, we popped a tire. I don't know about this town. I don't know if we're going to be able make it through. Shit!" He whacked the steering wheel again.

The buildings on the far side of the park were too far away to see any evidence of living people, but he didn't see any movement. He shouldered his rifle, grabbed the backpack, and opened the door. He left it open as he crouched beside the car that was pinned against the side of the van. The front left tire of the van was blown out completely and sat on the rim. There were two spares in the back along with a hydraulic jack, but the little Civic that was wedged against the van was right at the tire. He knelt again, feeling for the indent on the bottom of the van where the jack fit in. The tire rim sat in a deep pothole, with muddy rainwater splashed about. Simon stared at the pothole, and things began clicking in his mind: the perfect lane for his van to follow, the tire popping at the right moment …

"Oh, shi—"

A *bang* echoed out over the park, and the rear windshield of the Civic exploded, sending a shower of glass shards over Simon's back and dancing upon the pavement.

Simon dropped and rolled to the rear of the van. "Winst-Winston!"

Half-submerged in the grimy puddle water in the pothole, was a short plank of wood with nails sticking out. Long, sinister nails.

The shooter could be anywhere, but judging from the sound of the shot and the direction of the falling glass, Simon speculated that the shooter was in one of the far buildings across the park. Or maybe in the park itself, hiding in the tall grass.

Winston did not come out. The dog was terrified of loud noises and probably sitting on the floor of the van with his ears pinned back, trembling.

"Winston! Winston!" Simon's back was against the rear of the van. Another crack-like explosion ripped through the air, and a bullet walloped into the side of the van, just around the bend, only a foot away from his face.

"Jesus!"

Simon dove to the ground, and before he knew what he was doing, he was on his feet and running as fast as he could. He weaved in and out between cars, jumped over bodies, all the while screaming, "Winston! Winston! Winston!"

He was out of town the way that he came—among the line of vehicles on the interstate—and he continued running. He looked behind him and saw Winston fast at his heels, his tongue flopping out of his mouth and his ears pulled back tight. As terrified as Simon was, seeing his dog behind him removed a giant weight from his heart.

Coming to a halt, he dropped to a knee behind a car and grabbed Winston at his scruff, pulling him in close. The dog trembled against him. Simon held his rifle in one hand, his body low to the ground, and grabbed at his binoculars with the other, scanning the road. He saw nothing. Just the buildings at the town's entrance.

Then he heard another bang, and at the same time, the pavement beside him erupted in an explosion of concrete chips.

"God damn!"

Some pebbles struck his knuckles and he flinched, moving his fingers to make sure they still worked. Blood sprang to the surface. He jumped behind the car, shielding himself.

"Down, Winston! Down!" The dog was already down and staring at him with huge brown eyes.

After a moment, Simon heard the crackle of static, then a booming voice come over a megaphone.

"*Amigo! Hey, hey! Amigo!*"

Simon didn't say anything.

"*Cómo estás? Lo qué le trae por aquí?*"

He looked at Winston. "Fucking Spanish?" Simon took one year of Spanish in high school and remembered next to nothing.

"*Hey!*" came the voice, "*Deje el camión, girar y salir.*"

Simon did not know if he was supposed to answer.

"*Se deja el coche, perra estúpida americana. Se puede entender una palabra que estoy diciendo? Nosotros tenemos rodeado, podemos matar fácilmente. Matarte muertos! Correr y dejar el coche donde está! No vuelvas.*"

Simon knew what *muertos* meant. It occurred to him that he had been shot at three times, and at least two of the times the shooter had a clear line of sight, yet he missed. They were warning him, driving him away.

He spoke, shouting, "What do you want? Do you speak English?"

There was a pause, and then, "*The van. It is ours.*" His accent was thick. "*This town; it is ours. We will kill you no problem, comprendes?*"

"Don't shoot, okay? Don't shoot!" Simon began to stand. "Don't shoot!" He looked to his left and was shocked to see three people sitting just a few feet from him, on the side of the road.

"Jesus fucking Christ!" He jolted, falling on his back, and swung the rifle in their direction. He stared at them, his hands trembling on the rifle, and realized they were long dead. Crusty blankets were draped over their shoulders, and their bodies were nothing more than dusty shells—dry and empty leather.

"Take the van; it's yours! I don't fucking want it!" It occurred to Simon it would be better to not sound hostile. "I'll leave. Okay? I'll never come back."

There was silence.

Simon repeated, "I'll—"

"Yes, you go now."

Simon hesitated and then stood with his hands up over his head. He looked at the entrance to the town, toward the voice for only a moment. There were four men, all dark skinned and wearing matching army-green uniforms with black tactical vests. The man with the megaphone had a potbelly and wore a cap, while the others wore helmets. Two men kneeled, holding machine guns pointed right at him, and the other stood at the potbellied man's side.

Simon turned and began walking away with Winston at his heels. A shot rang out, hitting nothing but the sky, but Simon started sprinting away. The men laughed, and the microphone crackled, *"Andale amigo!"*

They laughed and Simon ran.

Chapter 15
The Waterside

Running while wearing the pack was difficult, and the distance between Brian and Steven grew until Steven was only a blur of movement in the distant woods before him. Brian shouted for him to slow down, but whether Steven heard him or not, he did not reply. They were over two miles outside of Odyssey when Steven slowed and Brian caught up.

Steven was doubled over, holding a tree for support. Labored breaths came wheezing out of his mouth, and he was dry-heaving thick strings of saliva. Brian fell to his knees beside him, grabbing at the stitch on his side.

After a moment, Brian said, "That was some shit."

Steven wiped his mouth with a sleeve.

They sat catching their breath for several minutes, still fearful that men were on their heels. Steven stood first, and then Brian labored to his feet and pulled out his map, finding a route to bypass Odyssey.

Brian knew without a doubt that the two men in the river outside of Odyssey were dead. The other two men in the house might also be dead. With any hope, they were *all* dead, and their bodies would not be discovered for a long time.

Brian walked beside his cousin. "You did the right thing back there."

Steven did not answer.

"I shot that one in the water stone dead. You see him? Jesus. He came out of nowhere. That boy had you dead in his sights."

Still, Steven did not answer.

As they walked on, Steven slowed, trailing behind Brian, and staring off in the woods. Brian wanted to keep him talking, but there was no use. Steven was prone to fits of silence; this was nothing new. The first time his silence had worried Brian was after Steven's parents died and Brian moved in with him. Steven barely spoke for a month. But the world was different back then, and Brian was able to get Steven out of the house for a few drinks here and there. He recovered in time.

The second time Steven's silence had worried Brian was all too recent—down in the bunker. The first few weeks underground weren't that bad, all things considered. The bunker was designed to hold six people, so they had plenty of space to move around and room for privacy. They worked out once or twice a day, played ping-pong and poker, watched movies, and read books.

Things changed that fateful day when the visitor showed up at the bunker door. Brian knew neither of them would ever be the same, but it had affected Steven in a different way. He became somber, quiet, and restless. In the months following the visitor's departure, they continued playing cards and working out, but it was like Brian did these things alone.

As they neared the two-year mark, Steven was improving remarkably. He was smiling and lifting weights with such vigor that Brian could hardly keep up. They were talking about leaving and starting to make plans. Steven was excited—so much so that he barely slept and twice almost collapsed with exhaustion at the weight bench. They had to go. They had to leave the bunker.

And now Steven was quiet again.

They walked all day without taking a break, putting the town of Odyssey safely behind them. At night, they made a small fire buried deep underground and heated a can of chili for supper. They'd left most of their gear in Odyssey, except for one scout pack. Rations were slim. They would have to start hunting and filtering water.

That night, they slept back to back on the ground, using the one sleeping bag spread open as a blanket. Neither slept for more than two hours, and in the early morning they continued, cold and stiff.

The forest was void of anything human—no garbage, no cold campfires, no tracks. Nothing. It was quiet out there, and with the absence of rain, it was eerily still.

Brian said, "I reckon we have to start hunting."

"I reckon so."

"You wanna start looking for tracks, or continue on a ways?"

"Continue on."

"All right." Then, after a pause, Brian asked, "You know what's strange?"

"What's that?"

"You seen any deer about, or rabbits? I ain't seen a single deer this whole time."

Steven looked in the woods about him. "There's birds in that tree."

Brian looked up. He could hear the birds. "Yeah, I reckon so. It's strange we ain't seen a deer though, don't you think?"

"I think it's plenty strange."

"You think—"

"I reckon I don't know, and I reckon I don't want to know."

That concluded their conversation for the day. They ate a small lunch in the afternoon, and as the evening approached, the rain returned.

***

They were stopping now six to eight times a day, so tired and exhausted that when they hit the ground, their legs and feet throbbed in pain.

Keeping watch at night was now a must, so they took shifts, each man remaining vigilant of their surroundings as the other fell to fitful rest. It was then, when Steven was alone, that his mind turned dark with rambling thoughts and vivid images—blood and gore, torn limbs, sinewy corpses, broken necks, charred baby hands eaten off the bone by rotten teeth, demons of all manner. These demons were in his mind, and in the tree branches above, and crawling across the muddy ground, and whistling through the air carried over by the breeze. They came out at night; all the evil of the world came out at night and danced around in Steven's head and before his eyes. Sleep was far at bay.

That night, as Brian slept and Steven sat with his back against a tree, people long dead emerged from the darkness, stretching and ripping their taut, leathery skin. They came out of the trees and slithered in the grass, clawing at his feet, foul rotten flesh falling from their bones.

They're coming, Stevie, they're coming to dance on your grave, going 'round and 'round, and then you, Stevie, can join in the dance. You too can join them.

***

If Brian was hungry before, he was starving now. Steven's sister Bethany was close, only a matter of days. She would have supplies in her bunker. Food. Water. Medicine.

They fell often, slipping on rocks and mud. Both men had cuts on their hands and fingers, scraped knees, and feet so torn up that there was little they could do to heal them. They never stopped to hunt, partially because they never saw tracks of any large game, and partially because they were so close to Bethany that it kept them moving forward.

Rations consisted of high-calorie survival bars, which tasted and looked like particleboard sprinkled with lemon zest. They split one bar a day, which was far less than the number of calories they were burning.

Several days passed with them in a hypnotic, near delirious state.

The rain had momentarily ceased as they walked up a steep hill on all fours, their hands grabbing at rocks and branches to pull themselves along. They could hear running water under the rocky terrain from the runoff of a pond at the summit.

Steven slipped, rolling backward a few feet before stopping himself on a boulder. He got to his feet and continued along the path. Brian looked back, but when he saw that Steven was able to pull himself up, he did not bother asking if he was hurt. They were both hurt, bruised, and bleeding. Brian reached the summit and waited, catching his breath as Steven lumbered to meet him. They both sat, slumped over and breathing hard, watching the pond water ripple.

They filtered water into their canteens and found a small clearing beside the pond to sit and take a break. Brian took off the backpack, and they sat in silence with their eyes closed for many minutes. Then they took off their shoes and grimaced as they peeled back their socks. Their feet were wrapped in strips of cloth cut from their undershirts. The cloths were stained red, and Brian gagged at the septic stench.

Then Brian heard something in the brush, not far. Both men sat rigid.

For a few moments, they stayed where they were, hidden from sight behind the tall weeds and trees, and listened to the sound of someone walking, legs scraping plants and brush. Creeping to the edge of the clearing, they peered out. A tall man stood beside the water's edge, maybe six foot three and lean, yet muscular.

The man knelt before the pond, splashed water over his face, then he opened the clasp on a shaving kit, and began lathering his face with a bar of soap. He was quick about it, studying his reflection in the water and swiping the razor over his skin with precise strokes. When he was done, he began washing himself with more and more water, much more than necessary. He kept splashing water over his face and head until a raspy voice rang out, "That's enough, Charlie. Get yer ass back here!"

The tall man slumped back on his heels. He grabbed a small stick from the ground and began poking at his reflection in the water.

"Damn it, Charlie!"

The man dropped the stick and stood, walking back the way he came. He took his time, stopping to pick flowering weeds, and stood marveling at a small tree for a moment. He scratched at his dark gray hair, cut short like a military flattop, then shuffled off.

Brian and Steven looked at each other. There was a smell in the air. At first it was just smoke, wood burning, but then there was something else. Food cooking. Brian's stomach groaned, and his mouth watered.

He grabbed his rifle and crawled through the weeds, Steven right behind him, until he could see smoke rising. It wasn't far.

They stopped when they could see two people—a much older man and the tall skinny one called Charlie. The old man sat on a log by the fire, a cane over his legs. He stirred something in a pot, which was bubbling with steam. Charlie sat with his legs crossed on the ground as he tossed small twigs into the flame.

Steven reached for his belt, unsnapped the button on his knife sheath, and began unsheathing the blade. Brian grabbed his wrist and shook his head, but Steven pulled his arm free. Brian hissed, "No, Steven—no."

Steven looked at Brian. "He's a retard."

"Don't, Steven. They ain't done nothin'."

"They have food."

"No, Steve. Wait."

They turned back to the two men. The travelers were squinting in their direction. Nobody said a word.

"Come on." Brian stood with his rifle up. Steven stepped beside him, raising his gun.

"Hey there," Brian shouted across the clearing.

The old man nodded, but did not smile. Charlie stood.

"Hey, hey, take it easy." Brian pointed the gun at him, but he just smiled from ear to ear.

"Hi," Charlie said.

"Charlie, sit yer ass down," the old man said.

Brian looked at the two, inspecting their possessions. They had one large bag and one smaller one. Charlie's jeans and flannel shirt looked clean, almost new, but the old man was filthy, his hair twisted about and his long-white beard streaked with dirt. There were no firearms to be seen, just a knife the old man was using to stir the pot and a cleaver resting on top of the smaller bag.

"We're unarmed." The old man scratched his beard. "We ain't gonna do you no harm."

"Where you headed?" Brian asked.

"Where *you* headed?" the old man replied.

Neither answered. They stared at each other, and after a moment, Brian lowered his gun. Steven yanked on his shoulder and leaned in close to Brian's ear. "Let's get out of here. They ain't right, these two."

Brian shrugged him off. "We're hungry," he said. "We would be thankful for anything you could spare."

"Can't spare nothing." The old man looked at Steven, who was staring at him. "Everyone's hungry. Always hungry." He did not flinch from Steven's gaze. "Tell you what." The old man sighed. "You put them guns down and we'll spare you a bowl full, but that's plenty. You be on your ways after."

Brian nodded. "Much obliged."

"*Brian,*" Steven said in a hiss.

Brian walked to the fire, and Steven followed. Charlie was playing with pebbles. He reached across the fire to hand one to Brian. "That's for you," he said. His facial features resembled those of a child, with a large forehead and chin that jutted out past his tiny nose.

Brian smiled. "Ain't that kind of you."

The old man passed tin plates and gave everyone a ladle of stew from the pot. It was a thick and rancid-looking stew, the top coated with a yellow layer of grease.

The old man asked, "Where yer shoes at?"

"Just yonder," Brian said.

Steven poked at a bit of meat with his spoon and picked up a chunk. He brought the spoon to his mouth, blowing back the steam, and nibbled at the corner. Brian did the same, weary of the smell. The meat was tough and fatty. He gagged.

"It's coon meat." The old man watched Steven eat. "I never said I could cook worth a damn."

They were so hungry that they ate with abandon, and afterward, Brian's stomach felt hot and queasy.

He sat back, looking the two over. "Must be tough traveling, just the two of you."

"It is," the old man said. "This one here is a pain in the ass."

"He your son?"

"My *son*? No, he ain't my kin. I found him curled up naked in the middle of the woods. You remember that, boy?"

Charlie nodded. "Mary was with me. My sister."

"That's enough of that," the old man said.

"Can I go to the water?"

"Go on, then."

The tall man went to the pond and started splashing water over his face.

"He likes to shave, for some reason. Can't get him to stop. He shaves four, five times a day. Scrubs his face whenever there's water. Cleans his clothes at every opportunity. I think if I left him by some stream, he'd stand in the water until he drowned. I got a mind to do just that."

"He looks healthy, considering you found him in the woods. How in the world did he survive all this time?"

"Beats the hell out of me. Must have been with some folks before I found him. The boy's strong as a bull, carries all our gear like it don't weigh a thing."

"What happened to Mary?"

"Who?"

"His sister. Mary."

"What do you think?"

"She dead?"

"She is. Everyone dies. She was young, six maybe. Don't know how she lasted as long as she did."

"She die a while back, from the disease?"

"Died yesterday."

Brian could feel Steven's eye's staring at him. They exchanged glances and stood.

"Thanks for the food. We'll be on our way."

"Right."

Brian shouted to Charlie, "You take care now."

The tall man laughed and beat at the water with a stick.

"Knock that shit off, Charlie!" the old man yelled.

They left the fire. Brian looked over his shoulder, and the old man stared at them until they disappeared. They retrieved their shoes and gear.

"Let's get the hell out of here," Steven said. "Something ain't right with them."

"I reckon you're right."

Chapter 16

Namaste

Simon contemplated getting rid of his backpack, stripping down to his pants, knife, and pistol, and continuing the trek in the manner of a scout, dressed with mud and charcoal and becoming the wind—invisible, safe, and dangerous.

But he didn't do that.

With Winston at his heels, traveling like a scout was out of the question. He was traveling light as it was; no sense in getting rid of what little supplies he had left.

His backpack contained dried kibble for Winston, a canteen, a water filter, emergency ration bars, bags of dried grain, a few supplies like ammunition, fishing lines, and a wool blanket. Enough to keep him and Winston healthy and safe.

After traveling several miles away from the town overtaken by the Mexican soldiers and feeling relatively safe, a calm came over Simon that he had not felt in a long time—not since leaving the cabin. He was in control. He could hear and see his surroundings without them streaming by in a rapid blur. Perhaps it was better that the van was taken from him. Perhaps it was the earth's way of protecting him.

Several days and nights went by without incident. On foot, Simon bypassed towns when he could, maneuvered through them when he couldn't, and slept at night in parks and woods.

Winston kept up, happily trotting beside him, sniffing charred rocks and random spots of grass along their journey.

"How you doing there, buddy?" Simon asked, looking over to his dog and ruffling his head. Winston looked up, panting and lapping at Simon's moving hand.

"Getting tired? Me too."

As night approached, Simon inspected his map and found a large park inside the town they had just entered, named Poricy. He made a debris hut by placing sticks against the side of a fallen tree, forming a ribcage-like structure, and then piling the construction high with branches and leaves. Next, he stuffed the inside with more fallen leaves to form a mattress, and snuggled inside with Winston, wrapping the wool blanket tightly around them. It was warm in there, and Simon slept better than he had in days. The fear of people seeing the van and lurking into the camp to murder and steal from him had been extinguished.

In the morning, he scattered the debris hut and started scouting the area around camp for food. He found small patches of wheat stalks mixed in a field of wildflowers, and picked every one within reach, scattering about many of the seeds from the grainy heads to continue the plants' life cycle.

Simon thought he had heard running water as he entered the park the previous night, and sure enough, after backpedaling a short ways, he came upon a flowing creek. He filtered fresh water into his canteen, then found a thicket of wild goldenrod on his way back to camp. Although the plant was not in full bloom, he collected what he could of the small brilliant yellow flowers, crushing some in his hand to breathe in the fragrant, slightly sour scent. After collecting the flowers, he picked a handful of the plant's leaves, to be used later, either boiled down like spinach or eaten raw.

At camp, he gathered wood and started a small fire. He added the goldenrod leaves, along with a handful of pine needles, to the water. Simon breathed in the pleasant aroma of anise and pine, wafting the steam over his face.

When the tea had finished seeping, he relaxed, leaning against a fallen tree and letting the warmth of his drink spread throughout his body.

"I bet you're hungry, buddy." Winston's ears perked up. His mouth opened and his tongue panted out. "Who's my hungry boy? Are you my hungry boy?"

Simon found in his pack the large sack of dehydrated vegetable and jerky-meat kibble, and held out a handful for Winston to gobble up. He popped a few pieces in his mouth, letting his teeth sink into the small pieces of dried meat. Winston ate three handfuls before Simon packed the bag away. The fire was out, and a faint trail of smoke whispered in the air.

Simon was contemplating whether to grind the heads of the wheat stalks now or wait until later … when he heard a noise in the woods.

He froze. Winston's head perked up, looking sharply into the underbrush.

Breathe in. Breathe out.

There was more noise, movement. The sound of something brushing up against plants.

Is it a deer? No, too big … too many. Too clumsy.

It was people—humans—not far. Approaching. Simon slung the pack over his shoulder, grabbed his rifle, and tapped Winston on his back, motioning with his head for him to follow.

They cleared the thicket surrounding the camp and crept up behind the side of a large maple. Simon pressed his body against it, one eye looking over the side, watching his camp, holding Winston by his scruff. He breathed, his chest expanding in and out against the hard side of the tree, his breath flowing like the wind, going in and out of the world, gently blowing with the branches back and forth.

I am the wind. I am the rock. I am the tree, and my roots grow deep ….

People walked into the clearing, around the fire. At first two people, and then three. Then four, and then six, and then more—over a dozen. Some had long hair and beards and others were shaved bald. There were both men and women in the group, and … yes, Simon could see a child. The majority of them were wearing something like a monk's robe—simple cream-white colored clothes—and none of them appeared armed.

They walked into the camp, examining the smoke trailing out of the extinguished fire, and looking all around into the wilderness. One of them toed the smoldering twigs, and a few of them spoke, but it was hard for Simon to hear what they were saying. One of them picked up the cup of tea that Simon had been drinking and held it to his nose. He looked at the man beside him, offering him the cup. The next man took a deep breath then placed it back on the log where they had found it. The child at the man's side wore a miniature version of the monk's robe with his head shaved bald, and bent down to inspect the contents of the cup.

As they spoke, a few of them removed necklaces made of thick beads, mindfully passing the beads between their fingers. They all seemed to be looking at one man, and stood tall and straight and were silent as he spoke.

After a moment, they changed course and walked in the direction of the water.

When they disappeared from view and Simon could no longer hear any noises or disturbances, he turned to Winston. "Stay, Winston. You have to *stay*." He opened his pack, put a handful of kibble on the ground, and with slow steps, he left the shelter of the tree to follow in their direction.

They were at the pond's edge. One was starting a fire, and a few others gathered water in pots to be boiled. Some wore small backpacks over their shoulders, and others carried only bedrolls tied at the ends with rope. The congregators who were not working on the fire and water were sitting on the ground with their legs crossed. An old man in a white robe faced the rest of the group, and after they gathered themselves on the ground, he made a gentle, guttural noise.

"Ommmmm."

Then they all took a deep breath and exhaled in unison: "Ommmmm." They repeated this several times, no one moving or fidgeting.

Simon was fascinated, and when he looked to the leader, he saw his eyes were open—not fully, but open in a relaxed manner—and he was looking right at him. Simon clung to the rock he was hiding against.

The group repeated, "Ommmmm." The sound seemed to resonate in the ground, vibrate through his feet and into his chest. The old man smiled, a thin and humble smile, and nodded. He then looked away, straight ahead, and held his beaded necklace in his left hand, feeling one of the round beads between two fingers.

This went on for some time before Simon stood. There was one man left tending to the fire as the others sat in meditation. That man looked at Simon, but showed no sign of emotion as he turned back to tending the flames. Simon stood apart from the group as they chanted and looked to the man in the front. His eyes and face were expressionless, lost in another world. Simon sat, crossed his legs, and chanted along with them.

***

When the meditation was over, the group stretched and a few stood, moving at a slow pace. Some of the men and women nodded to Simon, several bowed, and one even hugged him. "Namaste, brother," he whispered. They did not ask him any question, not even why he was there. They stood, talking softly to one another. The man at the head of the group was still sitting, yet he was no longer locked in meditation. He motioned for Simon to approach.

The man smiled as Simon sat at his side, and Simon said, "Hello."

"Hello," the man answered.

"Where are you guys headed?"

"Wherever our feet take us."

Simon took that in. "Are you in charge?"

"No." The man laughed a gentle laugh. "No one is in charge. Everyone does as they wish, and so far, we wake up every day and *wish* to continue walking."

Simon looked the group over. No one was starving or injured. "You guys look healthy."

"We are blessed."

"Are you armed?"

"No. We do not participate in violence."

"You're Buddhists?"

"No. We are nothing. We live surrounded by inward and outward peace. We meditate to keep our minds healthy and walk to keep our bodies in motion. And so our bodies and mind are in unison."

"What do you do for food?"

"We eat."

Simon laughed. The old man laughed too and continued, "I understand that our principles can be met with confusion. We don't carry much, because when we carry belongings it makes other people interested in us. If we have nothing to take, we are left alone. We hide the boy under our robes when we pass others, and we give our possessions willingly to anyone who may want to take them. We've had many of our brothers and sisters killed for no other reason than someone wanting the shirt off their backs. People have used violence against us for what we offer freely."

"I'm sorry to hear that."

"Don't be." The man smiled. "What is done is done and cannot be lamented over."

Simon nodded. "Looks like you have things figured out."

"No, we don't, and we don't want to. We just choose to live so that the earth can heal from its wounds, and we encourage all others we meet to do the same. Tell me, do you believe in karma?"

"Well … to a degree, I guess."

"It's much more than just negative and positive reactions. It works on a global scale. Humans have inflicted so much damage and negativity to the earth that nature did what it had to do—it eliminated most of mankind with a disease."

"You think?"

"Yes, I do. Tell me." The old man smiled. "What is your name?"

"Simon."

"Well, Simon, for centuries the human race has been devastating the Earth. We've killed whole species of animals without giving it any thought, stripped away entire forests, polluted the air, and poisoned our streams. We engaged in nuclear warfare, burning and ravaging anything that stood in our way. The earth's karmic scale has been tipped, and the result is what we have witnessed. A mass extinction."

"Is that what caused the virus? How?"

"It came from the Earth."

"Right. I mean—is that the final verdict?"

"There will never be a final verdict."

"Okay, I see what you're saying." Simon pondered these words as the old man counted the beads on his necklace. "Well," Simon went on, "thank you for sharing your thoughts. I will think about what you said."

"That's exactly right," the old man said. "You *must think*—and think with a positive mindset. When you meditate, focus your thoughts, you remain a constructive element of this Earth and are destined to reposition the karmic scale. Even if you do not know it, that is what you are doing."

Simon nodded. There was a commotion behind him, and Simon turned to see the young boy running up to Winston, who had just emerged from the woods. The boy was giddy with laughter as he hugged Winston around his neck. Winston's tail was a fury of wagging, and he licked at the boy's face with abandon.

"You see?" The old man nodded toward Winston and the boy. "What do you feel when you see a young boy and a dog playing together? Positivity is the key. Positive karma is essential. There are still many good people left in this world, but there are also many who are evil. More evil than good, it seems, but there is still some balance on the scale. It has not yet tipped fully in either direction—although it may appear to have done so.

"When you see a young child hug a dog, your heart grows warm with love, and it is *that* love that we must embrace. Love is the feeling of all humans being the best possible humans that we can be. If that is hard to comprehend, then you must think of one person. Imagine that this one person is healthy, happy, and achieving greatness—even if that greatness is only to gather water from a stream or to hug a dog around the neck. That feeling of love you get in your heart is how all of us—all humans—should feel at all times."

Simon didn't know what to say, so he nodded that he understood.

The old man patted Simon's knee, and Simon could tell that their talk was over. He stood and walked over to Winston, who was beyond happy with the little boy. Everyone in the group was taking turns scratching his head and having their face and hands licked. The old man was focused again in meditation, counting beads, and staring at nothing in particular. Winston came over and sniffed the old man's hand, gave him a lick, then walked away. He then turned, bent, and bit at a tuft of grass that the old man was unfocused on.

The old man blinked and then said, "Ha! And so it goes with the impermanence of all dharma. Leave it to a dog to teach the ways." He laughed and stood. "I'll take that as a cue that it is time to move on."

A few members of the group talked to Simon and made it clear that anyone could join them on their walk, although they did not know where it would take them. They had been heading east, like Simon, but in a little more of a southern direction. The path would be the same for several days, unless the group decided to veer, which weather or terrain might dictate. Simon took out his map and showed them where he was heading. A few in the group glanced at the page uninterested, then smiled and walked away.

The old man asked Simon, "What do you expect to find when you get to your destination?"

"My family," he answered.

The old man nodded, not showing the slightest range of emotion. "That will remain in my thoughts," he said.

They started walking, and Simon followed. They walked for hours, following the creek, in long stretches of tranquil silence. When they stopped for the night, Simon went off to gather some of the cattails that were growing all around. A few in the group studied him from afar, and then walked closer.

"What are you doing?"

"Getting dinner." Simon showed them the cattails. "These are edible."

"Could you show me how to do that?" one of them asked.

"Sure."

Simon showed a small group how to harvest and cook the cattails and pointed out the wild wheat that was growing everywhere, mixed in with the brush. The group gathered around Simon as he spoke, and their numbers grew until the entire congregation was sitting and listening to his every word.

Simon started by boiling water in a pot and added the young, tender cattail shoots. Then he removed the flower stalks at the top of the cattail from the green-sheath leaves that protected them and added the stalks to the water. He let everything cook for a few minutes and then strained the water, leaving them aside to cool. The roots, which he cleaned in the stream, he now roasted over a flame. When they were cooked and had cooled, he cut back the charred skin to reveal the creamy white interior.

"Here," Simon said, handing out pieces to the crowd. "How does it taste?"

The man closest to him chewed. "Kind of like a potato crossed with celery." He took another bite. "It's good."

Simon ate the last piece. "They're just as good raw."

The young shoots had cooled, and Simon passed them out among the group, along with the flower stalks, which were eaten like small corncobs.

"See," Simon said. "Easy, right?"

The audience nodded and thanked him. Some went off to gather cattails to practice on their own, leaving many behind in the soil to keep the balance of nature alive, just as Simon had instructed.

Simon looked around for Winston and, not surprisingly, found his dog wrestling around with the young boy. Winston's tail was flying.

Simon walked up to them, bending over to scratch Winston's belly.

The boy asked, "Can he sleep with me tonight?"

"Sure." Simon smiled. "If he wants to." He saw Winston lap at the boy's face as they played. "I think he'll like that."

They slept that night beside the water, and in the morning, they sat in meditation before eating breakfast. Many of the travelers knew how to forage for some of the wild grains and herbs that were all around, but Simon showed them more species that they had no knowledge of. He showed them how to make goldenrod tea and pointed out the wild plantain grass that grew everywhere along the ground.

As they walked, the old man spoke to him.

"There is a weight inside of you," he said.

Simon swallowed.

"There is a sadness in you that is weighing down your soul and your mind. It collects with the global sadness of the world."

The words struck a chord. Simon felt a weight that he had not known was there, and the feeling nearly brought tears to his eyes.

The boy that I killed ... the cabin ... my parents ... my brother ... that boy that I killed, oh Lord ...

"This is a violent world." The man took slow and deliberate steps as he walked, and Simon stayed at his side. "Although we have decided to remain without violence, I know that nonviolence is not a practice everyone can follow. I pray that one day we can all live in harmony, but until that day comes, we must deal with the fighting and hatred that is now a part of our lives. We must remember that there can be two types of conflict—one that causes damage, and another that causes it to cease. Being a warrior is a noble quest, but very few can accept the true responsibility that it entails and use it correctly."

Simon wanted to speak, but words would not form. The old man continued, "Some of us are monks, and some of us are warriors. You, Simon, come off as a teacher, but I see fierceness inside you that you may not be aware of. You must be careful, because that fierceness can tip your own scale in either direction—the way of destruction, or the way of ceasing destruction. Something bright burns inside of you, and you must take good care of that flame to see it grow into a blazing fire of your own choosing."

With those words, the old man left Simon to his thoughts.

They walked for another day. Simon felt at peace as he absorbed the harmony, mediation, and wisdom that the group shared. He was sad when he checked his map and compass and saw that the group was now veering away from his course.

It was time to go.

Simon said goodbye to them all in turn and stood leaning against a fallen tree as they took up their trek. The boy hugged Winston around his neck, then went off to hold someone's hand in the group, looking back over his shoulder with sadness. Winston stood to follow, but Simon called him back. "No, buddy. You have to stay." Winston sat, looking up at Simon and over to the boy, back and forth. "No, Winston." Simon scratched at the dark spot on his dog's head head, but Winston was not interested. He made whimpering sounds, watching the group walk away.

The old man called to the young boy, and bent low to whisper in his ear. After a moment, the boy ran back to Simon. "Mister Simon," he said.

"Yes?"

"I was told to give this to you. Can I give it to Winston?"

"Sure you can."

The boy gave Winston another big hug, then slid a thick black-beaded necklace over his head.

Simon said, "We thank you for that."

"Namaste." The kid pressed his hands together in prayer before his chest and bowed.

"Namaste," Simon replied.

He watched the group walk off until their white robes had vanished into the woods. When they had left, Simon stayed leaning against the fallen tree, listening to the gentle rustling of the leaves and the faint chirping of birds, which were all around.

Chapter 17
Two Years Prior: The Bunker

"Best three out of five?"

"You're on, if you're keen on losing."

"Yeah, yeah. No bragging. Serve the damn ball, Steve."

Steven held the ping-pong ball between two fingers, squinting one eye in preparation to serve.

Throughout his entire life, Steven had excelled at any sport he decided to play. If it were not for the pressure of having hundreds of people watching him out on the field, he would have prospered playing football. The same went with wrestling; he had been on his way to receiving a full scholarship.

Table games, such as poker and billiards, were typically not Steven's strong suit, with the exception of one: ping-pong.

They finished their fifth game, and Steven won 3-2.

"Can I brag now?" he asked, bouncing the little plastic ball on his paddle.

"Yeah, go ahead. You're a real fucking ballerina when it comes to table tennis."

"Ha! Best five out of seven, then?"

"No, you win. I'm quits. It's time to hit the bench."

"All right. I'm gonna eat. Let me know when you need a spotter."

Over the past month below ground, the need for a daily routine had become evident. After the first three weeks of doing nothing other than listening to the radio, drinking bourbon, and chain-smoking cigarettes, they had begun picking up their lives as best as they could. They showered and shaved daily. They ran on the treadmill in the mornings and lifted weights later in the afternoons.

Steven put a can of chili on the stove and flipped through *The Joy of Cooking*, his new favorite book. He was getting the hang of this whole cooking thing. Among the spices, he added a dash of chili flakes and a scattering of garlic powder.

When I get out of here, he often thought, *when life gets back to normal and me and Brian are back home, I need to get some decent cookware.*

He was glancing over a recipe for a pan-roasted venison loin wrapped in bacon, when a banging noise echoed throughout the bunker corridors, nearly startling Steven to drop the cookbook.

Bang, bang, bang … bang … bang … bang, bang … bang

Steven looked at Brian, who paused in the process of racking a forty-five-pound weight.

"Is-is that … is that …?" Steven stuttered.

They heard it again, the same knocking pattern as before.

Bang, bang, bang … bang … bang … bang, bang … bang

Steven put the cookbook on the counter and clicked off the burner. They ran to the entryway and looked up the ladder to the hatch door.

"Was that it? Was that the code?"

Brian nodded. "I reckon so."

He felt paralyzed, staring upward at the shiny, circular handle and bolt lock.

"What should we do?"

"I don't know."

Brian and Steven had given Nancy and Benjamin Hendricks, as well as Stanley Jacobs, a code in case they changed their minds and decided to join them down in the bunker. The option was viable for a few days only, maybe a week tops.

Brian craned his head upward. "We've been down here thirty days," he said.

"Thirty-three."

"What?"

"Thirty-three days. We've been down here thirty-three days."

"Right, thirty-three. What should we do? Uncle Al told us not to—"

"He told us," Steven said, "to do the right thing by Nancy and Ben, and I reckon we damn well heed his words."

122

"Yeah, but what if it's not them?"

"Who else knows the knock?"

"Someone could have found—"

The banging repeated and the men recoiled from the hatch door. Right above the half-foot slab of metal was someone who knew about the bunker and was out there staring down at the octopus etching.

"I'm opening it." Steven started up the ladder.

"Hold up, we got to put the suits on."

They grabbed two neon-yellow hazmat suits off the hooks in the entryway, stepped into the wide openings, and sealed up the zippers. They grabbed their rifles and secured the entry room for decontamination.

Brian stepped onto the ladder while Steven stood at the bottom with his rifle aimed at the hatch door. It was cumbersome holding the rifle with the thick gloves, and Steven was worried that he couldn't feel the trigger as he well as he should.

When Brian reached the top, he tapped on the metal underbelly of the hatch door with his pistol, holding it like a hammer.

Bang … bang … bang, bang … bang … bang, bang, bang

There was a long silence.

"You think they're—" Steven began to say, when a reply came booming from the door.

Bang, bang, bang, bang … bang … bang … bang, bang

Brian looked down. "That's it. That's the reply." His words sounded foggy to Steven, muffled. "You ready?"

Steven swallowed and nodded.

The clear plastic faceplate of his hazmat suit was wet with droplets of his sweat, and getting blurry.

Brian turned the handle and slowly, leading with his pistol, he cracked the door open.

"Who's up there?" Steven shouted. "Brian, Brian … who is it?"

Brian held the hatch door open on his shoulder.

"Dear mother of God," he said.

Steven pressed against the tunnel wall, just able to catch a glimpse around Brian. It appeared to be a person lying collapsed on his side next to the hatch door, facing away. The body moved, turning to face Brian, and Brian recoiled.

"S-Stanley, is that you?" Brian said.

The face of Stanley Jacobs was swollen and black, with open sores seeping both clear and red fluid.

"Stanley …"

"Brian," Steven said, fidgeting, trying to look past his cousin's cumbersome suit. "What's going on? Brian!"

Stanley pushed himself up on his elbows and mumbled incomprehensible words through thick strings of red drool. With some effort, Steven could just make out Stanley attempting to get to his knees, Brian helping him, but then Stanley's balance faltered and he tumbled face-first into Brian's chest.

"Shit!" Brian said, his feet slipping on the ladder rung with the weight of the hatch door pushing him down. Brian fell backward, crashing into Steven below, and both men collapsed on their backs. Stanley fell halfway inside the bunker before the hatch door crashed down on his thighs, catching him in mid-air so he dangled upside down. He made a sound like, "Aaahhhgghhh!"

Stanley's arms were swaying over his head like a macabre marionette puppet with blood trickling from his face and fingertips, falling like raindrops over Brian and Steven's suits and face masks.

"Holy shit!" Steven yelled. "Is that blood? That's blood!" He began recoiling back, trying to get Brian off of his chest.

Then the hatch door relented and Stanley Jacobs's body slipped free. He crashed on top of them like a ragdoll.

They cut away Stanley's filthy clothing in the entryway, and sanitized him in the decontamination shower with a chemical sponge bath.

Stanley's eyes were rolling around under his eyelids.

"Stanley," Brian kept saying. "Stanley—answer me, man. You in there?"

But Stanley was incoherent, his head bobbling about, his lips forming jumbled sounds.

They carried his swollen and blistered body across the bunker all the way to the spare bedroom intended for Nancy and Ben Hendricks. They dropped him on the bed, his body trembling in violent spasms under the sheets, and left to set up an inflatable pool outside of the room, filling it with the same chemicals used in the decontamination shower.

They stood outside the closed door.

"We're dead, man; we're dead." Steven's voice shook. "We shouldn't have opened the hatch door. We shouldn't have opened it."

Brian seemed to be thinking the same thing, but he kept his mouth shut.

"We're fucked, man. We're so fucked."

It was stifling hot inside the hazmat suit.

"Uncle Al warned us about this—this disease," Steven said. "Why the hell did we open the door?"

"I don't know."

A deep, guttural cough came from the room, and Steven flinched. They stared at the door. The coughing resumed, gurgling with fluid. The cough turned into heaving and panting, and the retching sound of vomit and liquid hitting the floor.

"Oh, Christ … oh, Jesus Christ," Steven said.

Then they heard a voice. It was Stanley's voice, only it did not sound like Stanley. "B-Brian? Brian? You out there? Stevie?"

Steven shook his head. "I ain't going in there."

Brian reached for the handle. "You sure as hell are. He's our best friend." He turned the knob and opened the door.

The room looked like a slaughterhouse. The wall beside Stanley's bed was plastered with a dark mixture of blood and disease, as was the mattress beneath him. He looked already dead, lying in a pool of his own gore. The sheets had been kicked off his body and Stanley was sprawled naked and wet with perspiration. The sores on his groin were horrific—putrid boils and blisters, swollen, black, and leaking fluid.

"Stanley," Brian choked out the words. "We're here, Stanley. It's Brian and Steven."

They took a step forward.

"Stanley … can you hear me?"

His eyes were open, looking at them, and his eyes were brittle red orbs.

"What's with the masks?" he muttered.

Brian swallowed, but did not answer.

"They won't help you. This bunker won't help you. Everyone … everyone's dead."

"What-what do you mean?" Steven said.

"They're dead, man, all dead. People, they just—" He started coughing and Steven jumped back to the door, gripping the handle. "The people,"

Stanley continued. "They died where they stood. Dropped like flies. There was nothing … nothing anyone could do. The scientists on TV, all the politicians and generals … they told us nothing was happening. They told us, when people started getting sick, that nothing was happening. They lied to us … and now everyone's dead. And so are they, all the scientists and doctors, the generals … they're all dead. Oh Jesus, you got to help me … I had-had nowhere else to go … the hospital is filled, spilled to the streets. All dead …"

Steven wanted to ask about Nancy and Ben, but he couldn't form words.

"What can we do, Stan?" Brian asked, almost pleading. "Tell us what to do, how can we help you? What do we give you?"

Stanley's eyes were fluttering beneath the lids. "Me and Emma, we'll go … Momma ain't far off … doctors and generals, all dead …"

"Stan?"

"It's … tomorrow, Momma. Tomorrow …"

Steven exchanged glances with Brian and they backed out of the room. They closed and locked the door, leaving Stanley to ramble in delusion upon the thin mattress.

***

They brought him water and antibiotics, unsure of what else to do. They made chicken broth and tried to feed him spoonfuls, but he only coughed and sputtered it back out. Brian tried to talk to him, but it was hopeless. The only words that came out of Stanley's mouth were from some distant corner of his brain. He vomited often and had explosive diarrhea that looked much the same as his vomit and smelled of decay. Brian and Steven did their best to clean up after him and even attempted to bandage his wounds. But it was pointless. The fluid never stopped seeping. At night they took turns keeping watch outside his door, more so to keep him contained than to look out for his well-being.

Two days passed, and in the midst of a particularly loud, fluid-filled coughing fit, Stanley started laughing … and he did not stop. He was laughing so hard that he choked and spit up gobs of red drool. He was rigid on the bed with his back arched in a dramatic tetanus pose, his chest twitching to inhale air, and his throat screeching loud with each attempt. Then his body went slack, with just a slight twitching of his fingers.

Steven looked at Brian, his hair soaked against his forehead with perspiration behind the clear plastic mask. "What the hell was that?"

"I don't know."

Stanley was not moving.

"Stanley, hey Stan? You all right, man?" They inched toward him.

"Stan—"

Stanley's body began convulsing in violent spasms. Steven fell backward and pulled himself up at the doorway, grabbing at the handle. Stanley's body was thrashing, quaking, shuddering.

"He's having a seizure," Brian said. "What do we do? Steve—*what do we do?*"

Steven clutched the door handle as if he'd fly off the face of the earth if he let go. He did not speak a word, yet a whimpering sound issued unintentionally from his mouth.

Stanley's seizure stopped as abruptly as it had started.

They stood motionless, staring at their friend.

Brian crept forward. "Stan?"

He gingerly strapped a blood pressure cuff around Stanley's arm, checking for a pulse.

"It's barely there," he said.

Less than an hour went by, and Stanley Jacobs died.

They did not try to revive him.

For many minutes, they stood in the room and stared at his dead body. Then they left and closed the door, locking it behind them, and scrubbed their suits in the kiddie pool.

"What the hell are we gonna do?" Steven asked. "We ain't opening that hatch to get him out. We're never opening the hatch door again."

"Don't get yourself riled—we're not opening it. Come on, help me with the supplies."

In the supply room, they took an industrial-size roll of plastic wrap and several gallons of decontamination chemicals. They wrapped Stanley Jacobs in his bloody sheets, and then used the plastic wrap to go around and around his body. The mattress, spoon, bowl, glass—everything that had touched him—was put in a plastic bag, tied shut, and wrapped in plastic wrap until airtight.

After decontaminating themselves, and spraying everything with the chemicals from the shower, they carried Stanley Jacobs's body to the storage room, past the rows of shelves, to the walk-in refrigerator in the rear. Inside the refrigerator on the far wall was a second door, which led to the walk-in freezer. They had previously cleared the freezer of the frozen meat, moving it to several smaller plug-in freezers, which Uncle Al had made sure they purchased for that very reason. They hefted Stanley Jacobs's body onto a wire shelf in the freezer and stuffed the mattress next to him. Using small, handheld squirt bottles, they sprayed everything that they had touched with the chemicals.

There was a drain in the center of Stanley's room, as there was in every room, and cleaning was not difficult. They threw buckets of chemicals and soapy water on the walls, floor, and even the ceiling and scrubbed everything with bristle-brushes. They found plastic sheeting and duct tape in the supply room and sealed off the doorway. When they were done, they stepped out of their hazmat suits, put them, the kiddie-pool, and all the cleaning brushes into a landscaper-sized plastic bag, sprayed it, and put the bag in the freezer next to Stanley.

They closed the freezer door and dragged a metal rack into the refrigerator to block the entrance.

Steven avoided even looking in the direction of the walk-in refrigerator for the remainder of their stay.

Late at night, when the bunker was dark and quiet, ominous thoughts would emerge and play havoc in his mind. Lying in bed, curled in a ball, Steven fought away images of Stanley's frozen hand cracking the refrigerator door open … the hinges creaking ever so slightly. He swore at times that he heard movement coming from the supply room, and he almost woke Brian up on several occasions to tell him so.

Those nights were the darkest. Steven had to fight with his own mind to chase away the horrifying images both real and imagined. It was a battle that would continue to rage the duration of their stay underground. Some things can be unseen, but the death of Stanley Jacobs was not one of them.

There was no funeral or eulogy given. Stanley Jacobs's corpse was left frozen to the marrow of his bones, deep underground in the bunker, where he would remain forever in darkness.

Chapter 18
Two Years Prior: The Cabin

The snow just kept falling.

It was the last week of March, and the storms blanketing the area had kept Simon stuck in the cabin for three days straight. He sat at the table by the window, staring as if hypnotized by the blustering snowfall accumulating outside. It fell so heavy at times that Simon could not see the ridgeline of the forest in the near distance. Everything was white. Blindingly white.

"You know what's cool about snow?" he asked Winston, who lay curled near the stove. "It lets you see the wind." Winston was fast asleep, but Simon continued. "I mean, you can feel the wind, and you can see tree branches swaying in it, but you can't actually *see* the wind as something three-dimensional." Winston still didn't care.

Simon glanced at the calendar on the wall as if it were incorrect. "How the hell is it still snowing like it's January?"

Simon stayed at the window as the snow piled high. Soon it covered the front porch, and later it reached the bottom of the windowsill. Simon made another cup of tea and added wood to the fire as the accumulation rose, inch by inch, slowly cutting off the natural light from the outside world. When the snow covered the windows entirely, a degree of fear rose in Simon's chest, and he had to focus on his breath to calm his trepidation. There was, after all, enough food and supplies in the cabin to last weeks, if not months.

The bedroom was full of split wood, more than enough to keep the main room of the cabin warm. That little cast-iron stove did a hell of a job. Once hot, it only needed a small flame to keep the heat pumping.

As far as food went, he had a full shoulder roast, a flank, and some of the loin and rump roast left from the last deer he butchered. He also had two skinned and cleaned rabbits, still whole. The meat was secure in the refrigerator in the ground, sealed away from insects, and kept frozen by snow packed along the trenches between the fridge and the earth.

Besides the fresh meat, he had a sack of dried jerky, two sacks of flour, and several sacks of dried vegetables from last year's harvest. Branches of wild sage, goldenrod, catnip, and all manner of herbs hung from the bedroom ceiling to dry, making the room smell deliciously pungent. Various containers and sacks stocked the shelves—all full with wild clover, chicory, dandelion, hazelnuts, maple syrup, hickory nuts, and cattails.

Although Simon was wary about picking wild mushrooms, he knew several edible varieties … and a few poisonous ones to avoid. He collected some black morels, oyster mushrooms, lobster mushrooms, and apricot-jelly mushrooms. The black morels were Simon's favorite, and he was planning to use them in a stew with one of the rabbits or the rump roast of the deer. Probably soon.

Apart from these harvested supplies, there were still many boxes filled with processed survival foods, along with plenty of packaged water—although water would not be a problem with all of the fresh snow.

What worried Simon was not running out of wood or food and water; it was the seclusion of being trapped in the cabin with nothing to do but stare at the walls and talk nonsense to Winston for days on end. If only that dog could talk back.

What Simon feared most was losing his mind, but the fear of losing his mind was more dangerous than actually losing it. It was fear that had driven him mad the previous winter—the constant worry, the feeling that he was trapped in a box for all of eternity. Like he was in purgatory. Like the cabin was his tomb. Nonsense feelings.

Despite Simon's anxiety, he tried to make the best of his situation. He knew there were monks who hid away in small caves, happy to meditate alone for days on end. So Simon stared at the walls for hours and days, breathing in and out. Focusing. Calming his mind and body. Sometimes the meditation sessions went well. Other times his mind was jumbled and he could not sit still, and he would end up pacing around the cabin in anguish like a lunatic.

That last winter had taught him much about dealing with seclusion, and he felt better prepared now because of it. He was alive, in good health, and if that winter didn't kill him, this one certainly wouldn't.

As the snow covered the windows, a pale, white light filtered through. The snow seemed to glow against the glass, but as it kept falling, the cabin grew darker, until it was impossible to tell whether it was day or night.

Simon brushed his teeth with tea made from boiled black alder bark and went to sleep. When he woke, the cabin was still dark, and he had no idea what time it was. Winston was awake and lapping water from his bowl. Simon stood and stretched and saw that Winston had pooped in the corner of the room where he was trained to poop during these periods of isolation. *Good boy.* The fire in the cast-iron stove had burned down to hot cinders, and Simon guessed it was the next day.

"You hungry, buddy?" he asked Winston, who was wagging his tail and panting.

He fed Winston, relit the fire, and went to the bedroom where he opened the window. The snow was so dense that only a scattering fell in. He used a folding shovel to begin digging a tunnel, packing the excavated snow all around the fridge. When he could not pack any more, he pried up several floorboards beside the fridge and stuffed as much as he could underneath.

Simon was making good progress. He was now standing on the windowsill, and the snow overhead was becoming translucent. He struck at the ceiling, and after a few jabs, the snow collapsed. Bright sunlight filtered down the passageway. When he stood with the tips of his toes on the windowsill, he could just pop his head outside. The land was a sea of white, set in a tall drift against the house and piled even higher against the trees in the distance. The mound of snow covered much of the roof with the top of the chimney producing a steady stream of twisting smoke. Simon ducked back inside, closed the window, and nailed the floorboards back in place.

"Well, Winston, at least we have sunlight and fresh air."

***

"Gory, gory, what a hell of a way to die! Gory, gory, what a hell of a way to die! Gory, gory, what a hell of a way to die! He ain't gonna jump no more!"

Simon was singing and marching back and forth in the main room. Winston sat by the stove, watching.

"Gory, gory, what a hell of a way to die!"

He had been doing this on and off for an hour, and it was becoming boring for both Winston and himself. Days passed, over a week, and the snow outside was now melted below the windows. Simon had ventured out several times, using a pair of snowshoes he had made the winter before out of young saplings and woven string. They worked all right, but he fell to his waist beneath the drifts more than once and decided it was not worth venturing far from the cabin.

He was in desperate need of a bath, and his hair and beard had grown wild.

There was still a good amount of food, but he would have to get more soon. Most of his traps would be collapsed by the storm, and soon, maybe the next day, he would venture farther away to check the ones shielded under trees.

Simon stopped at the window, looking at the glaring reflection of the sun against the blanket of white.

"Melt, you bastard! Melt!"

***

There was nothing in any of the traps. Two weeks now, and nothing. Zero. Zilch. The snow had melted to a manageable level, and the air was starting to feel warmer. Soon, he would have to bathe. The water was frigid, but he would have to endure it. Washing his face and skin with a washcloth was no longer acceptable.

He turned to Winston. "You want a bath? Hmm? You want a bath, my idiot bud-bud? My bud-bud-buddy?" Winston's tail was going crazy, but if he could understand what Simon was saying, he would not have been so happy.

They were walking a path that Simon had ingrained in his memory—the animal trap trail. The course first followed a stream, then veered around a wide field before looping back toward the cabin.

They had just entered the field when Simon saw something.

He stopped midstride. There was movement in the middle of the field. Two dark figures. Not deer. Deer would be by the tree line, grazing where the grass was shielded from the snow. They were human.

An unsettling wave of panic struck him; the air seemed to be taken out of his lungs in a gasp. The people were far off, but it appeared that they were trudging in his direction with their eyes cast to the ground.

Simon stepped behind a tree trunk and motioned for Winston to get lost, which the dog promptly did. Simon grabbed the lowest branch and hoisted himself up, climbing the tree with the fluidity of an animal that belongs up there, until he was far overhead.

The two people were walking erratically. They stumbled, hunched over and clasping ragged garments over their shoulders to their chests, not having an easy go of the winter terrain. Simon could tell they did not belong in the woods. They wore many layers of clothing, and as they came closer, Simon could hear them snuffling and coughing. They looked feverish and ill, and they were deathly skinny. Simon himself was skinny, but his body was lean and strong. Their faces looked like flesh canvases stretched over bone frames. He could smell their pungent odor beneath their soiled rags as they neared. They smelled like death.

They were directly beneath him, and Simon could feel his heart thumping against the hard side of the branch.

Then one of the men stopped in his tracks. "What's that?" he said, pointing to the woods.

"What's what?"

"There, look."

Simon looked as well. From his vantage point, he could see Winston meandering back over, his tail wagging and his nose sniffing the air.

Simon almost screamed. He almost shouted down to Winston, but he did not. He kept his mouth shut tight.

I am the wind. I am the rock. I am the tree, and my roots grow deep ....

"I don't see ... wait ... is that a *dog?*" The man looked around in all directions but up. "What the hell is a dog doing out here?"

"Who cares why he's here." The man had a rifle over his shoulder, and in one quick motion, he swung it around and pointed it at Winston. "He's the only animal we've seen in days."

"I ain't eating no dog."

"You not hungry enough?"

The man seemed to think it over. Then he swung his rifle off his shoulder and aimed.

Simon carefully swung his own rifle from his shoulder, aiming it down. Sweat was dripping off his face, and he felt like he was about to burst. Screaming Winston's name was on the tip of his tongue. Then one man fired and the other did the same.

But they'd shot prematurely. Winston was too far off, and the bullets went wild. Like a flash, Winston was gone. Simon felt nauseous. His hand was trembling on the rifle, and the trigger was slippery with the perspiration dripping from his face and trailing down the length of the rifle. If they had hit Winston, or if they had taken another half-second before firing, Simon would have killed them both. They would never have seen him coming.

If Winston had died, Simon didn't know what he would have done. He would go crazy for sure. Images of himself bashing in the skulls of the two men with his fists rushed through his mind … and it made him feel good. They had no idea how lucky their bad aim had been.

One man started to run in the direction of Winston, but the other called out, "It ain't worth it, Roger. You ain't gonna catch him. Come on now, let's go."

The man stopped running and stood scanning the woods. "I don't see nothing."

There was no wilderness in these men. These were no men at all. They were monsters, and Simon felt he would be doing the world a favor by leaping down and striking them dead … but if he did, he too would become a monster. The evil extinguished by their deaths would be reborn in his heart.

He watched as they walked off, then got down from the tree and followed their tracks. He stalked them for two miles until he was certain they were far past the cabin and still walking straight. He backpedaled until he got to the trail with his traps, and then jogged until he was back at the cabin. When he was in the clearing, Winston ran over to meet him, his tail wagging wide.

"Winston!" he shouted. "My God, Winston, are you hurt?" He looked the dog over, but he was fine. "You asshole, Winston! I told you to stay! You never listen—you never listen to a word I say!" He grabbed Winston around his neck, hugging him tight, the dog's mouth panting hot air in his ear. "Don't do that again. You can't leave me, you hear? You can't leave me." Simon was crying into Winston's fur and squeezing him tight. "Don't do that again."

He let Winston go, opened the door to the cabin, and let him inside. Out of the corner of his eye, Simon saw the van. Maybe it was the rush of emotions still coursing through his mind, but he closed the cabin door, telling Winston, "I'll be right back," and walked to the van.

The tarp was heavy with snow, but he pulled it back enough so that he could get to the passenger-side door. He opened the door and searched on the ground for the duffel bag his father had given him the day before he left his home. He found it and held it tight to his body as he walked back to the cabin. This was a bad idea.

***

It was late and the night was dark.

The front door of the cabin flew open, crashing back on its hinges. Simon stood shirtless in the doorway, staring up at the heavens, his chest exposed to the frigid cold.

A scream erupted from his mouth that was barely human; the sound roaring from somewhere deep inside him. Plumes of steam escaped from his mouth to the stars above. Tears rolled down his face. He was not in his mind. He was not in his body.

Simon took off from the doorway, running without shoes or socks, his feet beating upon the frozen earth. His vision pulsed with his racing heart, and he grabbed a long stick from the ground as he ran. As he came upon the first figure-four trap he had set under a bush, he bashed it with the stick, not stopping his pace.

The path was illuminated in the full moonlight and dazzling stars above. Simon went from trap to trap, bashing them with the stick, kicking them with his feet, and scattering the precisely cut and positioned pieces of wood with his hands. He ran so fast that his memory alone drove his feet forward as he jumped over the familiar fallen trees, splashed across the small streams, and slid over the frozen pond to the circular-cut holes in the ice with the X-shaped fishing traps above.

On the table in the cabin, illuminated by a single candle, were the contents of the duffel bag. The stacks of money were now scattered on the floor from when Simon had smacked them off the table before running out the door and losing his mind in the night.

Beside the flickering flame was an array of photographs his dad had put in the duffel bag without Simon noticing. Simon had first seen them during his drive two years prior, and he vowed that he would not become obsessed, stare at them day after day, mourning the departure from his old life while far away in the solitude of British Columbia. So he had left them in the van and vowed to not look at them until it was time to leave for home.

Moments ago, he had broken that vow. Subconsciously, he knew that it was time to leave the cabin.

He looked from picture to picture, all of his family, all with smiling faces and love in their hearts. There were pictures of him next to his father—arms over each other's shoulders, smiling for the camera. He looked younger, softer. Chubby even. There were baby pictures of him and his brother—one of him being washed in the kitchen sink, his mother with her hair held back in a bandana smiling beside him. His mother's face was so young, so bright, so cheerful, so proud, no lines of worry or age. She had so much to look forward to back then—two babies, a well-established family business, and the naive security of youth.

There was a picture of his dad in a white V-neck T-shirt—not a suit—laughing, as a young Simon sat in a high chair, his face and head covered with what looked like spaghetti.

Simon looked through the photographs, and the emotions that raged inside him took control.

He leapt over a fallen tree, screaming, crying, and bleeding from small cuts on his arms and face. He crashed through a cluster of bushes to a clearing on the other side, which was vast and reflected the light of the moon along the curves of the snowy ground.

Then he came to a dead stop. He had burst through the bushes and nearly run straight into the side of a full-grown moose traversing that moonlit plain.

He fell on his back in a mound of cold snow.

The frightened moose reared up on his hind legs, the moon behind the animal shrouding it in shadow so that it appeared mystical against the intense starlight of that crisp night. Clouds of steam escaped from its snorting nostrils as it bucked. This was the closest Simon had ever been to a moose, and the size of the beast was both awe-inspiring and terrifying. The deep earthy smell of the animal's fur and steaming breath lay thick in the air. The negativity and hopelessness that had pervaded Simon's thoughts were gone in a flash.

The animal came back down on all fours, its antlers looming huge over its head. There was a glint of the moonlight in the wetness of its eyes, as they stared at each other for what could have been an eternity. Then the beast turned and lumbered off, vanishing into the brush.

For some time, Simon did not stir. Then Winston appeared, nudging up against his back, licking the wet snow from his face.

"Winston. Ohhh, Winston. I miss them … I miss them so much."

He hugged his dog tight.

"It's time to go home, Winston. It's time to go home. We pack tomorrow."

Chapter 19
Wicked Things

The feeling of sunlight on their pickled flesh would have been marvelous, only there was no sunlight to be seen. The rain was sporadic as the day progressed into evening, but in the intervals when it ceased, a heavy fog rolled in, and Brian and Steven were miserable.

The old man and Charlie were a full day's walk behind them. Under a massive tree, with the ground dry and shielded from the onslaught of rain, Brian could make out the faint tracks of the old man's cane beside his footprints. This gave Brian some hope, because if the old man could traverse the coming path, they would have no problems. And so far, the walk that day had been the easiest since leaving the bunker.

Brian's throat was swollen and his nose was congested. Steven had to stop at times with fits of coughing and sneezes.

Steven said, "I'm getting sick, Brian."

"Me too."

"You think—" Steven paused to cough and hack up a ball of phlegm in his mouth, and spit it off to the side of the trail. Brian closed his eyes. Steven had so many bad habits—many that he used to perform in public without the slightest hesitation. This grunting, sinus-clearing noise he was one of them. It was disgusting.

Christ, I'm gonna punch him, Brian thought. *He's a fucking animal.*

Steven finished clearing his sinuses and continued, "You think we got the … you know, what Stanley had?"

"No. Don't talk like that. We're just sick, is all."

"Yeah, but—"

"We don't got the disease. Don't get yourself riled. If we did, we'd be dead already. Would have died in the bunker, right after Stanley."

"We had those suits in the bunker. Maybe the disease is still around, out here."

"Those suits didn't amount to jack. The doctors and scientists, they had better hazmat suits than the ones we wore, and they're all dead. If we were gonna get sick, we'd know by now. I reckon we're immune, like the others we've seen."

"But—"

"That's enough of that."

They were close to Bethany's town of Aurora. If they could get to her bunker before a fever broke, they would be all right. Her bunker would be well-supplied, just as their own, and there they could recover and rest. Rest, above anything else.

Only a few more days of this hike … only a few more days.

Brian stepped over a cumbersome rock, stumbling for a moment before catching his balance. "Let's start looking for camp," he said.

Steven nodded.

They continued on the path another mile until the ground opened to a flat clearing. In the center of this clearing was a circle of rocks.

"Campfire," Brian said, walking over. He leaned and touched the rocks, and felt the cinder with his fingertips. "The rocks are barely blackened. Used once, maybe twice."

Steven asked, "When?"

Brian felt the coals. "Several days. That old man and Charlie might have camped here. Look." He pointed to areas of scattered dirt that the rain had not washed away. He saw faint telltale imprints of a cane. "Nobody else has been here. Not today at least. I reckon we're safe."

Steven stood on the edge of the clearing.

"Come on now, let's get a fire going. The rain stopped."

"You sure it's safe?"

Brian looked at the trees circling the clearing. They were tall and thick.

"I think so."

Steven walked to the center of the clearing and sat heavily on a log by the fire pit. Brian sat next to him. The log was spongy with water.

"Let's get wood," Brian said. "Lots of wood. We need a big fire tonight, for sure."

"I'm so cold I can't feel my feet."

"Let's get on with it."

They gathered a small pile of wood, and Brian dug away the ash that had turned to mush in the center of the fire pit. He crunched together a ball of dried grass and pine needles, placed it in the center, then draped a few twigs and small sticks over it. He dug his lighter out of his bag and lit the dried tinder.

The tinder took to flame, and Brian fed the small fire until it was burning steady. Once it was burning on its own, he continued gathering wood with Steven. They had a full hour of sunlight before it would become difficult to venture far from camp, and Brian wanted to have more than enough wood to burn through the night. He wanted a bonfire. He wanted heat and security, and the feeling of warmth on his cold, sodden skin. A fire would cure them; a fire would dry the wounds on their feet and restore their spirits. A fire would—

A scream jolted him from his thoughts.

A scream so guttural and surreal that panic struck him deep in his core. It took him a moment to realize the sound did not belong to an animal, but came from Steven, who was a short distance away collecting wood.

Brian turned to see his cousin stumbling backward from beside a tree he had stopped to urinate against. Steven toppled over on his back, scrambling backward with his legs kicking, grabbing at his fallen pants.

"Steve!" Brian dropped the wood in his arms and swung his rifle up. He darted across the clearing. "What is it?"

Steven was still kicking himself backward.

"What is it—*what is it?*"

Brian was kneeling beside him, his rifle darting and scanning the woods.

Steven got to his feet, pulling the front of his pants up, then fell over on his hands and knees and began vomiting in the brush.

"Steve! Steve! Talk to me, Steve!"

Steven spit up bile and strings of saliva, with nothing much to eliminate from his stomach. He began to raise his hand to point, but doubled over in another round of gags.

"What—"

Then Brian saw it.

No more than a foot away from the tree that Steven had been leaning against to urinate was a pile of human remains. Thin bones were arranged in a neat pile. Some were boiled stark white, while others were deeply charred. Leaves were scattered over the carnage, but it only took a breeze to blow them away, and they looked … fresh.

Behind the remains was a tree stump, the top of it stained dark red. Brian's eyes darted between the hack marks on top of the stump to the hack marks on the bones.

"Oh, Jesus Christ …" Brian stepped away. "Holy shit." His head was spinning. "Come on, Steve." He grabbed Steven under the arm. "Let's get the fuck out of here."

Steven rose to his knees and shoved Brian off. "Fuck!" He hollered, "Fuck, fuck, fuck, FUCK!"

Brian stepped toward him again, "Come on, let's—"

"Fucking coon stew!" His eyes were dark slits as he glared at Brian. "Fucking coon stew! You trusted him, Brian! You trusted that old fuck!"

Brian's stomach wrenched, and bile rose to his throat. "Oh, Christ," he said. "Steve, we have to get out—"

"You fucking asshole!"

"What did I—"

"You fucking piece of shit!" Steven was on his feet, walking toward Brian. "I fucking told you! I told you we shouldn't be talking to that old man! I told you we should move on! What was her name? Mary? And the retard, he's next! Why else have him around? You don't listen; you never listen! Even when I told you we shouldn't go into Odyssey, you didn't hear a word I said!"

"Now wait just a damn minute." Brian was stepping backward. "You never said we shouldn't go into that town. You wanted shelter too. I didn't do nothing, Steve. Keep your voice down, for Christ's sake."

"All my life, *all my life,* it's *you* that fucks everything up for me!" He had that look in his eyes, that faraway gaze, eyes that were looking straight through Brian to the wilderness beyond.

"Come on, man … let's get our stuff and move on."

"Ohhh," Steven let out, and then began screaming to the heavens.

"AAAHHHH!" He let it all out, screaming until his lungs ran out of air.

"You, Brian. You!" He walked toward Brian, pointing. "You never listen to a word I say! Every decision you make is for yourself!"

Brian's hands formed into fists. "Now, you wait just one goddamned minute."

"We wouldn't have eaten that fucking stew if you'd listened. Look at them bones! We wouldn't have spent that night in the house! We wouldn't have killed people! You're an arrogant bastard, Brian! You only care about yourself!"

"Care about myself? Care about *myself*!" Brian's vision throbbed with the quick beating of his heart. "What the fuck are you talking about? Do you hear yourself?"

They were inches away—red eyes locked with red eyes.

Brian went on, "All I've *ever* done my entire goddamned life is help you, protect you. I've never been able to actually have a life, *Steve*, because you're so fucking helpless. I moved in with you when your parents died because you couldn't fucking deal with living alone, and you still can't. Did you ever wonder if I wanted to be there, in your house? I'm a grown man; we're both grown men. I could have had a life, a family, but I gave it all up. I gave it up to take care of your sorry ass."

"Bullshit!"

"Fuck you, man. You want to know why I make all the decisions, why I don't ask for your opinion? It's because you're incapable of making decisions for yourself. I do *occasionally* ask what you think just so you don't get upset and throw a fucking temper tantrum. You're an oversensitive, inconsiderate, fucking child!"

Steven's face was stone cold and bright red. His hands were clenched. It was too late now. Things had been said that could not be unsaid. A wheel had been set in motion, and there was no way of stopping it.

"Nobody tells you the truth about how much of a baby you are because the only way you know how to deal with negative feedback is by beating people up. So everyone smiles, pretends that they're your friend so you don't cry and act like you're not just a big dumb—"

Steven punched Brian hard in the face. Brian's head jerked violently, the whacking sound loud in his ringing ears, the pain electric. He stumbled back on his heels but caught himself. Warm blood dribbled from his nose and his eyes teared up.

Steven snarled, his teeth clenched, breathing so heavily that strings of drool flew from his lips. Brian knew Steven had passed the line. He could not speak if he wanted to; he could not think if he wanted to, or control his actions. Steven's vision was now pure crimson. What Brian had no way of knowing was that all the demons that had tormented Steven's mind for so long were now out to play ... and letting them take control ... felt ... so good.

Brian swung a powerful right hook at Steven's jaw, making a sickening crack. Steven wobbled and his head turned, but his feet didn't budge. A drip of blood trailed from his lips. His eyes were wild, crazy—the most terrifying thing Brian had ever seen.

"Oh ... shit," Brian muttered and braced himself.

Steven sprang forward and Brian crouched low. They gritted their teeth like wild wolves and lunged. They met halfway and grabbed at each other, swinging their arms and gouging at each other's faces. Their hands felt for eyes, ears, anything to grab ahold of. Steven's teeth searched for Brian's nose.

Brian bobbed, swerved his face, hauled his head back, and struck Steven square in the nose with his forehead, producing an awful cracking noise. Stars flashed before Brian's eyes, and blood poured from Steven's splintered nose, but the strike only seemed to strengthen his cousin's resolve.

Brian looked at him ... and Steven smiled. He smiled wide through the flowing red blood, making his teeth shiny and terrifying.

Steven grabbed Brian under his armpits and tossed him away. Brian stumbled back and caught his footing, but right as he steadied himself, he saw a streak of Steven's fist as it walloped his eye socket.

Intense brightness enveloped his vision, and pain struck Brian's nervous system like lightning bolts throughout his entire body. He stumbled backward, his heel caught a rock from the edge of the fire pit, and he fell over, landing hard on his back. The wind knocked out of his lungs.

Before he could inhale, Steven was on him. His large body straddled Brian's chest and his massive palms locked around Brian's throat. The eyes staring down at Brian were not the eyes of Steven Driscoll. They were the eyes of a blind man, of a man without a mind, incapable of control. There was no way out of this ... Steven would kill him for sure, and would not even remember doing so.

Blood from Steven's face was dripping over Brian's eyes, making everything red and cloudy. Brian kicked his feet frantically, and Steven pressed his weight down harder, crushing Brian's esophagus. Brian's head felt like a balloon; his chest was in spasms trying to take in air.

He punched wildly at Steven's head, causing more blood to flow down upon his eyes, but Steven was like a stone, an effigy of madness. Brian's vision was turning from red to white to black, and vivid with a strange twinkling pixilation. His eyes were ready to burst from his skull.

This can't be it … this can't be the end.

Brian grabbed at the ground, scratching at the earth with bleeding fingertips. He grabbed handfuls of dirt and mud, grinding it into Steven's eyes, his nose, his smiling mouth. Brian reached his hand out far along the ground, his mind fading, and felt something hard against the tips of his fingers. He grabbed it—something heavy and warm, almost hot in his palm— and with every ounce of strength he had left, he swung it upward …

Steven's eyes flashed wide and his neck twisted violently to the side. Brian felt a splash of hot blood fall over his face and chest, and Steven jumped to his feet.

Brian kicked at the earth, pushing himself backward, while taking in gasping breaths. The air felt like razor blades against his raw throat.

Brian wiped his eyes and saw through a red veil, Steven standing, his body twisted as if he was looking for something behind him.

"S-Steve …"

Steven collapsed. His body seized and twitched, and then became still. Blood pooled around him.

Brian was unable to move. He stared at Steven in shock, as his cousin's body grew cold and gray with the coming of night.

***

When Brian came to his senses, he was crouched on the ground, his mouth agape and his eyes staring at the body sprawled on the dirty ground before him. The fire had burned down to a light crackle, and darkness had settled in.

Brian rushed to his cousin, his fingertips fluttering over Steven's wound, the blood pooled about him. His vision was a haze, his mind speeding in circles. He realized he was still clutching the grapefruit-sized rock in his hand. The side was red and sticky, as were his fingers. He dropped the rock as if it were a thing on fire and smacked his palm against his leg, chasing away the flames.

His trembling hands searched over Steven's neck and wrists for a pulse, but he felt nothing. The shock that he was touching his dead cousin made him recoil.

The night had grown pitch-black.

In a panic, his mind told him to run like hell. Brian snatched his rifle and backpack from the ground and ran, ran like a man set ablaze. He felt eyes staring at him from the brush, observing and judging. He ran through the woods like a blind man, every branch, both big and small, seeming to find him and whip at his body and face as he sprinted forth.

Then he just stopped and stood where he was, unable to comprehend what had happened, what he had done, what he would do now. Guilt washed over him, and the unimaginable pain of his crime sank heavy in his chest.

This is all a dream … it has to be a dream. This can't be real.

But it was not a dream.

I killed him. I killed my … cousin … my brother …

Brian stumbled in the darkness, over rocks and brush, not sure where he was going or in what direction. He tripped twice, and the second time, he remained where he fell. He sat up in the darkness, feeling the eyes of demons all over his body, examining and judging his soul.

I'm all alone.

Flashes of the fight shot through his mind. The feeling of Steven's grip around his neck was still very real. He saw Steven's body twisting unnaturally, all the blood that flowed from his head. He watched him lie there so eerily still.

I didn't mean to kill you. Lord … what have I done?

He pictured Steven at that very moment, his unblinking eyes facing the stars above, his body cold on that same earth that Brian now shivered upon. The dirt around his cousin's body laying claim to his flesh, accepting him with the onset of decay.

"I won't leave you there, Steven," Brian said. "Why did I run? Jesus Christ, I ain't right."

What have I done?

Brian stood.

I'm coming back, Steve. I'll bury you proper.

It was too dark to see more than a few feet into the bramble, and Brian had no idea from which direction he had arrived in that place. After taking only a few steps and tripping over something on the ground, he stopped and sat back down.

He had to wait for a long time, hunched over, his knees pulled to his chest for warmth. His own wounds from the fight were barely noticeable, but the weight of his cousin's death was crushing his soul.

At first light, he stood, grabbed his pack and rifle, and followed his stumbling tracks. As he walked on, his head felt dizzy and faint, and his own injuries began to throb.

I don't deserve to live … Steven, I'm so sorry … I'm a monster.

Brian followed his tracks into the morning hours. He didn't remember running as far as he had, and it took some time until he saw the familiar thicket of trees surrounding the campsite.

"I'm here, Steven. I'm here."

Brian didn't want to see his cousin dead on the ground. There was a real chance that he would faint. But the thought of leaving him out there for the wolves and the bugs to consume made him boil in despair.

Brian crashed through the brush and into the clearing.

"Steven, I'm so—"

He looked about.

"Steven?"

His cousin was not there. The campsite was empty, wiped clean.

"S-Steve?" Brian swung his head around, looking into the woods. "Steven, Steve? What the … Steve?" He began shouting into the woods. "I'm sorry, Steve! I'm so sorry!"

Brian's eyes darted everywhere, but there was no trace of his cousin. All the gear he had left was gone. The sleeping bag, the food, everything.

Did it really happen? Am I going insane?

Brian scanned the ground where he had left Steven. Sure enough, the soil was dark with blood.

Where? How? He was dead … wasn't he? Didn't I check his pulse?

It occurred to Brian that his hands had been trembling and were torn-up raw from the fight, but still …

He was turning all gray. He wasn't moving or breathing … There's no way …

Brian studied the ground around the camp.

What the?

There were hoof prints in the spongy soil and several piles of fresh dung that smelled sharp. These tracks had not been there when he and Steven had first entered the campsite; they were fresh and deep in the wet dirt.

"Horse tracks," he whispered to himself. "Riders. Four, maybe more." There were plenty of human footfalls to go with them. Brian went to the edge of the clearing and walked in a circle, studying the ground until he came to where the riders had entered and exited the campsite. They had followed a similar path as Brian and Steven.

Brian walked fast, rifle up, listening to the wind as he followed the tracks. There were deep ruts carved in the soft ground. Perhaps a cart, but the marks looked dragged.

The prints went on for miles, and the morning went by in a blur as Brian followed them. As the afternoon progressed, the sky turned dark. A rumbling sound echoed from the thick heavens. Rain returned, and fell beating to the earth.

"No, no—No!"

Brian watched as the prints before him began to wash away and vanish. The water soaked the already saturated ground so fast that small streams sprung up all over.

Brian ran up a ways and watched the farthest track get wiped clean, turning to a slate of wet mud.

What now?

The rain was cold. Brian's core shook and his jaw chattered. He ran up farther, attempting to guess the path that the riders would have taken, but there was no evidence to suggest that he was right in his assumptions.

What the hell am I supposed to do?

A voice inside his head spoke, *He's dead, Brian. He's got to be dead. But Bethany isn't. You get to them. You stop this foolish pursuit. You don't got any food or water, and you're dripping cold.*

"He's dead," Brian whispered. "There's no way he's not."

He shook his head.

"I'm so sorry, Steven. I'm so sorry … I'll never forgive myself. I love you, brother."

Brian raised the hood of his poncho and turned back the way that he came.

Bethany was waiting.

Chapter 20
Monticello

Far north was the city of Chicago, like a great evil looming over the land. Simon dared not entertain the very notion of going near that city. It would be ravaged far, far worse than anything he could imagine.

At a junction of interstates, several miles outside of Monticello, Simon saw a tremendous white tent erected along the distant horizon like a great white mountain. The tent was the size of a football field, possibly larger. He stopped and studied it through his binoculars.

From his distance, he could see an abundance of military vehicles—ambulances, Hummers, and mobile offices—left abandoned around the tall fence surrounding the tent. A gigantic red cross was painted large on the broad side of the tent, and signs attached to the chain-link fence read:

QUARANTINED AREA. RESTRICTED ACCESS.

Simon put the binoculars away and continued on the path. He looked over his shoulder as he walked, glancing at the gigantic tent, and his pace quickened. The inside would be worse than anything he could imagine, and the images his mind produced were horrific—infested and diseased corpses, creatures emerging straight from the bowels of hell.

He hastened his steps until the tent was well behind him and gone from sight.

A few miles later, he came to a vantage point where he could see the town of Monticello in the distance. A black and cratered land led to a burned crisp of a town. Hundreds of tanks and vehicles were scattered in the valley like an infestation.

Simon studied his map. It would be easy to bypass the center of town. All he had to do was stay northeast and he would skirt along the border, but he would have to walk straight through the cold war zone.

"All right, buddy," Simon said to Winston. "You ready?"

Simon started walking with Winston at his heels, sniffing the air.

They walked into the fields of battle, and Simon quickened his pace. The land had been cratered and burned so long ago that new bright green plants and little colorful flowers were now sprouting from the charred and barren soil, and between the cracks of machinery. Corpses—some shredded beyond recognition—had been overgrown with vining weeds. Tall sprouts emerged from ribcages and poked free through hollow eye sockets.

Halfway across the field, Simon was soaked with sweat. The dark and twisted metal of destroyed machinery rose from the earth like the claws of a thousand demons, scratching through the land from the netherworlds. A line of transport vehicles lay in ruins, crisp and rusted, many still holding the remains of the passengers they had carried. Some were blown apart, with scraps of metal and bone fragments fanning out in circular arrays.

Simon looked at Winston.

"You okay, buddy?" Winston stayed at Simon's heels, panting with his ears pinned back. "We're almost across, boy. Stay with me." Winston dared not venture off. This was a poisoned land.

As Simon neared the northern border of town, the field of war diminished. They would have to pass through a small portion of Monticello to enter the wooded park on the far side. Once there, they would be able to stop to eat and take a break before continuing onward. Simon's stomach was grumbling and his mouth was parched. He was certain Winston felt the same.

He took a long drink from his canteen and poured some water in the cup of his palm for Winston to lap up, before crossing a desolate highway. A strip of businesses lined the other side of the road—a truck stop, the White Wheel Diner, and the Monticello Park Motel. He and Winston walked along the expansive paved lots before the truck stop, scanning the windows and shadows for movement, but there was nothing to be seen. Past the truck stop were several blocks of homes. Winston's head was low and troubled.

"Come on, boy. We're almost out. I can see the trees."

This was true. In the distance, Simon could see a wall of green that bordered the town from the wilderness.

They neared the edge of a tall building, constructed in a semicircular shape. It rose three stories high, and just beyond was the wilderness. The dozen or so abandoned ambulances at the rear entrance indicated that this had once been a hospital.

As they neared the corner toward the front of the building, Winston began whimpering.

"What? What's the matter? Let's move, buddy."

Winston slowed and sat. Simon walked on a few yards and then stopped to survey the land with his binoculars. "Winston … come on, man. There's nothing there." Winston sat panting with his big tongue hanging from the corner of his mouth. He whimpered and even barked a low bark.

"You all right, buddy?"

Simon walked back to him and ruffled his head. Winston stood and started walking back in the direction they came. "No, Winston. We're not going back." Simon looked in the direction of the hospital. He again scanned the windows, the park in the back, and what he could see of the field in front of the building. "There's nothing, Winston." He put the binoculars away and gripped his rifle. "Come on, let's go."

Simon walked, and reluctantly, Winston followed, lingering behind.

As they neared the edge of the building, Simon kept his distance—and then he saw the front of the hospital. He stopped midstride.

"Oh, Christ …"

Piled high in the semicircular space before the entrance were bodies in such volume that Simon could not venture to guess the number. Many were in body bags and some were wrapped in sheets. Others lay where they had been tossed, heaped in piles. Three ambulances were stranded among the sea of death along with two garbage trucks and several flatbed pickup trucks. Corpses were everywhere. Bodies burst from the parked vehicles, spilling out. Dozens of wheelbarrows and carts were heaped in overflowing piles. The corpses covering the sidewalk were piled so high that the wheels and license plates of the vehicles could not be seen. They had been brought here like garbage at the dump.

Simon quickened his pace.

He couldn't help but stare, though he tried to steal his gaze away. The large double doors of the hospital entrance had stretchers jammed into the doorway like corks, disappearing into the total blackness beyond. Above the door was a sign, spray-painted on a large board and nailed over the entrance:

Monticello Fields Hospital
Quarantined
Bring Your Sick Only

His stomach turned, and Simon fell to a knee and heaved. He tried to stand, wanting to be far away from this awful place, but his stomach cramped.

"Winston ..." Winston was far to his side, his tail between his legs. Never had they witnessed such death. Simon tried not to imagine what the inside of the hospital looked like—the corridors, rooms, and the morgue in the basement. But his mind produced images nonetheless.

Simon got to his feet and moved, jogging. Then he started running, and so did Winston. Winston passed him in a rush, and he did not stop until he reached the woods. Simon gritted his teeth and sprinted, not looking back, not wanting to see or know the reality of the world that he faced—the reality that he knew was only going to get worse.

Chapter 21

Aurora

The town of Aurora sprawled beneath his feet.

I'm here. I'm finally here.

Fever had developed fast after Brian continued on his trek, and was worsening as he entered the town. First, he felt like his flesh was burning. Then his head felt scorched—the skin on his face, his nose, and ears stinging. And now his brain seemed to be boiling in his skull.

It's just so damn hot … .

He passed building after building, one burnt-out shell after the next. Piles of debris sat where homes had once thrived, and the roads were jumbles of craters with large sections of pavement strewn about. The town was like a scattered jigsaw puzzle, with factories, businesses, and whole city blocks reduced to rubble.

Brian's mind swam in a realm of delusion. His feet stumbled over the ground, seeming to move on their own. His vision was choppy and bright, and when he looked from one thing to the next, pings of panic and pain surged through his body and mind.

This is it … Do I have the disease? I must … This is the end …

He fell, collapsed on the ground, feeling the warm earth on the side of his face. Comfort overtook him. Numb tremors vibrated down his spine, making his hands and feet tingle. It felt good. It was warm and inviting on the ground. He could feel stress pour out of his body, exiting through his hands and feet. He could stay there forever.

I wonder if I'll see a white light …

But no white light came, just darkness, pure black—an all-encompassing void of reality and time. When Brian's eyes fluttered back open and he remembered *where* he was, *who* he was, and *what* he was doing, he got to his feet and stumbled forward. He could not account for the fact that he was still alive; some otherworldly force kept his legs moving and prevented his eyes from closing permanently.

How long have I been out of food?

The last thing he had eaten was a packet of cheese sauce belonging to some military rations from some meal long ago. Brian had found the packet while scrounging for crumbs in the backpack, going from pocket to pocket repeatedly as if food would magically appear. He sucked the neon-yellow paste straight from the packet. As the cheese sauce digested, his stomach cramped, and soon he was vomiting. A shaking developed deep in his core, and he twisted and turned on the ground, clenching his stomach, rife with pain. A severe case of diarrhea followed.

Somewhere along the way, along the dreamlike walk that felt like a distant memory, the weight of the backpack became heavier and heavier, pulling him backward toward the earth. He let it drop to the ground. There was nothing much left in it anyway. All he had now was his rifle, his pistol, spare ammunition, a few sips of water, a knife, and the clothes on his back.

He looked to the sky and could see the clouds thinning. No rain in sight. His soiled clothes were plastered to his skin, soaked with sweat despite the constant chills and the uncontrollable trembling in his core.

A large field lay before him, beside a structure that must have been a school. Two soccer goals stood out from the overgrown grass. Military vehicles lined the ground bumper to bumper. The procession of parked vehicles was pockmarked by craters, blackened from old explosions, and covered in grit. Small tents were constructed on a separate turf adjacent to the soccer field, a running track bordering the edge. One tent remained intact, its white canvas walls torn open and flapping in the wind, a red cross still visible on the side. The others had been burned down to their metal frames.

The school looked sinister, deviant. This scene of destruction before him, mixed with his conjured images of children playing in an environment intended for education, made anger boil up in his chest.

Why … Why did this have to happen?

It was the eternal question. The one everyone had asked at some stage or another. The question without an answer. *Why?*

Brian inspected the intact medical tent, but it had been wiped clean. He skirted the field, stopping at a shady patch of grass to catch his breath, and unfolded his map, now weathered and frayed to something illegible. The fever that was raging inside his body brought with it confusion and disorientation. He squinted, trying to decipher the path he'd marked before leaving the bunker. The map looked fuzzy, unreadable—a jumble of lines, shapes, and some colorful patches that seemed to leap out from the pages. Brian read the town names, but it was difficult and the words didn't register any specific meaning. He wiped the sweat from his brow and watched his finger tremble over the page. Overhead, the overcast sky was boiling, blindingly white.

He closed his eyes. His mind was swimming in a sea of disease, going a hundred miles an hour.

Images flashed through his mind: Steven staring down at him ... hot blood dripping over his face and in his eyes ... the reverberation traveling down his forearm as the rock hit skull ... Steven's body, lifeless ... his own body, lifeless ...

He shook these thoughts out of his head.

I deserve to die. I deserve to have the disease ... Now I understand why humanity was wiped from the face of the planet. Humans are awful. We do horrible things. We don't deserve to live on this earth.

Despite these feelings, Brian stood and continued walking. Bethany was only a few blocks away.

He tried to walk with stealth, in the shadows, cautious of his environment, but he was loosing control of his feet and hands. As he neared Bethany's home, with the piles of debris encompassing whole city blocks, he fell and tripped often over the irregular terrain.

Carpet bombed, he thought. *Aurora looks like it was carpet bombed.*

The outlines of the buildings left intact were blurry, and the glimmering of shattered glass was blinding. Everything was so bright, it hurt to keep his eyes open.

At some stage, he unbuttoned and peeled off his sweat-soaked shirt, letting it fall to the rubble, making a wet sound as it hit the ground. He saw the street sign for Park Avenue and took a left. Several streets with fruity names followed—Apple, Pear, Cherry, and Orange—and he made it all the way to Elm Street. Through the rubble, he counted what house numbers he could decipher: *Twelve, fourteen ... twenty.* He crossed the road. *Twenty-four ...*

He climbed a mound of fallen bricks, using the side of the house's foundation for support. Past the house, the backyard had some property to it. Nothing like Steven's home in Nelson—or any of the homes in Nelson—but it was a large parcel of land for Aurora.

Then Brian saw what he was looking for.

In the corner of the yard was a shed identical to the one in Steven's backyard. A flimsy wooden structure a little bigger than an outhouse.

He felt like he was walking in a dream as he shuffled toward it, each footstep an eternity.

Then he was standing before the door. He touched the splintering wooden planks.

The air inside was stagnant, stifling, and thick with dust. The room was barren. He went to the corner and felt along the ground for the loose floorboards. Sweat poured from his face, leaving dark droplets on the dry wood. His mind was racing, like his brain was being swept away in heavy gusts of wind. When he closed his eyes it was like being on a roller coaster.

The loose floorboards came up with a gentle pry ... then he stared down at the etching of the octopus on the hatch door. He tried the handle, but it was locked. Brian unholstered his pistol, holding it like a hammer in his palm.

This is it.

This was the end of his journey and the beginning of a new one. Either Bethany was inside or she was not. Either way, he could not go on any farther. Brian would either be saved or this flimsy shed would become his tomb.

His eyes began to shut while kneeling there and he snapped them open.

He brought the butt of the pistol down, crashing it against the metal of the door, and the familiar pattern played out.

Bang ... bang, bang, bang, bang ... bang ... bang, bang

The handle did not move.

Several minutes passed, then he repeated the knock.

It was becoming hard to hold the pistol; his grip was weakening. He put the gun down and rested on his side, curling his knees to his chest, watching the hatch door through narrow eyes. The floor underneath him was cool.

Brian closed his eyes, and all went black.

Chapter 22
Sullivan

There was no longer a singular nightmare that tormented Simon's mind, but rather a conglomerate of several that made his time since leaving the cabin an assortment of terror.

Flashes of memories plagued his thoughts—images of the Mexican soldiers kneeling with machine guns and the terrible feeling of fleeing from gunfire, the piles of bodies on the sides of roads, buried en masse under stretches of land, and piled high before the doors of the Monticello Fields Hospital.

Then, there was the boy.

The boy at the gas station and his friends in the woods. Images from that day, those minutes, were forever frozen in Simon's mind—the cloud of red mist and cotton fiber that hung stagnant in the air as the boy's feet left the ground, the bullet intended for Simon whizzing by, the other children dragging away the body ...

It seemed like such a long time ago. Or like a dream that had never happened.

One horrible experience replaced another, and the nightmares were now overlapping.

Sometimes at night, Simon cried. He tried not to. He tried to keep it bottled up, but he couldn't. He cried for himself. He cried for all of humanity. He told himself, like the millions before him and the few who even now still had tears to cry, *This just isn't fair ... Why?*

There was no answer to that question. Unlike a *koan*—a question or phrase made to test a person's mind during meditation—this *koan* would never be resolved. It was the universal *why*. It went through everyone's mind, time and time again in endless loops. It could not be settled, even with years of meditation. There was no single answer. And if there was an answer, if someone out there knew why humanity was forced to suffer and face extinction to leave only a small fraction to endure, starve, fight, and commit atrocities against their fellow man, that person was not talking.

After leaving Monticello, Simon began seeing other survivors, and their numbers were increasing. They were easy to spot from a distance, giving him time to evade them. He could hear them whisper and see the flight of birds and the scurrying of squirrels off in the brush well before the travelers were close enough to see him.

Most people he saw traveled in groups, two to four, along with the occasional solo traveler. They all looked the same—filthy, vile, skinny. They wore dirty rags and all were armed. They were death. They were destruction and decay, and they left the earth a contaminated place as they passed. Simon dared not utter a sound until they were out of sight.

Parks and shadowy corners of backyards became his campgrounds. He had to be aware, cautious of every corner, dark window, and shadow.

Simon's biggest concern, however, was not running into a random stranger—they were still few and far between. His biggest concern was that he had not seen a single animal track—anything much larger than a squirrel—in quite some time. Not since leaving the cabin. This frightened him. He had enough food to complete his journey as long as he could still scavenge plants and herbs in parks and lawns, but his rations of dried meat would run out soon, and he would have to start hunting. He could survive indefinitely on foraged plants, but feeding Winston was another matter.

But hunting could wait, because the end of his journey was within sight. In a few days, he would arrive at Ridgeline Road, with its majestic views of the Ridgeline River in the distance past the houses and estates bordering the road. He would see the mansions dotting the opposite bank, the familiar businesses that he had observed countless times growing up.

Simon was almost home.

At present, he was in a town named Sullivan—a large town connecting to other large towns with little parks and fields in between. The map showed a park not far from where Simon stood, the name on the map reading Livingston Park.

He made his way through Sullivan, past the many once-ornate homes that now sat in decay and ruin.

Signs of more recent life were evident—piles of shiny litter blown about, the occasional bullet shells, and several steel drums used to hold fire, all charred, rusted, and decomposing. Sullivan was lucky because the town was still intact. Corpses were littered about, but the buildings had evaded damage from the war. This gave Simon some hope. If Sullivan had survived, then maybe his own hometown had survived as well.

"This is a good sign," he told Winston as they walked. "Better chance Mom and Dad will be waiting for us when we get there. They gotta be."

Simon and Winston entered Livingston Park and passed the scattered campfire circles dotting the field. Most were old and overgrown with grass. He passed a parking lot, a pair of tennis courts, a single basketball court, and a soccer field before entering the shade of the thick woods. The farther he walked, the less trampled the trails became, and traces of garbage diminished.

"You know what's strange?" Simon told Winston, who was paying more attention to the scent of the trees than to Simon's voice. "People, I've noticed, are afraid to sleep in the woods. They would rather sleep in the fields beside them. It's the stupidest thing they can do. It's *far* safer sleeping in the wilderness than out in the open. Animals are better to be around than strangers."

Winston looked up at him with his tongue lolling out of his mouth. His ears were raised and he looked happy. Simon smiled and ruffled his head.

Judging by the map, Livingston Park was large in comparison to the two other parks in Sullivan. Simon went straight to the deep brush where no human tracks or trampling could be seen, and found a small clearing to camp for the night. The comfort of seclusion put his mind at ease, and he let out a sigh.

"Hey, my buddy." He looked down at Winston. "You hungry?" Winston's tail went wild.

They ate and then slept in a lean-to shelter that Simon put together out of sticks and leaves. In the morning, he scattered the shelter's remains so that the terrain looked much the same as it had before being disturbed. They followed a narrow stream that cut across the center of the park. A mile or so on, the path intersected an old dirt road. It was overgrown, almost absorbed back into the wild.

They walked on their own path, following the stream as a guide, and at times Simon could see the dirt road parallel to him through the brush.

A structure in the distance became visible well before Simon came upon it. The crest of a roof rose above the distant tree line. Simon neared, and he soon came to the expansive back wall of an old barn, the white paint chipped and peeling off in sheets. It was over two stories high, and judging by the width, the barn was massive. Simon walked on the pathway beside it, keeping everything around him in constant surveillance. There seemed to be no need to worry. The birds in the trees chirped without care, nothing scurried, and there were no voices to be heard or signs of a recent human presence.

Simon rounded the corner, taking his time as he neared the front, and when he did—when he saw the land before the barn—he stopped short.

"Holy hell …"

Chapter 23
Riders

Time was not relevant. It had no meaning or existence.

The world was black, a clean slate. And then consciousness came rushing back.

Steven's eyes fluttered open, and he stared unfocused at the swaying treetops far above—a blurry sea of green against a cloudy backdrop.

His mouth opened, but sentences could not form. Then one word escaped, "B-B-Brian?"

There was no reply.

His hand moved. Pain spread.

"Easy now, lad," rasped a deep voice.

Steven looked away from the treetops. Two men sat across from him, a campfire in the middle. He was lying uncomfortably straight on some sort of makeshift stretcher with the top of his head touching the scratchy bark of a tree. Agony was becoming evident all over his body, inside and out.

What happened?

"Relax, lad," said the same rasping voice. The man who spoke sat upon the side of a fallen tree, stroking his fingers through a graying beard. He wore something of a uniform, a compilation of various dark military fatigues. The other man looked at Steven, and then cast his eyes back to the fire, stoking the flames with a stick.

"What ... Who are you? Where's Brian?"

"Is that the other lad's name? Brian?" the bearded man asked. Upon hearing the conversation, several faces appeared in the woods, looking down at him where he lay. In the distance, Steven could hear the whinnying of horses.

"What happened … What …" Panic was fluttering in Steven's chest.

"W-who are you?"

"My name is Captain Thomas Black, first battalion. You are in the custody and care of General Metzger, by God's good grace."

The words escaping the man's mouth were pure gibberish. This rough-looking horde, all staring down at him, were well-armed and wore similar uniforms.

The bearded man stood and dusted his battered cavalry hat on his knee before placing it on his head.

"Where were you headed?"

Steven didn't answer.

"The other one." The man walked before Steven with his hands clasped behind his back. "Brian, you say? Where is he headed?"

Steven looked away.

"He left you for dead, you know. When we found you sprawled out in the dirt, we were certain you were dead. You lost a lot of blood. Your pulse is still weak, and you may not live to see tomorrow. If you're lucky, we will arrive in Odyssey before you expire and the doctor can patch you up."

Steven's eyes grew large.

Odyssey …

The adrenaline coursing through his body helped him muster his strength.

"You gonna kill me?" Steven's face set in a scowl. He tried to raise his body from the ground, but fighting through the jolts of pain was like cutting wire tied to keep him down. "Go on and try."

"Christ in heaven." The bearded man stepped forward, motioning for Steven to lie back down. "Easy does it, now." He looked back to the others. "Stout lad, ain't he?"

Steven collapsed on his back. His head pulsed with pain, throbbed against a tightly bound bandage, and he thought he was going to vomit.

"I'm not gonna kill you. By the looks of it, killing you is no easy feat. Your friend tried plenty hard."

Steven tried to think back to his last memory, and through the patchy clouds of red, he saw a scene—fragments of bone and organ meat tossed beside a bloodstained stump. The image churned his stomach.

What happened?

"W-what happened?" he asked.

"I rightly do not know, other than your friend trying to murder your ass and leaving you to die alone."

"Brian would never—"

"But he did, lad. He did. That's a fact."

Would he? Did he?

The fear in Steven's mind was changing, evolving, turning to courage and strength. Anger was boiling to the surface.

"What do you want with me? I know who you are, I saw you back in Odyssey. I saw you parading through town with all them murdered bodies. I ain't stupid."

The bearded man laughed. "Son, I'm not sure what you *think* you saw, but I assure you, we have never murdered a soul. Honest to the Lord high above. Not one. Killing is a God-given right in this day and age, as long as the reasons are just. Those people you saw dead were guilty of crimes against the very nature of humanity. What you saw was an illusion created in your mind by your own fear. We are not bad people; to think otherwise is a fault in the way you processed events. And, son, I do believe that if murder was still a punishable offense, you would most certainly be found guilty yourself. Am I wrong in saying so?"

The man stared at Steven with crisp, blue eyes.

"I ain't never killed a person. I protected myself is all."

"Did those people that you killed try to harm you in any way?"

"I ... those people are dead?"

The captain nodded. "All dead, lad. All dead. Do you believe that a jury of your peers would find you innocent? What if we were to try you in a court of law?"

"I ain't done nothing wrong. Where's Brian?"

"He's gone. I told you as much. He left you for dead, took your gear, and moved on. We'll send some scouts after him if it suits your desire, but the man has turned his back on you and has disappeared."

"That ain't true ... he would never—"

"But he has, lad. He has."

"What ... what do you want with me?"

"Well … we were tracking you to get justice for the men that you killed. We were going to tie your hands and feet to trees and stretch you out in a star. We were then going to take a sharp blade and make a cut down your back, from the top of your head to the base of your spine, and then over your arms and legs. Yank the skin off your muscle and bones.

"Some say that if you do it proper, the person will still be alive to witness their own skin piled before them. But if that's possible, we've never been able to achieve it. We start with the head and face, take it slow. Show you your reflection in a mirror before you expire."

Steven gritted his teeth and pushed himself to his elbows.

"You go on then and give it a try. See what happens. I'll kill the lot of you! You'll all be dead—"

"Easy, lad. Easy." The man looked back to the others, issuing a laugh. "A live wire we got here." He looked to Steven. "We've had a change of heart. You killed four men back in Odyssey. Three with your bare hands, and the other was shot. Those were not easy men to kill. One you punched so hard his skull was shattered like broken glass." He held his hand to his heart. "Honest to God, I've never seen a punch thrown like that."

Steven didn't mention that it was Brian who did the shooting. And he did not mention that it wasn't hard killing any of those men, not in the slightest.

"Those men, were they unlike yourself? Struggling to survive? Now, our organization is prosperous. We are the largest known assortment of fighting men, and we thrive on strength and numbers. You are nothing of a weakling; am I wrong in saying so? You come off as a smart lad. Smart and cunning indeed."

All the exertion was catching up to Steven and his eyes wanted to shut. The bearded man walked back to the fallen tree and sat down by the fire. The man stoking the flame added a fresh log. The wood hissed and crackled.

Then a short and stout man with a straggly red beard came into the clearing to stand beside Captain Black. He rested his hand upon the gleaming rosewood handle of a machete.

"Get him ready, Captain, we're moving out."

Captain Black nodded. "Yes, sir."

The stout man looked at Steven, and then disappeared into the woods, toward the sounds of the whinnying horses. Captain Black turned to Steven as Steven's eyes fluttered with exhaustion. "You rest now, lad. You rest. If you are still alive when we arrive in Odyssey, we have much to talk about. I see a bright future for you. Bright indeed. You will be a prosperous man. All the food you can eat, all the alcohol you can drink, and all the women you can stand. This world"—the man stroked his beard—"is ripe for the picking. It belongs to you. Always has. Just reach out and take it."

Chapter 24
Bethany and Carolanne

Two faces popped up from the ground. The eyes staring out from behind the foggy face masks were huge. It took a moment for Brain to remember where he was.

The hatch …

He tried to speak, but words were lost on his tongue. The two people in the hazmat suits spoke to him, but all Brian could hear were muffled noises.

He closed his eyes.

Hands were on him, moving, pulling. He felt weightlessness, and then he felt pain. At times, his eyes cracked open, but all he saw were flashes of color so bright that he had to shut his eyes again and go back into the pleasant void of unconsciousness.

Then there was water all over his body. Warm at first, then hot. So hot it burned. Brian was trembling, convulsing, and he knew he was speaking, but whatever words were escaping his lips were unknown to him. Blurred figures moved before him—bright orange blobs in human form. They were touching his naked body, holding him down as he thrashed about in the burning water.

Then everything went dark.

The next time Brian woke up, he could not control his arms and legs. They were moving about, shaking, and rubbing up against … sheets? He was on a bed. The smell of clean cloth and starch and the feel of soft cotton against his skin.

I made it to heaven.

***

"Is he dying?" Bethany asked. "Oh, God, is he dying?"

She was biting the tips of her fingernails. "He's got the disease, doesn't he? Oh, Christ, oh, no … no, no, no. We're dead, aren't we?"

Carolanne unzipped the side of her hazmat suit, breathing in the cool air of the bunker. She finger-combed her sweat-soaked hair out of her face. Her cheeks burned bright red against her pale complexion. "Beth. Bethany. Relax. I don't think he has the disease."

Bethany was fanning her face with her hand. It was hot in those suits, and her dark, wet hair was soaked. They were both pale as ghosts, long forgotten down in the bunker.

Bethany said, "But he's dying; I mean, look at him. He's got to be dying."

"Well, he's not dead yet. He has hypothermia and maybe pneumonia. But his skin is clear of welts and discoloration." She shook her head. "I don't think he has the disease."

They stood in the hallway in front of Brian's room. Their suits were unzipped to their waists, and the bottoms looked large and silly in contrast to their skinny torsos poking out from the tops. Their wet T-shirts clung to their bellies, displaying the ripples of their ribcages.

"Go to storage and find three canteens," Carolanne said. "I'll boil some water."

"What for?"

"We have to keep his temperature up. We'll use the canteens like heating pads."

Bethany turned to leave. "I'll find them."

They filled the canteens and submerged them in a pot of boiling water until they were warm, then stood outside Brian's room.

"We don't need those," Carolanne said to Bethany, who was partway into her hazmat suit. "He doesn't have the disease."

"How can you be sure?"

"Remember what George was like when he got sick? This is nothing like that."

Bethany thought it over. "Maybe it's changed. You know, mutated. Diseases do that, right?"

Carolanne shrugged. "If it has, the suits won't do us much good. The bunker was most likely contaminated the moment we opened the door."

Bethany looked around, as if she'd be able to spot the germs in the air.

"Besides," Carolanne added, "the disease had the chance to kill us once. Like I said two years ago, I think we're immune."

Bethany didn't look so sure.

They wore latex gloves, doctors' scrubs, and disposable surgical face masks instead of the hazmat suits and entered Brian's room. He was still on the bed, but the sheets were kicked off and his skin was sticky with perspiration. Bethany went to his side and cradled his head while Carolanne held an antibiotic pill to his lips. Once he opened his lips enough to let her insert the pill, she tipped a glass of water against his mouth. Brian sputtered and coughed, and the pill fell to the mattress.

"He needs an IV," Carolanne said. "Desperately. He's severely dehydrated. We'll have to tie him down if he doesn't stop thrashing."

Bethany looked at Brian twisted in the sheets, her cousin, her brother's best friend. His skin was clammy and pale, almost blue. He was skinny … so skinny. Yet, there was still strength inside him. She could see the muscles in his torso twitching and convulsing.

"I just …" She trailed off, her eyes growing wet. "What happened to him?" She was shaking her head like she didn't understand. "He's so sick." Tears rolled down her face, soaking her surgical mask. "And where's Steven?"

Carolanne put one canteen under each of Brian's armpits and one by his groin. They stayed in the room with him, tucking the sheets back around his chest when he kicked them off and reheating the canteens when they cooled. They used a sponge to feed him tiny sips of water, drops at a time. His kicking subsided, and Carolanne connected a bag of IV solution to his arm.

He slept for a long time.

All the while, Carolanne and Bethany never left his side. They stroked his hair, sponged the sweat off his body, and consoled him with gentle words.

Hours passed, almost a full day. His eyelids fluttered and his face and head twitched. They stared down at him as his eyes opened, darted around the room, then focused up on their faces. Carolanne shone a penlight in his pupils.

"Brian?" Bethany said. "Brian, can you hear me? Are you awake?"

She patted his cheeks.

"Brian … talk to me, Brian."

His mouth opened and closed.

"I …" he said. "B-B-Beth …" His voice was a dry squeak.

Tears returned to her eyes. "Yes, Brian, it's me. You're safe."

His lips moved. "T-t-thirsty."

"Here, drink." Carolanne held a glass of water to his lips. He tried to move his arm to hold the glass, but was shaking too much to do so. "I got it. You just drink."

His lips touched the rim of the glass, and he took a sip. Then sipped again and again, his body eagerly absorbing the moisture. Bethany thought of a dry sponge.

"Here, Brian. Take this." Carolanne pushed an antibiotic tablet in his mouth. He didn't seem to notice. He kept drinking until the glass was empty, and then he rested his head on the pillow.

"Good. That's very good." Carolanne put the empty glass on the side table. "Go back to sleep. We'll be here when you wake up."

***

When Brian was finally able to sit up in bed, he found a bowl of chicken broth on his nightstand. For the first time since he'd woken up, he was alone in the room. He grabbed the bowl and began sipping the warm liquid, blowing back the steam from each spoonful. The warmth in his belly spread further throughout his body with each sip, down to his fingers and toes. The shakiness subsided.

A great veil seemed to have been lifted from his eyes and mind, and he felt better than he had in days.

When he finished the last of the soup, he put the empty bowl on the bedside table. His stomach now grumbled as if it were a bottomless pit that needed to consume endless amounts of food and water. There was a needle in the crook of his arm, connected to a long, clear tube leading to a bag of IV solution hanging on a rolling stand.

For a few moments, he sat there staring up at the ceiling. A dull, almost pleasant sensation emanated from his forehead as the pain and fever melted away. He let his eyes close and took several deep breaths.

Then he sat up and inched his feet off the side of the bed, letting them dangle before touching the ground. He sat like that for several minutes, his bare feet feeling the carpeted floor. Then, using the metal pole of the IV stand for support, Brian pulled himself to standing. There was an initial wave of dizziness as he steadied, and his knees took a moment before regaining some strength. The soles of his feet felt like pincushions. He looked down at the pajamas he was wearing. He didn't remember putting them on. In fact, he didn't remember much of the last few days. Even the time leading up to finding the bunker was hazy—a jumble of choppy images.

Brian shuffled to the door, holding the rolling IV stand, and turned the handle. The hallway outside looked exactly the same as the hallway in his and Steven's bunker in Nelson. A strange feeling washed over him, as if he'd gone back in time, as if he would see Steven walk across the far end of the hallway at any moment. As if the last few weeks had all been a fever dream.

But as he exited the hallway, Steven was not there.

There were two women in the kitchen, one pouring a pouch of dried soup powder into a bowl of boiling water, and the other watching.

Bethany.

He wanted to stay off in the corner forever just watching the two of them. This was a victory. The first stage of his journey had been completed. It had nearly killed him, and it had killed Steven …

He didn't want to think about that right now.

He wanted to watch the women. He wanted to soak in their presence. Brian knew Carolanne, had even met her once at Bethany's wedding. She was Bethany's neighbor and her best friend.

They're so skinny, he thought. *They look like twigs.*

They both wore jeans and tank tops and were barefoot. Their hair was up in ponytails that hung down to the centers of their backs. Carolanne's hair was a strawberry blond, much lighter than Bethany's, and Bethany was an inch or two taller, but besides from that, they looked almost identical from behind. They might have been sisters.

Carolanne turned, and a look of surprise washed over her face.

"Brian!" She rushed over.

Bethany turned off the stove and followed. "What are you doing out of bed?"

"I'm okay, really."

"No," Carolanne said, grabbing his elbow. "You're *not* okay. Sit."

She led him to a recliner.

"I feel all right."

"You still have a fever. You have to rest. You have to go back to bed."

"I promise I will. Just let me sit here for a few minutes."

Carolanne seemed to think it over, then went to get a throw blanket and draped it over his lap. She got an ear thermometer and told him to stay still while she took his temperature. As she leaned in close, the fragrance of her clean hair and skin gave Brian goose bumps.

She smells like the beach, he thought. *Somehow, she smells like the beach.*

Brian asked, "Are you a doctor?"

"No, I'm a nurse. Almost. I was still in school."

Brian's eyes darted around the bunker. It had the same octopus layout as his in Nelson, with the central room round like a dome and corridors, like tentacles, extending out to the various bedrooms and storage.

The main difference, Brian saw, was that there was no weight bench, and Steven's dirty shirts and socks were not left on the couch. The women's bunker was clean and organized. He never thought that their bunker in Nelson had been messy, but now, seeing this one, he knew that it was. All their DVDs were set in perfect rows on a shelf by the TV and not left in piles. Their kitchen counter was clear of books, and the sink was not full of dishes. Plus, there were cheerful paintings and pictures hanging on the walls and plastic flowers in vases on the kitchen counter, coffee table, and, well ... everywhere.

Carolanne said, "You still have a fever, but it's gone down."

"Good," Brian said. "That's very good. I need to get better. There's a lot to do before heading out."

The girls swallowed and went silent. Just like Brian and Steven not long ago, the girls had been alone for a long time, with no sunlight, no real air ... no outside world. The thought of leaving was both terrifying and exhilarating.

Bethany broke the silence. Tears were welling up in the corner of her eyes. "Oh, Brian." She hugged him tight. "I can't believe you're actually here."

"I'm here, Beth, I'm here. And I'm not going anywhere."

Carolanne brought Brian another bowl of broth and promised they would make a solid meal for dinner. As Brian sipped at the steaming bowl, a silence filled the room that was thicker than the soup.

It was time they talked about their experiences. It was time they talked about war and disease.

Brian looked up at Bethany. "Your brother …" he said.

Tears welled up in her eyes.

Brian cleared his throat and shook his head. "I'm sorry, Beth. He was like a brother to me … my best friend."

She dabbed at her eyes, surprisingly solemn. Carolanne took her hand and held it tight.

"How'd it happen?" she asked.

A pang of sorrow and guilt struck Brian's heart. He pursed his mouth. He wanted to tell her; he wanted to tell them the whole story from start to finish, the way it should be told. He wanted to confess his guilt and hope that they would understand and give him absolution and not be frightened or remorseful of him. He wanted them to wash away his sins.

But he didn't. It wouldn't do them any good knowing that the last moment of Steven's life was rife with insanity, delusion, anger, fear … murder.

"He was shot," Brian said. "It happened in a flash. I … he was shot … and I ran. I had to. I had to leave him. There was nothing to be done."

Bethany nodded and looked at the ground, tears falling from her eyes to darken the carpet in round droplets.

"Who shot him?"

"Some desperate sons of bitches. I don't know who they were."

She continued nodding.

She was prepared for this, Brian thought. *She was prepared for me to be dead too. Probably thought she'd be underground forever.*

Brian cleared his throat and changed the subject. "Nelson's nothing more than a ghost town."

"Nelson wasn't much more than a ghost town when I knew it," Carolanne said.

Bethany smiled and so did Brian.

"Seriously," she went on, "how the hell did you guys live there?"

Brian chuckled. "It's picturesque, they say."

"Who says that? It's hicksville, if you ask me."

Bethany laughed and wiped her eyes. Carolanne squeezed her hand.

As the mood lightened, Brian found that the women had a million questions about his journey and the outside world. He answered their questions as best as he could, not wanting to sugarcoat anything. They would be leaving soon, and they needed to know what to expect.

"You see many people out there?"

"Some."

"What are they like?"

"It's best to avoid 'em. I'm sure there's still plenty of good people out there, but I ain't seen any."

Brian took a deep breath; it was his turn to ask a question. "And George?"

Bethany looked at the floor. She didn't look up, just shook her head.

Brian couldn't remember the name of Carolanne's husband, but he remembered her having one. Maybe they split up before she left for the bunker? He didn't think so.

Bethany answered the question for him. "Same with Robert," she said.

Brian nodded. The girls looked solemn, but they'd had sufficient time over the past two years to mourn and comfort each other, and had come to terms with the deaths of their husbands as best as they could.

"They were both sick before coming down here," Bethany said. "They were sneezing and coughing, but it didn't look like anything other than a common cold."

"The disease got them?"

"The disease got George." Bethany took a deep breath. "I'll start from the beginning. When the fighting first began, and the walls were shaking with all of the bombings, Robert got nervous. Not just because of the bombings, but because he still had family up there. We begged him not to go. We begged and begged him, but he said his Aunt Valerie had raised him like a son and he just couldn't leave her up there to die, just couldn't do it.

"After a long break in the bombings, he went to the ladder. Even George was giving him hell, but Robert couldn't be swayed. He said he'd be fine. He promised he'd be back in five minutes, with or without her. He was smiling even, reassuring Carolanne. So he took the shotgun and left. We waited by the hatch door, staring up at it. Five minutes passed, and then ten. After a half hour, George said he'd go out looking. We begged him not to leave, but he went anyway.

"Ten minutes later, George returned, white as a sheet … and he was alone.

The bombings had resumed, and he didn't see a trace of Robert anywhere. George said the whole town was on fire and looters were rampant in the streets, sick and dying, and killing each other faster than the disease could get to them. Two days later, George got sick. We cared for him the best we could, but ..." Bethany was shaking her head.

"I seen what the disease does to people," Brian said. "I know how bad it is. I'm sorry that you girls had to go through all that."

The girls nodded, staring at their feet. Brian took their silence as a sign that the conversation was now complete. That was fine. Brian had just arrived—this was a time to be happy, not dwell upon the dead.

Chapter 25
Livingston Park

Simon was looking at two barns and one stable: each structure large, each structure, old.

The buildings had stopped being used for their intended purposes many years ago and had been converted to offices and storage for the park rangers and staff. Simon did not know this, because what he saw before him was a more recent conversion: a military outpost.

The three structures formed a horseshoe configuration, with the two barns facing each other, the stable in the rear, and a field in the center that had been paved over. Dozens of dark green military vehicles sat in rows, new and unused, as if sitting at a car dealership. Many were fitted with tarps tied about them.

Grasses and weeds emerged through cracks in the pavement, some vining up between the vehicles' treads and tires, and a thick layer of pollen covered everything. Whatever army or platoon had been stationed in Livingston Park was long dead, and this assemblage of machinery had been forgotten.

Simon walked between two rows of tanks, feeling the cold metal with his fingers, leaving trails across the dust.

He recognized the Abrams tanks and counted twelve Hummers, six of which had machine guns mounted on top. Four attack helicopters sat on separate detachable flatbed trailers with their rotors tied back for transport. There were vehicles with rectangular rocket launchers on top, a few tow trucks, medical transports, and about a dozen vehicles that Simon didn't recognize.

He walked to the front of the barn he had approached from the woods and wiped away the grime from a smoggy window, cupping his hands over his eyes to see the cavernous interior. Pillars of light filtered down from windows high above. Row upon row of boxes and supplies towered tall.

"Holy crap, Winston. You seeing this?"

Winston was off by the tanks, sniffing the tires and treads. He turned upon hearing his name.

"It's okay, boy. Go on."

There was a tall sliding door at the front of the barn, and Simon grabbed ahold of the handle and pulled, leaning his body weight into the task. The door creaked and inched open, gritty dust falling from the track high above. He entered and walked to the center of the barn, trying to decipher one box from the next.

They were mostly wooden, but some were metal. Others were plastic. Random numbers and letters marked each box in military jargon. Simon walked to the closest container and unsnapped the hinges. Inside sat a glistening pile of arranged projectiles, each the length of a football. Simon gently picked one up, rolling it in his palm. It felt cold and weighed about the same as a grapefruit. When he put it down, his fingers felt greasy and smelled like oil. He wiped his hand on his pants and walked to the next stack of boxes. Inside were even larger ordnance—tank shells, or missiles.

He went from box to box, opening over a dozen. They all held large-caliber ammunition.

Simon went back outside and walked across the lot to the barn on the opposite side. Winston was sniffing around from vehicle to vehicle, but he ran over to Simon for a quick scratch on the head before going back about his discovering.

After clearing the filth from a window, Simon peered inside. The room was roughly the same size as the previous barn, but there were no towering stacks of boxes. Some cots were strewn about and what looked like garbage mixed with the soldiers' personal effects.

The door slid open like the last, and Simon sneezed as the gritty dust fell over his face from the overhead tracks.

Picnic benches lined the far wall, and metal cups and mess kits were scattered about. Up against the wall was a line of military carbines, with bandoliers left in orderly piles.

Simon picked up an M16. It wasn't new, but it wasn't old either. He looked at his own M1A strapped over his shoulder. The M16 felt so light in his hands, and there was more than enough ammunition in the bandoliers to fill his backpack. The M16 was a superior rifle and fired on automatic. But …

He put the rifle down and swung the M1A up in his hands. The smooth wooden stock and the cold metal barrel felt comfortable in his grip. He had shot the M1A hundreds of times and knew exactly how it fired and where to aim. He knew how to take it apart and what to do if it jammed. It was like an appendage of his body.

This was not the time to learn how to use a new weapon.

What if it jams when I'm under fire?

He went along the line of guns to a collection of pump-action shotguns, all jet-black. He picked a .12 gauge Mossberg, and pumped the forestock and checked the ejection port and magazine. The action was smooth. He would take it apart and oil all the parts later, but this gun would fire without hesitation. Among the stacks of ammunition, he found boxes of .12 gauge shells and took enough to fill the empty space in his backpack.

Back outside, he crossed to the stables. He whistled low for Winston. "Hey," he shouted. "Where'd you go?"

Winston was curled in the grass. He stood and stretched his back, bowing low, then ran over to meet Simon. "Don't disappear on me, buddy."

The glass window of the stable was thick with grime, and he wiped a section before peering inside.

"Oh … fuck," he said.

It was now evident what had befallen the soldiers of this lost battalion. Inside each individual stable, and lining the open walls, were dozens of cots. Twenty, forty, *a hundred?* Simon couldn't see to the back of the room. Upon each cot lay a corpse, covered from head to toe with a blanket. Bags of IV solution and medicine still hung from metal racks—the bags drained and wrinkled—with the plastic tubing still connected to dry veins. Twisted feet stuck out past the bedsheets like dehydrated tree roots. This had been a hospital once, but was now a morgue. The air in the stable was thick with stagnant dust illuminated in shafts of light, as if time did not exist inside that morbid structure.

Simon stepped back.

He turned to Winston. "Hey, let's get out of here."

The urge to be far away was apparent.

After a few yards, he stopped and removed the map from his pocket. He traced the green splotch that comprised Livingston Park until he came roughly to where he was standing. He took a marker from his backpack, pulled the cap off in his teeth, and marked a black dot.

Chapter 26
Water on Glass

The next time Steven Driscoll opened his eyes, he was lying on a gurney in a hospital bedroom, looking out the window at the trees swaying in the wind.

A short, balding doctor came in wordlessly, rifling through a kit of medical supplies.

"Open your eyes," he said, shinning a penlight into Steven's pupils. The beady-eyed man checked the bandage covering Steven's forehead and inserted a syringe into the injection port of the IV tube running to the crook of his arm.

"What's that?" Steven asked.

The doctor packed his things and left. Steven was alone in the room with only his thoughts.

However, his mind was quiet. Calm, even, for the first time since … he wasn't sure. He was back in the town of Odyssey. Rain had begun to fall outside the window, and the thick droplets plunked against the glass, exploding like burst grapes.

Steven sighed and closed his eyes.

Later that day or perhaps the next, he heard footsteps approach from down the hall.

Captain Black entered the room. "Well," he said, shaking the rain from his hat, "by the looks of things, they've put you back together proper."

Steven stared out the window.

"Hell of a lot of blood you lost. Hell of a lot of blood. Would have made the doctor's job a lot easier if you'd told him your blood type."

The rain was now battering the window, and the trees were contorting in gusts of wind.

"Hell, son, say something. We're only trying to fix your broken ass."

"I don't know," Steven muttered.

"What's that now?"

"I don't know my blood type. Reckon I was never told."

"That's fine, lad." The captain dragged a chair across the floor to sit beside the bed.

"Still got a headache? Well, the doctor said you're healing fast. I even got some food on its way for you. How's that sound? Put some meat back on those bones."

At the mere mention of food, Steven's stomach growled. "When?" His eyes looked to the captain, huge, pleading.

"We'll feed you proper, lad, don't you worry. I promise. I bet you're hungry. By the size of you, one meal may not suffice."

The captain crossed his legs high and placed his cavalry hat upon his knee.

"Son, I'm going to tell you a few things, and I do recommend that you listen. I know you're not one for talking, so just listen. You need to rest. You need to heal, and I will give you ample time to do so. As you recuperate, I want you to dwell on your future. What will you *do* with your strength when it returns? The world is a dangerous place, as you are well aware. Your own family has turned its back on you and left you for dead. You are alone. A destitute soul in a decrepit world.

"We'll get you back on your feet, but you must decide where those feet will take you. By my calculations, you'll survive on your own for a week, maybe two. What a shame that will be. What a waste, spending all of this time and resources fixing you up. When you rest tonight, I want you to think of your new family—us here, in Odyssey and beyond. We are not the awful people you might have thought we are. You and me," the captain motioned between himself and Steven, "we are one and the same. Survivors. I do believe that I can show you the benefits of becoming part of our brotherhood. Family is important; am I wrong in saying so? Family is all you got in this world, and our family is large."

Steven opened his mouth to speak, but the captain continued, "You rest now, lad. You rest. We'll talk more tomorrow, see if we can't get you back on your feet. I have a whole new world to show you."

Captain Black stood and shook out his wrinkled hat.

"Till tomorrow, lad." The captain turned and left, leaving Steven alone in the quiet room.

Steven knew that he should leave, that he must continue on his journey, the journey he was tasked with. He must reach Bethany and Uncle Al ... only ...

Shit ...

Steven knew Bethany lived in Aurora, but where *exactly* was Uncle Al?

Where's my map?

The last time Steven looked at his map, the black ink used to line his path was smeared and fading. The waterproof material on the paper had begun to disintegrate, and the paper was soft underneath. The map was just a jumble of lines and colors to him anyway. For a second—one fleeting second—a thought crossed his mind.

I need Brian.

He pushed the words out of his head.

Did he really try to kill me? My own cousin ... my brother?

Steven couldn't remember. The events of their fight were lost to him among a sea of sweltering red. But one thing was for sure—he had awoken with his head cracked open, and his cousin far from sight.

Why, Brian? ... Why? ...

Red was returning to Steven's vision with each beat of his quickening heart. But exhaustion calmed him back down, and his eyes struggled to stay open. He felt numb all over, inside and out, in a good sort of way. A pleasant numbness. His body was relaxing, his muscles soft on the mattress. Steven closed his eyes and sleep overtook him.

Dreams did not come. Only a pure and utter void.

When he awoke some time later, the room was dark. Whatever pleasantness he felt earlier had evaporated. His head throbbed. Ached. His brain seemed to pulse against his skull, too large and ever-expanding to stay confined.

They're all dead, Stevie. They're all dead ...

Sickness struck the depth of his stomach. Nausea. Everything hurt, all over his body.

Brian—he's dead. Uncle Al, Bethany, everyone you've ever known—they're all dead. If you go venturing off in the woods, you will join them. You will see them again in the pits of hell. You will rot with them.

Steven gritted his teeth against the pain.

An hour went by, and a man came in carrying a tray. He turned on the lights.

"Holy hell," he said. "I'll go get the doc."

The man returned with the beady-eyed doctor. He looked Steven over and took a bottle of medicine out of his bag.

"Here," he said, offering Steven two white pills and a glass of water.

Steven took the medicine and shut his eyes against the throbbing in his head. The doctor and the man left, and as time went by, the pain subsided. The scent of food on the table was beginning to smell appealing. Soon, Steven forgot he had ever been in pain to begin with as he took the cover off the plate and beheld a thick slab of meat, charred around the roast edges and leaking juices to pool underneath. A gentle whiff of steam rose in the air. Steven picked up the fork and knife and cut away a slice.

The earthy scent overtook him, and he grabbed the chunk of meat in his hand and sunk his teeth into the moist flesh, ripping it apart, unable to stop his carnivorous appetite. He gnawed at the meat, devouring whole pieces that were barely chewed, and sighing deeply as the warm juices coated his mouth and flowed down his throat.

***

Steven walked beside Captain Black. The captain was showing him the town of Odyssey—the parts of the town that he had not seen from the window high on the hill that one dreadful night.

"This here is the barracks." The captain pointed to a wide brick structure. It had once been an old apartment building, or maybe a department store. "We'll get you set up with a room if you decide to stay."

Steven watched the men gathered before the building, standing around a fire built in a rusted barrel, many smoking cigarettes. They were dirty and ragged, yet most looked well-fed and strong. He watched a black man with long, skinny dreadlocks tied down to the small of his back walk by on spring-like toes. The gathering of men straightened their backs as he passed, and some nodded or saluted.

"Who's that?" Steven asked. "That the leader or something?"

Captain Black turned to see the black man turn around the side of the barracks and disappear. "He's a lieutenant," he said. "You'll meet him in due time. The general is the leader, Steven, the man that you met."

Steven had met many people over the last several days. The captain brought them into his room—people with names and ranks that Steven could not remember. The captain would say things to them like, "Stout one, ain't he? Look at the size of those arms." And the men would nod and walk away.

On one particular morning, maybe two days prior, Steven awoke bleary-minded from the pain medicine and met the general in a fog. The conversation was lost to him, but he remembered the man's voice, deep and soothing, using words Steven did not know the definitions for. The general smiled straight white teeth down at Steven as he lay on the bed, and he stood tall—as tall as Steven, yet leaner. The whole meeting was veiled by Steven's foggy memory, lost with the passing days and the doctor's strong pills.

"You have to make up your mind soon, lad," the captain explained, leading Steven back toward the infirmary. "We don't let outsiders stay for any given time, but in your case, I've asked the general to grant a few days of amnesty. There's something inside of you, Steven. I see greatness in your eyes. You're a big lad, maybe the biggest man in all of Odyssey. You have a chance, if you stay with us, to prove to yourself that you are capable of achieving things that most men only dream about. There is exhilaration in warfare, something I do not think you've had the pleasure yet to experience. It's addictive, the rush. It's euphoric. There is no drug that can produce a sweeter high than the one you experience in battle. You achieve true power over all things—yourself and others.

"And you, Steven, were designed for this life. You were designed for warfare; it's in your blood, your DNA. You should not fear it—you should embrace it. I'll show you how. I will show you how to reach the true apex of your existence here on this godforsaken earth. You, Steven, will flourish among our ranks. We have spared your life despite the crimes of murdering four of our men so that you may redeem yourself by replacing their numbers among us. Now, I'm not sure where you were headed when we found you, but—"

"I was going to see my uncle," Steven cut in.

"What's that now?"

"My uncle. He's supposed to be waiting for me on the East Coast, or that's what he said. I'm not sure exactly where. There should be people there with him, kind of like this."

Steven had found his map in a pile of his personal belongings. The paper was saturated in dried blood and crumbling away with water damage. It was incomprehensible.

"On the East Coast? There's not much left of the East Coast, not in the cities at least. You sure he's alive?"

"No …"

"Well, one thing is certain. *We* are alive. Now, why is your uncle making you go all this way to get to him? If he has a gathering of people, why not send a convoy to escort you?"

"I …"

"Doesn't sound promising, if you ask me. Sounds like you're fixing yourself for disappointment. Marching to your own death. Your uncle—what did you say his name is?"

"Al. Albert Driscoll."

"It doesn't sound like Albert Driscoll cares much if you get to him or not."

Steven shook his head. "It ain't like that. He's in the army."

"There is no longer a United States Army, lad. But … perhaps I am wrong. Where exactly did you say your uncle is waiting for you?"

"He's … I don't know."

"You think you could point it out if we show you a map? We could send a scout to check out the land, then perhaps an envoy. We have camps close to the Northeast, much like this one here in Odyssey."

"I reckon so. Maybe."

They approached the infirmary.

The captain held the door open. "Another time. Tomorrow."

Steven walked through. He thought of Bethany and wondered if she was waiting for him, or if she had perished along with the majority of the population.

Were Brian and me stupid for even trying? Did we actually think Beth and Uncle Al would be alive? Hell, there ain't barely nobody left in all of the world … Why would they be spared?

The pain in Steven's head was creeping back. He put his hand in his pocket, rolling around the two painkillers the doctor had given him. The sides felt smooth against his thumb as he popped one in his mouth and ground the bitter, chalky pill between his teeth. The sensation sent a shiver of euphoria down his spine as the medicine absorbed into his bloodstream.

Chapter 27

Whispers of Smoke

Expansive farms and cornfields followed outside of Livingston Park. The corn had long ago lost its battle for life, and the old dry stalks jutted out from the land, strangled with vining plants whose broad leaves reached out to the heavens.

Winston frolicked over the ground, sticking his nose deep in the soil, smelling the plants that had once prospered in the fields.

Simon was so close to home that he marched on into the evening, and the sun now hung low in the far horizon over the endless fields. For a moment, he missed the West, where the sky was large and unhindered by buildings and power lines, much like it was here.

A small garage caught his attention, far in the rear of a property, behind one of the ample cornfields. Thick woods bordered the back of the structure like a fence. In the distance, he could see the spectacular farmhouse once belonging to the property. He continued toward the garage, with Winston lagging behind, tired from the full day's march.

Simon stopped to scratch Winston's head. "I'm sorry, buddy, we're almost done. We'll take it slow tomorrow. I promise."

Once Simon was in full view of the building, he could see that the small garage had once belonged to a larger structure. Connected to the sidewall were the charred remains of a building that had long ago been consumed by fire. The bricks and mortar had been blackened to dust, and portions of the enclosure were strewn about. Yet the garage remained intact, except for the rear corner where flames had crumbled away a minor portion at the base.

Simon knelt beside the hole in the wall and inspected a rock from the ground. He felt the grit of old fire in his palm and could still smell smoke when he held it to his nose. He peered into the blackness behind the hole, but he couldn't see anything of the garage's interior. The opening was rather small, and he doubted he would fit if he tried to squeeze his way inside.

The sliding garage door on the front was padlocked shut. Simon thought about trying his new shotgun on the lock or smashing it away with a rock, but there was no reason to go inside. The rear of the garage shielded him from sight of the road, and the woods were close behind, forming a semicircle around the clearing.

Simon built a fire as Winston went about smelling the remains of the burnt building. Simon whistled him over. "Come on, boy."

After unrolling his wool blanket, just beside the charred gap, Simon gathered as much wood as he could manage before the night grew dark.

Home, he thought. *In just a few days … I'll be home.*

He fed Winston, who fell asleep curled up on the blanket the moment he finished eating. Simon put a cup of water on the fire and made pine needle tea to accompany his dinner of jerky and a salad of baby clovers, arugula, and dandelion greens, which he'd harvested while gathering wood.

The water was steaming on the fire, and Simon removed the cup with his knife, setting it aside to cool. He patted the front of his pocket, and removed the pictures, leaning in close to the light of the flames. They were all there— his mother, his father, his brother. There was also a picture of him and Emma back when he was a little boy. She looked old even then.

He thought about his brother often, although maybe not often enough. They had grown apart over the years, and deep down, Simon knew that if Marty was still alive, he was far away.

Sadness struck Simon's heart thinking that there was a good chance his brother had died in France, or some distant land. Images of their childhood together flooded his memory—he and his brother playing in the park as Emma watched, late-night comic book reads with them sharing a flashlight.

As teenagers they barely spoke. Marty went to business school and Simon went to the woods. When Marty left for college, they only saw each other during the holidays. The thought of his brother dead as an adult didn't bother Simon as much as when he pictured the little boy he'd grown up with no longer being around.

Simon flipped through the pictures and landed on a photo of him and his dad. Simon was thirteen, maybe fourteen. He looked strange even to himself. He was wearing a button-up shirt and khaki pants, and his hair was parted. He smiled for the camera, although he remembered that at the time, he had not wanted his picture taken. The acne on his face was embarrassing. His father, though, looked the same as he always had. He was wearing a suit and tie, with one arm over Simon and the other holding a briefcase. They were outside the house, near the front door. His father was smiling, and his hair was not as gray as it would later become.

Simon smiled, laughed even, despite being on the verge of tears.

Winston's head popped up, but Simon didn't pay him any mind. He blew back the steam from his tea. Winston let out a low growl, looking off to the woods. He was tensed, his nose wiggling in the air, ears pinned back.

Simon looked up. "What is it, buddy?"

Winston stood, his eyes fixated on something in the darkness. Simon followed his gaze, but all he could see was the border of the forest and nothing beyond.

Winston's growl grew in intensity, and the fur on his back stood on end. He was up on all fours, his muscles taut, his lips snarled, fangs glaring.

"What is it? What do you see?"

Simon crouched on his knees and shielded his eyes from the light of the fire.

He saw movement. Faint and dark, like whispers of smoke in the night.

Then he saw them in the woods; saw the twinkling of eyes.

"Oh shit," he muttered.

The growling of wolves emanated from the shadows.

Chapter 28
The Exit

The haze and pain that had spread over Brian's mind and body from the fever diminished, vanished even, and he could now stand witness to his crime with a clear mind. He had killed his best friend, his cousin, his brother.

Brian was a murderer.

A monster.

He was death.

I left him there, out in the cold. I didn't bury him. I didn't throw a blanket over his body. Something dragged him off…. This could have been avoided. What if I had backed down from the fight? What if I had run and let him cool off? What if I hadn't hit him so hard with the rock?

But Brian had not backed down from the fight, and now he had to accept his guilt, and endure the anguish and torment.

And he would have to endure these feelings alone, for the events surrounding Steven's death must remain a secret. The women needed Brian now more than ever. They needed someone to guide them to Uncle Al—to safety, to humanity—and it was Brian's task to do so.

If only I had Steven to help shoulder the burden.

Brian rested upon his bed, attempting to rationalize the death of Steven Driscoll: if Steven had survived that day—killing Brian instead—it was unlikely that he would have made it much farther in the journey, let alone to the bunker. The demons in Steven's mind had overtaken his senses, and his fear and anger had become uncontrollable. The man that died that day was not the same Steven Driscoll whom Brian had grown up with … he had become a monster. The poor man's soul had been tormented until he himself became the evil that he despised.

Steven's death had saved the lives of Bethany and Carolanne.

Brian made a vow to himself that his life was now dedicated to the survival of the two women, at any cost to his own well-being. He did not know what amount of strength lay dormant in his body, but he would use all of his power to get the girls to Uncle Al.

He would not let them down.

***

They ate canned ham, pancakes with rehydrated fruit, pasta with tomato sauce or tossed in olive oil and garlic powder, biscuits, fresh-baked bread, peanut butter and jelly, canned peaches—anything and everything. There was enough food in the pantry to last another year. Brian was so hungry that he craved every type of food at once—every taste and flavor combination in his mouth at the same time, and he could not seem to get full no matter how much he devoured.

After a few days, his body was taking shape again. His battered feet had begun to heal, with all the open wounds and popped blisters hardening to calluses, and he could walk without pain shooting up his legs. The women had a few light dumbbells in the living room, and in the days prior to leaving, Brian set them up with a workout routine. Curls, pushups, pull-ups, and squats. Basic stuff. There wasn't enough time to make a big difference, but at least their muscles would be awakened.

Bethany's legs were strong and she would be fine marching with gear. Carolanne, however, was struggling. After ten squats, her cheeks would turn red and her breath would come out in huffs. Brian would have to keep a close eye on her.

Their weapons were assembled and laid out on the dining room table, and a lesson was given on how to take each firearm apart and keep them from jamming. Brian had his assault rifle and automatic pistol. The women had two .22 rifles—both good firearms, especially for hunting small game. One of them, the Ruger, had a compact yet powerful scope. The women also had a .38 snub-nose revolver, which they kept lodged in the railing below the hatch door. Bethany had always been a crack shot, even when she was a young girl. Brian had no doubt she would be fine handling any gun on the table. Carolanne looked at the pistols and rifles as if they came from a foreign land.

Brian inspected their weapons, counting the ammunition and feeling the cold and heavy .38 snub-nose revolver in his palm. "This is a good pistol," he said. "Is this everything?"

"We had a shotgun," Carolanne said. "But … it's gone now."

The girls looked at the floor.

Brian waited for an explanation, but they did not offer one.

Disappeared along with Robert, he remembered.

"Okay, this is what we're going to do," Brian said. "I've set up a target down the hall. We're each going to fire a few rounds from the .22s. It's going to get smoky in here, so we're only going to fire off a few." He faced them. "You know how to fire a gun?"

Bethany rolled her eyes. "Please. I grew up in Nelson."

"I was asking Carolanne. You ever shoot a gun, Carolanne?"

She flushed. "I … no, not really. Not ever, actually."

"Now's the time to learn. Beth, you need to watch too. I reckon you never handled an assault rifle."

He showed them how to load each firearm and how to take them apart for cleaning, with Bethany helping dismantle the .22s. Then he stood at the range and aimed down the barrel at the box filled with books and crushed tin cans. The loud *pop* of the gunfire made Carolanne jump.

"Easy, see?" He looked at Carolanne. She didn't seem so sure.

Bethany fired next. It was her rifle, although it had belonged to Steven when he was a boy. Somehow, over the years, it had wound up in her care. Brian remembered the gun fondly from his own childhood—a Marlin, with a smooth wooden stock and solid metal barrel.

"This is the only rifle George allowed in the house," Bethany explained. "He thought guns were unnecessary, that they should be eliminated from the world—an obsolete need and a danger to society. They should only be used by soldiers and police, he thought. However, after firing it himself at tin cans and paper targets, he grew to enjoy it as a sport and later he bought the Ruger."

She turned toward the target and fired a few rounds, in expert fashion.

"Okay, Carolanne," Brian said. "You're up."

Carolanne took the rifle. She rested the butt of the stock against her shoulder, but she was shaking and her stance was off.

"Hold on," Brian said. "Here, let me help."

He showed her where to put her feet and stood behind her holding her forearm.

She squeezed the trigger, and her eyes went large.

"That's it. Breathe. Stay steady."

She fired again, and again. Brian stepped back, and she continued pulling the trigger. When the firing pin clicked and the magazine was empty, she loosened her grip.

"That's fun," she said. Her cheeks were flushed against her pale skin. Brian laughed.

***

When the women emerged from the bathroom, they had tucked their hair into hats and were dressed in olive-drab jumpsuits and bulletproof vests.

"How do we look?" Bethany asked.

They were wearing size smalls, but the jumpsuits were loose around their waists, and the sleeves were too long.

Brian laughed. "Like a couple of teenage boys."

"Better we look like teenage boys than young girls."

"Not if we run into a band of priests."

"Brian Rhodes!" Bethany laughed.

Brian had replenished much of his strength, and the girls were eager to see the light of day. The time had come; they were packed and ready to leave the bunker. They went over the route they would be taking until it was ingrained in their memories, and each of them could retrace the line on a blank map by recollection. Brian stuffed the large military stuff-sack with more supplies than he thought they would need and packed smaller backpacks for the women. He gave Carolanne the Marlin rifle, and Bethany the pistol and the scoped Ruger.

He asked them both, "You ready?"

They wore grave expressions, the collars of their jumpsuits forming dark rings. They looked similar to Brian and Steven when they had left the bunker in Nelson.

Brian turned to the ladder. "Let's get on, then."

***

Bethany stopped dead in her tracks a few feet outside of the shed and just stood there. They were next to an old garden, the rectangular outline still visible from a waist-high grass border.

"Beth, we got to move on." Brian looked to her house in the near distance, reduced to rubble. "I know this is a lot to take in, but we gotta move."

She didn't budge. Carolanne went to her side. "Give her a minute," she told Brian.

"All right, but we—"

Carolanne shot him a fierce look, so Brian reluctantly walked away to scan the road ahead. He looked back; Bethany was kneeling beside the garden, her head bowed in solemn contemplation as more tears fell to the earth. Carolanne was rubbing her shoulders. He walked back.

"Is everything okay?"

"It's …" Bethany said.

"What?"

Brian looked at the garden. It was hard to see, but when he studied the ground, he saw a rectangular-sized mound under the tall weeds and a basketball-sized rock at the far end.

George …

He didn't say another word, but walked off to keep watch. The surreal image of the two girls digging a hole in the garden while wearing neon hazmat suits flashed in Brian's mind.

Ten minutes passed, and Bethany rose. They walked over to where Brian stood among a fallen section of Bethany's house. He wanted to ask Bethany if she was all right, but he couldn't find the words. The looks on their faces told him to remain quiet.

He was happy to oblige.

***

It took some time, but they made it to the outskirts of Aurora. After several hours of walking, the women were not as shaky as they had been when leaving the bunker. They complained at times that they were tired and sore, but their adrenaline kept them moving. They were headed for the woods near the Adirondack trail. The walk so far was nothing in comparison to the trail Brian and Steven had endured since leaving Nelson. The land here was flat, the rain had ceased, and the air was clear and dry. Plus, the distance between Nelson and Aurora was much farther than the distance between Aurora and the East Coast. In just a few days, maybe a week, they would make it to Uncle Al.

"You think God killed them?" Carolanne asked.

"Who?"

"Everyone."

"God? I don't know."

"If not God, who then? Did *we* make the disease? Did humans do this?"

"I suppose we'll never know. Maybe. Probably."

Carolanne shook her head. "Why? Why would we do that?"

Brian shrugged. "Maybe we didn't? Maybe it just came about, just happened."

"*Just happened?* There has to be a reason. I heard on the news—back when there was news—that it started in the Middle East."

"Could be. Reckon I heard that too, but that could've been a load of bullshit. Propaganda. Maybe it wasn't anybody's fault. A disease can come about without the aid of people. Usually happens that way, I imagine."

Carolanne frowned. "No." She shook her head. "We did this."

They were quiet for a while, and then Carolanne went on, "What if we get to Uncle Al's and nobody's there?"

"We can't think like that," Brian said. "Uncle Al made a plan. He knew what to expect. We're doing all right so far, ain't we? We survived in the bunkers for two years, and now we're following the route he laid out for us. We're a part of Uncle Al's plan, one way or the other, and because of that plan, we've survived this long."

"I guess so." She bit at her lip, and then continued, "Not everything's gone according to plan though. We've lost a few along the way."

Brian's voice dropped. "Yeah ..."

They were quiet.

Then Carolanne continued, "Sorry I brought that up. I sometimes ... talk a lot when I'm nervous. Words seem to slip past me."

"Hey, that's no problem. You were only being honest. Talk away."

She bit at her lip again before continuing, "What do you think it will be like when we get to your Uncle?"

"Shit, I don't know." Brian held back a branch so it wouldn't whip the girls as they passed. "I reckon there will be other people. Probably a good number. Survivors, like us."

Carolanne giggled.

"What's so funny?"

"Nothing. Sorry. I just never heard someone say *reckon* so many times before."

Brian smiled, but he felt his cheeks turn red. He knew the stigma attached to coming from the Deep South.

"I don't think it's bad or anything …"

Bethany laughed.

A few minutes later, when Carolanne took out her map to give it a study, Bethany whispered in Brian's ear, "She never knows when to shut up."

***

They made camp deep in the forest. Brian gathered wood for a small fire, and they heated cans of soup on the hot coals.

"We're going to take turns keeping watch," he told them. "You two will go first, together."

Bethany interrupted, "We can each take a turn."

"No, and it's not up for discussion. You two will keep watch together for five hours, then it's my turn." Brian continued, "Keep the fire low, and wake me if you hear anything. *Anything.* Okay?"

"Okay," Carolanne answered.

Bethany kept her mouth shut.

They ate and the night grew dark. Brian crawled into his sleeping bag and was asleep within minutes. Half an hour later, he was snoring.

They kept the fire low and sat close together as the night wore on. A small crackling noise caused Carolanne to jump, but Bethany calmed her down. "It's nothing," she said. "A deer or something."

They woke Brian after five hours, and he sat up in his sleeping bag, his eyes puffy with sleep. His voice hoarse. "All right. You girls get to bed."

Brian yawned and tossed some sticks in the small fire.

It was a long night, and all Brian could think about was Steven. How he had left him staring up at the sky, and then came back to find him gone.

Did animals drag him off?

But those were horse tracks, and people.

He reminded himself that he could not afford to let his mind dwell on terrible thoughts, lest he suffer the same madness that had befallen Steven.

As the first rays of sunlight approached, Brian filled his tin cup with water and set it before the glowing coals. When the water began to steam, he removed the cup and sprinkled some instant coffee on top. He stirred it with a twig and tossed the twig in the fire, where it sizzled.

He heard movement, but not from the woods. A moment later, Carolanne was sitting up in her sleeping bag.

He whispered to her, "Go back to sleep. You have more time."

She shook her head and yawned. After a moment, she scooted herself in her sleeping bag closer to the fire. Bethany was fast asleep.

"Good morning," she whispered.

"Good morning."

"What's for breakfast?"

"Powdered eggs." Brian chuckled. "How do you like your powdered eggs? Soggy or damn near drowned?"

She wrinkled her nose. "Gross."

They were quiet as Brian heated a cup of coffee for Carolanne. The instant coffee was premixed with powdered milk and sugar from the bunker and didn't taste half bad. Brian preferred his coffee black, but just having coffee, any coffee, was an amazing boost to his morale. When the coffee was hot, Carolanne held it under her nose, breathing in the rich vapors and blowing away the steam.

"It's weird being out of the shelter," she said.

"I know. It takes some getting used to. I've been out for a little while now, and I'm still not used to the outside world. Don't know if I ever will be."

"You think there are more people out there? Good people like us?"

Brian thought of the old man sitting by the fire, stirring the rancid stew, his cane resting over his knees. He thought about the town of Odyssey and the awful-looking men marching with weapons fashioned out of metal poles, dragging naked prisoners along down a road lined with executed corpses hanging from streetlights and crucified on poles.

He said, "I reckon there are good people out there."

They sipped their coffee. "I never said thank you." Carolanne's voice was low. "I never thanked you for coming to get us."

Brian looked surprised. "You don't have to thank me. Hell, it's me that owes you some thanking. I would have died outside your bunker for sure if you hadn't taken me in and cared for me the way you did."

"I liked having something to do. I was glad to have a purpose."

"Well, thank you."

As the sun came up, the morning dew turned into drifts of low rolling fog.

"I'm scared, Brian."

He looked at her. Carolanne was looking into her coffee, lost. She went on. "When George died and Robert disappeared, I thought Beth and I would soon die for sure. Thinking we would have to wait two years for you and Steven to show up—if you showed up—and that we would have to spend those two years alone down there, waiting … scared the shit out of me. All I kept thinking about was getting the hell out of that bunker. Now, though, now that I'm out … I kind of want to go back. But I also want to be as far from it as possible. I know it's stupid, but I'm … terrified."

"That's not stupid. I understand." He envisioned them—Carolanne and Bethany, alone in the bunker, comforting each other, spending weeks and months mourning their husbands.

"I never lost a loved one the way you and Bethany lost your husbands, so I'm not trying to compare, but I know the feeling of losing someone you care about while there ain't a damn thing you can do about it. Nancy and Ben Hendricks—they were like parents to Steven and me, and we had to leave them above ground in Nelson. All that time in the bunker, I kept thinking about them and what they must be going through, cursing myself for not forcing them to come with us, although I thought the task impossible at the time. Then came Stanley … Stanley Jacobs, my best friend after Steven. He came to the bunker sick with the disease and died down there. I saw firsthand what the disease was doing to people. It was the most frightening display I ever seen. Knowing that Nancy and Ben might have died that way … it just about killed me thinking about it."

Carolanne nodded, looking into the fire. "I want for things to get better. I *need* for things to get better so incredibly bad. It's time to move on. Beth and I, I think we've come to terms, but I need something to believe in again—

a sign that humanity hasn't truly seen its last days on earth. I hope to God that there are good people in Uncle Al's camp … but, I have to admit, I'm terrified to get there."

Brian played with a stick in the flames and looked up at Carolanne, hugging her knees to her chest inside her sleeping bag. "I promise you," he said, "I'll do everything in my power to get you girls to safety. I promise, with all of my heart, with all the strength I can muster, that I will do everything I can to protect you. I'll never leave you, Carolanne. Neither of you. I will get you to shelter or die trying."

"I know." She choked back a tear. "I know you will."

Chapter 29
The Alpha

"Get back, Winston! Get back!"

Winston's body was rigid, his muscles taut.

The muzzles of the wolves were now looming out of the shadows like insidious devils belonging to the night.

Simon had to act fast.

He grabbed the wooden end of a stick burning in the fire and threw it hard in the direction of the wolves. It crashed against the side of a tree and burst like a firework, raining down an avalanche of hot sparks. The wolves scurried.

Move, now!

Winston was ready to lunge. Simon grabbed him hard at the base of his neck with one hand and scooped him up under his ribcage with his other. Winston was thrashing about in his arms, but Simon managed to stuff him in the hole in the garage wall, and blocked the entrance with his foot. As Simon turned, the wolves were back, sprinting out of the shadows, dark and evil.

Oh, my God!

The alpha wolf was in the lead, snarling. His wet fangs glistening a bright white against his fur that was black as night.

Simon grabbed the shotgun, aimed into the fire, and pulled the trigger. The burning wood exploded in a frenzy of sparks and burning coals, fanning out in a semicircle before him.

The wolves stopped as if they had hit a wall.

Simon turned and dove headfirst into the hole. His shoulders scraped the sides, but his torso cleared the opening. Then he felt a snag around his waist. He was stuck. It was pitch black inside the garage, blindingly dark. Simon couldn't see Winston a foot in front of him, although he could feel the heat coming off the dog's growling breath. He groped the floor of the garage for anything he could use to pull himself forward, but all he felt was the cold, cement ground.

He thought he could hear the patter of paws approaching, the wolves drooling over the meat of his exposed legs. The teeth would sink in deep, rattle his body about, and shred away whole chunks of calf and thigh meat before ripping him free from the hole to devour him in a frenzied swarm. The prize would be his brain, broken free like a walnut from the shell.

Determined, he struggled, tearing his shirt and breaking a brick free. He scurried inside, then turned to face the hole. Winston lunged forward, but Simon grabbed him around the neck. "Winston!" he shouted. "No, Winston! No!"

The fire outside illuminated the break in the wall. He held the shotgun steady in his right hand, gripping Winston around the neck with the other.

He waited.

"Come on, you fuckers. Come on ..."

A mouth of snarling white teeth and foaming saliva lunged into the opening, its jaws snapping in the air, desperate to clamp onto flesh and bones. The air filled with the pungent odor of its rank fur and breath.

Simon pulled the trigger. The head of the wolf splattered in a red mist, and its body flew backward from of the opening.

The shotgun buckled out of Simon's hand, and the sound the shot produced in that small space was tremendous. Winston yelped, tore free from Simon's grasp, and ran somewhere behind him. Simon grabbed at his ears and shouted, "Fuck!," but he couldn't hear his own voice. He found the shotgun on the ground, pumped a new shell into the chamber, and turned back to the opening. The alpha was dead, but they might regroup. The beta would take the lead, becoming the new alpha.

Five minutes passed and the brilliance from the fire outside had burned down to a gentle glow.

Simon didn't have his flashlight. He did not have any of his gear. Everything was outside with the wolves. His breathing felt labored; the air was thick, smelling of cold smoke. He patted his pockets and felt the rectangular smoothness of his lighter.

He flicked it on, and the small flame sent shadows dancing along the walls. "Winston, where'd you go?"

Winston was in the corner with ears pinned back, scared but unharmed.

The garage was small, with enough space to house the one car that was parked in the center of the room, draped with a thick canvas sheet. Along the walls were metal shelves and stacks of various-sized boxes. The lighter was starting to burn his thumb, so he let it cool as he stood still, his eyes adjusting to the darkness.

Using his hands and feet as guides and flicking on the lighter now and again, he took several boxes from the shelves and crammed them into the gap until it was sufficiently blocked. Anything trying to come through would struggle enough for Simon to fire off a shot.

He pulled the canvas material off the car, scattering dust in the air that tickled his nose. Simon tried the back handle. It was unlocked.

"Come on, boy; get in."

Winston walked over and paused before the open door.

"Get up."

Winston jumped in and Simon followed.

***

Light filtered in through the one rectangular window near the ceiling. Winston was awake before him, panting. The interior of the car was stifling hot.

Simon sat up in the backseat, rubbing his eyes and peering at the hole in the wall. The boxes were unscathed. He opened the car door, enjoying the cool air that flooded the interior. With the sunlight streaming in, Simon could see the garage clearly. The wall around the hole was black from where the flames of the old fire had poked through. The rest of the garage had fared well, with only a few boxes and a shelf next to the opening burnt and melted.

Simon listened outside. It was quiet. He moved the boxes and knelt to look out. The wolves were gone, from what he could see, except for the body of the alpha—a massive, dark gray beast.

Simon crawled through the gap, through the dried gore, and came out the other side with his shotgun aimed and ready. He picked up his M1A rifle from where he had left it, and shouldered the strap. Winston followed through the hole and went straight to the dead wolf, burying his nose deep in its musty fur.

The wolves were gone. If they were near, Winston would know before Simon, and Winston didn't seem bothered.

The campsite lay in ruins.

"Oh, shit, Winston. Oh shit, shit, shit …"

Simon lifted his blanket, examining it. Cinder from the fire had burned large holes straight through. He followed various scraps of material until he found his backpack lying like something dead at the edge of the woods.

The food was gone—all of it. The binoculars were nearby, with teeth marks sunk deep in the plastic and rubber material. He put them to his eyes and could see well enough, yet the lenses were scratched. Ammunition was scattered about, along with most of the inedible contents, but the food was gone, and the backpack itself was shredded to pieces.

He kicked at the dirt. "Crap, Winston. Damn it all."

Simon picked up an undamaged brick from the burnt foundation and went to the front of the garage. He swung at the padlock. The noise the brick made against the padlock and metal-shutter door was louder than he anticipated. He hit it again and again. The face of the padlock scraped and the door dented, but the lock would not break free.

Simon tossed the brick. "Fuck it." He stepped back, unholstered his Colt .45, and took aim. The gunshot rang loud in the air and the padlock burst into pieces. Simon turned the handle and the door rolled upward.

Various tools and boxes filled with automotive parts lined the shelves, and Simon went through them until he found a beat-up, heavy-duty duffle bag. He opened it, emptying the car jack and tools to the floor. Before leaving, he took a Coleman cooler off a shelf, making sure the inside was clean and empty.

Simon gathered what supplies he could salvage, putting them in the duffle bag, and turned to Winston. His dog was done sniffing the dead wolf and sat staring up at Simon with large brown eyes.

"I know you're hungry, boy. So am I."

Simon gathered wood and built a fire. He dragged the dead wolf by its hind legs to a flat stone and proceeded to skin and butcher the animal. There was little meat on the wolf, but he cut away what he could.

"This is all we have right now, Winston." He skewered the dark meat on sticks and set them near the flame to roast. The animal had been dead for hours on the ground and had to be cooked thoroughly.

The meat sizzled and browned, and when it was charred on all sides, Simon removed it from the flame. He diced the meat into manageable pieces and offered it to Winston. He put what was left in the cooler and went out to the woods to forage food for himself. Winston sniffed at the dark meat, unsure, but without further hesitation, he devoured it all.

***

The car was a dark blue, almost metallic, Buick Regal. It was old, but looked like it had been well kept. Simon flipped the sun visors and looked through the glove box. He found the keys on a hook by the sliding garage door. The starter clicked when the key turned, but the engine would not turn over.

Simon popped the hood. The engine looked clean—not that he knew enough about car engines to know if something was wrong. On the shelf where he had found the duffel bag were two car batteries, still in their boxes. Jugs of motor oil, washer fluid, and transmission conditioner sat in a neat line. Whoever had once owned this garage knew a thing or two about car maintenance.

Simon reached for a battery, and then stopped.

What am I doing?

He didn't have an answer. He was moving on autopilot. Home was only a few days' hike, but with a car, he could be there … that night?

Cars are trouble. Cars are moving targets. Remember the van?

But his food was gone, and the meat he had cooked for Winston would last only a day before it was finished or spoiled. If they were going to survive, he would have to stop often to hunt, set traps, fish, gather wild plants and grains, and smoke any meat that he caught. It could take days, especially since deer tracks, or tracks of any animal large enough to keep them fed for a long period, were nowhere to be seen.

He could do that—set up camp, and hunt.

Or he could be home in a few hours.

Simon took the battery off the shelf, letting the box fall to the ground.

This might be fate, he thought. *Everything happens for a reason. I can't disregard the chain of events leading to me standing right here, right now. If I can't get the car to run in an hour, I'll give up and prepare camp.*

Changing a car battery was one of the few mechanical skills he knew how to do, along with checking the oil and changing the wiper blades. He went to the driver's seat. "Here goes nothing."

The engine rattled, made a gurgling noise, kicked, and then started up. Dark bluish smoke sputtered from the exhaust. The radio turned on, loud, and Simon went through the dial before clicking the static off.

"I'll be damned."

Simon let the car run for a few minutes, then killed the engine. The gas tank was three-quarters full. In the corner of the room, next to a lawn mower—and only feet away from the black and charred hole in the wall—were two five-gallon gasoline jugs. Judging by the black patterns on the wall, the flames had come perilously close to burning these cans, even licking their sides. How this room had survived devastation was beyond him.

With an old rag, Simon brushed away the cobwebs covering the cans, watching the little striped spiders scurry about. One can was full, five gallons, and the other was about two-thirds from the top.

Fate, he thought.

Back outside the garage, he found Winston curled in the shade.

"Hey, buddy, you want to go home?" Winston's head perked up, and his tail wagged against the ground.

"Want to go home, you big dummy? Want to go home?"

Simon ran up to his dog and scratched his head with both hands, letting Winston lick at his moving palms.

Chapter 30

Fade to Black

Brian, Bethany, and Carolanne followed a stream until it brought them to a little pond. The day was nice, and the surface of the water rippled ever so slightly. A battered wooden sign sticking out of the ground read *Sunfish Pond*.

Brian looked at the sky, shielding his eyes against the glowing white with his hand. The warmth felt glorious on his skin. "Think it's about noon," he said. "Let's take a break and try some fishing."

Despite the overcast, the days of never-ending rain seemed a thing of the past. A dream. A nightmare.

If only the clouds had cracked for Steven to see the sky, just once, just a crack. Just one time … things might have gone differently.

The women were happy to take off their backpacks and sit along the bank of the water. It was tiring to walk all day, but they were well fed and had to admit to themselves that most of the walk was scenic and peaceful.

As much as Brian did not want to admit it—hated to admit it—not having Steven around to gloom and go into one of his silent moods was making the trek that much nicer. The women got tired often and complained their fair share—especially about their blistering feet and aching backs—yet they kept a positive attitude. And when they did not feel like being positive, they were honest about what was bothering them.

They sat in silence, letting the minutes pass, watching the hypnotic ripples flow across the pond. Carolanne picked up a small pebble and plucked it into the water.

"All right," Brian said, "let's get our lines."

Carolanne opened her bag, looking for the fishing gear. "Fishing?"

"There's nothing to it." Brian smiled, looking at Carolanne's face staring at the bobbers and line. "You never fished as a child?"

Carolanne wrinkled her nose. "Umm, not that I remember."

Brian gathered three branches, and they tied their lines to the ends, sticking the poles in the ground. The girls sat back and watched the bobbers float about in the water while Brian stood up and stretched.

"I'll be right back," he said, walking up the embankment behind them. "I'm going to gather some wood." The girls sat with their backs against the slope, unable to see Brian only a few steps away.

"So," Bethany asked, "how are you feeling?"

"I guess all right. My feet are killing me."

"Yeah. Mine too."

They watched the fishing lines sway in the breeze.

Bethany cleared her throat. "I have to say, you're handling being out of the bunker pretty well."

Carolanne nodded.

"You're doing good, Carolanne."

"Thanks. I feel ... I don't know. It was time, I guess. Brian's talked to me, helped calm my nerves."

"What did he say?"

Carolanne shrugged. "I don't know ... nothing really. Just that he promises to get us to safety, to watch over us."

"I ain't never heard you two talking."

Carolanne raised an eyebrow at Bethany. "*Ain't?*"

"Hey, I am from Nelson. It comes out once in a while."

They looked back to the water. One of the bobbers was wriggling about.

"We caught something!" Carolanne jumped to her feet and grabbed the pole.

Brian returned down the embankment with an armful of sticks. He dropped it and walked beside Carolanne.

"Go on, reel it up."

Carolanne pulled the short line out of the water, and a small fish, maybe six inches, was thrashing about on the end of the line.

"I got a fish!"

"You did. Good job." Brian took the line from her. The little fish was shaking water on them. "It's a sunny."

"A what?"

"A sunfish. Like the name of the pond." He nodded toward the sign.

"Oh, right."

"Just a few more like this and we'll have a meal."

Carolanne laughed. "So, how do we clean it?"

"I'll show you." Brian was removing his knife from the sheath when Bethany said, "I'll finish getting the wood."

"We don't need much more. Maybe some kindling, but there's no rush. I'll make the fire in a minute. You don't have to leave." Brian looked up from the wriggling fish.

"I know how to make a fire. Plus ... I got to pee." She started up the embankment.

"Wait," Brian shouted after her. "Stay close. Don't go past that big oak tree up there. And don't forget your rifle."

"Yeah, I got it." Bethany grabbed her rifle, and disappeared up the embankment.

Brian turned to Carolanne. "Ready?"

She nodded and smiled.

Brian put the still-wriggling fish on a rock and expertly chopped off the head in one stroke. "I would normally leave the head on, but it's more humane to kill it quickly." He then proceeded to cut it along the belly and wash away the guts in the water.

Carolanne's face went sour.

Brian laughed. "I thought you wanted to learn."

"Yeah ... well."

He skewered the fish on a stick and went about sorting the wood, getting the kindling and tinder ready.

"This, I can help with," Carolanne said and squatted next to Brian, her side just touching his.

Then a muffled scream carried over the embankment.

Carolanne startled. "What's that?"

"Beth ..."

Carolanne's face washed pale.

Brian rushed to the dirt bank, pressing his body flat against it. He peered over, then ducked back down. *"Shit, shit, shit,"* he said in a hiss. "Stay here and stay down."

Carolanne grabbed her .22 and hugged it to her chest. "I-I-my heart is pounding, Brian. I'm gonna faint. I'm—"

"You're not gonna faint." She was staring at him with huge eyes, trembling. "Breathe. Stay here. Keep your head down."

With that, he jumped over the embankment and moved forward, his rifle up and his stance low.

Three men were running, stumbling, in the opposite direction. The one in the middle held Bethany around the neck with his forearm, while the one in the rear was struggling to hold on to her kicking legs.

Brian rushed forward. "Stop! Stop! Stop right there! STOP!"

The three men hesitated when they heard his voice, and the two in the rear glanced back, but they did not stop. They held the terrified and flailing Bethany in their grimy hands.

"Stop! Right now!" Brian took aim at the man grabbing at Bethany's ankles, who was also holding Bethany's .22 as he ran, and steadied his breath. *In and out ...* He fired. The shot hit the man in the side, spinning him around and dropping him hard to the ground. The man made a deep, guttural noise and clasped his hands over his lower ribcage where blood was seeping through his shirt.

The two other men stopped and turned. The one in the rear stepped to his side, fanning out, and swung an AK-47 in Brian's direction. The one holding Bethany produced a large knife and held the glimmering blade against her throat. He grabbed her hair hard with his fist, yanking her head backward. He was only a kid, Brian saw. Just a tall kid, skinny as bones, with flaming red hair.

He aimed at the man with the rifle, a much older man, but for some reason he did not fire and neither did the man.

"Let her go," Brian commanded.

The man stared at Brian, his mouth not moving behind his bristly gray beard. He seemed to ponder his options, and then when he spoke, Brian saw the deep wrinkles in his face move as if cracking free from his weathered flesh.

"I think not," the man said.

The man Brian shot was holding his wound, his legs flailing at the dirt.

"M-Mike," he choked through cries. "Mike, get me outta here, Mike. Oh, sweet Jesus, oh, Jesus. M-M-Mike … Mike, I'm dying, Mike …"

Mike did not answer.

Brian's thoughts were rushing like river water, and he tried to slow his mind. Enough bad choices made on his part had gotten people killed and had made Steven go crazy. "What do you want?" he asked.

"We already have what we want. Turn back and go away."

Brian looked at the boy with the knife. His eyes were huge against his freckled and pimple-covered face, and the top of his curly red hair seemed to be twitching. Brian studied the blade, studied the boy's grip.

Bethany cried out, "Brian! Brian! Fuck these motherfuckers!"

"Shut her up!" the man commanded, and the boy put a filthy hand over Bethany's mouth, squeezing her head into his chest. Her hands went up, clutching at the boy's forearm.

Brian wondered if he could get off a shot at the boy's head. It would be tough, but not impossible. He would certainly be killed while doing so, and Bethany still might be dragged away. Carolanne would also be taken, to be raped, tortured, and eventually killed. Maybe cooked for dinner.

The thought made Brian mad as hell.

The man told him, "Son, lower your gun and turn away. This don't concern you. She's coming with us. There's more of us yonder. The longer we stand around, the sooner they'll come looking. Lower your rifle. Go away."

Brian remembered Odyssey. He remembered the people dragged by their necks and the others crucified and left to rot.

Clarity washed over his mind.

He looked to the boy. "Hey, you—boy!"

"Don't talk to him," the man commanded.

Brian ignored him. "Boy, I'm talking to you! You don't have to do this. Put the knife down and get on. The only way this is going to end is with you dead. All of you. And if there are any more of you fuckers back behind them trees, they're all gonna die too."

The boy's eyes were large, but he did not speak. Brian had been eating regularly and working out. His clothing was new and military issue, and his face had been shaved before leaving the bunker. He looked like a soldier. The boy's expression spoke fear.

"Listen," Brian said, "just turn away. I have food and water. You look hungry. I'll feed you. I promise."

"You're a good ol' boy, ain't ya?" the old man said. "Listen. We ain't letting her go, so go on and fuck off."

The anger inside Brian boiled over. "I'm not talking to you! There are twenty more in our group, in the bushes on either side of this clearing."

The man said, "Bullshit." But his twitching eyes betrayed him.

"I'll kill you both if you don't let her go! I'll kill you first, boy, and let your friend down there on the ground bleed out while he watches you die!"

"Who, him?" The man laughed—actually laughed—and turned to his friend on the ground who was writhing in pain. "Who gives a shit about Larry?"

He aimed his rifle at the man's chest.

"Mike! M-Mi—"

Mike shot Larry in the chest. His body jumped on the ground and twitched, and blood began gurgling from his mouth.

Brian saw Bethany's hand come out of her pocket. She was holding the snub-nose pistol. In a flash, Brian's mind outlined his next move.

The man was turning back to Brian after shooting his companion, and Brian took aim and fired, hitting him square in his right shoulder. He twisted and fell face-first in the dirt.

Bethany lifted the pistol to the boy's elbow, just below where he held the knife. She pulled the trigger, but had miscalculated the distance, most likely afraid of shooting her own ear. The bullet grazed the boy's forearm, not shattering his elbow as she had intended. Still, the boy shrieked, dropped the knife, and loosened his grip over Bethany's mouth. The shot had echoed loud.

Bethany fell to the ground, holding her ears tight in her palms.

Brian sprinted forward.

The boy composed himself in a rush and scooped up the knife from the ground, not sure what else to do. As he straightened up, Brian was on him.

Brian took hold of the boy's wrist in one hand and grabbed the front of the boy's shirt with the other, latching on to something like an ammunition belt that was strung across his chest. He drove the kid backward until his back hit the side of the nearby oak tree.

The boy was terrified, but he pushed back, attempting to shove the blade of the knife in Brian's direction. But the boy was weak, malnourished, and young.

Brian grasped on to his wrist and firmed the grip on the ammunition belt with his other hand. He pulled the boy away from the tree, and then slammed him back against it. He did it again. Hard. Their eyes were locked. Brian could smell that the kid had soiled himself.

The blade loosened, and Brian grabbed on to the boy's relaxed grip. With a final shove against the tree, Brian plunged the blade of the knife into the boy's throat, and pushed it down to the handle. The point of the blade hit the hard side of the tree. Brian pressed forward one more time, and the blade stuck into the wood.

The boy's hands fluttered to the knife handle as blood foamed and spattered from his lips. He looked shocked. Death was impossible, inconceivable—yet fast approaching and certain.

Brian stepped back.

The events that followed seemed to happen in a dream.

Brian let go of the ammunition belt slung across the boy's chest and felt something fall, making a *ping* sound. He heard a grunt from behind him and turned to see that the old man had raised himself up on one knee, his right arm dangling and immobile. He was holding a pistol in his working hand.

Brian glanced back to whatever had fallen from the boy's ammunition belt and saw a hand grenade bounce and roll under his feet. Although he did not realize it, the pin had already fallen from his palm when he released the boy, and the handle had sprung free.

His heart was beating so fast that the flashes of red in his vision were like a strobe.

Brian grabbed the hand grenade, cocked his arm back, and threw it off toward the tree line. As he did so, he heard the popping of gunfire.

The grenade made it just past the oak tree, then exploded in midair. The whole side of the tree erupted with splintering wood, blowing the boy's body in the air like a rag doll and hitting Brian in the chest with a barrage that felt akin to being struck by a car. Brian's feet left the ground, and he crashed violently on his back.

The explosion looked impossibly white in Brian's eyes before turning to darkness. And then his mind shut off.

Chapter 31
1421 Ridgeline Road

The Buick was a good car, despite its age.

It had strength and speed and drove like it was made out of solid metal, not some composite plastic. The V6 engine whispered like a well-maintained machine as Simon sped over the cracked asphalt.

He saw the White Sparrow Diner with its neon lights now dark and cold. He passed the old armory, a wide brick building built to manufacture ammunition during World War II but converted to a roller-skating rink sometime before he was born. Simon had been there, in that rink, for countless birthday parties and had eaten at the White Sparrow Diner with his parents for many meals.

As Simon drove on, he swung the radio dial back and forth, listening for any whispers of human civilization, but all he heard was static. An endless flow of static, like water in a moving river. It never stopped.

Simon clicked the radio off as the road brought him to Bronson Bridge. The bridge was significant to Simon because the water that flowed beneath it was the Ridgeline River. He was close. Miles. Not weeks or days, or even hours—miles.

Simon crossed the bridge.

Ridgeline Road was now under his tires and it would take him straight to the driveway of his house, just a few towns over.

The ride became scenic as Simon entered Alice Springs Park. The western portion of the town of Alice was wooded with a bountiful reservoir that supplied the drinking water to the neighboring towns. It was a large park, a beautiful park, and Simon adored it. He had spent much of his childhood there, and as he grew older and took an interest in survival and the outdoors, the park served as his escape and recluse from the everyday world. He knew the trails like the lines on his palms.

Entering the park, as the road swept under a canopy of trees and the landscape on either side of the highway became thick overgrowth, Simon let out a sigh.

"We're in Alice, Winston ... we made it to Alice."

The road curved left and right, then went straight for several miles over slight mounds in the hilly woods. It was the most beautiful road in the entire county—at least, at that moment it was.

On the far side of Alice Springs Park was the town of Alice itself, a small community with one school, one church, and one grocery store. It was once a popular town for the middle class—small, quaint, and surrounded by nature. Past Alice, in the town of Fairview, the mansions along Ridgeline Road would appear, with Simon's home among them.

At the present moment, Simon was content with enjoying the trees and scenery. Sunlight broke through the canopy of branches in flickering intervals, illuminating the road in shafts of brightness. Simon rolled Winston's window down, letting his dog smell the familiar air and trees.

The road itself was in good condition, without many potholes or much debris. A few random cars sat on the side of the road like ancient relics, and occasionally Simon had to slow to bypass larger branches.

The road made a sharp turn, and Simon was confronted with a fallen tree blocking most of the two lanes. The leafy top was just shy of the far left shoulder.

Simon drove on, careful not to scrape the side mirror.

He passed the fallen tree and was confronted again by another tree blocking the road a few car-lengths before him. This one had fallen in the opposite direction so that the leafy top reached the right shoulder.

Wait ...

A thought struck him like a bullet shot.

At the same time, he saw what he feared in the distance.

Another trap.

"Oh, shit."

Past the fallen tree, obscured from sight through the branches jutting into the air, Simon saw a line of concrete dividers stretching from one side of the road to the other. He thought he could see two, maybe three, domed helmets peering over the top.

"Shit, shit, shit, shit."

Winston's ears were alert as he huffed the outside air.

Simon scanned the horizon on either side of the concrete divider for any signs of inorganic shapes—anything man-made—and sure enough, there were two gazebo-like structures, one on either side, tucked in the thicket of trees. They were concealed with camouflaged blinds, and although Simon could not see them, he was sure there were armed men behind the fortified walls.

He put the car in reverse.

But then a voice boomed through the air from a loudspeaker.

"PUT THE CAR IN PARK AND YOUR HANDS ON THE STEERING WHEEL."

Simon glanced at his rearview mirror at the tree he just bypassed. If he tried to peel out, he would surely be shot before he could maneuver past the narrow passageway.

Maybe I can run?

"DO AS WE SAY AND YOU WON'T BE HARMED. PUT THE CAR IN PARK AND YOUR HANDS ON THE STEERING WHEEL. WE HAVE YOU SURROUNDED."

Then figures emerged from the trees as though the plants had come alive. They were well-camouflaged and armed with assault rifles. He thought he might cry.

"Winston … oh, Winston … I fucked up. Again. I'm so sorry. I fucked up."

In his side mirror, he watched a man wearing army fatigues approach the driver side door, aiming an M16 with precision.

"Put the car in park and put your hands on the steering wheel," the voice commanded. Simon did as he was told. His hands were shaking and he glanced over at the shotgun on the seat next to Winston. The chamber was loaded.

He could see at least four men—one at each corner of the car—kneeling with rifles pointed. They looked like things of the earth—ghostly apparitions contrived out of warfare and the wilderness. Winston was growling. The fur on his back stood on end.

"No, Winston. No."

Winston was not listening; he let out another growl.

"No," Simon said in a hiss. "Winston, down. *Down.*"

Winston looked at Simon, his eyes large at the tone of his voice, and he curled up on the floor beneath the passenger seat.

A loud rapping at Simon's window startled him. Simon half-turned to see the muzzle of a rifle pressed against the glass, inches from his face.

"Lower the window. Slowly, please."

Simon obeyed.

"Where are you going?"

"I'm …" Simon swallowed back a lump in his throat. He wanted to turn to face the man, but he did not dare move his head. "I'm-I'm going … home."

"Home? Where's home? There's no one living around here other than the delegates of Zone Blue. No sir, you're going to have to turn this car around and head back the way you came."

Zone Blue?

"Sir, turn your car around."

Simon's hands became steady on the wheel. He was trying to think of another way to bypass Alice.

"I-I live just up the road in Fairview. It's not far."

"Sir, no one is allowed to pass or enter Zone Blue without permission. Where in Fairview?"

"Fourteen twenty-one Ridgeline Road."

The soldier did the math.

"That area is unoccupied, but it's still in the protected perimeter. I cannot permit you entry."

Cannot permit me? Cannot permit me! I've almost been killed trying to get here, and I've … I've had to kill …

"Sir, this is the last time I'm going to ask. Turn this car—"

Simon turned his head, looking straight into the guard's face. He was wearing an olive-drab cloth over his nose and mouth, but Simon could see his eyes.

"Sir! Turn around this instant!"

"Please, I'm begging you … I've come a long way. I've almost been killed."

"Who hasn't? Turn around and move on. *Now.* You have ten seconds to get off our land."

"Oh, Christ, please, you have to allow me to pass. I've waited years …"

"I told you, that area of Ridgeline Road is unoccupied. There's no one living there. And no one can pass without the direct consent of General Byrnes."

Simon's eyes went wide.

Byrnes?

"Wait—what did you say? Byrnes? Tom Byrnes?" The framed picture in his dad's office flashed in his mind: his dad and good friend Tom Byrnes, fishing. The same Tom Byrnes who had warned his father to leave the East Coast. The same Tom Byrnes with *alleged* CIA affiliation and a military background.

"Is it Tom Byrnes?"

"Sir, you can't enter without—"

"Let me talk to him, please. I know him."

"I'm afraid that's not possible."

"But I know him—I swear." Simon could hear the squelching sound coming from a radio in the background.

"Call him over the radio. Call him, please. Tell him Simon Kalispell is here. Tell him Simon Kalispell, Anthony Kalispell's son."

"Sir—"

"I promise I know him. Just call him on the radio. It will only take a minute of your time. I'll stay right here with my hands on the steering wheel. I won't move an inch. If he says no, I'll leave. I promise. I'll turn around and leave."

The guard was silent for a moment. Simon thought he was about to be forced to put the car in reverse, but then the soldier said, "Keep your hands on the steering wheel. Don't move."

"Yes, sir."

Simon watched the soldier in the side mirror step back and unclasp a walkie-talkie from his belt.

***

Sergeant Jeremy Winters met Simon at the entrance to Alice Springs. Simon was not permitted to enter the center of town, but was given permission to walk under escort to his home.

Simon parked where he was told and exited the Buick.

A guard offered him a cigarette, but Simon shook his head. After a moment, he looked back at the car and then all around him.

Winston?

"Winston? Hey, where are you, buddy?"

The guard cocked his head. "Who?"

"My dog." Simon poked his head in the car and looked under the seats. "Winston?"

"What dog? I didn't see any dog when I approached you. Wouldn't he have barked?"

"He was on the floor of the car. He was …" A flash went through Simon's mind, back to the gas station.

Why didn't you bark, Winston? Why didn't you bark?

Simon saw the men in the woods in British Columbia; felt the way his heart beat against the tree branch as they aimed their rifles at Winston in the woods.

Not possible …

"My dog, Winston … he was right there."

The guard took a pull of his cigarette.

I can't have been imagining … no, no, it's not possible. I'm not crazy. I'm not—

His skin broke out in a cold sweat.

The guard cracked a smile. "There's no dog in your car."

Simon felt faint.

"He's over there." The guard nodded off to a gathering of soldiers, not far. The man chuckled. "He snuck out when you opened the door. Good-looking dog."

Simon fought the urge to punch the guard in the face, but seeing Winston with his tail going crazy as all the soldiers circled around him, scratching his head, made Simon feel overcome with happiness.

"Just fucking with you," the guard said.

"I might just take you up on that cigarette."

"What kind of dog is he?"

"A stupid one."

"Ha!"

Winston trotted to them, and the guard scratched Winston's back. "No, you're not dumb, are you, fella? You're not dumb."

Sergeant Jeremy Winters stood taller than the other soldiers and was not wearing a helmet or cloth around his face. He was dressed in simple, dark green fatigues, clean and pressed and tucked in around the waist, with an M16 slung over his shoulder. He was built like an athlete, like a quarterback or a rugby player—slim, strong, and tall.

"Mr. Kalispell, I'm Sergeant Jeremy Winters." The man walked over, scratching the graying stubble on his chin.

Simon shook the sergeant's hand. "Nice to meet you, Sergeant. Please call me Simon."

"Likewise. Call me Jeremy." The calloused palm of Jeremy's hand squeezed firm. He smiled as they shook, and Simon noticed a scar running from below his left eye down the center of his cheek. It was not discolored or awful to look at. Rather, it seemed fitting on the man, as if he had been born with it. A badge or indication of rank.

A guard next to Sergeant Winters said, "Mr. Kalispell, you'll have to leave your firearms at the gate before entering Alice."

"That won't be necessary." Jeremy shook his head. "He's been given inclusive access from General Byrnes himself."

The guard nodded. "Yes, sir."

Jeremy turned to Simon. "Mr. Kalispell—Simon—would you like to proceed?"

Simon looked up at the man. "You have no idea."

"This way, then."

Simon turned and whistled to Winston. "Come on, boy."

One of the soldiers scratching Winston's head turned to Simon. "He can stay here with us if you want. Until you get back."

Simon looked at his dog licking at the guard's hand and laughed. "I think Winston wants to see his home too. Come on, boy."

Simon and Jeremy began walking north from what was labeled *Checkpoint Z*, and after a few steps, Winston came running up to Simon's side.

"Nice-looking dog," Jeremy said.

With the checkpoint behind them, there was no one else around. The road was vacant. It was strange for Simon to be back on a familiar road, one he had driven countless times, but was now so desolate, quiet as a tomb. The lane had once been well-traveled. Cars, joggers, kids on bikes going back and forth at all hours.

The quiet felt surreal. Simon shuddered. Fairview was vacant, like an eggshell without the yolk, ready to crack.

They turned on Ridgeline Road, and Simon's heart sped up. His hometown. They passed a home that had fascinated Simon as a child. The massive house itself was hidden from view up a long and overgrown driveway, but a large, old carriage house was in the corner between the road and the driveway. There were four semicircular windows up high, near the ceiling, with four gigantic chandeliers visible in the room's interior. A medieval-looking crest was painted on the wall facing the street, large and magnificent.

There was no electricity powering the chandeliers, and the windows were now dark and barren.

Jeremy offered Simon a cigarette and pulled one out of the pack with his teeth for himself. Simon declined.

"You been here long?" Simon asked.

"You could say that." Jeremy flicked a battered brass Zippo lighter, and inhaled the cigarette to life. "Served with the general a long time."

"Mr. Byrnes?"

"Yes, sir. Tom Byrnes."

"What is it you guys have going on here?"

There was a pause as Jeremy inhaled.

Jeremy answered, "In Alice? Alice is Zone Blue, a faction of survivors. We're trying to get life back to normal … or as normal as possible."

"Normal?" Simon's mind wandered, remembering normal: hot showers, dinner at seven o'clock, electricity, plumbing …

"That's right—normal. A government, you could say, although the concept of an organized government is not the most appealing idea to most people these days. I'm not supposed to be telling a non-member any details, but General Byrnes gave me direct orders to make you feel at home. He said you're old friends."

"He's a friend of my dad's."

Jeremy nodded, scratching the rough hairs on the side of his cheek. "Your dad must be a good man. General Byrnes is top-notch."

"He's in charge, I presume?"

"That's right. He's in charge of Alice, along with his son."

"Right, I think I remember him. Nick, was it?"

"That's right. Lieutenant Nick Byrnes." Jeremy tossed his cigarette to the ground, letting it burn out on its own against the pavement. Simon had noticed earlier that Jeremy walked with a stiff leg, but it didn't seem to slow the man down.

Simon's heart fluttered as they neared the edge of his family's property. The long iron gate surrounding the border was covered in vines, with the broad flat leaves extending into the air. This was going to be more difficult than he'd thought. For a moment, Simon debated asking Jeremy for a cigarette.

Jeremy sensed his trepidation. "This is it, right? Fourteen twenty-one Ridgeline Road."

Simon nodded.

They came to the entrance. The automatic gateway was long without power, and the vines had sewn the two gates into one. They each took a side and pushed and pulled, using their knives until the vines snapped apart and the driveway leading to Simon's home became visible.

Winston took off, running into the yard like a lunatic and stopping to sniff at familiar trees and bushes.

Simon took a deep breath and stepped onto his property.

"You okay?"

Simon nodded.

… no one's going to be here …

They walked down the driveway. Green plants had sprung up between the brick pavers.

"Just a quick question," Jeremy asked. "What is your plan after this?"

"Excuse me?"

"I mean, what's your plan? If your family is not here, what are you going to do?"

"I … I haven't thought that far ahead."

"It's not that far ahead. It's right in front of you."

"I don't know."

"Okay, no problem. Let's just do one thing at a time. We'll help you figure things out later, when we meet up with the general."

Simon remained quiet.

The driveway turned, and all at once, the majesty of his old estate came into view.

He saw it all: the circular driveway around the fountain, the garage far to the left, and the house itself—the massive and beautiful European-style home with stone veneer and dark wood accents and trim. For a moment—just one fleeting moment—Simon thought he would see his parents standing in the driveway where he had last seen them, dressed in robes and pajamas, holding each other tight.

But they were not there. The driveway was barren, and the ground where Simon had last seen them standing was green with grasses sticking up between the brick pavement.

It was dark. Even in the daylight, the house looked dark, and the windows were like hollow eye sockets.

They approached the front. Winston ran across the driveway, his tongue bouncing out of his mouth.

"I'll be out here keeping an eye on Winston." Jeremy walked to the fountain—now green with algae that covered the three stone goddesses up their torsos—and sat on the rim, his stiff leg outstretched. He pulled another cigarette from the pack with his teeth, then contemplated, put the cigarette back in the pack, and produced a cigar from his breast pocket.

"Gonna be here a while," he said. "Take your time."

Simon walked forward toward the entrance.

Each step of the porch felt like an eternity until he reached the front door.

He closed his eyes and reached for the handle.

Chapter 32

Blue Skies

The sentence escaped in a jolt, "Where are the girls?"

The thoughts that followed were: *Where am I? What happened? Where's Carolanne?*

A man's voice spoke to him, "You're awake. That's good."

"The girls—"

"They're in the other room. They're safe. You're safe. Please relax. My name is Doctor Liam Morris. Do you remember what happened?"

Brian remembered. At least he thought he remembered. Images rushed through his mind, although the course of events was choppy. There was the boy. The rotten-toothed boy with dirty red hair. Brian saw the kid's stare—his eyes at first shocked by the reality he was facing, then fading as death became inevitable.

Brian remembered the injured man on the ground pointing a handgun in his direction. The grenade rolling under his feet. He picked up the grenade and threw it. There was a burst of bright light combined with the sounds of gunfire. A flash of the boy's body being tossed in the air like it weighed nothing. That was it. His memory ended there.

"I remember," Brian said. "I think I remember."

"You were knocked unconscious and injured in an explosion." He felt the doctor's fingers on his temple. "But you'll survive."

"I can't see anything." His fingers went up to touch a cloth covering his eyes and forehead.

"Your vision is fine. I'm removing the bandages now. You sustained a laceration on your left temple, and down the right side of your cheek. You're lucky you didn't lose the eye."

Brian tried to do a body scan, feel his toes and feet, legs and hands. He could wiggle all his appendages, but there was stiffness in his body and pain throughout. "Where am I hurt?"

"Most of your injuries are the result of wood fragments, primarily to your torso—"

"Be frank with me, Doctor; how bad is it?"

"I was being frank. The bulletproof vest you were wearing absorbed most of the impact, but your chest is deeply bruised. You have a fractured rib and several lacerations on your right shoulder. All of these injuries will heal in time. The bruising on your chest and your injured rib will hurt the most, but they're the least of your injuries. What we are concerned about is a piece of shrapnel still lodged beside the bone in your right kneecap and lower thigh. Without a proper x-ray, it's difficult to determine just how close the shrapnel is to the popliteal and femoral arteries."

"So ..." Brian tried to place the pain he felt in his body to the corresponding wounds. "What do I do now?"

"You rest. Tomorrow—"

A voice interrupted the doctor. "Brian?"

It was Bethany. "Carolanne, get over here!"

"Brian, you're awake!" The voices of the women rushed into the room.

"Are you girls okay? Are you hurt?"

"We're fine, Brian," Bethany said. "Are *you* okay?"

"I ... don't know."

"Hold on just a second, ladies." The doctor was cutting away the bandages. A blinding brightness grew greater in intensity as each layer of cloth was removed. "There," the doctor said. "You can open your eyes. It will take some time to adjust."

Brian's eyes were like slits. All he could see was an impossible whiteness. He blinked, tried to focus. Shapes began to take form. He saw the girls on the left of his bed, holding his hand. Tubes were running from bags down to his arm, and the doctor on the other side of him did not look like a doctor at all. He was wearing army fatigues, with close-cropped hair and a day-old shave.

Brian looked at the girls. Tears rolled down both of their cheeks, but they were smiling.

"We did it Brian. *You* did it," Bethany said.

"Did what?"

The doctor picked up a canvas medical bag from the ground. "I'll be back in an hour to change your bandages. Don't try to walk. Don't exert yourself. Rest. We want that shrapnel staying right where it is until we get an x-ray at the hospital."

"Hospital?"

"I'll let the ladies explain. I'm sure there's a lot for you to catch up on." With that, the doctor left.

"Where are we?"

"We're in a house," Carolanne said. That much Brian knew. The walls were made of pine, which Brian could smell before he had his eyesight back, and there was a large stone fireplace across from the bed with a brilliant fire burning. Carolanne continued, "Let's start from the beginning."

"Okay ..."

"It happened so fast. You were fighting with that guy—the guy holding Beth. A grenade fell."

"I remember. But that man on the ground; he had a pistol aimed at me. He was still alive. The last thing I saw was him about to pull the trigger, and I thought I heard gunfire."

"That," Bethany cut in, moving to the opposite side of the bed, "was Carolanne. She shot the man before he could pull the trigger. At the same time, the grenade went off and the side of the tree exploded. You flew backward. We rushed to your side, but you were unconscious and bleeding all over. We didn't know what to do. It was ... awful."

Brian squeezed Beth's hand.

She continued, "As it turned out, that grenade that almost killed you— would have killed you, if not for Dr. Morris—also saved our lives."

"How is that?"

"Let me explain. We heard noises and voices close by and remembered what those disgusting men said about there being more of them. Carolanne and I tried to drag you away, hide in the bushes. But you were bleeding so much .... When we moved you, you started convulsing.

"We heard gunfire. A lot of it. It seemed to last forever. Then, after a brief pause, a group of men came into the clearing. They looked different from those awful men who tried to capture me. These men looked like soldiers—real soldiers. They were pointing guns at us and yelling and screaming. They made Carolanne and I put our hands on our heads while they searched the area. All the while, you were bleeding to death right in front of us, and they wouldn't let us move to help you.

"When they determined that we didn't belong to that gang of hideous men, they began to leave—leave us and let you die—when Carolanne started shouting for them to help. How could they just leave us while you were dying right before their eyes? They said there was nothing to be done. They couldn't spare resources on the already dead. They all left, except for one. A young soldier named Silas who was missing half his right hand. He gave us some bandages, and despite being reprimanded by the other men, he helped us stop the bleeding on your leg. The other soldiers had left the way they'd came when Silas said he had to go, that he had to leave us. He already broke protocol by giving us first aid and supplies. Carolanne was a mess—"

"We," Carolanne interrupted, "were both messes."

Brian's heart sank, knowing that Carolanne would now have to live out her life having shot and killed someone. There was no coming back from that. He looked at her face, a thin smile on her lips and concern in her eyes.

Bethany continued, "She pleaded with Silas, who was walking away. She started shouting things—things we'd been through in the bunker, and things we were supposed to do. Then she shouted a name: *Uncle Albert Driscoll.* Silas stopped and turned. 'How do you know General Driscoll?' he asked. I told him that General Driscoll is my uncle. He looked shocked, and asked our full names; then he called something over his radio. Seconds later, all of the soldiers came running back into the clearing, and started bandaging your wounds and got you on a stretcher."

"Uncle Al is here?"

"Not exactly. But he's close."

"We ... did we make it? Where are we?"

"We're in the house of Miss Ingrid Snow. She lives in the woods near Uncle Al's territory. The soldiers explained it to me, but I don't really understand. Uncle Al—or General Driscoll, as the soldiers call him—lives in some Zone or something."

"Zone Red," Carolanne said.

"Right, Zone Red. It's not far, they say. There are other Zones too, with more survivors. This house—Ingrid Snow's house—is a forwarding post. We're not technically in Zone Red."

Brian nodded.

"Now," Bethany continued, "getting back to how the grenade that almost killed you also saved your life—all of our lives. The soldiers were on patrol when they heard the explosion. They came to inspect the noise and came upon a group of men, who were on their way to the clearing. Uncle Al's men intercepted them before they reached us."

"I don't believe it. I can't believe the luck."

"You did it, Brian," Carolanne said.

"I ... don't think I did. Carolanne, you had to shoot someone."

She shook her head, looking down. "We're safe. That's all that matters."

***

Whatever drugs they gave Brian must have been weak, because his body was in constant pain. They put him on a stretcher, strapped him down, and moved him to the kitchen to wait for transportation.

Ingrid Snow was at the counter. At first Brian thought he was hallucinating when he smelled pastries cooking. Then, sure enough, the pleasant old lady removed a baking sheet of cookies from the oven.

Fucking chocolate chip cookies.

It didn't seem possible that such things still existed in the world.

"We keep trying to get Ingrid to come to Zone Red, but she refuses," a soldier told Brian.

"Seems pretty safe here."

"It's safer in Zone Red. Besides, the other soldiers don't know what they're missing." He motioned toward her platter of cookies.

Brian looked at the man, younger than him, with a close shave and short hair. He was sitting on a chair beside Brian's stretcher, his helmet resting on a knee. His right hand was mangled with old scars, fingers missing.

"You Silas?"

"Yes, sir. Sergeant Silas Powers."

"Reckon I owe you a debt of gratitude."

225

"No need."

Ingrid Snow was walking on small, shuffling feet toward Brian. She held out a cookie on a napkin.

"Eat, eat," she said in a thick accent.

Silas was about to intercept, since Brian was not allowed to eat anything before transportation arrived, but he nodded his consent.

"Thank you," Brian said. *You have no idea ...*

"She doesn't speak much English," Silas said. "She's Polish."

Ingrid hovered over Brian until he took a bite. The melted chocolate was warm and covered his tongue. Brian thought he might cry. "Oh, my ..."

Silas laughed and stood to take a cookie off the plate on the counter. "She uses milk and butter from her cows. They're better than my own mother used to make."

Ingrid smiled, satisfied with Brian's reaction, and went back to the sink to clean the baking dish.

Brian turned his head toward Silas. "What's it like in Zone Red?"

"You'll find out soon enough. It's heaven compared to the rest of the world. We have a hospital, an apartment building for a barracks, and some homes connected to power."

"Sounds amazing."

"And hot water ... most of the time."

"How far?"

"By foot, two days. But we'll get there in no time at all by truck."

A few minutes later, Brian heard an engine rattling, growing louder as it approached. Bethany came in from the front door.

"They're here," she said.

Silas stood. "Okay, let's get you ready."

Silas and another soldier wheeled Brian out the door and secured his stretcher on the flatbed of an idling pickup truck. Bethany and Carolanne sat on either side of him, along with Dr. Morris and another soldier. Silas closed the rear door and smacked it with his palm. "Have a safe trip."

"Silas." Brian tried to look up, but a shooting pain from his injured rib made him rest back down. "Thank you for everything."

Silas nodded and walked off.

There was another pickup truck in the lead loaded with soldiers. The first truck started moving down the dirt driveway, and then their own truck inched forward. The vibration coming through the truck bed rattled the pain into a frenzy throughout his body.

Brian could see the outside of Ingrid Snow's house—her cabin set in the woods. A dozen or so soldiers walked about her property, looking over maps, having discussions. The old lady was shuffling to a chicken coop on the side of her yard. Smoke from her chimney rose and dissipated in the clear sky, and soon, his view of the cabin disappeared.

Dr. Morris leaned forward with a needle. "This will help you sleep through the ride. It's a bit bumpy." He injected Brian, and then put the needle away.

Carolanne was brushing her windblown hair out of her face, smiling as bright as the sun shining through the branches overhead, flicking its warmth on Brian's face.

"I ate a chocolate chip cookie," he said, and heard her laughter as the drugs started kicking in.

Carolanne's hand touched his own, the fingers coiling around his palm.

"I just remembered something," Brian said, his eyes shutting.

"What's that?"

"Something that came to my mind when I first woke up. It was *you* … you were one of my first thoughts; that I might never see you again."

Carolanne smiled and blushed in front of the other passengers in the back of the pickup truck. Sleep was coming fast, but he felt Carolanne squeeze his hand tight, and fingers combed back his hair. Overhead, the sky was a brilliant blue and the sun felt warm on his skin.

Chapter 33

Eyes of the Damned

As the seasons changed, the dying land reborn, Steven himself emerged as something reinvigorated. His body had mended and the tormented thoughts that once had plagued him were vanquished. With the passing of time, and help from Captain Black, he had grown to understand that in order to master his fears he must accept his mind for what it was.

That night when he and Brian had seen the town from high above seemed like a distant memory—an event that never happened.

Brian was dead. And that uncle of his was probably dead as well. If not, what did it matter? Uncle Al had left him to fend for himself in a decaying and diseased world that wanted to kill him at every step.

Where had Uncle Al been his entire life? This uncle—his own family— had not only deserted him in the end, but had deserted him ever since he was a child. No one ever loved him. Maybe his sister did, but she had moved away a long time ago, and what did it matter now? She was dead along with the rest. Steven was alone. He had been alone for a long time. His only friend, his cousin, the man he once called *brother,* had left him for dead on the cold ground ...

Steven shook the thoughts away.

It was rare these days that he gave Brian, Uncle Al, or his sister any thought at all. At first, they were all that he could think about, but over time he attained peace by accepting that they were out of his life for good. Finally, he could make his own choices. Be his own man, without the interference of his know-it-all cousin.

He was strong now, stronger than he had been when down in the bunker—or even before. Captain Black had explained that taking hold of that rage inside of him was not such a bad thing after all. His *seeing red* was a thing to be proud of, not ashamed about. It meant he could tap into his true inner strength, unleash the storming fury that most men had a difficult time mustering.

He owed these men a lot—his soon-to-be brothers. Not only had they saved his life, but they had nursed him into an even better man than he had once been. A man no longer ashamed of who he was. A man no longer afraid of demons in the night.

As Steven walked down the main street with the corpses on either side, he was reminded of what Captain Black had told him.

"Lad," he had said, "this is the way the world works. Don't you think any different about it. These bodies here are just things and nothing else. They are what remain of those who stood in our way, who wanted to take from us our very lives. Don't think for a moment that any of these rotting, putrid corpses would not have crucified you if given the chance.

"We're living in a world where you either dangle the noose or put your own neck against the rope. That choice is up to you. If you want to die, get yourself killed, go right ahead. I won't stop you. There's plenty dead—more dead than alive. What's one more to their numbers? Now, if you want to live—and live well, not like some starving cretin—you heed my words and advice: lend us that strength inside you, and become a member of our community. You, Steven, belong here as one of General Karl Metzger's fearless soldiers."

Those words rang true in Steven's ears. Karl Metzger knew things that Steven did not. He could teach Steven things that he yearned to know. The men in Odyssey could teach him how to survive, how to become fearless.

It was time to join their brotherhood, their family.

And that's where Steven was heading—to the sandy lot before Odyssey's police station where he could now see Captain Black waiting for him along with a number of men. Karl was among their numbers, and so were his lieutenants, all standing in a half-moon formation.

Steven flicked his cigarette to the ground and walked before them. A light wind swept up the dusty sand.

"So," Captain Black said, walking toward Steven while brushing the grit from his battered hat. "You stand before us, ready to join in our ranks?"

Steven nodded.

"Stout lad as you may be, it's a formality to display your devotion to our organization. Are you prepared to do so?"

Steven again nodded.

Captain Black turned, his hands clasped behind his back, and motioned to his men. A moment later, the half-moon wall of soldiers parted, and two armed guards dragged forth a ragged and battered prisoner—a putrid and loathsome worm. He was shoved wild-eyed to the center of the dirt lot and thrown to his hands and knees before Steven's feet. Steven could smell the awfulness wafting from this man in waves, and a spike of anger went off within him.

The captain stared at Steven. "This man has been found guilty of crimes against our society and of society-at-large. He fought against us in battle and he has lost. His being alive is in direct violation of the laws of humanity."

One of the guards produced two rusty and battered machetes and tossed them to the ground between Steven and the ragged man. The man jumped at the blade and held it waveringly toward Steven, his body jerking and his hands trembling. Steven didn't move, only stared at the man.

"Steven," the captain said, walking back to the gathering along with the two guards. "Add another body to the line on the road. Be the great man you deserve to be, who you always were. Embrace yourself."

The ragged man's eyes were watering, looking up at the towering Steven Driscoll, whose biceps were wider than the man's legs. The man collapsed on his knees, his hands clasped before him.

"Oh, Jesus Christ," he said, and Steven stepped toward him.

The End of Part I
Journeys Conclude and Others Begin

Far to the east of Odyssey, where Steven contemplated the course of actions that would further seal his fate, lay the town and people of Alice. A wheel had been set in motion that could not be stopped or hindered, for the lives of many would soon be decided by the choices of a few. Simon Kalispell and Brian Rhodes were not yet aware, but the strength that resided inside them would soon be tested, and destiny will call for their lives to be forever intertwined.

Part II

Fire Horizons

Chapter 34

Tom and Nick

Nick tapped his papers together on the table and stood, securing them to a clipboard. Martin Howard had just finished outlining his presentation to bring solar power to all of Zone Blue by mid-year the following year, but Nick wasn't buying it. Martin's team had not yet brought solar power to the apartment building, and that job should have been finished three months ago. How did he expect to convert the entire town?

Martin and his promises.

Martin and his diplomas, his schooling, all amounting to nothing.

A college degree was as good as tinder for the fire.

As second-in-command after his father, Nick Byrnes had vetoed Project Yellow, denying Martin Howard and his team permission to begin construction. While Nick *did* want the town of Alice to lose its reliance on Zone Red's supply of oil and gasoline, he felt Project Yellow required too many able-bodied men—the same men who should be building and fortifying the town's defenses.

Attacks on the town were still common. Although the small bands of marauders never broke through the perimeter, danger was still out there, still real—a certainty. The vast majority of attackers had no idea they were charging into a well-defended town, but Nick knew the day would come when a group of intelligent adversaries would pose a real threat to the town's safety, and when that day came, Nick wanted Alice to be ready. He didn't want to ever have to say, "I told you so."

Every available body and all of the town's resources should be used to construct taller guard towers, additional bunkers, and strengthened walls in the labyrinth of trenches that barricaded the town from the wild beyond. Project Yellow could wait. Solar power could wait. Zone Red kept them well-supplied with gasoline, and the buildings that needed power were not in danger of running out of fuel. Not by a long shot.

Nick had said this all before. And it had fallen on deaf ears.

The men comprising the Round Table—the men elected to lead Zone Blue and all of Alice—were proving themselves to be old, incompetent, and useless. Giving them an equal vote in serious matters—with only Nick's father able to veto—was a terrible idea. They trusted the aged defenses of the town, which had not been upgraded since the Zone was first established. One day they were all going to be sorry they had not heeded the warnings of Nicholas Byrnes.

"All right, gentlemen," Nick said, addressing the six men around the table. "Is there anything else?"

The men all shook their heads, and Martin began removing his diagrams and blueprints from the easel.

A guard opened the door for Nick to pass, and when Nick looked over his shoulder, he saw the familiar barrel chest and white hair of his father, Tom Byrnes—*the general*—at his heels. Nick looked at his watch.

"Lights out in half an hour."

His father nodded.

"Don't you think we're pushing these meetings a little late?"

"Don't put off until tomorrow what you can accomplish today, son. These meetings are important. We'll do them by candlelight if need be. Hopefully soon, we'll have enough solar panels to not worry about such things."

Nick rolled his eyes. *Or maybe Zone Red can give us enough fucking gasoline to get through the nights.*

"Martin's presentation went well, wouldn't you say?"

Nick shrugged.

"I know this project has never been at the top of your agenda," Tom said. "But it's important that the people in Alice have electricity and hot water twenty-four hours a day."

"Yes," Nick agreed. "It *is* important. Imperative, even. But until we have the town's defenses running at their greatest potential, we shouldn't be wasting our resources on such extravagances. Defense first, comfort later."

"I agree with you, Nick. However, the people need reassurance. They need to know that we're constantly progressing. A hot shower at any time of night and electricity whenever it's needed will give the people hope, something to fight for. It's not enough for the town to be running at a tolerable level. We must always be advancing."

"We can have electricity twenty-four hours, if only—" Nick cut himself short. It was pointless raising the same argument over and over. "Besides," he continued, "the people of Alice should still be impressed with the progress we made at the reservoir. Running water—clean, filtered, running water—all throughout Alice. Water. Is that not the greatest achievement we could ask for?"

"Yes," Tom agreed. "But we fixed the reservoir over a year ago. The people need to see progress at every opportunity."

What people really need, Nick thought, *is security and safety. Even if they don't see the reinforced bunkers and trenches on a daily basis. Those are the improvements they should be thankful for.*

They were walking down the dim hallway in Alice Elementary School toward the double doors at the end. The school served as a hub for Zone Blue's administrative staff and as a learning facility for the few children who resided in Alice.

It was nice this time of night, Nick thought, when it was dark outside and the hallways in the school were deserted, with only a few emergency lights illuminating the corridor at intervals. Tom and Nick were quiet, listening to their footfalls resound on the linoleum tiles until they neared the exit. They pushed the door open, feeling the cool night air wash over them.

A guard outside nodded. "Sir," he said, addressing them both.

Nick nodded and Tom smiled, saying, "Good night, Richard."

"Good night, sir."

They walked to the edge of the schoolyard, where one out of every three streetlights remained lit. Tom squinted at his watch. "Want to grab dinner?" he asked. "They'll just be putting it away now. We have time before lights-out."

Nick shook his head. "Nah, you go ahead if you like. I'll eat at home."

Out of the shadows they both saw a figure, a soldier, jogging toward them.

They stopped where they were under the streetlight until the man was within earshot.

"Sir," he stopped and saluted.

"Yes," Tom said. "What is it?"

"We have reports of possible movement. Section Three."

Tom nodded. There were reports of movement often, and it usually amounted to nothing; but still, it had to be inspected.

"Inform Frank Morrow," Tom said. "Have him send some Rangers to check it out."

My dad and his beloved Rangers, Nick thought.

The Rangers were comprised of men who were adept at hunting and stalking and had distinguished themselves as being capable of moving about undetected in the woods. They were not as tough as Nick's brigade, his Dragoons, named after the cavalries of old, but Nick had to agree with his father's decision. Sending the Rangers to inspect the disturbance was the best call.

The soldier said, "Frank is still away on hunt, sir."

"That's right," Tom remembered. The Rangers, along with the town's farms, were responsible for supplying Alice with their fresh meat. "Get Kalispell then. Have him assemble a team. Now."

"Yes, sir." The soldier saluted, and took off in the shadows.

Simon Kalispell, Nick thought. *Dad's little prodigy.*

In the time since Simon had arrived in Alice, over a year ago, he had climbed the ranks. He was now second-in-command under Frank Morrow, a middle-aged Special Forces soldier who led the Rangers. Simon had no military background whatsoever, and it infuriated Nick to no end that he had been promoted to second-in-charge. But, he had to admit that Simon's abilities in the wilderness were unmatched, and Simon had the love and respect of his peers. Besides, the Rangers were not strictly a fighting force. They were best at reconnaissance and hunting.

"Well, Dad, good night."

Tom shook Nick's hand, and Nick walked out from under the streetlight.

"Good night, son."

After a two-block walk, Nick arrived home. His residence was half of a subdivided house bordering the large, rectangular brick apartment building that housed the soldiers and residents. Some of the officers and delegates were allotted homes bordering the barracks, but not many.

He opened the door and walked in the kitchen tired, hungry, and weary. A familiar voice called out from the bedroom, hoarse with sleep.

"Nick? Is that you?"

Nick closed his eyes, his temples throbbing. *Who else would it be?*

"It's me," he answered. "I'm home. Go back to sleep."

He heard the mattress creak from the bedroom, and Stephanie came to the doorway, tying her silk robe around her waist.

"How was your day?" she asked, yawning. Her dark hair was tousled with sleep.

"Fine," Nick answered, swinging his AK-47 off his shoulder and leaning it against the table. He undid the clasp of his leather holster belt and placed it on the table. Nick carried a brown Smith & Wesson .357 revolver, the black metal clean and polished, and the sleek brown handle gleaming out from the holster. The belt was an old-fashioned brown police belt, which held the pistol low on his hip. The town had a large arsenal of automatic pistols, but Nick felt his sidearm made him distinguished. And it did. His pistol and belt were iconic among the residents, along with his pressed military fatigues, always tucked in and fitted around his tall, strong frame.

Stephanie stood behind Nick as he sat in a chair, untying the laces of his boots. She smoothed back his dark hair.

"Tough day?"

"Something like that."

"Was it your father again? I'm sorry, baby, you deserve so much more. You deserve—"

"Stephanie, honey." Nick closed his eyes against the drumming in his temples. "Now isn't a good time."

Stephanie backed away. She knew better than to anger Nick when he was in one of his moods. She was lucky to have him—the prize catch in all of Alice.

"Okay, baby. Okay." She walked back toward the bedroom. "I left a can of soup on the counter, if you're hungry."

Nick stared absently at the counter, exhausted. After a moment, she disappeared into the dark bedroom. "Good night," she said.

"Good night, Steph." He was happy for the silence.

He kicked off his boots and sat in the chair for many minutes. He was both hungry and tired, and craved the soup but did not want to get up from the chair to get it. For a moment, he debated calling Stephanie back to the kitchen to heat it up for him, but then thought better of it. *I'd rather it stay quiet.*

Taking a deep breath, he closed his eyes, and exhaled.

All right, Nick, he thought. *Time to eat.*

He had just begun to stand when all at once the lights overhead turned off, and the room went dark.

Fucking lights-out.

He reached for the flashlight on the table, feeling the cold metal in his palm. He paused, then sat back down and let out a long breath. Nick sat in the chair for a long time, a shadowy figure absorbing the pitch-black.

Chapter 35
Dead Leaves

Simon crouched low in the bushes, keeping his distance from the sleeping travelers that had come close to Zone Blue's perimeter the previous evening. It was the glow from their campfire in the woods that had been spotted by a soldier high up in a guard tower. Simon had left in the dead of night to investigate, along with one other Ranger named Justin Waters.

The campfire was small and far enough away from the town's border to suggest there was no immediate threat. And the fact that they had lit a fire at all led Simon to believe that the travelers had no idea how close they were to any other human beings.

Simon and Justin had spent the long hours leading to morning concealed only several yards away from the strangers.

Nearby, Simon could hear the moving water of a small creek, which ran east into the reservoir behind the defended border. The reservoir then ran north, streaming into the Ridgeline River, creating a natural border for Alice and the portion of Alice Springs Park that comprised Zone Blue. The river made their job of defending the town that much easier, with the zigzagging trench line only needing to form a semicircle below their property, connecting to the river at either side. No one had ever attacked Alice by water, and it was doubtful that any large force of men would try—with the banks being as steep as they were—so the northern border was left lightly defended with machine gun nests and guard towers in intervals. In an instant, one of the two mortar brigades near the center of town could be radioed in to target any point along the line and a short distance beyond.

Mortar Battalion Alpha was issued the coordinates of the sleeping travelers as soon as the campfire was spotted, and if a problem were to present itself, Simon could call in an artillery barrage that would decimate, or at least scare the hell out of any hostiles.

The sun was now rising, and the campfire had been a smoldering pile of ash for some time. The group had been quiet all night long, and despite that there were over a dozen of them, no one had woken up to rekindle the flame.

With the coming of morning, a few began to stir, and one man stood, yawning into the damp air. He was tall and skinny and had a great, long beard with shoulder-length hair.

Simon looked back to Justin Waters, who was crouching beside a fallen tree with his assault rifle resting across his lap. He raised his hand, signaling to Justin that there was movement.

The man in the group stood for what might have been five minutes, staring into the woods with a blank expression.

He's praying, Simon thought.

After a moment, the man bowed his head and then shuffled toward the campfire. He added a handful of leaves and twigs to the smoking ground and gently blew life back into the old fire.

A few more travelers awoke and quietly, one after the other, sat up and rose, joining the bearded man around the fire. A few stood like the man before, staring off in prayer, arms raised in a stretch before falling to their sides. Others sat up in their bedrolls, their backs straight and their arms resting on their knees.

Wait a minute …

Simon sensed Justin's tension from behind. The young Ranger had readied himself, shouldering his rifle.

A minute passed, and Simon half-turned to Justin. He waved his hand back and forth, open palmed. *No threat.*

Simon stepped forward and continued until the travelers turned to see him approach. He entered their campsite and stopped, surveying the group.

"*Namaste,*" he said.

They nodded and replied, "*Namaste.*"

The group shuffled under their robes, not sure who this soldier with the darkened, mud-streaked face could be. It was the boy who recognized Simon first.

"Simon—it's Simon!" He tugged at the hemmed robe of an adult beside him. "Where's Winston, Simon? Where's your dog?"

The boy ran forward and hugged Simon around his leg. Simon patted the young boy on his bristly, shaven head. "He's sleeping, probably. Back at home."

An old man stepped forward from the group, smiling. "Teacher Simon," he bowed. "*Namaste.*"

"I can't believe we're meeting again," Simon said to the group. "What are the odds?" He reached into his pocket and felt the thick black beads of the necklace they had given to him all those months ago. The necklace—or mala, they were called—had a calming effect when he passed the beads between his fingers.

The old man laughed. "As is the *dharma* in all things. You cannot expect the same occurrences to happen twice, as it is the nature of the world to constantly change. But when they do occur twice, it is a joy to behold."

The group met Simon, each one hugging him or shaking his hand, and told him of his teachings that they had taken to heart: how to gather cattails and edible plants, as well as how to avoid the poisonous ones.

Simon shook off their praise. He looked back at Justin, who was bewildered at the people before him, unarmed, dressed in robes, and appearing clean. Simon gave him a quick rundown of his meeting with them and explained that it was they who had given Simon the beaded necklace that Justin had seen Simon roll around in his fingers countless times.

Justin nodded. He was a bright boy. All of the Rangers were bright, Simon thought. Even though many of them were soldiers, they all displayed a connection with the Earth that was deeper than most others. This is what made the Rangers a calmer and more levelheaded force than the others in Alice, though still dangerous.

Justin took his handheld radio from his belt and clicked it on.

"We're all clear," he said. "Group is non-hostile."

"*Roger,*" crackled a reply.

As the group gathered around Simon, talking and telling stories from their travels, several went off to collect branches of fresh goldenrod from the woods to brew a pot of tea. Simon pointed out an area where he knew wild mint was growing, and a few went off to find the plant. They returned shortly with a handful of leaves and crushed them into the water to seep. Once done, they ladled cups of steaming tea for everyone, including Simon and Justin.

Many in the group had formed a circle around him, and Simon guessed that they were hoping he would have more to share with them. Simon indicated the simple acorns that covered the ground, pointing to where many lay underfoot. A man from the group said, "They're too bitter. We've tried them."

Simon nodded. "They are bitter. However, boiling them in several changes of water takes away the bitterness. Once the water boils without a reddish tinge, the acorns should be good to eat."

Simon took a handful of acorns, cracked off the tops with his knife, and exposed the little nuts hiding within. He explained how to roast them and grind them up to be used as flour. He went on to explain that the first boil of water should be saved, since it could be used as an astringent for an assortment of skin maladies.

"The bark of the tree can also be boiled and used to help throat infections, fevers, and stomach ailments," he told them. "It can be made into a powder to treat wounds or mouth sores."

The group was quiet as Simon spoke, watching as he pointed to a large oak tree only a few feet from where they sat.

When they had finished their tea, the group began to rise, one by one going off to secure their bedrolls and meager belongings. They each stopped in turn to thank Simon and wish him luck and good fortune.

The old man stayed, sitting cross-legged on a section of blanket. When the gathering dispersed, he spoke to Simon in a low voice.

"I know you cannot tell us about where you are living, otherwise you would have already done so."

Simon took a deep breath, glancing at Justin. It was forbidden to say anything about Alice or the Zones to an outsider.

The old man continued, "And I would not want for you to tell me. But, I am interested to know, did you find what you were looking for? Did you find your family?"

Simon looked at the ground. "It's … a long story."

"I have all the time in the world." The old man reached out, patting Simon's knee. "Unless, of course, it is a story that you do not wish to tell."

"No," Simon said. "No, it's nothing like that. I just don't know where to begin."

"Start wherever you feel comfortable."

Simon thought back to the day he arrived in Alice, defeated at first, then hopeful when his friend Jeremy Winters showed up. Simon had never talked to anyone other than Jeremy and Tom Byrnes about that day, but when he looked at the old man's face, he saw genuine concern. His eyes flickered to Justin, who sat listening intently.

"Okay," Simon sighed. "Let me begin …"

***

"Take your time," Jeremy said, sitting on the edge of the fountain with the algae growing out over the stone goddess statues.

Simon walked toward the porch. Winston was off, running back and forth in his old yard, smelling familiar smells.

Each step felt like an eternity until Simon reached the front door.

He closed his eyes and reached for the handle.

It turned, unlocked. Simon opened the door, walked inside, and closed it behind him. His eyes were shut tight, his back pressed hard against the front door. A layer of sweat had formed on his skin and felt sticky against his clothing.

Breathe, Simon … breathe …

As he opened his eyes, all in a flash, he knew instantly what he had known all along.

Nobody is here.

The foyer was dark and deserted. All the paintings and furniture that had once made this entrance lively were gone, and the air smelled warm and stale.

From where Simon stood, he knew in his heart that the entire house was empty. He had known it outside, walking up the driveway. And he had known it back in the cabin when he'd flung the door open in disillusioned rage to beat upon the night with his frustration and anger, only to be stopped short by the broad side of a huffing moose.

But perhaps the house had not been empty for long. Maybe his parents had returned at some stage—months ago—and left a note behind or a clue about their whereabouts. If not … if they were still down south, then maybe he could find the address.

Simon pushed himself away from the front door, walking first through a sitting room with couches and coffee tables all covered in drop cloths, and next through the majestic dining room. The solid mahogany table was still there, draped in a canvas sheet.

Next, Simon entered the kitchen—the real family room of the house. It was this room where everyone gathered, sitting side by side at the small table by the window. They ate their meals there and talked about their days, marveling at the view of the expansive backyard and the Ridgeline River off in the distance.

The window in the back was now shattered; the remains of a branch that had long ago broken off from the locust tree outside protruded into the room, looming out over the table and chairs.

There wasn't a note on any of the counters. Simon checked the refrigerator door for any clue hanging by a magnet, then the cabinets and drawers, before sinking to his hands and knees and scouring the baseboards for anything blown about. There was nothing. The kitchen was barren. For a moment, he almost opened the refrigerator out of instinct, then thought better of it. The smell would be acrid even if there were only crumbs in there.

Simon went from room to room, but there was nothing left behind. In his parents' bedroom he stopped, sitting on their king-sized bed. One of his mother's silk scarves had been left on top of the dresser. He held it in his hands. It still smelled of her lilac perfume and those little Chinese bars of soap that she used so often. He held the cloth against his face, breathing her fragrance in. His eyes welled up.

Get it together, man. Get it together.

He left his parents' room, searching the entire second floor before turning to his own bedroom. Inside, all his childhood possessions came rushing back to him: his trophies, books, and twin-sized bed. The room was just as he had left it, only it smelled musty, a time capsule cut off from the outside world.

A feeling that Simon did not expect washed over him. He felt uncomfortable. He didn't want to be standing there looking at his possessions, his old way of life. There was a picture of himself on the dresser, posing with his baseball team when he was maybe ten years old. It did not seem possible for such trivial things to have ever existed. Baseball. Trophies. Photographs. A gathering of smiling children.

He left and went downstairs to his father's office. It was stripped clean, with the built-in shelves void of electronics and family pictures. All that remained was his father's mahogany desk and chair. Simon opened all the drawers, one at a time, but found nothing but loose rubber bands and paper clips.

For several minutes, Simon sat in his father's chair, leaning backward. The room was dark. The whole house was dark.

It was not his home any longer.

With a deep exhale he stood. He knew what he had to do; he had to check the underground vault.

The only sunlight streaming into the hallway came from the glass portion of the door to the greenhouse, otherwise it would have been pitch-black. As Simon opened the door and began moving the gardening bench and tools from the small cinderblock shed, he was aware that Jeremy Winters was probably almost done smoking his cigar. He would have to be quick. He didn't want Jeremy coming in to check on him while he was down there.

Sweat had darkened the front of his shirt as Simon removed the last of the pavers hiding the trap door. He unlocked the locks and swung the metal door back on its hinges.

A draft of earthy air traveled up the stairway and cooled Simon's face. He descended the steps and stood at the bottom, blinking into the dark cavity of the room.

Several long metal flashlights were on a shelf to his side, and Simon grabbed one, clicking it on. The flashlight worked like new.

He opened each of the three safes in turn, looking over the stacks of money and the artwork tied in canvas cloths. It was worthless—all of it. Just paper. In the last safe were the important possessions: the pictures and albums. Simon glanced over them, then went back to the shelf at the bottom of the staircase and grabbed an empty duffel bag. He filled the bag with the family albums, finding along the way the framed photograph that used to sit in his dad's office. It was the picture of his father, himself, Tom Byrnes, and his son—Nick—back when Simon was a young boy. They had all gone fishing together and were smiling at the camera, holding up their catches. Simon put the picture in the bag and closed and locked all of the safes. There was nothing else he needed down there, not now. The emergency food rations and spare hunting rifles and ammunition could stay where they were.

things that you have seen—a light will always be shining bright deep down in the darkest recesses, for I will always have you in my thoughts and prayers."

Simon felt his throat constrict. "And I you," he told the old man.

The man nodded and said, "There is no way to change the past. One can mourn it, and in mourning will come great tribulations. It is your mind that conjures up painful and negative emotions; outside circumstances are only *things*, illusions. It is possible to remain positive in the worst circumstances, no matter how terrible the outside circumstance may seem, once you peel back the veil of negativity that falsely covers your mind. You are in charge of your own thoughts and emotions; they are not guided by circumstance or the outside world. A universe is within you, and you may do with it as you please."

As Simon thought this over, the old man reached forward, clapped a hand over his knee, and stood on agile feet.

"We thank you, Teacher Simon, for your lesson. If our paths ever do cross again it will be for the benefit of us all." The old man spoke these words, bowed his head, and turned toward the congregation with a thoughtful smile.

Chapter 36
Alice Bound

General Albert Driscoll, *The General,* was responsible for establishing the three Zones. The now white-haired man resided in Zone Red, several miles north of Alice, controlling the ports in a town named Hightown.

Zone Red controlled the import of fuel.

Zone Blue controlled the water.

Zone Green had not yet been fully established, but the plans were for it to restore the factories and large farms far south of Zone Blue. Zone Green's primary objective was ensuring long-term canning, food processing, and the eventual assembly line approach to food, weapons, parts, medicine, and personal goods. Presently, only a small faction of well-qualified engineers and soldiers resided in Zone Green, setting its boundaries and deciding which factories need the minimal amount of work to get running.

Brian, Carolanne, and Bethany were provided residence in Zone Red the day they arrived, and after being given time to heal, they were issued work details.

Brian was now in the trade grounds, crossing over the broad paved lot used to unload the goods coming in from Alice. Once a week, sometimes twice, a convoy of trucks left Hightown to drop off their share of gasoline, oil, and other necessities to exchange with Zone Blue. They filled their own tankers with Alice's clean water and packed the backs of the flatbeds with boxes of produce from Alice's ample gardens. Plans were in the works to construct pipelines between the two Zones, delivering fuel and water back and forth, and eliminating the need for armed convoys. But that day had not yet arrived, and Zone Red still relied on Alice for the majority of its fresh water and food. Although Hightown had its own small farms, the inhabitants did not maintain a quarter as many of the plants or livestock as Alice.

It was Zone Red's responsibility to send the convoys, since their surplus of fuel was plentiful, and Zone Red's soldiers were better equipped and trained. Hightown's supply of armored cars and vehicles dwarfed Alice's fleet, and Zone Red's men were real fighting men, and not the fifty-year-old teachers-turned-warriors that comprised much of Zone Blue's fighting force.

The convoy was now returning from Alice. It was Brian Rhodes's job to take inventory of the produce delivery, as well as lead the kitchen as *sous chef* under Chef Nick Remo at the communal mess hall.

Brian tucked a paper in his clipboard and stepped down from the back of a flatbed truck as soldiers began unloading the crates. He checked his watch as he limped toward the exit: three hours until he was expected back at the kitchen to prep for dinner. Plenty of time.

At the gated entrance to the trade grounds, Brian nodded to the guards and walked a short way toward the residential section of Hightown. Most of the soldiers were barracked beside the port or near the border, but the few residents who were not soldiers were permitted housing farther away from the front line.

The pavement underfoot was bumpy, and Brian was relying on his cane more than he liked. His leg had been stiff all that day, and the walk was taking longer than usual.

"Hey, Brian! Wait up." He turned to see Bethany running along the sidewalk to catch up to him.

"You done already?" he shouted to her.

"Yup," she said. "Your leg feeling all right? Haven't seen you use the cane in a while."

"A bit sore today, but I'm fine. It's getting better every day."

"Good. I'm glad."

Brain asked, "What did ol' Patrick say about the potatoes?"

"He said there's no signs of mold on the new harvest. It's under control. Two weeks until we're back to normal."

Brian nodded. "Good. That's good."

Patrick O'Hern was the chief of agriculture in Zone Blue and was as honest a man as Brian had ever met. If Pat said two weeks, he meant two weeks and not a day longer.

"How's he looking?" Brian asked.

"About the same. Maybe a little better."

"I reckon a man his years should be spending less time plowing the fields and more time making sure someone else is plowing them."

"He's not *that* old. I think he's in his early sixties. But I agree with you; he should be spending more time teaching his craft and less time working at it."

When Brian asked Pat why he still tended the fields, he would reply in his faded brogue, "Why wouldn't I?" Then he'd shuffle off on feet that appeared too heavy for his body to handle.

Brian had nothing to say to that. And Pat was right, because however frail he might look, no matter how droopy his weathered skin appeared on his bones, the man still knew how to use a plow. No one could make things grow better than Patrick O'Hern.

"How was the delivery?" Brian asked. "Any trouble?"

"Nah, it's quiet out there."

"Glad to hear it. You keeping inventory with the cargo team, going back and forth to Alice, still makes me nervous."

Bethany shrugged. "Is Carolanne home?" she asked.

"She should be." Usually during the gap between deliveries and dinner prep, Brian had some alone time with Carolanne back at their house.

A surge of heat fluttered in his chest when he thought about what he'd normally be doing with her about this time. It would have to wait until later that night, when Bethany was fast asleep in her bedroom down the hall.

He was thinking about this when Bethany asked, "What's for dinner tonight?"

"I, umm ..." He cleared his thoughts, his vision of Carolanne's dirty blond hair fanned out over the mattress as she lay with her back arched ever so slightly, elevating her breasts, her natural scent like the beach in the air. "Stew again," he said. "No potatoes, of course."

Bethany looked at the ground as she walked at Brian's slow pace. She was fiddling with her hands, and Brian was about to ask her what was wrong, but then she said, "Hey, listen ... I have a question for you."

"What's that?"

"I've been thinking …" She cleared her throat. "Well, I've been thinking … you know …"

Brian looked at her. "No, I don't know. What is it, Beth?"

"It's just …" She took a deep breath. "I'm thinking about moving to Zone Blue."

Brian watched her cheeks flush red.

She continued, "It's just that, I mean, you know how happy I am that we're living in safety—an actual safe town, with food and water, and—"

"You don't have to explain," Brian interrupted.

She looked surprised, but continued. "I think I would be happier over there."

"Have you mentioned this to Uncle Al?" Brian looked around, making sure no one was around to hear him say *Uncle*. Only a few people knew Bethany's true identity in Hightown, and no one in Alice knew it at all. It was Uncle Al's intention for it to stay that way: to have the eyes of a trusted family member oversee trade without being identified. Bethany being related to the general was strictly confidential.

She nodded. "I did. And Carolanne. And now you."

Brian was surprised. *How did Carolanne not tell me? The woman who shares my bed keeps secrets from me?*

He smiled and said, "Hey, if that's what you want to do, then by all means. Zone Blue is nice. It's much calmer; it's more like a real town. I understand." He stopped and thought for a moment, then continued. "Up here, it's all soldiering. The three of us don't fit in with this lifestyle, but at least Carolanne and I have each other to pass the time. You could socialize a bit more down in Alice. I hear they have a stage where they play music after dinner and all sit around and talk."

"It's true. Pat O'Hern told me the same thing. Listen, there's one other thing I have to mention to you. I asked Uncle Al—just to see what he'd say—I asked him if you and Carolanne could move down, too … only if you want to, of course. He was reluctant at first, since the soldiers aren't allowed to transfer unless it's by assignment, but he relented. We're not soldiers. He would let us all move to Alice."

Brian was struck silent. He had never thought about moving—it had never seemed to be an option. He was just glad to be living in safety. Brian had been to Alice a few times but had seen little of it.

"It will be nice to see some trees," Bethany continued. "Most of the town is in a park; Alice Springs."

Brian knew this, of course. That's where the clean water came from. He looked about as he walked; in every direction he saw smokestacks, machinery, paved lots, warehouses. Zone Red was almost entirely industrial, with the ports taking up the vast majority of the space.

"Reckon I'll have to ask Carolanne," Brian said. "Do you know much about Tom Byrnes?"

Bethany shrugged. "Only that everyone in Zone Blue loves him. It was him and his son who established the town, under order by Uncle Al. They led a small company of soldiers to clear out any threats, then established the borders and built up the perimeter. Tom is responsible for fixing the reservoir. That much I know—that much everybody knows. I've seen him during deliveries. He's about Uncle Al's age, but he's got a big barreled belly." Bethany smirked. "He's kind of handsome in an old man sort of way."

Brian raised his eyebrow at her. "I've heard good things about him. A few of the cooks spent time in Alice, settin' up their kitchen. Reckon he's a born leader. You sure Uncle Al doesn't mind us moving down there?"

"Tom Byrnes and Uncle Al are friends from before the war," she said. "Tom doesn't mind. They could use help in the kitchen, and Carolanne would be of use in the infirmary. Plus, they always need help in the garden. Everyone in Alice has to spend time in the fields, one day a week, minimum. Doesn't sound so bad, if you ask me."

Brian nodded. "Well, I'll talk to Carolanne. When are you planning on leaving?"

"Next week—next delivery. But you guys can come down whenever is good."

"I would have to train a new *sous chef*, but that wouldn't be hard." Brian was quiet for a moment, and then smiled. "I think Carolanne will like it in Alice."

Bethany reached out and squeezed his hand. "I think so, too."

Chapter 37

Tomatoes

The large fields in Alice Springs, several of which had once been soccer and football fields, had been tilled, turned over, raked, plowed, and planted. The acre-sized rectangular fields were now crowded with row upon row of vegetables. Lanes wide enough to drive cars down were cut straight through, sectioning the various gardens. At times—especially when the corn was in harvest—the fields looked able to produce an endless amount of food.

Not far away, just a short walk through the woods, was the reservoir itself.

Today was Simon's shift in the gardens, and he'd just spent the previous three hours hunched over, pulling weeds from spaces between the budding tomato plants.

Soon, he thought, *soon, they will all begin to flower.*

He couldn't wait.

The heirloom tomatoes were particularly fascinating with their wide range of colors and unique shapes. Almost like tiny pumpkins, Simon thought, or tomatoes left to the imagination of Matisse or van Gogh. Simon longed for the day when he could pick a ripe tomato straight off the vine, feel its warmth in the palm of his hands, hold his nose next to the skin on the fruit and smell the sun and earth and water baked into its flesh, all the while standing among a sea of glistening red tomatoes shimmering in the summer sun.

But it was too early in the season to be daydreaming of such things.

Off in the distance by the tool shed, someone rang a bell to indicate lunchtime.

Simon stood, stretched his back, and wiped the sweat from his forehead with the back of his gritty hand. He picked up his rifle, swung it over his shoulder, and wove in with the workers emerging from the rows of plants to walk down the center lane. Simon stood in line to return his plow to the tool shed, then made his way with everyone else toward the mess hall in the center of town.

Although every resident was given a share of the raw produce, the majority of the harvest went straight to the kitchen at the Alice Volunteer Fire Department, where three meals were served a day.

The firehouse stood in an expansive grass field, and a buffet line was set up in one of the vacant, long garages formerly used to house a fire truck. In the clearing before the tall firehouse doors were dozens of park benches arranged in straight lines, many underneath a tarp awning.

In the rear of the building and to the side, bordering the woods, a plank-board stage had been constructed, with the open field before it stretching to the street. Speeches were given there, town addresses, and weekly news reports issued from Tom Byrnes himself. Several of the town's residents often gave impromptu musical performances in the spring and summer evenings, when the sun provided enough light for everyone to gather around after food service.

Simon stood in line with a tray until he was given a scoop of stew—a mix of just about every conceivable vegetable and meat, including small birds and squirrels. Large wild game was scarce.

Before exiting the food line, Simon was given a thick slab of freshly baked bread, which smelled earthy like sage and was producing vapors of steam from its fleshy side.

He headed to the benches in the front, finding Jeremy eating with several other men. Shortly before Simon came to town, Jeremy Winters' previous two roommates had been killed while out on patrol searching for supplies in a neighboring town. Simon had been issued lodging in one of the spare rooms.

"Jeremy," he said, "how's it going?"

"All right, Simon. Enjoying your day of hard work?"

"Every day is hard work—not like you lazy Guards."

"Oh, is that right?" Jeremy raised an eyebrow. "You and your Ranger friends going for a leisurely stroll through the woods after dinner? Holding hands, maybe? Be sure to bring a guitar."

Another guard at the table, Mark Samuel, interrupted them. "Will you two get a room?"

Jeremy and Simon both turned across the table to Mark.

"Shut up, Mark," Jeremy said before laughing.

The banter between the various infantrymen was a common and sometimes annoying occurrence. The three main divisions of men in Zone Blue were the Guards—the men on the front line, day in and day out; the Rangers—to which Simon belonged; and then the Dragoons—Nick Byrnes's hand-selected special operations, much smaller in number than the Guards but larger in number than the Rangers.

The Guards joked that the Rangers were all hippies, and the Rangers liked to call the Guards lazy and stupid. It was as simple as that. Only the Dragoons rarely participated in the banter. They were of a different breed. Fighting men, but with something else to them, and not just the privileged elitism that went along with being Nick Byrnes' hand-selected few. They were hard men, and many of the tasks that they relished doing would be described by others as … unsavory.

It was not uncommon for the Dragoons to sit alone during meals, only socializing with one another. They wore a circular patch on their left shoulders to differentiate themselves—a simple uppercase *AD* in red stitches against a black background, standing for *Alice Dragoons*. They were fiercely loyal to Nick Byrnes. They were *his* men; they had fought by *his* side on countless occasions. It was Nick and his early brigade of Dragoons who had led the charge into Alice when the town was first settled, clearing out the infestation of hostile men who were hiding in houses and shelters like maggots in a ripe apple. The Dragoons answered to Nick Byrnes above anyone else—except, of course, for General Tom Byrnes. And the Dragoons' bravery could not be questioned. They had showed their effectiveness in warfare many times over by brutally slaughtering any and all who stood before them.

The Rangers and the Guards mixed freely and got along well. Despite the slight discord between the men, they all came together over one thing: their loyalty to Alice and their praise for General Tom Byrnes, whose quick rationale and fierce determination had made their lives here a reality. The men, women, and children in Alice owed the aging, barrel-chested man a debt of gratitude that could not be put into words.

"So," Jeremy said, steering the conversation away from their repartee, "any luck with the hunt?"

"Nothing new," Simon answered with a mouthful of bread. It was a common question. Everyone wanted to know about the hunt—about food.

"I heard," Jeremy continued, "that there were sightings of deer south of here near Zone Green."

"That's news to me."

"You think—" Jeremy's words were interrupted.

The foghorn in the fire department tower cut through the air like a bullet shot. Everyone on the firehouse lawn startled and then erupted all at once in a frenzy.

Jeremy and Simon exchanged glances.

Alice is under attack.

Each and every man had a position on the line, in the trenches, in guard towers and armored bunkers, and above the tall wooden fences and walls. If an enemy was encountered that the forwarding guards could not handle, they fell back to the front line and let the invaders follow. Whoever was trying to attack Alice would then come face to face with the town's artillery and defenses.

The number of blares on the foghorn indicated that the enemy had been spotted in the northeast.

The lunch crowd took off in a frenzy, everyone running to their positions, trays left behind. Simon, being second in command of the Rangers, had been issued a two-way radio. As he ran, he heard the crackling of a voice over the speaker: *"All Rangers report to position N.T. I repeat, all Rangers report to N.T."*

It was hard to make out the words through the roar of the crowd, and Simon had to stop and cup his ear over the speaker as the message repeated itself.

N.T., he thought. *Shit. That's the trade grounds.*

***

The first time Simon had heard the foghorn blare was two weeks after taking up residence in Zone Blue. He ran behind Jeremy, who shouted at him to keep up, until they reached the line of trenches. The scramble of people all around him was enough to make his head spin, and he would have gotten lost for sure if not for Jeremy pulling him along.

Simon jumped into the cavity of a trench, his body flat against the earthen wall, hugging his rifle tight to his chest. He dared to peek his head over the top, over the sandbags lining the rim, and look out at the field beyond. The area in front of the trenches was a grassland, barren of trees or large rocks so that an approaching enemy would have no cover when coming out of the woods.

For several heartbeats, nothing happened.

Then Simon saw movement. A few ragged men ran out of the far woods, unaware that a whole army was waiting for them. Then there were more men, and more. They might have only numbered a few, but at that moment, they appeared to Simon like a swarming brigade of well-armed soldiers. A whistle was blown, and the sound of gunfire erupted. Simon fell back, his body pressed against the trench wall. His sweaty skin turned the dirt to mud against him.

"Stand up," Jeremy yelled through the roar of gunfire. "Get on your feet, and fire your weapon!"

Simon did not move.

"You have to shoot!" Jeremy shouted over the gunfire. "Stand up and shoot!"

Jeremy reached down, grabbed Simon's arm, and yanked him up to face the melee. The invaders, now realizing they were running straight into a wall of gunfire, either clung to the earth, desperately shooting over their heads, or attempted to run back into the woods for cover. The ground was a boil of erupted dirt and grass as bullets and mortars rained down. Simon shouldered his weapon and tried to aim down the barrel, but there was so much noise, so many guns firing, so many voices shouting and swearing. Sweat stung his eyes, blurring his vision.

"Pull the trigger," Jeremy shouted, firing his rifle. "Squeeze it!"

Simon pulled the trigger. Blindly, he fired his weapon, and he continued firing it until the magazine clicked and was empty.

"Reload," Jeremy commanded.

Simon began to reload, his heart beating out of his ears, until the sound of a whistle cut through the gunfire.

Up and down the line, men began yelling, "Cease fire! Cease fire!" The popping of gunfire slowed until it stopped altogether. The bodies in the field were riddled with bullets and blown to unrecognizable shreds.

Simon's whole body was trembling. His face had been pressed so hard against the rifle stock that he could feel a line imprinted across his cheek, and his front was covered in dirt.

Jeremy had taken a seat beside him, pulling a cigarette from his pack with his teeth and clicking open his Zippo.

He offered Simon a cigarette, but he declined. Not because he didn't want one, but because he thought his hand was shaking too much to pull one from the pack.

Jeremy leaned close to Simon's ear. "You don't have to actually shoot anyone," he whispered. "But you have to pull the trigger."

To this day, and after a dozen or so opportunities, Simon had never killed a single human being. Not one. Not after the boy. Not after the incident at the gas station.

Jeremy was the only person aware of that fact.

As time passed and encounters with hostiles became somewhat regular, Simon stopped trembling so easily, yet fear remained.

***

Simon remembered his first encounter as he listened again to the radio repeat the message: *"All Rangers report to N.T."*

Frank Morrow, along with some Rangers and an assembly of Guards and Dragoons, was already at the northeast checkpoint as Simon approached. He heard gunfire from the front line and off in the woods. A convoy from Zone Red came rushing through the tall chain-link fence surrounding the trade grounds as Simon joined the other Rangers.

"Simon," Frank said. "I was just explaining—this convoy here came under attack less than a half mile out. The soldiers guarding the trucks neutralized the majority of the attackers, which we estimate to be over a dozen. The hostiles who were not neutralized by General Driscoll's men attempted to follow the convoy into Alice, and as you can hear, are still being dealt with." Frank paused, his finger in the air as he gazed upward, listening to the now-sporadic gunfire. "One of General Driscoll's men has been killed and three wounded. One of the convoy trucks crashed in the melee, and two of the occupants took off on foot and are missing. That's why we're here. We're going to find them. Suit up; we're heading out."

Frank turned toward the gathering of men; some from Zone Red's convoy team were running over to join them. There were over twenty soldiers assembled, and each man was checking his rifles and gear just as Simon was doing.

A guard swung open the gate, and Frank shouted, "Move out!"

The men jogged into the wooded terrain just outside the gate with weapons up. Simon felt the sweat build up on his body. He hated this part: the possible encounter with an enemy out in the open. He was much better alone or with just a few Rangers.

Outside of Alice's perimeter, the men neared the area of attack—a single-lane road in the woods of Alice Springs. Bodies lay sprawled on the ground where they had been shot—all of them skinny, filthy, and wearing nothing but rags. They already smelled of death and decay, even though death had just claimed them. The convoy truck's broad side was peppered with bullet holes and crushed against a massive tree. The soldiers circled the ground, scouting and securing the area. The leading officer from Zone Red spoke to some of the Dragoons, and the rest of the men squinted off in the distance, looking for any signs of the two missing soldiers.

Simon approached the convoy truck, mindful of the ground. Frank Morrow eyed him trailing off, and stayed a few steps behind.

There are too many people here, Simon thought. *The tracks are getting scattered.*

Simon stepped off the road and into the woods, passing the convoy truck, and then he stopped. "There," he pointed. "That's where they ran off."

Frank peered around him. The officer from Zone Red saw Simon pointing and broke off his conversation with the Dragoons.

"What is it?" he asked Frank Morrow. "What's he pointing at?"

"That, right there." Frank gestured to a low plant about shin height.

"What?"

"That's where they ran off. Look at the branch; it's broken in two."

The man squinted and stared for a moment. "It's merely a twig." Then he turned to his soldiers. "Markus, stay here with the men. Johnson, Reed, follow—hey you, stop!" he shouted to Simon, who was walking off into the woods, alone.

The officer walked toward Simon, but Frank put up a hand to stop him, shaking his head. "Let the lad go. If anyone is going to find them, it'll be that boy there."

The trail was easy for Simon to follow. The men who were missing wore combat boots and had beat upon the ground in haste. Simon didn't want to say it out loud, but he saw something troubling along the trail: blood. The ground was dark in spots, and much of the underbrush was covered in red. The wound was low, Simon figured, judging by the way the blood splattered the leaves.

The trail became different, broader, and it took Simon only a moment to decipher that the marks on the ground indicated one person had begun dragging the other.

Simon followed the marks, being mindful to overlook the noise the men were making behind him. Not far in the distance, Simon saw a dark outline on the ground like a rock in the tall grass, but as he neared, he knew that it was not a rock. The person who had been dragged lay dead. Bullet holes riddled the man's stomach and thighs. Simon motioned to the men behind him and moved on.

The blood on the trail did not cease, and there were marks where the other person had stumbled and fell. He was getting close. The sides of shallow depressions—knee marks and handprints in the dirt—were still moist.

Simon heard a noise behind a cluster of trees.

A person. Ragged breathing, sighing. Anguish. Not words.

He raised his hand to signal the trailing men to stop.

Instantly, the men dropped to their knees and the woods grew silent. Simon listened to the wind and the voice that it carried. The person was injured.

This was the tricky part—sneaking up on a person, friend or foe. It was easy to wind up shot in a rush of fear and confusion.

Simon neared the trees, crouching low, his feet touching the ground in soft, deliberate steps. The sounds grew louder: panting and choppy breaths.

Simon pressed his chest into the side of a tree and craned his head around it.

He saw a woman, her back against the thick base of an oak. Her leg was bleeding, and she was turning a tourniquet around her thigh with a strip of torn cloth and a stick. She had a rifle over her lap and clenched her jaw with such ferocity that her face was bright red and contorted. Instinctually, Simon could empathize with the pain she was feeling as if he were experiencing it himself. She was tough, all right.

He took a deep breath and exhaled, preparing himself to step out from behind the tree. He had expected her to not see him until he spoke, but then she grabbed her rifle and swung it up at him.

Simon exclaimed, "I'm a friend! I'm a friend! I've been sent to find you. Don't shoot." He held his rifle out in his open palms in a gesture of offering.

She stared back at him in disbelief, her finger trembling over the trigger, her eyes wild.

"Where—how the hell'd you sneak up on me?"

"I was sent from Alice to find you. I'm a Ranger—a scout."

For a moment they stared at each other.

She's good, Simon thought. *This girl knows a thing or two.*

She lowered the gun and a tear escaped down the side of her face. Her body was jittery.

Simon walked to her side and kneeled down, inspecting her leg. "You're okay," he said. "You're going to be fine. The wound isn't bad. If the bullet had hit the bone or an artery you wouldn't have made it this far."

"I f-fucking know that," she said, and then closed her eyes and took a breath. "I-I'm sorry …"

"I understand."

She nodded and rested her head back against the tree. Simon helped apply a bandage as the rest of the soldiers caught up.

"Let's get you out of here," he said. "Take my hand."

Simon grabbed the woman under her arm and helped pull her up to one wobbling leg. She winced and held on to Simon's shoulder. Another soldier came to help, and they carried her out of the woods with her hopping on one foot and spitting out obscenities in long chain-link sentences through clenched teeth.

"Oh, ohh, you fucking, mother-fucking-bitch-face!" she screamed at the pain.

Simon suppressed a laugh.

She turned to him. "What the hell is so funny?"

"Nothing. I'm sorry. I've seen men shot through the chest that didn't curse as much as you. You're a tough one; I'll give you that. I didn't know there were women on the convoy team."

"Yeah? Well, there are. One."

They made it to the road where a stretcher was waiting. Simon helped her down, and before the soldiers took her away, she turned to him.

"Hey, look," she said between labored breaths. "I'm … I'm really thankful. You saved me … I'll never forget that. You're a damn good scout; didn't hear you coming. What's your name?"

"Simon," he said. "Simon Kalispell."

"Thank you, Simon. I'm Bethany. I owe you, big time."

Simon shook his head. "You don't owe me a thing."

Chapter 38
Lone Rider

"They're bringing the girl back now," Nick said, holding the handheld radio to his ear.

Tom Byrnes nodded. "Good," he said. "That's good." He let out a sigh, put the binoculars down, and turned his back from the observation post on the guard tower.

"Let's go," he said to Nick.

As they descended the ladder, Nick called out, "Who is she?"

"Who?"

"The girl—who is she?" His father had shown obvious concern when he heard the convoy had been attacked, but there was something else, a certain urgency in his mannerism. And when he had heard it was a girl who had gone missing, he had grown quiet. Then he ordered for a team to be assembled at once.

"A new resident of Alice. I don't remember her name."

"She's moving to Alice?"

Tom shrugged. "What of it?"

It wasn't unheard of for people to move between the two Zones, but it was infrequent. The residents were issued jobs and rarely allowed to pick and choose where they wanted to live. They were lucky enough to be alive, and even luckier to be living somewhere safe.

"You just seemed concerned is all. Why is she moving to Alice?"

Tom reached the base of the guard tower and waited for Nick. "She's here to help organize trade. Her name is Liz, or something. Beth, I think."

Nick stepped off the ladder and saw his father's face. He was hiding something. Alice didn't need help with trade. But apparently, his father didn't feel like elaborating.

"Come on," Tom said. "Let's get lunch while it's still hot."

Nick nodded. "It was Kalispell who found her," he said.

"Simon?"

"Yes. Simon."

"He's a smart kid, that one. Good at the hunt."

"Maybe. But he needs to keep that hippie Buddhist bullshit to himself."

"It's not his fault people ask him questions. And I don't think he's a Buddhist."

Nick shrugged. Just yesterday he'd overheard a few of the other Rangers discussing Simon's preaching over dinner, that violence of any sort—even negative emotions and thoughts—was something that needed to be eradicated if humanity was to ever rise from the ashes. Nonviolence was a big part of Simon's belief system—whatever system that may be. No violence. What a silly notion. The world was a violent place, and Nick needed men who could use violence as a means of self-preservation, as a tool, and not shy away from it. It was a necessity.

As they walked away, Nick remembered that his father and Simon's father had been old friends. Tom told Nick that he had met Simon when they were young, but Nick had no recollection of that. When Simon first arrived in Alice, his father had made a big to-do over it. The Kalispell family owned Kalispell Sports, a company that had been all over the world pre-disease. Simon had given Nick the addresses of several warehouses that he knew of, and Nick led a contingent of Dragoons to scour for goods. But there was nothing left in any of them. They were stripped clean down to the cold cement floors.

"We got lucky this time," Nick said.

"How so?"

"It was a small group that attacked, and we didn't suffer any causalities."

"No, but they're reporting Zone Red had casualties, and we're one and the same."

Nick rolled his eyes but agreed with his father for argument's sake. Zone Red held its precious resources over Zone Blue's head, as if their fuel was more important than Alice's water. The soldiers in Hightown were a bunch of elitists, making inflexible rules and regulations in favor of themselves as if they deserved better treatment than the people of Alice. The only thing Zone Red had over Alice was more men. Numbers. Nick would contest the strength of his Dragoons against Zone Red's soldiers any day.

"Yes," Nick agreed. "So we did lose some men. We're lucky that the fools who attacked us knew nothing of warfare. We killed, what? Seventeen? Twenty?"

"We'll know the exact number at briefing."

"You know, one day it won't be a group of ragged miscreants who come marching to our front door."

"Our line is strong, Nick."

"Our walls were never completed. Against the usual assortment, yes, our defenses are well equipped, but there are others out there, Dad. Many more who would love nothing other than to slit our throats and strip our fields."

"Nick, I know what you're getting at—"

"We need to reconsider bolstering our line, adding numbers to our fighting men."

This was a fragile conversation, Nick knew. As far as everyone was aware, the three Zones compromised the largest number of survivors working together to rekindle humanity in an organized assemblage.

But there *were* others.

Bands of men. Organized groups.

A man had presented himself two weeks ago, arriving alone at the checkpoint. He came riding on the back of a massive buckskin horse, the animal's coat a light gray, its eyes even paler. The man came unarmed, smiling a mouth full of teeth like gravestones. He was a spectacle to be seen, standing a full head in height above the tallest guard on duty. He bowed to them all and spoke in such a way, with such eloquence, that the guards decided to radio headquarters rather than turn the man away. Tom and Nick had met the rider at the checkpoint and listened to what he had to say.

When they approached, the man had been holding his stallion by the reins, the muscles on the beast's side rippling like steel wire under its taught skin. The man was lean, yet the width of his shoulders displayed his strength. He was older than Nick, and when they shook hands, Nick felt a grip like iron wrap around his fingers. When the rider smiled, the skin on his face creased with the roughness that his years on this earth had accumulated.

The man spoke to them in a deep, smooth voice that came out from his throat with the bobbing of his Adam's apple.

"Sirs—General and Lieutenant," he formally addressed them, standing straight. "I come to offer you the services deserved of your fine establishment here in Alice. I offer you myself and my men. A proposition you will find most appealing.

"I am the leader of a band of well-trained and well-armed mercenaries who will do anything asked of them in exchange for lodging and food. There will never be a question raised. They will kill, defend, and construct—run in circles if it is so wished." The man paused, then went on to give a rough estimate of their numbers, the abundance of weaponry they maintained, and a short tale of their exploits.

"I leave you, Sir General, with a proposition and nothing more. The fate of your people is for you alone to decide. My men are eager to soil their hands at your bidding. You will rest at night knowing my soldiers watch the gates. They are the finest assortment of fighting men alive in this world. I assure you that. I will leave you now to organize your thoughts and will return in two nights' time to further discuss the future of Alice and the grandeur that it shall forever achieve."

Nick was enthralled, or at least curious to hear more. An army. Ready to fight and obey his every command. All they wanted in return was food and water, and Alice had plenty of both.

But Tom would not stand the notion.

"Not a chance," he had told Nick as they walked off with the man trotting away. "That man ... there's something not right with him."

That was the end of it. Tom would not listen to Nick's logic. He shook his head and said, "No. End of story."

Tom refused to return two nights later.

As they distanced themselves from the guard tower, Tom again stated his objection.

"If you're suggesting that we find that man and his band of mercenaries, you can forget it."

Nick felt his face flush red. His father could be so stubborn. Never did he let Nick offer an opinion.

"Then, Father"—he sighed—"if that is your final say … I'll leave it at that."

"It is, and always has been, my final say."

"Fine. But I hope that when a large enough threat presents itself, you'll be wise enough to consider the man's proposition. We have more than enough food and enough housing to maintain three times their numbers."

Tom stared ahead, and Nick knew the conversation was over—for good.

As they walked off, Nick's personal guard and secretary of sorts, Will Holbrook, struggled to keep up.

"Will," Nick said, turning to let the young soldier come close.

"Yes, sir?" Will stood rigid before his lieutenant.

"Go get something to eat and take the afternoon off. Find me before the evening meeting, at my house."

"Yes, sir," he said.

Nick and Tom Byrnes distanced themselves from the front line, leaving Will standing at attention.

Chapter 39

Progress

"It was the damned Chinese," a Ranger named Mark Camps said. "Those bastards were ruthless."

"Nah," Justin Waters argued, shaking his head. "It was the A-rabs. That's where it started, in the Middle East. That's what the news said."

"Fuck the news. Those asshole reporters and the scumbag politicians, they lied to us all. They lied about everything."

Simon watched Frank Morrow suppress a laugh as the two Rangers went on. Frank was the oldest Ranger in all of Alice. Perhaps not by much, but he held himself with such a degree of decorum and poise that other men knew upon meeting him that they were in the vicinity of a wise and learned man— a natural leader.

Frank asked, "What if it was neither?"

The two Rangers looked at him. It was common banter among the men to pick a party responsible for creating the disease. It was the eternal question, as eternal as the other questions of *why? Why* did humanity nearly perish? *Why* did I lose all of my loved ones? *Why* am I still alive? These questions were asked in endless loops, but answers never came.

"Maybe," Frank continued, "it was *us* that created the disease. The United States of America."

"That's crazy talk." Mark dismissed Frank with a wave of his hand. "If anything, it just happened. You know, like from God or something. Or like the earth had enough—enough of the war and us killing everything—and shook us off like a wet dog shaking itself dry."

Simon was not interested in joining the discussion today. It was the same discussion, all day, every day. But his ears did perk up at Mark's observation.

They were finishing the perimeter inspection and were now nearing the checkpoint. In the past, Simon had enjoyed talking to the other men about the disease and the fate of humanity, and the men took interest in what he had to say. Many had even begun meditating—contemplating that a constant cycle of violence, no matter how small in comparison to the disease and war, could be just as dangerous. One negative thought could spiral out of control like a snowball down a mountain.

No matter how many times it was discussed, the fact remained the same: the war and disease *had* happened, and nothing could be done to change the past. It was best to accept reality, move on to deal with the pain and suffering, and find ways to prevent their small remnant of humankind from repeating history.

As they passed the checkpoint, they stopped so Frank could dismiss them, and then they split up in different directions.

Simon was in a hurry.

In under an hour, Bethany was going to be released from the hospital. Her leg was healing remarkably well. For some reason, Tom Byrnes had kept her in the hospital for six days, much longer than needed. Typically, an injury like hers was patched up, and the person was soon sent on their way. She told Simon she didn't know why she was getting such personal treatment, but if she had to take a guess, it was because Tom Byrnes wanted General Driscoll to know that Alice takes good care of its people.

Simon reached the hospital and made his way down the corridors to Bethany's room. His eyes glanced on the clipboard on the door before entering. Sure enough, the name *Bethany Rose, Female*, was typed across the top.

Simon opened the door, knocking lightly at the same time.

"Bethany? Did I wake you?"

Her eyes darted open as he entered. Simon had visited her after her leg was sewn up, and seeing her lying on the bed alone without even a window made his heart ache. He brought her a book the next day, and each day following had dropped in to chat. She was a curious girl, asking Simon plenty of questions about hunting and stalking. He told her that he could kill a deer with only a spear, and she didn't believe him. She had a few good stories herself and told Simon all about the incident next to Sunfish Pond.

"I'm awake," she said. "Just resting my eyes."

He walked over to the side of her bed.

"I'm leaving soon." Her face was radiant.

"I heard. You must be excited. This wasn't a good way to be introduced to Alice." He laughed, and so did she.

"Listen," he said, pulling over a chair to sit down. "Tom came to talk to me early this morning—"

"Tom Byrnes?"

"Yes. He came to talk to me. He mentioned that you have two roommates arriving in Alice in a few weeks. In the meantime, he wants you under guard."

Her face went sour. "I don't need anyone—"

"It's not up for debate. It's an order from the General. You're injured and will need help getting around."

"I can get around fine. I can get to the bathroom, and I've been showering by myself for the last two days."

"That's why you're not moving in with a female soldier. He asked me personally, as a friend, to take you in—just until your roommates arrive. You'll have a bedroom to yourself. I share the apartment with a roommate, Jeremy Winters. He's moving out of the larger room, so you can have it while you stay."

"I don't need the larger room. I'm fine in a smaller one."

Simon rolled his eyes. "Fine—you can have the smallest room we can find."

"I … I'm sorry. You're being nice, and I'm being … a bitch. It's just that, you know, I've been staring at the walls in here for days. Honestly, I don't care where I go, as long as it's out of this hospital. You say that Tom Byrnes is a friend of yours?"

"Our families were friends before the disease. I have a picture—rather, I *had* a picture—of Tom, my dad, Nick, and myself all fishing. I gave the picture to Tom a long time ago, before I was an official resident."

She nodded and looked up at Simon with a smile. "Thank you, Simon. You're helping me again. It's nice to find a friend here so quickly. I can't wait for you to meet my cou—" She cleared her throat. "Sorry. I can't wait for you to meet my roommates, Brian and Carolanne."

Simon smiled. "Well, until then, how about we talk to the doctor about getting you ready to leave? Jeremy is going to come by in a few hours to give us a hand."

Simon thought she was about to say, "I don't need any help," but she didn't.

"I can't wait," she said with a smile.

Chapter 40

The Foghorn

Nick checked his watch. The minute hand seemed to be ticking away at lightning speed. In half an hour, he and his father had a lunch meeting with Martin Howard to discuss the speech they were slated to give later that evening about the impending shift in manpower to Project Yellow—solar power throughout Alice. Nick had lost the majority vote, and the project had been given the green light.

Currently his father was making his afternoon rounds, checking in at the reconnaissance office—the eyes and the ears of Zone Blue—set deep in the woods. Tom's rounds were punctual, starting with the various posts along the front, then the water filtration plant, and lastly, the recon office. Nick knew he had less than five minutes until his father would be leaving for the meeting, and he intended to catch up with him at the office.

He checked his watch again. *Tick, tick ...*

Behind him, Will Holbrook was a few yards away.

"Will," he shouted without turning. "If you can't keep up, why bother doing your job at all?"

"S-sorry, sir," he said, panting. Nick would have to reconsider whether Will was best suited for the job. He was just a kid, after all.

Nick sighed. "I have to catch the general before he leaves—hurry it up."

"Yes, sir."

They cut straight through the gardens, down the wide lane in the center, with some of the workers stopping to salute or nod their greetings. Nick waved them off and watched them move aside as he barreled forward.

The sun shone straight down throughout the fields, unhindered in a clear sky, and especially in the center lane where there were no shadows at all. Nick was sweating only a few steps in, despite the cool breeze in the air. After about a minute, his undershirt was sticking to his chest.

"Will, hurry it up," he shouted behind him.

Will jogged after Nick, his rifle bouncing over his shoulder as he ran, until they reached the woods on the opposite side of the abundant vegetable gardens.

The trees grew thick, and there was no manicured path to the reconnaissance office, but it was an easy enough walk up and down a few shallow hills.

Nick could just make out the structure ahead. The old concrete ranger station looked more like a small windowless bunker with thick wires snaking out into the woods than the central hub for all of Alice's communications. It was intended to look that way—like nothing important.

The few men working in that office were responsible for relaying information from one front to the other, issuing reinforcements, and supplying the two artillery brigades with coordinates for an attack. Artillery ammunition was scarce, so bombardments had to be precise.

A lot of activity went on in that little room.

Nick checked his watch again. He was close enough to see the two guards stationed outside the door standing at attention. His father must still be in there.

Just in time, he thought.

The door opened, and his father stepped out while still speaking to one of the officers. He was holding a clipboard, and when he looked up, he made eye contact with Nick standing atop of a rocky mound.

His father smiled and waved.

Nick looked at the old man, *his* old man. The old soldier still looked good—stout and strong despite his barreled chest and rounded stomach. His cheeks burned red with the cool air against his morning shave. He was wearing a windbreaker and his white hair fluttered in the breeze.

This old man was responsible for the safety and security of all of Alice. He had accomplished so much in his lifetime—more than Nick could ever hope to achieve, although he would try.

A flurry of memories overtook him—the grainy photographs of his youth with his much younger and skinnier father, who only had streaks of gray in his dark hair at that time. He pictured his dad posing for the camera, beaming as he held his baby boy in his arms. He saw his father in his crisp army fatigues and remembered the deep pride that he'd felt as a child seeing his father the soldier; and even more pride when later, his dad had become a private investigator. He remembered his father's pain, and his own, when his mother had gotten sick and succumbed to cancer.

Nick stood there in the woods, his father in the doorway waving his hand, with a smile on his face that showed nothing but genuine affection.

Tom waved, and Nick waved back. Then, there was a noise.

Nick looked in the air. He heard a whirling, whistling sound. Faint, but growing louder.

Nick saw his father look up, followed his gaze, his hands shielding his eyes from the sunlight flickering past the tall canopy of trees.

The whirling sound grew louder, and panic came flooding over Nick. "Ohhh, shit—"

He took off in a run toward the windowless office.

"Dad!" he shouted. "Dad! Get down! Get down!"

Will sprinted behind him. The guards in front of the building were scanning the skies, looking for the noise and panicked to see Nick rushing toward them.

"Run!"

Tom grabbed the doorway and was jumping inside when the first mortar hit.

"No! Dad—no!"

The mortar round was large—possibly a 120 mm shell—and in an instant, Tom Byrnes vanished in a lightning-fast blaze of fire. The roof of the small concrete structure exploded upward in a thousand pieces, and debris of all kind shot out from the doorway like cannon fire. The guards at the front were blown off their feet. One lay where he fell, motionless, burning, as the other scrambled to get back up.

"Daaaad!" Nick screamed, still running.

The guard had made it two steps from the office when another shell hit the ground, followed by another, and then another. A few hit the trees overhead, sending large splintering branches crashing to the ground. The guard vanished, and a wave of torrid force struck Nick so hard that he fell on his back.

He shielded his face as another shell landed nearby. The fierce heat seemed to singe his skin. Something heavy hit his shoulder, rocking him, and then something else hit his leg, tearing away the material of his pants near his knee. He moved and twitched his limbs; everything seemed to still be attached and he didn't feel the hot, slippery sensation of massive blood loss.

Firm hands grabbed his shoulders, and he looked up to see Will Holbrook dragging him into a shallow depression in the ground. He now remembered why Will had been appointed as his personal guard—the boy was strong as an ox.

They made it to cover as a shell ripped into a parked Jeep beside the recon office, producing a gigantic fireball that scoured the tree branches high above.

Nick and Will pressed their bodies against the ground, as if they were trying to meld with the earth. Waves of dirt and debris splashed over them.

Then the explosions ceased and the air grew still.

They cautiously lifted their heads and could feel the heat emanating from the leaping fires of what had been the recon office. They stared at the dancing flames for some time, open-mouthed, as if inside that fire lay the doorway to hell itself, and at any moment, legions of demons would spring forth to poison the land.

In the distance, the foghorn blared.

Chapter 41

Karl Metzger

Karl Metzger rode into Alice on the back of his buckskin horse.

His lieutenant, Mark Rothstein, rode at his side, heeling a brilliant chestnut stallion along, its muscles rippling beneath its broad shoulders. The short, stout man had a great red beard down to the center of his chest, streaked with gray. One hand rested on the rosewood handle of an ornate machete.

To Karl's right rode his other lieutenant, a man they called Sultan, his real name unknown even to Karl. Sultan's slim body rode straight-backed atop his jet-black stallion, his own skin just as dark. With each step of his horse, his long dreadlocks bounced over his shoulders. He scanned the land before him with an ever-present smile on his face.

Riding beside Sultan was Dietrich—the Priest. The Priest looked somber, sitting atop his Palomino horse, the color similar to Karl's stallion and similar to his own gray-white hair. The Priest hummed to himself, adjusting the black eye patch that covered one eye.

Behind the riders marched a small procession of soldiers, all well-armed and advancing in two columns. Between the two columns, five prisoners were forced forward, their wrists tied behind their backs so tight that blood seeped from around their wire bindings. Gags had been stuffed into their mouths, and strips of cloth covered their eyes. They wore filthy rags, and two of the prisoners were barefoot and limping with bloody feet. These five men were all that remained of the force that had attacked Alice.

They were led to the dark prison cells in the basement of Alice's police department and put under guard. Many townsfolk camped outside the building for just a chance to lay witness to these miscreants. Anger boiled so thick in the air that many felt they might not be able to stop themselves from tearing the flesh from these men's bones if presented with the opportunity to do so.

As evening approached and the prisoners shivered in their damp, pitch-black cells, Nick Byrnes sat alone on a folding chair in a small office on the second floor of Alice's volunteer fire department.

His wristwatch sat coiled in the palm of his hand, the bands hanging below his fingers. The second hand kept ticking away: *tick, tick, tick ...*

The barren office was beginning to grow dark as the last ray of sunlight became blocked behind the tall trees in the distance. The air in that room was thick with stagnant dust, illuminated in the shaft of sunlight from the room's one window, motionless, as if time did not exist there.

Nick's dinner plate sat undisturbed and cold on the carpeted floor. He looked up from his watch, letting his eyes glance over the drab interior of this unused room. The walls were paneled in wood, and stacks of folding chairs lined the wall behind him. Next to the door was a painting of a cabin in the woods, which might have come with the frame. The room was uncomfortable and seemingly forgotten, but there was something in the ugliness that made Nick feel relaxed, like he could disappear in there and let the woes of the world proceed without him.

From outside the window, Nick could see the stage and the woods bordering it in the rear of the firehouse. There were several men on the stage adjusting the podium and testing the microphone. He could not see the gathered crowd, but knew that every single resident of Alice was there, waiting for him.

They were waiting for assurance. They were waiting to hear that Alice was safe. They were waiting to know justice would be served to those found guilty. The air was alive with anger. The people wanted blood, and Nick was going to give it to them.

Nick's reflection looked back at him in the window. Despite not sleeping for the past twenty-four hours, he looked okay. His hair was combed back, showing his temples in dramatic fashion. He had not shaved that morning, and the stubble on his face cast a dark shade with a slight silvery hue that he thought would look good if grown into a beard. It was time he showed his age, his power, his wisdom, and his strength.

He closed his eyes and took a deep breath. It was now or never; the crowd was growing impatient. He inhaled deeply and opened his eyes.

Take what is yours, Nick. This is your time … take what is yours.

He stood from the chair, adjusted his pistol-belt, and walked to the door.

Outside, Will Holbrook jumped to his feet as Nick walked past without stopping. He went down the hallway to the staircase.

Four men were waiting downstairs beside the glass doors leading outside—Karl Metzger, Mark Rothstein, Sultan, and the Priest. They wore similar dark fatigues, and Karl stood the tallest of them all, his back straight and his arms clasped behind his back. His head had been shaven near bald, and his eyebrows looked bushy and large in comparison.

"General." Karl bowed and smiled as Nick stepped to the landing. "General, we follow your lead. Mr. Rothstein." He turned to his lieutenant, "If you would, please."

Mark Rothstein moved on quick feet, despite what his large body would suggest, and opened the fire door for Nick to pass. Nick walked outside.

The distance from the fire door to the stage was short, and the sea of people gathered before it grew quiet as Nick approached the podium. Seated behind the podium were the men of the round table, as his father had called them, and they stood as Nick readied himself to speak. Karl Metzger and his lieutenants followed Nick onstage and stood by his side.

For a moment that seemed like an eternity, Nick was silent, his palms resting on the podium. When he lifted a hand, the low murmurs in the crowd ceased. The crowd stretched so far back that many stood in the road before the firehouse and could not be seen.

Take what is yours, Nick … this is your time.

"People of Alice." His deep voice boomed from the loudspeakers. "Today, the world is a different place." He paused so that the crowd could absorb the immensity of these simple words, and then continued, "This morning I performed a task previously unthinkable; I sent an emissary north to Zone Red to inform our allies that our beloved leader … my father … had been killed in a ruthless attack against this great town of ours.

"Following the bombing that destroyed the reconnaissance office and killed our general, along with six soldiers who lost their lives, a well-armed force attacked our front line. Nine more men perished as a result of that battle, and there would have been many more if not for this man who now stands beside me." Nick stepped back, gesturing to Karl Metzger, who bowed solemnly.

"This man," Nick continued, "and a small contingency of his fighting force were camped nearby due to a meeting they were scheduled to have with both General Tom Byrnes and myself. When they heard the explosions and gunfire, they marched to our aid, flanked our enemy, and delivered upon them a quick death. Karl Metzger, too, lost men in the melee. We thank you, Karl, for your help and sacrifice. We mourn your losses."

Nick faced the crowd.

"It was the enemy's belief that we would crumble without the aid of our reconnaissance office and without the leadership of our beloved Tom Byrnes. It was also the attackers' intention to target me—to eliminate both general and lieutenant, father and son. But the enemy got two things wrong.

"First, the size of our fighting force, the number of men and women living in Alice and defending her lines. The second and most important factor was the extent of our resolve—the extent to which we are willing to defend our town and our lives. They thought we would crumble. They thought Alice was weak. They thought we would break, but they were wrong. Let it be heard by both friend and foe that an attack on Alice or any of its people will be met with extreme retaliation."

With those words, the crowd stirred. A few townspeople clapped. Nick's voice rose in pitch.

"As many of you know, the enemy did not work alone. Someone in Alice is responsible for supplying them with information. For one, the exact time and moment that Tom Byrnes and I would be visiting the reconnaissance office. It is believed that whoever divulged this information did so for their own personal gain, as they evidently lied to the enemy about our numbers and defenses. Let me make myself clear, whoever you are and wherever you may be, listen to my words; you will *not* destroy Alice. You will *not* hurt our people. You will *not* destroy our hearts, our minds, our wills.

"I have assembled a task force to investigate General Byrnes's assassination to the fullest extent. The guilty party can be assured that you might run, you might hide, you might cower in the night, or you might stay here in Alice, confident that your heinous secret will never be revealed—but let me tell you this, you will never know a restful night's sleep for as long as you may live.

We will hunt you down." Nick paused, his finger in the air. "You will not know safety for the rest of your days. You will find only dismay and death— a grueling, unimaginable death that will befit the severity of your crime. Your days are numbered. Oh by God, I swear it."

The crowd erupted in applause, which Nick attempted to quell with his open palms.

"Know this," he shouted. "Know this: you may have killed our leader, but the torch has been passed, and those who choose to oppose Alice will be at odds with the beast which you have awoken.

"We must recover both our town and our spirits, and it will not be entirely up to me to fix. It will be up to you, the people, to keep your chins high no matter how dark the night may seem. The world may be a different place now, but Alice is still safe because our enemy has failed. They have not and cannot break our spirits; destroy our pride. They will not best us in combat.

"As I stated earlier, both my father, General Byrnes, and I had a meeting scheduled with this man, Karl Metzger. It was General Tom Byrnes's wish that Karl Metzger's men integrate with us here in Alice to help fortify our defenses and prove that our soldiers are not only a *capable* fighting force, but *the best* fighting force in all of the known United States. In all of the world. We are going to honor General Tom Byrnes's final wish by following *his* plan for integration.

"As a show of good will, Karl Metzger has personally delivered the five prisoners captured from the attack for us to do with as we see fit. These five men have done nothing to proclaim their innocence, but have only further fueled their desire to cause us harm by laughing in the face of our interrogators and stating their happiness over the death and destruction that their actions have caused. They have been found guilty of murder and will be executed tomorrow morning at dawn before the memorial for General Tom Byrnes and the many others who gave their lives so that Alice may live to see another day."

At this, the crowd roared with thunderous ovation.

"Karl," Nick shouted over the cheering. "Karl Metzger and his men are welcome in our community, for they are our allies and number a great deal of strong, fighting men. They will help build our walls, line our trenches, and reinforce our posts. We owe them a debt of gratitude and a warm welcome into our beloved home."

with red strips of cloth tied below the sharpened points, creating ragged flags that fluttered in the wind.

Some in the crowd threw rocks and fistfuls of dirt at the prisoners, and by the time the guards had prodded the miscreants forth to reach Alice's fire department, many were bleeding from deep lacerations.

When they reached the firehouse, Nick, Karl, and the two lieutenants dismounted their horses. The marching columns of men turned to form a barrier between the townspeople and the stage, which had been given a recent addition of a hastily put together gallows.

The prisoners were forced up the steps, prodded along with the points of the spears. The rope connecting one man to the other was cut, and large guards forced the condemned to stand on chairs placed below the dangling ropes. Two of the men had to be picked up and made to stand, as they thrashed about, attempting to speak around their gags. One looked to Nick and Karl in exasperation, opening his clasped hands.

As the guards slid the circled ends of the corded ropes over their faces, tightening the nooses around their necks before binding their ankles, Karl turned to Nick and whispered in his ear, "Quite a civility you've managed to attain here in Alice." He chuckled, looking over the sea of people frothing with rage. "Looks as if we'll have a proper execution this fine morning. The people are ripe for it."

Nick stared at the prisoners through narrow eyes, then moved toward the podium, the palm of his hand resting on his sidearm. He stood stone-faced before the townspeople with the prisoners behind him quivering on the flimsy chairs. He waited until the crowd grew silent—and then he waited a moment longer. Even in the silence, the coming of violence could be felt as if it were something alive.

Nick spoke.

"Behind me stand the condemned. They have been charged with murder and found guilty of their crimes by a jury of their peers. They are sentenced to death by hanging. May God have mercy on their souls."

Nick nodded to Karl and walked away from the podium.

Karl turned to Mark Rothstein and Sultan, giving them each a dramatic stare before nodding his head, and moved to stand beside Nick at the edge of the stage. The Priest walked before the condemned men, standing tall with his arms open wide and his head bowed as if he were conducting a symphony of the damned.

He spoke in a bellowing voice, "Most sacred heart almighty, I accept from Your hands whatever kind of death it may please You to send me this day with all its pains, penalties, and sorrows in reparation for all of my sins, for the souls in Purgatory, for all those who will die today and for Your greater glory. Amen."

The Priest walked with echoing footfalls to stand beside the generals. Mark Rothstein and Sultan issued whispered orders, and the guards moved the podium off the stage so the condemned could be seen in full witness of the crowd.

Mark Rothstein stood behind the first man and kicked the chair out from under his feet. The man dropped and wiggled about like a fish on a hook. Mark proceeded to the next man, and then the next. When he came to the fourth man, he kicked, but the chair only budged. The man's legs wavered and his knees buckled before straightening back out, and he cried out loud behind his gag. Mark kicked again, but the chair didn't dislodge. Sultan reached his long arms around the man's trembling knees, then Mark kicked a third time, and the chair splintered into pieces. Mark moved to the last man, who stood tall upon his chair, staring at his friends expiring by his side. Mark kicked.

All of the condemned now hung by their necks, dead or writhing about. The fronts of their pants grew dark as their bladders emptied. Nick watched as Karl leaned in close to his ear.

"They're pissing themselves, Nicholas," he whispered, his lips curled.

Time passed as the men swayed and twitched until they all hung motionless. The crowd remained stone silent. Guards brought the podium back out and Nick approached it.

"Justice has been served. The condemned have fulfilled their sentences." His deep voice bellowed. "Tom Byrnes—my father—can now rest at peace."

With these simple words Nick exited the stage.

Karl followed.

The crowd cheered.

***

Following the execution, a large force of Karl Metzger's men entered Alice. They wore a variety of military fatigues—a mixture of camouflage and tactical gear. No two men looked alike; however, they resembled each other enough to suggest cohesion.

The men shouldered large backpacks and carried machine guns, knives, mortars, rocket launchers, machetes, shotguns, and all manner of weaponry. Several Hummers drove in along with supply vans and two automatic grenade launchers capable of firing over two hundred rounds of 25mm grenade ammunition or .50 caliber machine gun ammunition a minute.

These soldiers were tall and well-fed. Many had visible scars, were missing fingers, or had mutilated ears. All of the men had fashioned a red handprint above their hearts by slapping a paint-covered hand over their shirts and jackets. The handprints were thick and cracked, reapplied dozens of times, with red trails dripping down the fronts of their chests.

Karl introduced his force as the Red Hands, and himself as their leader.

The Red Hands shared with the people of Alice an assortment of plundered goods out in the big field before the fire department. Endless amounts of hard alcohol, dried meats, tobacco, soda, and beer circulated among the crowd. A whole cow and several pigs were delivered on the back of a truck and slaughtered outside the kitchen door.

Everyone was given the day off from work, with the exception of Karl's men, who were taking up their new positions on the line. Even trade had been postponed. The Priest took Karl aside under the shade of a maple tree and they spoke at length. Following their conversation, the Priest walked with urgency across the lawn to saddle his horse, and he galloped out of Alice with a contingency of men.

"Where's he going?" Nick asked.

Karl smiled, laying a hefty arm over Nick's shoulder. "That's not your concern, Sir General. Please, have a drink with me."

As the afternoon progressed, spirits were high, fueled by alcohol, cigars, and fresh meat. Karl Metzger stood tall over the congregation of men, quieting them down so that he could address Nick and the Dragoons. Men came forth, carrying sizable wooden crates, and set them down on the park tables before Nick and Karl. All watched as Karl opened a crate with a pry bar and stuck his hand in to remove a glimmering steel pistol from the padding of hay. Karl held high a six-inch barrel Colt Python revolver. The stainless steel glistened, and the black grips were sleek and new.

"These pistols"—Karl's deep voice boomed from his bobbing Adam's apple—"are suited for only the hardest of men. Men who have proven themselves on the battlefield time and time again. They are a present to you, Nick, to distribute to your Dragoons. A deserved sidearm for men of such high caliber."

The Dragoons closest to Karl and Nick were handed their new pistols and ammunition along with dark brown leather chest holsters. The pistols rested prominently on the torsos of the Dragoons, glimmering in the sun like sheriff badges.

***

Simon headed to the gardens as the party on the firehouse lawn progressed. He had seen enough. Standing in the crowd amongst a torrent of people caught up in a maddening revelry was the most frightening display of barbarity he had ever witnessed.

What Simon needed at that moment was to be solitary, to lighten his thoughts in the joyful meditation that only making things grow could provide. He went back to his apartment first to bring Winston along, who was all too happy to be out in the fresh air.

"Come on, buddy," Simon said, reaching down to ruffle Winston's head. "Want to help me garden?"

Winston licked at Simon's palm.

As the sun glimmered overhead, and Winston wandered around to smell the various plants and piles of dirt, Simon busied himself picking the weeds between the rough leaves of the kale plants. A few times he had to reprimand Winston for digging in the soft ground, and his dog looked up at him with dirt on his nose and a cocked expression.

Then he heard a familiar voice.

"Simon? Hey, Simon."

Simon half-turned to see Jeremy Winters approaching through the narrow lane. Winston was already trotting to meet him, his tail swaying wide.

"Yeah, Jeremy. Right here."

Jeremy walked over, carrying something long and skinny and wrapped in cloth. He scratched at Winston's head and smiled.

"I've been looking all over for you," he said to Simon. "You alone?" He looked over the expansive field.

Simon nodded.

Jeremy took a seat on the ground across from him.

"You hungry? They made a feast at the firehouse. I snagged this for you." He unfolded the cloth to display a loaf of freshly baked bread about a foot long. Simon's mouth salivated.

"You're missing all the fun." Jeremy laughed, tearing off a chunk of bread.

"Yeah? Maybe."

"You don't look so sure."

"I'm not." Simon was quiet, not able to find the right words at witnessing such a violent display mixed with the overwhelming revelry by the townspeople.

They chewed on the crusty bread and Jeremy said, "Hey, listen … I don't know what's going on …."

Simon looked at Jeremy, who was shaking his head. "I mean … I didn't even realize it, but I was screaming along with the crowd, and then, as they were stringing up the prisoners, it struck me: What the hell is going on? What am I doing? Why are we not only accepting this execution, we're lusting for it? This isn't the way we did things in Alice. We have laws, rules. We don't execute people. We try to better ourselves, better humanity, to prevent the past from repeating itself. With Tom gone, it's like we've all gone insane."

Simon looked at Jeremy. "I've got a bad feeling in the pit of my stomach. We're changing—Alice is changing, and it's not for the better. And worse yet, it's being accepted with open arms."

"Look," Jeremy glanced about, despite the fields being barren, "if this is the way we feel—before we start talking openly—I think we need to establish something."

Simon nodded.

"With everyone in a frenzy, we need to be careful who we talk to."

"Okay."

"We should only speak in private, to each other. No one else."

"I agree. I think everyone is distracted by the death of General Byrnes. If they hear us saying anything bad about Karl or his men, we might feel the sharp side of his spears. I don't think the town's bloodlust has been satiated quite yet."

Jeremy nodded. "If we do talk to other people, it can only be those who we know and can trust." Jeremy sat upright, as if a thought had unexpectedly come to him. "Where's Beth?" he asked. "I thought you were watching her?"

"Home. She's fine, I checked on her before coming to the fields. She's sleeping. Lucky for her, she missed the morning's festivities."

"Maybe she knows someone in Hightown who can help. Maybe someone over there knows more about these Red Hands, about Karl."

Simon thought it over. "I'll talk to her."

"Good." Jeremy tore the remainder of the bread in half, handing Simon a chunk. "Nick … he's blind right now. He can't see past his pride and anger."

Simon tore his remaining bread in half, giving Winston the larger of the two pieces.

"I couldn't agree more," he said. "I'll talk to Bethany tonight."

Chapter 43
987 Ridgeline Road

"I'm so proud of you, baby." Stephanie Kern bent over Nick, kissing his cheek while rubbing his shoulders. Nick took a sip of his morning coffee.

"You're a great leader," she said. "Better than your father."

Nick jerked away.

"My father was a great leader," he said. "I can only hope to be nearly as good as him."

But I will be better, he thought. *I am better.*

Soon, Nick would leave to make his rounds while Stephanie sat at home doing whatever it was that she did while he was working.

Nick used to encourage her to go outside and mingle with the townspeople, but Stephanie seemed to enjoy her reclusiveness. She read books like they might disappear from the face of the earth, and if she was to venture outside, it was only to go to the Alice Public Library. It was that same library where Nick had found her, all that time ago when he was clearing out the town, building by building. She was huddled in the corner surrounded by blankets and candles, piles of empty food cans nearby. She was like a hermit, living in a cave of knowledge. When he later asked her, "How the hell did you manage to stay alive?" she replied, "No one comes looking in libraries, it's the safest place. I foraged for supplies at night, and spent the days hiding in the dark."

Nick put his coffee down and asked, "Are you going out today?"

"I don't know." She stared off. "I have a headache."

Her migraines were getting worse, keeping her bedridden in the dark for hours, sometimes days.

She rubbed at her temples. "What else did General Driscoll say?"

"Nothing I haven't already told you."

"You really are the king of Alice." She beamed.

Nick sipped his coffee. He had traveled to Zone Red to meet with General Driscoll late the previous night, before dawn. The general had heard the news of Tom Byrnes's death and returned to Hightown as soon as he could. Nick told him that he had been put into power by the townspeople after the death of his father, and when asked about Karl Metzger and his band of mercenaries, Nick told him, "They're only a few dozen men. Just to bolster our line."

The stony-faced general had nodded gravely, lost in thought. He ordered Nick—*ordered*, actually *ordered* the leader of Alice—to bring Karl Metzger to a sit-down meeting. Nick obliged.

"Of course." He smiled. "I'll talk to him today, get it scheduled."

Nick stared into the steam rising from his coffee.

I was the next in line. I'm taking what's already mine—what I fought to establish. I don't have to bring Karl to a meeting. I don't have to answer to anyone.

Nick left General Driscoll being wished the best of luck—not that he needed any luck. Not that he didn't notice the way the general talked to him like a child.

They think we're a town of feeble peasants.

Oh, how wrong they are.

"When's your first meeting today?" Stephanie's voice shook Nick from his thoughts.

Nick checked his watch, not actually looking at the time. "In about an hour," he said. His afternoon meetings with Martin Howard had been cancelled for good, but Stephanie didn't know that. She didn't have to know anything, really—it was best to keep her in the dark.

The day after the memorial service for his father and the party following, Nick conducted his usual evening meeting with the round table … only he brought along Karl Metzger and a detachment of well-armed Dragoons to circle the room, their new pistols gleaming over their chests.

At long last, Nick set the men at the table straight.

He told them that the Guards were ordered to fall back to domestic responsibilities, replaced by the Dragoons and the Red Hands on the line. The people of Alice were needed to spend extra time in the gardens, rebuild guard towers, strengthen the trenches with cement and wood, and build stronger turrets. Leave the fighting for the soldiers.

Nobody at the table had a chance to speak, and no one dared to utter a word. Nick never sat down. He stood tall at the head of the table with his hands clasped behind his back as he spoke, Karl Metzger standing to his side like a giant, menacing shadow. The startled old men answered him, "Yes, General."

The respect felt good, despite that it was coming from the aged members of the round table, which still consisted of the same people his father had put in charge—Martin Howard, the electricity man; Douglas Banks, the architect; Stephen Knight, his father's old war buddy; Tim Chester, once a public relations officer in the Army; and Chris Lockton, a one-time urban developer.

They had once served a purpose, but they were no longer needed. His father should have set them straight ages ago. They were given too much power, too much say in the way Alice conducted itself. All they did was make progress difficult.

Don't just act the part, Nick reminded himself. *Become the general—be the leader that you already are.*

Nick told the table that Project Yellow—Martin's solar project—was now placed on permanent hold. The group nodded, remaining quiet, as Nick explained that the town of Alice was being put on lockdown until the person or persons responsible for feeding the attackers information were brought to justice. This meant that a curfew was in place, and the Rangers would not be allowed outside the perimeter on their regular patrols.

The men at the table looked grim and sipped at their glasses of water.

Good, Nick thought, smelling the fear in the room. *The executions showed them that I'm in charge—that my men respect me, and will obey my every word.*

As Nick walked toward the door, leaving the men sitting at the table, he heard a voice dare to speak. "Nick." Douglas Banks stood. "I have an idea."

Nick stood outside the open door and nodded his consent for Douglas to continue.

Douglas went on, "I still have my original blueprints for improvised defenses. If we have the manpower, maybe they could come in handy?"

"Good thinking," Nick replied. "Give them to Will Holbrook. I'll look them over when I can." With that, Nick had left, followed by Karl and the Dragoons. Nick remembered Douglas Banks' old blueprints—catapults and arcane medieval type defenses. They were laughed at when he first bought them up, but something pleased Nick when he envisioned the fear in the enemy's eyes at seeing a barrage of rocks rain down on them.

Psychological warfare.

The more weapons, the better. The time was ripe for a shift in power, for Zone Red to stop hovering above Alice. It was time for Zone Red to recognize the strength gathering behind the walls, even if it meant withholding from them the one resource more important than all the fuel Zone Red could ever supply—water. Zone Blue controlled fresh water, and plenty of it. Enough for hundreds of people, thousands … or none at all if he should choose.

Nick checked his watch again.

Today, the only thing on his agenda was to meet with Karl to discuss how to quell the discontent over the recently imposed curfew. They had waited several days after his father's death to give the news, but still the ruling was met with audible grumbles, and the murmurs of restlessness were becoming louder. Nick had to think over his options. He would have to use force if there were no other choices.

He swirled the few sips of coffee remaining in his mug when he and Stephanie both heard the rumbling of an engine. They exchanged glances and went to the door.

"Who the hell is driving a car? I didn't authorize the use of anything from the garage, especially through town."

They stood on the porch as the rumbling grew louder, and soon he saw a Jeep approaching from down the road. Several soldiers in front of the barracks across the way stopped what they were doing and stared. Nick had the feeling that soon, every window in the barracks would be lined with faces.

The Jeep approached and stopped before Nick and Stephanie's little home.

The door of the Jeep opened and Karl Metzger stepped out, flashing a broad smile as he looked up, seemingly enjoying the sunny day.

"Ah. Good morning, Sir General," he said with a slight bow. "A beautiful day, is it not? Stephanie, you look radiant as always." He stopped before them.

Stephanie blushed and smiled.

The house was gigantic. Nick could not imagine how many bedrooms were inside, and the yard was vast in either direction on a field of rolling grass. There was even a tennis court on the side behind a tall chain-link fence.

"What do you think, Sir General?"

Nick looked around. "I think you should have told me about this."

"How can a gift be considered a gift if it is not a surprise? There is no reason to be upset. I do believe you will find the house more than adequate."

"*Adequate?* It's huge! Look at the size of it; why in the world would you think that Stephanie and I would need all of this space?"

"It is your home," Karl explained, "but it is also *our* new office. A better office than that awful little school. There's a whole wing set aside for you, completely private. And look up there." Karl pointed to a broad plate glass window near the roof, three stories high.

"That's the attic," he said. "It's a complete house in itself with a kitchen and walk-in bathroom. It has floor-to-ceiling windows on three of its sides looking out over the yard, the gardens, and the river in the rear."

"We're far from the center of town. I'm not sure how safe it would be living here."

"We are well behind the front line, Nicholas. And behind the house is an old lighthouse you might have seen driving in."

Nick nodded. He had seen the top of a pointy structure towering out from above the house.

Karl continued. "It was never a real lighthouse, but had been constructed as an observation deck, looking out over the river and the property. We've fortified the walls and manned it with a sniper and a machine gun nest. In the yard, we'll put up a fence and dig a few trenches—nothing major—but nobody will break through. Now come, follow me." Karl walked toward the front door. Stephanie took off ahead of them, disappearing behind the doorway.

"This is all well and good," Nick said, turning to Karl, "but no more surprises. If you want to do something like this again, you make sure I'm aware. I need to know these sorts of things in advance. Besides, we have more pressing issues to attend to."

"You're referring to Priest Dietrich, I presume?"

"Yes. I don't know how much longer the people in town will put up with the curfew. Their discontent is growing louder by the hour."

For a moment, the ever-present smile vanished from Karl's face, and he turned to Nick with darkness in his eyes. "You should not trouble yourself with matters that do not concern you. Let me worry about controlling the people of Alice, and you go on continuing to be the general. Understood?"

He pressed his body close to Nick, and Nick could feel the heat from his breath. He did not respond.

Then Karl broke away, slapping Nick on the back and issuing a laugh. Nick flinched.

"Come, my boy," Karl said. "Come look at the house my men have tidied up for you. We've put together a welcoming present inside. Bottles of the finest liquor, boxes of cigars, chocolates, and fresh preserves."

Nick stepped toward the door, and Karl stopped. "Go on ahead. I need to speak to Mr. Rothstein for a moment. I'll be right behind you."

Nick stood in the doorway.

Stephanie called to him. "Nick? Nick, come on!"

He turned and vanished inside.

Karl spun to face his lieutenant.

"Mark," he hissed. The red-bearded man snapped to attention.

"Sir?" Mark adjusted the rosewood machete on his belt so his palm rested on the handle.

"Where the hell is Dietrich?"

"The last scout reported Priest Dietrich and his men have left Masterson, but they're still two states over."

Karl's face turned a boiling red.

"Jesus Christ. He was supposed to be here two days ago. What the hell is going on?"

Mark looked grim. "Things … didn't go as planned in Masterson, sir. As you know, the enemy force numbered well over what our intelligence reported. When the Priest arrived things were in bad shape, but he's mustered the men. Masterson is conquered."

"I damn well know that, Mr. Rothstein."

Mark swallowed.

"How many casualties?"

"Ninety or so, I believe."

"You *believe*?" Karl stepped toward Mark, his tall, lean body towering above Mark's wide frame. "You are supposed to *know*—not *believe*."

"Y-yes, sir. The number is ninety-seven, sir. From the last report."

"So when the hell will they arrive?"

"A forwarding detachment of a hundred men left Masterson two days ago and should be arriving in Alice soon—tomorrow night. The rest of his forces will arrive shortly after."

"You know I don't like it when a plan doesn't go exactly as it should."

"Yes, sir. I do."

Karl sighed. He thought of his gray-haired lieutenant general—the Priest. It was hard to envision that the man was allegedly an ordained minister before the war, as his bloodlust was extreme. It was common for Dietrich to cite whole verses of scripture while knee-deep in battle and gore.

Karl's face relaxed. "No bother," he said. "This doesn't change a thing; it's just a slight delay. Never dwell in the past, Mr. Rothstein." Karl Metzger looked straight into his lieutenant's eyes. "Concentrate on how to better the future. The forward detachment of Dietrich's men will be enough to calm the gripes of these fucking peasants in Alice."

Chapter 44
Moonlight

Simon placed a few small logs on the fire now that the night had grown dark. They would keep the flames small, although no one ever ventured into the gardens this late. And even if they did, it would be difficult to see the gathering's location in the center of the cornfield where the stalks had grown near six feet in height.

A circular clearing was set around an old stone well beside a newer waterspout, with plenty of room for the congregation to gather. The group now consisted of Simon Kalispell, Jeremy Winters, Bethany Rose, Frank Morrow, Pat O'Hern, and the most recent additions from the round table, Martin Howard and Chris Lockton.

And there was a new inductee that night, Will Holbrook. Will had been fired that same day—not that it was either surprising or unwelcomed. He had explained to Simon earlier that evening that he had hated working for Nick Byrnes, even before Tom Byrnes was killed. Nick took Will's quiet nature as a sign of his abiding loyalty, but that was not the case. Nick treated him like his personal servant, his slave. He seemed to get a kick out of making Will stand at attention for hours on end, and ordered him to keep his uniform pressed and his boots shined without so much as a spot. No one in Alice put as much emphasis on their uniform or appearance as Nick Byrnes—it was a compulsion. He berated Will for his own personal enjoyment, just to see his authority respected.

Martin Howard was the first politician to join the group after speaking to Frank Morrow. It was no mystery that Martin Howard and Nick Byrnes didn't see eye to eye, so accepting him wasn't a hard decision. Martin later introduced Chris Lockton after listening to Chris's complaints about the curfew and his openly questioning Nick during a speech when Nick announced the disintegration of the round table in favor of a newly elected congregation to take its place.

Nick had stood before the podium, addressing the townspeople, when Chris Lockton spoke up from the front row. "With a transition of leadership comes revision and change, yes, but why must it be revolutionary?"

With this and the noticeable agreement stirring in the crowd, Nick answered in a calm voice, despite the fire in his eyes. "Chris, this is not a revolution—not in the slightest. This is a minor modification, a time to reconstruct and advance our development and progression as a society in whole."

"But we are still only in the infancy of our establishment, and the laws and ways of our town have helped construct our society. A complete reversal in policy and representation at this point could be disastrous."

Nick smiled. "I am only in favor of doing what is best for Alice—for everyone. I will take your words into utmost consideration. If newly elected officials are not what the town wants, I will not force elections to take place. I leave it to you, the people—the heart of Alice—to make the decision. For now, the round table shall remain in place. In the weeks to come, we will hold a general vote to see if the people want a change of representation."

The crowd applauded these words, nodding their approval. Ultimate power—controlling the balance of all matters both big and small—was a tremendous responsibility and one which Nick Byrnes reveled in. The man was a natural; his words could calm the crowd or stir them into frenzy. He was a born leader of the worst kind.

Chris Lockton's words that night had caught the attention of Simon and the rest of the group.

"Today—just hours ago," Simon said as everyone found seating around the fire, "we witnessed Nick Byrnes deliver a speech where he announced the greatest threat yet to us all. He took away our means for survival. He took away our weapons. And he did so under the guise of friendship, security, and the town's overall advancement. What's scarier yet is that the majority of people, our friends, don't see the danger in him stripping us of our power.

They applauded Nick's speech and handed over their weapons without the slightest reservation."

Frank shook his head. "I don't think anyone is being fooled, Simon, or supportive of what Nick is doing. They're scared. Terrified. This witch-hunt for the informant has been a source of constant fear. Margaret Alton—you all know Margaret, right?"

Everyone nodded. Margaret was in charge of the supply house and rationed out clothing, blankets, jackets, socks—everything.

"She's gone missing, taken in for questioning."

Margaret wasn't the first person to go missing. They were disappearing night and day. Vanishing. Gone. Nick stated that the individuals were being brought in for questioning. Nothing more. Just a conversation. Some were helping the cause, he said. Others were being held in suspicion of giving information to the enemy, causing Tom Byrnes's death.

"And we don't have to be reminded about Justin Waters," Frank added.

Everyone grew quiet. Justin was a good friend, especially to Frank and Simon, who had hunted with the young Ranger numerous times.

It had happened only two days ago, during another one of Nick's now-nightly speeches. From the podium, Nick had announced the disintegration of the Rangers.

Justin called out, "You're taking away our security? Our hunting for food? You're dismantling the eyes and the ears of Alice, leaving us vulnerable."

Nick answered with a smile, looking out over the sea of worried faces, "No, no, dismantling the Rangers will not leave us vulnerable. I am only doing it to protect you, to keep you from harm's way. Let Karl's men do the hard and dangerous work. Besides, has anyone gone hungry since they have arrived?"

It was true; Karl and his men had brought a small warehouse's worth of food and liquor into Alice, keeping the townspeople well fed and lubricated.

After Justin's outburst, he had gone missing. The next day it was rumored that Justin was being considered a possible suspect in the death of the beloved Tom Byrnes. Of course, nothing was made official. The townspeople had grown mute as stone. Submissive. Willing to go along with whatever Nick said.

Simon continued, "Nick says it's only logical for us to hand over our weapons. He says it's dangerous and unnecessary for the people to be walking around armed like it's the Wild West. *Civility,* he called it. A mark of a civilized society. But may I remind you, he spoke those words while resting his palm on the handle of that Smith and Wesson revolver of his."

"Not to mention," Frank Morrow cut in, "that if we don't turn in all of our weapons in the next twenty-four hours, we're threatened with punishment."

Following the speech, a group of his wild-eyed Dragoons had circled the townspeople, aided by the Red Hands, collecting weapons from the audience. Any additional firearms were to be brought to Alice's police department within twenty-four hours. Most everyone had their own assortment of personal firearms, not supplied from Alice's armory, and these too were expected to be turned over.

Pat O'Hern was the next to speak, his voice crackling like the fire, "Where the hell is General Driscoll?"

Nobody had an answer; yet, everyone had that same question.

Bethany looked at the ground, then her voice squeaked, "I … umm …" Everyone turned to her. She kicked at the dirt.

"What's that?" Simon asked.

"It's … nothing. I'm sorry." She shook her head.

After a moment, Frank spoke.

"I heard Metzger was a criminal," he said. "Before the war. I heard it from his own men. They say he's a crazy son of a bitch. *Really* crazy. A serial killer or something. They could be bullshitting me, but they came off convincing. His men talk, brag even, about the number of people Karl's killed. They say he's unpredictable, liable to explode at any given moment—even against his own men.

"They told me a story, and honest to God, they were laughing as they told it—about a young soldier out on a hunt who came back empty-handed for weeks. One day Karl just walks up to him during lunch and whacks him over the head with a rock. For no other reason than he was hungry. The boy sat there slumped over in a chair with his brain hanging out. They all turned their heads, just left him there. Karl ordered him removed when the stench and flies got to bothering him."

The group shook their heads, their eyes staring at the fire. Stories like this were becoming common, and it was impossible to determine whether any of them were true. If they were true, then the people of Alice needed the aid of General Driscoll without delay.

The meeting went on until the fire grew low and their supply of wood was depleted. The night felt darker than it actually was among the tall corn stalks.

"Well," Frank Morrow said. "I think we're done for the night. It's well past curfew, so let's get home safely. We'll meet tomorrow, and come up with a plan to reach General Driscoll." He stood and stretched, and the rest of the group followed.

Simon whispered to Bethany, "Is everything all right? What were you going to say earlier?"

"It's …" She swallowed. "I can't," she whispered, her voice trembling. "I can't tell you."

"Are you okay?" He looked at her with concern, and then took her elbow, leading her to the edge of the gathering. "Bethany, what's wrong? You can tell me."

"Oh Christ," she said. "I just can't keep it secret. I can trust you, Simon. I know I can. We've talked a lot since we've met. I've told you things … things about George's death that I've never told a soul."

Simon nodded. "I've told you a lot too. Only a few people know about my parents, and my journey to get here."

"That's why I think if there's anyone in Alice that I can trust, it's you. But please, you have to keep this a secret. Do you promise? I might … be able to help."

"Of course I promise." He looked around, making sure they were out of earshot. The rest of the gathering was still chatting, all except for Will Holbrook, who stood with his hands in his pockets.

"Simon," Bethany whispered. "I'm so sorry I didn't tell you earlier. I'm … I'm General Driscoll's niece."

"Wait—*what*?" Simon's voice rose.

"*Shhh.* I'm sorry I didn't tell you sooner, but I promised my uncle that I wouldn't tell anyone—*anyone*."

Simon considered this, considered the consequences of Bethany being related to General Driscoll. "He's right, your uncle. Don't tell anyone else. We'll talk about this at home."

Simon's head felt like it was buzzing. Jeremy prepared to lead the way out of the cornfield with a flashlight, and everyone gathered single file to follow. As they stood in a line, the shadowy form of Will Holbrook appeared before Simon.

"Simon?" His voice was low.

"Yes?"

"We need to talk."

"What's the matter?"

"Not here. Tonight, when we get out of the field."

Simon could hear Will's voice waver, but his thoughts were on Bethany.

"Will, I don't think tonight is the best time. I mean, we're under curfew. Sneaking back to our apartments is hard enough."

"Fine—take this then." He put something in Simon's palm, pressing it tight until he was sure Simon held it securely.

"What's this?" The device was small and rectangular, easily held in his palm, and Simon felt small buttons on one side.

"Put it in your pocket; *do not lose it*. I can't keep it secret anymore."

"Will, I—"

Jeremy spoke above the crowd. "All right, people. Let's move. Everyone grab the shoulder of the person in front."

Simon held on to Will's shoulder as they walked down the narrow row of corn. Whatever was in his pocket felt like it was growing heavier with each step. Halfway through the cornfield, Simon leaned close to Will's ear. "Okay," he whispered. "Meet back at my apartment."

time to react. The other two he exchanged blows with, but his strength crashed the blade down upon them. One prisoner fell missing the crown of his head, and the last trembled before Steven, too afraid to fend for his life.

Steven had laughed and tossed the man about like a cat plays with a mouse before ending his suffering with the sharp edge of his weapon. He was a god at that moment. The ability to take life was easy. The miscreants left scouring the earth deserved it. They were beneath him. He was the largest, toughest man in the entire world, and the delight he felt testing his strength and being victorious in battle was euphoric.

The red handprint on his chest was now covered over many times with both blood and paint. In Masterson he had killed dozens. Bullets whizzed by him, but he no longer feared death.

Steven Driscoll was an instrument of war.

***

The Red Hands arrived at the gated entrance of Nick Byrnes's mansion. Karl Metzger and his lieutenants greeted them as they marched forward, and the soldiers in the yard cheered at their arrival. They were guided past the rows of trenches being constructed that crisscrossed the yard and the fresh cement foundations for machine gun nests. Park benches from the firehouse were brought to the grassy part of the yard and arranged in a U shape.

Nick stood at the doorway of his house, watching the activity in the yard.
So this is the army I was promised?

The men dropped their gear, and bottles of hard alcohol surfaced all around. The air filled with tobacco smoke, and Mark Rothstein lit a bonfire in the middle of the U-shaped tables.

In tow with the army were a dozen or so prisoners, bloody and bruised and filthy. They were shackled around the wrists and gagged with cloth and thick tape. They were brought to the tennis court on the side of the property and placed inside the tall chain-link fence. Barbed wire had been added to the top earlier that day, and the bottom of the fence had been secured to the ground.

Soldiers produced food of all varieties, dumping everything on the tables, and the cooked and smoked meats were eaten with such relish that they soon disappeared. Trucks began making runs to the kitchen and storeroom, the men removing whole bushels of produce and gigantic slabs of meat. The soldiers fed piles of wood to the bonfire, and whole animal carcasses roasted over the flames.

Bottle after bottle of whiskey, vodka, and tequila appeared and were soon empty, tossed into the raging fire.

A few produced instruments and took up improvised performances while the men became drunker and drunker and the piles of shattered bottles and animal bones grew larger.

At the head of this debauchery sat Karl Metzger, his knees too tall for the chair that he sat upon. Beside him sat Nick Byrnes, slumped with a bottle of bourbon on the table before him. Glass after glass had been poured and swallowed. Sultan and Mark Rothstein joined them at this front table, tearing into the flesh of whatever animal was placed before them. Choice cuts of meat were served on platters, one after the other, along with anything else that could be cooked over fire and eaten.

Some of the newly arrived men presented themselves to Karl Metzger in turn. Karl introduced his men to Nick Byrnes, calling him the general of Alice. Trophies of war were presented to Nick until the floor around the table was piled high with revolvers, bottles of wine, champagne, various knives, an antique Japanese katana, whiskey, cigarettes, cigars, heroin, preserved meats and fruits, pornography, painkillers, cocaine, and marijuana.

Karl put the end of a thick cigar between his teeth and inhaled a plume of smoke.

"Ah," Karl said, "and here he is. Nick, may I introduce you to the fine gentleman who may very well be responsible for us being here today. Steven, come forth, my boy."

Karl waved Steven over, and without the slightest show of emotion, Steven reached down and shook Nick's hand.

Nick looked up through weary eyes at the man towering before him. He flinched as a knuckle cracked in Steven's palm.

"My pleasure," Nick said.

After a moment of silence, Karl spoke up. "The lad's the silent type."

He laughed, and Steven walked off. Karl leaned toward Nick when Steven was out of earshot. "He's the one I told you about."

Nick nodded, his vision hazy with booze.

"I saved the very best for last, my boy," he said, patting Nick on the shoulder. "Mr. Rothstein, Sultan, if you would please?"

The lieutenants stood from the table, Sultan smiling at Nick and saying, "Oh, you gonna like this, my man."

They walked off, and after some time, returned dragging behind two women with their hands tied together about their wrists. Their eyes were large.

"Here we have it," Karl said, his hand presenting the women. "The very best, despite the layer of filth on their skin. We will make them presentable before the night is done."

"Wha-what's this?" Nick slurred, narrowing his eyes to focus on the two women.

"A gift deserving of the king of the manor." Karl raised his voice to address the group. "A gift befitting the king of Alice, the general. My sergeants kept them unspoiled just for you. They are fresh."

Nick stared at the two girls. The blurriness made the fear on their faces difficult to process, and his mind could not decipher the unfolding events. Nick remained quiet, his gaze absent.

"Sultan," Karl said, "would you please have these ladies cleaned properly and then delivered to the general's room?"

"Shaw-thing, my man." Sultan walked away on bouncing toes, dragging the girls behind.

"Oh, and Sultan?" Karl turned to face him. "The general's *private* quarters, if you will."

"You got it."

Nick's private wing of the house had three bedrooms, a kitchen, and a wood-paneled library with deep, rich leather couches, a massive marble fireplace, and a private doorway to the backyard guard tower. A stairway at the end of the long hallway led to the attic-studio apartment, with the floor-to-ceiling windows overlooking the yard and river. This was where Stephanie had set up home and where Nick often resided—although he tended to enjoy nights spent alone, downstairs. Nick looked back at the house as Sultan dragged the two girls away. The attic windows were dark.

"Th-those girls—" Nick began.

Karl interjected, "Nicholas, ease your mind."

He poured a large swallow of bourbon into the tumbler on the table. Nick raised the glass to his lips and drank. Karl poured another.

"Eat and be merry, for you are the king."

Nick swallowed again and grabbed the bottle from the table, taking another swig.

He muttered something to himself, shaking his head back and forth.

"What's that you say?" Karl asked.

"What's … happening … to me? What … have you done?"

Karl snarled. "Only what you wished for, Nicholas. And now, with the army here, we can finally begin."

Chapter 46

Voices

Simon, Jeremy, Bethany, and Will Holbrook sat around the circular kitchen table in silence; the fresh cups of coffee steaming. The voice recorder lay before them with all eyes fixed upon it. They had just listened to the taped conversation twice, and then after, Bethany had explained to the three men that she was General Driscoll's niece.

This was going to be a long night.

Winston made a grumbling noise, curled up on a blanket by the couch, and Simon snapped out of his contemplation.

"How did you get this?"

Will stared at the cup of coffee placed before him, the vapors rising to his face.

"Nick gave me the recorder months ago so I could 'be more organized,' he said. I never used it. I felt stupid hearing my own voice reminding myself that Nick needed something. I was with both Tom and Nick the first time Karl Metzger arrived in Alice. I accompanied them to the checkpoint, where they had a brief talk with the man while I stood off to the side. I didn't hear a word they said, but I could tell that Tom and Nick came back from that meeting with a difference of opinion. Tom looked forlorn. Something wasn't right. Then, the night Tom was killed, Nick sent me to the supply depot to set up a table and chairs for a meeting and to make it private. He knew I wouldn't ask any questions, and I didn't, but I was suspicious. The supply depot is locked twenty-four hours a day, even when Margaret Alton is there, and only a few people have the key. At night, the place would be barren.

"I set up a table and chairs far back, between the rows of supplies. At the last minute—I don't know why—I just put the digital recorder between two boxes, next to the table. Early the next morning, before Margaret Alton arrived for inventory and after the meeting, I took the table and chairs away and put the recorder in my pocket. I should have told someone sooner … but I didn't know what to do or who to tell. Everyone was caught up in the revelry of the executions and accepting Karl Metzger and his men as heroes."

"Will." Bethany put a hand on his shoulder. "What's important is that you're doing the right thing now. There was nothing you could have done. Not by yourself. But now, with friends and numbers, we can help bring this recording to light."

"I was going to play it over the loudspeakers," Will said. "But now, it's too late for that. I should have done it before the executions, before we accepted the Red Hands into Alice with open arms. If I played it out loud now, I'd disappear with all of the rest. The people of Alice are unarmed. We can't face these men alone. This … is all my fault."

Everyone looked at Will, waiting for someone else to reassure him. The boy was young, about the same age as Simon had been when he'd left for British Columbia. That seemed ages ago—another lifetime.

Simon broke the silence. "Will, you can't dwell on ways of altering the past. Remain in the present moment and figure out how your current actions will shape the outcome of the future."

Will nodded.

Jeremy reached to the table for the recorder. "Let's listen to it one more time."

He clicked play.

***

The sound of Nick's boots clacking on the cement floor grew louder, and then it stopped. "Nicholas, my boy," echoed the voice of Karl Metzger. "All hail the chief."

After a moment of silence, Karl spoke to his lieutenant. "Mr. Rothstein, would you give us a moment, please?"

The sound of footfalls as Mark disappeared in the shadows.

"Nick," Karl spoke, "my condolences for your fath—"

"You son of a bitch," Nick said. "How dare you?"

Karl sighed. "I was only being cordial. This is no way to great a guest, Nicholas. No way to talk to your new partner."

"You were early. You were five minutes early. You fucked it all up."

"Hardly." The sound of a chair scraping the ground, and the creaking of the flimsy table. "Don't ... play ... coy ... with me, Nicholas Byrnes."

"We had a plan, an agenda. I followed my instructions to the tee. You—you were five minutes early. You killed him, you killed my father!"

"Calm your voice, Nicholas."

"This is all your fault, all your—"

"Calm your voice!" Karl's words bounced off the walls, and Nick grew quiet. After a moment, Karl spoke in a tranquil manner. "Let me set things straight. *You* had a plan—but it was not *the* plan. Your plan called for me to bomb the recon office right after your father's visit, and then my soldiers were to come in and save the day by flanking Alice's attackers. Then, you thought your father would have no choice but to let my men into Alice, and you would have the army that you always wanted. The people, these peasants, would see you as a leader—their leader. Even your father would say that you were right all along and that he wished he would have listened to your advice sooner."

"But you were five minutes early ..."

"Yes. I was. Your plan was ill-conceived, Sir Nicholas, so I set forth my own agenda to correct the ailments of your directives. With your father in charge, we would never be able to achieve our goals. This is something you know—something you have always known."

"No, it's—"

"You want power, and that's what I've given you. The people of Alice are going to accept you with open arms. Accept you as the general. The course of events that I have put into motion will ensure that our plan succeeds. We will control the oil, capture the gasoline supply line, and eventually own the refineries. I want Hightown on a silver platter. Resources are the new currency, and we—you and me, Nicholas—can have it all. We have enough water to last a lifetime, and soon, all of the fuel we could burn. We will own the land. Can't you just picture it? We will *own this world*. Only, we would never have succeed with your father still alive."

"You didn't have to kill him ... we could have made him step down."

"Correction, Nicholas. I *did* have to kill him. What did you expect? Do you think the peasants in this shithole town would have accepted us attacking Zone Red with him still alive? No. Such things are done with the use of force. Don't lie to yourself. You want Zone Red just as much as I do, maybe even more so. You hate General Driscoll and his elitist soldiers. The world is going to be yours, Nicholas—*ours*. You've known all along what the cost was going to be." The table creaked again. "You just didn't have the gall to kill your father yourself."

"*My father ...* " There was anger in Nick's voice, but he didn't say anything further.

After a pause, Nick continued. "Who is it that we're executing tomorrow? Who are those people you brought in?"

"They're of no consequence to you."

"They *are* of consequence to me. This is my town, Karl. Don't for a second forget that."

Karl lightened his voice and spoke in an amused manner. "Of course, Sir General. Please, let me explain. The men are nothing more than prisoners we've captured from previous campaigns. Awful human beings who deserve the punishment they are going to receive."

"And they're admitting that they planned the attack themselves—how the hell did you manage that?"

"I offered them fruitful promises," Karl answered. "They were made to think that Alice was much smaller in size than it is and that freedom could be achieved if their valor was displayed on the battlefield. We accept many of our conquered foes among our ranks. Any whom we deem as a potential threat we simply kill or keep around to serve us otherwise—the men do need their playthings, you know. We told these derelicts that if they went along with the plan, put up with a beating, and admitted their guilt, they would be whisked back to safety and either promoted to the brotherhood of the Red Hands or given the opportunity to leave as free men. Many of my best soldiers earned their ranks in similar fashion."

"But you're going to kill them?"

"Correction. *We're* going to kill them. Not all of my men get promoted in this method, only some. Do not pity these miscreants. They are slime. They are filth. They have fought against and killed many of my men ... your men, now."

"What if they don't go along with the plan? What if they don't confess?"

"What does it matter?" Karl's voice sounded whimsical. "Just tell the people that they offered their full confession. Case closed."

Nick sighed and then mumbled, almost to himself, "In the long run, I know in my heart that this will be in Alice's best interest. I know that I can lead this town to greatness." He sighed again. "Alice will be the capital of the world one day; I'm sure of it. I suppose it's unavoidable to dirty one's hands in order to achieve such progress."

"Good then," Karl said. "It warms my heart to hear you speak so candidly. We will become good friends, Sir Nicholas, I assure you. We will accomplish great things together."

"I can never forgive you for killing my father … but …" His voice lowered. "I see why you did what you had to do. But listen, no more secrets. If we're going to make this work—you and me—no changes in plan. You tell me everything."

"Yes, General Byrnes." A chair scraped against the floor. "No more secrets, I promise. Shake on it." There was a muffled noise and then the sound of footfalls falling over the cement floor.

***

Jeremy turned off the recorder.

Simon spoke.

"In light of what we've just heard, we know that our mistrust in Karl and his men is legitimate. Our little meetings in the garden are too feeble an attempt to stop the momentum that the Red Hands and Nick have begun. However, it may still be feasible to change the course of events. The army of the Red Hands and Nick's Dragoons combined don't outnumber Zone Red's soldiers. Karl and Nick would be insane to attack without a much larger army."

Will shook his head, and his voice choked out, "There're more coming … many more. An army's worth."

Everyone looked at Will, and Jeremy spoke. "How many?"

"I don't know. I've heard them talking, Nick and Karl. The Red Hands have an army, several hundred, maybe thousands, I don't know. They're locusts, these guys. They attack and kill and take everything they can before moving on to the next target. Their plan was to gain our trust and destroy

Alice from the inside, quickly, and then attack Zone Red with an overwhelming and unexpected force. They're aware that General Driscoll has spies among them and knows their numbers here in Alice, but the general knows nothing of the army that's set to arrive, and would never suspect a horde of men flooding his gates. If caught off guard, Zone Red couldn't hold out, even if they have superior soldiers."

"Oh, Christ," Bethany said, her fingers covering her mouth.

Jeremy shook his head. "Zone Red wouldn't be fast enough to mobilize the firepower to stop a force that size if they're caught unaware. They have some tanks and artillery, but that's about it."

Simon stared straight ahead, his mind whirling. He tried to stop and focus his breath.

What do we do … what do we do?

Then ideas began piecing together in his head like a jigsaw puzzle forming a vast picture of the future. He took a deep breath and said, "I have an idea."

Everyone turned to him.

"This doesn't leave the room."

He looked about, and everyone nodded. Jeremy said, "Nothing we've discussed leaves the room."

"I know how Zone Red can better arm itself and prepare for an attack. I stumbled on a place a long time ago along my journey to Alice. A field deep in the woods full of tanks, helicopters, and a warehouse stocked with ammunition. Everything was new, still in boxes. Dozens of vehicles. The army guarding it had died of the disease."

Jeremy's eyes opened wide. This was the first Simon had ever mentioned this.

"Where?"

"In a park—Livingston Park, in a town named Sullivan. It's not far, about halfway between here and Zone Red and a bit to the west. I'll show you on a map."

"Do you think it's still there?"

Simon shrugged. "I don't know. But it hadn't been touched in a long while when I was there. All you would need is fuel and trained soldiers to operate the vehicles, and that's something Zone Red has plenty of."

Bethany spoke up. "We have to get out of here. If Karl's army is expected any time, we have to warn Uncle Al—I mean, General Driscoll—now. We can't wait any longer."

"No, we can't," Jeremy agreed. "You, Bethany, have to leave right away. You have friends arriving from Zone Red on tomorrow's supply run, right?"

Bethany nodded.

"Then you're leaving with them, and you're taking the recording with you."

Will shook his head. "That's too risky. They're checking everyone coming in and out of the border for contraband. We can't risk letting both the recorder and the general's niece fall into the enemy's hands at the same time."

"Fine, then," Jeremy continued. "We'll split Bethany and the recorder up. Simon can sneak past the front line without a problem, can't you, Simon? If anybody can, it would be you."

"Well … yes, I'm sure I could."

"Then this is what we're going to do. Bethany, you're leaving on tomorrow's supply run. You've gone across the lines dozens of times; is there a safe way to get you out?"

Bethany thought it over and answered. "I think I could do it. I could forge a letter saying that I'm assigned to go on the next trade run. I know the exact wording on the paperwork, and it's all handwritten. Once I'm there and unloading boxes, I'll talk to my old coworkers from Zone Red and explain the urgency of the situation. I still have my Zone Red credentials, so I'll blend in when they're exiting and leave with them. It would be just like any other supply run."

"That's not a bad plan, but it's still risky," Jeremy said. "I trust your judgment on how to proceed."

Bethany nodded.

"Tomorrow night," Jeremy continued, "Simon will sneak over the front line with the voice recorder. You, Beth, have to speak to your uncle as soon as you get to Zone Red so they expect Simon's arrival. When General Driscoll hears the recording, he'll have no option but to act fast. In the meantime, Will and I will try our best to rally the people, get our hands on some weapons, and get the children and elderly into hiding."

Everyone was silent. It wasn't a bad plan. It was the best plan they would come up with at that late hour. Simon had no doubt that he could sneak past the guards and out of town at night.

"All right," Simon said. "Jeremy, you'll have to watch Winston while I'm gone." He sighed. "All I ever wanted was to make it home safe."

"You will." Bethany reached out and rubbed the top of Simon's hand. "You will, Simon. I'm sure of it. But your journey isn't over yet."

Chapter 47

Late Hours

"How can nobody know anything?" Carolanne was frustrated.

"I'm sure someone knows something, but they ain't talking."

"Did you talk to Pat O'Hern?"

"Pat wasn't there. There was nobody at the trade ground I recognized."

Carolanne huffed and pulled the covers up to her chin.

"Do you think it's still safe?" she asked.

"I don't know. I asked all around Hightown, and everyone's tight-lipped."

"The soldiers probably aren't allowed to give details."

"Probably not."

"So, what do we do? Do we leave tomorrow?"

"Look, this is what we do know: General Byrnes was killed, his son took power, and he's hired some outside mercenaries. Aside from that, we don't know much."

"The timing of it all just seems strange."

"I reckon it's plenty strange. With Tom's death, the town is going through a change in policy. Maybe it's nothing to get riled over."

Brian was tired. For over an hour they had been lying in bed, discussing whether or not to leave with the convoy team in the morning as planned. His eyes were now fully adjusted to the dark room. Carolanne had heard rumors at the hospital from doctors and nurses that daily life in Alice was getting rough. They said that Alice was on the verge of a revolution. But none of the soldiers had uttered a word, and Uncle Al had been too busy to talk.

Brian yawned, and then said, "The revolution stuff could all be hearsay.

People like to talk. Besides, Bethany is waiting for us. She's counting on us to join her, and we've given her our word."

Carolanne seemed to think this over.

"Yeah … I guess so."

Brian heard the trepidation in her voice. "If you're nervous … maybe we should wait. If you think it could be dangerous, maybe we should ask around a bit more. We could try sending word down to Beth—"

His words were cut short by a booming knock from the front door. Carolanne jumped and instinctively clung to his side.

"Who is that?" she asked.

"Beats the hell out of me."

Brian swung his legs off the side of the bed. The knock repeated.

"All right, all right. I hear ya."

"Brian—"

"I'll be right back."

Brian took his robe from the door hook and was tying it around his waist as he looked through the peephole on the front door. He saw the face of a soldier staring back at him.

Brian opened the door.

"Brian Rhodes, sir?" the soldier asked.

"Yes?" A car sat idling in the road behind the soldier.

"Sir, I've been given orders to escort you to General Driscoll."

"What, *now*?" He looked again at the car.

Carolanne came out from the bedroom, tying her robe around her waist.

"Brian, who is it?"

"I think, um," he called back to her, "General Driscoll needs me."

"Actually," the soldier cut in, "I've been ordered to escort both you and a Carolanne Rhodes to headquarters. Ma'am," he bowed slightly to Carolanne.

"Why? What's the matter?" Carolanne stroked the smooth side of her ring at hearing her new last name.

"Ma'am." The soldier took a breath and relaxed his tone, seeming to remember that these were civilians he was talking to. "I'm sorry to have woken you both. My name is Sergeant Irons. The general asked me to escort you to headquarters. I'm one of his personal guards."

Brian recognized the man.

"Okay … okay." Brian was starting to wake up. "Do you know what this is about?"

"Sir," Sergeant Irons said, "all he said was that you're needed urgently and that he has reason to believe a certain Bethany Rose might be in harm's way. I don't know if that means anything to you, but he didn't elaborate."

Brian turned in a hurry. "Let me get some clothes on."

Chapter 48

Askew

Will Holbrook left after several hours of planning, and Bethany sat at the table, hunched over in concentration, forging the paperwork she would need in only a few hours. When she was done and a dozen sheets of paper lay in a crumbled heap, she showed Simon and Jeremy the final product. They passed the papers back and forth.

"This is good," Jeremy said, squinting at the writing. "I wouldn't know that this is a forgery."

They then went through their belongings together, counting weapons and ammunition. They had ample firepower to arm themselves, and Jeremy had several thin, police-style bulletproof vests, enough for each of them. They decided that it was best, from here on out, to be prepared for the worst. Since firearms were outlawed, they would carry concealed pistols only.

The empty coffee cups on the table were cold, and the first rays of sunlight were fast approaching. Jeremy stood from a chair in the living room, where they had circled around the displayed arsenal. "We need to call it quits," he said. "There are a few hours left until morning, so I suggest we try and shut our eyes."

Simon and Bethany nodded from the couch, their eyelids heavy.

"I'll see you in the morning." Jeremy shook his head, walking toward his room. "This has been a hell of a night."

He closed the door behind him, and all at once the apartment became eerily quiet.

"I'm so tired I'm starting to tremble," Bethany said, her legs curled up to her chest under a throw blanket.

Simon sat next to her on the couch, his head reclined and his eyes puffy slits.

"I know what you mean. We should go to bed."

"I don't think I can sleep."

"Yeah … I hear you."

Winston slept curled in a ball on the rug by Simon's feet, his breathing the only noise in the room. Then Simon heard a gentle humming sound.

"Beth?" He turned to her. "You okay?"

She was crying.

"I'm just tired."

Simon reached over and rubbed her arm. Bethany wiped her eyes and sat up on the couch. "I'm fine. I'm fine."

"Hey, I'm scared too. Terrified."

Bethany shook her head. "I'm not scared …."

Simon put his arm around her shoulder, and she accepted, resting her head on his chest and curling back up.

"I have complete faith in you," he said. "You're going to wake up tomorrow and do what has to be done. You're going to be fine."

Bethany nodded against Simon's shoulder, and he felt the warmth of her tears. *Jesus,* he thought. *We have to succeed.* And then his next thought was, *Her hair smells incredible. My God …*

Bethany nodded. "You're a good person, Simon. You've been really good to me." Her eyes were shut, and she didn't move from where she sat curled against his body. Simon stretched his legs out on the couch beside her and pulled the throw blanket over their bodies. They lay curled together in the dark room, holding each other, listening to Winston's deep breathing.

Feeling the heat from Bethany's body pressed against his own was making Simon's heart pick up speed. They had shared so much together within a short period of time. A desire to protect her—to hold her forever on that couch and make the moment eternal—washed over him and calmed his mind.

Simon thought he would never fall asleep.

Then, his eyes snapped open with the morning rays of sunlight shining through the windows. Some time had passed. Winston's face was inches from his own, panting hot breath. His tail wagged in wide sways. Simon reached out and ruffled the dog's head.

Winston backed away and stretched his back.

Simon looked at the top of Bethany's head, the side of her face pressed against his chest. He tried not to move, to let her sleep, but then she said, "I'm awake."

Simon pulled the blanket up to her chin. "Try to sleep a little longer. It's early."

"No, I'm up." She sat up on the couch, rubbing her swollen eyes.

Winston was standing by the door, whining a low whimper.

"I have to take him out." Simon stood and stretched. "It won't take long."

"I'll make some coffee."

Simon took Winston outside, and the dog promptly did his morning routine in a small field across from the barracks. It was nice this time of the morning, with the dew dissolving in pale drifts over the grass. A slight chill remained in the air, but by all accounts, Simon could tell that the day was going to heat up fast.

"Come here, boy. Come here." Simon held out the end of a thick stick, and Winston came sprinting over with his tongue bouncing out of his mouth.

He still has so much energy, Simon thought. *He still acts like a puppy.*

Simon tried not to think about Winston's age, but it was always on his mind.

When Winston neared the stick, Simon grabbed him by his scruff and pulled him in close, rubbing him all over his chest and back. "You're a good boy, buddy. Aren't you? You're a good boy. I love you so much." He buried his face in Winston's fur, smelling the deep scent of the earth that his dog seemed to carry. Winston's tail and tongue were going crazy. Simon let him go and threw the stick.

He watched his dog sprint across the field, yet his mind kept wandering back to the previous night and the feeling of holding Bethany tight.

Keep your mind sharp, Simon, he told himself. *There's a lot to do today. Keep your mind sharp.*

About twenty minutes later, Winston was walking over the grass instead of running, his morning reserve of energy used up.

"Come on, let's get something to eat."

Back inside, Jeremy was awake, standing in the kitchen with Bethany. Both of them were bleary-eyed.

"The convoy will be here in two hours," Jeremy said, blowing back the steam from his coffee.

Bethany nodded. She knew it was time to go, but the thought of leaving was terrifying.

"I'm going to get dressed," she said, walking to the bedroom.

Jeremy called after her, "Remember to put on the vest."

"I will," she called back.

Simon turned to Jeremy. "My stomach is in knots."

"Mine too."

"I … what if there's a problem when I sneak past the guards?"

"There won't be. You can't think like that. If anyone can sneak over the line, it's you."

"Yeah, but—"

"I know what you're afraid of." Jeremy looked to the pistols and rifles laid out on the living room floor. "You don't want to use any of them—but if it comes down to it, you have to."

"I don't know." Simon shook his head. "I just don't know."

"If not for yourself, then for Winston, Bethany—for everyone in Alice. Even me."

By the window, Winston's head shot up rigid, and his fur stood on end. Simon saw this and listened to the sounds in the distance.

Jeremy looked at him with concern. "What is it?"

"Shhh—listen." They stood motionless. Then, in the distance, the slight rumble of an engine could be heard. They went to the window. They watched as two Jeeps drove toward the barracks.

"What do you think's going on?" Simon asked.

Jeremy shrugged.

The Jeeps drove closer. Then they slowed in front of the door to their apartment and came to a full stop. Jeremy recoiled.

"Come on; get dressed." Jeremy pulled Simon from the window, and they rushed to secure the white, police-style bulletproof vests around their chests and button up their shirts. Simon grabbed the voice recorder and slipped it into an open slit he'd made in the hem of his windbreaker the night before. There was no time to sew it up as planned.

Someone was knocking on the door while Jeremy was shoving the assortment of weapons under the couch. He tossed Simon his Colt .45 and grabbed a pistol for himself. Winston was barking, and Bethany came out from the bedroom with large eyes. Her shaking hands touched her lips.

"Who is it?" she asked.

"I don't know," Simon whispered. "But we have to answer."

The knocks echoed loud, sending Winston into a fit of barking.

"Winston, quiet!" Simon commanded. Winston disobeyed. Simon opened the door, holding Winston back with his leg.

"Hi," he managed to say. "Can I help you?"

The bearded face of Mark Rothstein smiled back at him.

Chapter 49

Delirium Tremens

Nick's eyes opened into slits.

He blinked repeatedly, hoping to produce some moisture between his raw eyelids that rubbed against his eyeballs like sandpaper. He needed water, but the slightest movement of his body caused waves of nausea and pangs of intense pain in his forehead.

After some initial uncertainty, Nick knew he was in his bedroom downstairs. He felt silk sheets plastered against his clammy skin and a mattress under his body. He had made it to bed the night before.

Thank God.

Slowly, he moved and flexed his feet and hands. His right hand stuck to the sheet at first before coming away with a sting of pain. He brought his palm before his eyes, squinting to focus on blood-covered fingers.

What did I do last night?

Nick racked his brain. Slight fragments of memory returned to him, but the last thing he recalled was sitting at the table outside as the bonfire grew large. The wood for the fire had run out, and the men commenced to burn anything that would catch fire. Chairs, tables, desks—anything made out of wood—were brought out from the house and thrown on top of the blazing inferno, for no other reason than to watch things burn.

That was Nick's last memory.

Now he was in bed, and his head was swimming. He pushed himself up to his elbows, examining the room. It looked as though a hurricane had passed through. A line of his clothing extended to the doorway—his shirts, holster, belt, and one boot. His other boot was still on and so were his pants, inside out and around the one ankle. Glass shards were everywhere from where he had apparently thrown and smashed the bottle of bourbon. The furniture was toppled over, the lamps on the bedside tables were destroyed, and bloody handprints smeared the walls. In the corner were the two women Karl had sent to his room, stripped to their underwear with their hands tied at their wrists around the radiator. When they saw Nick stir, they began to tremble.

He couldn't deal with this right now.

The pangs of pain in his head were overwhelming, and the threat of vomiting was real.

He got out of bed and wobbled to the bathroom, where he drank mouthful after mouthful of water from the faucet. It did not sit well, and within moments he was kneeling at the toilet making an awful mess.

After several minutes, he stood and took only a few slow sips of water. His throat was burning something fierce, and his palm was shaking as the tap water pooled inside. He stood and waited to see if the water would stay down. When it seemed it would, he stumbled back out with his palm pressed to his forehead, as if he needed to hold his brain still.

In the bedroom, he tried not to look at the two women tied in the corner, who had averted their eyes. He must have put on a spectacular show last night.

Nick gathered his clothing, his head throbbing each time he leaned over to pick something up, and swung his holster over a shoulder. A few steps out from the doorway, he stopped and tried to regain his mind. He put his clothing on the ground, removed a Buck knife from his holster belt, and returned to the bedroom.

The women shrieked as he returned, naked down to his underwear, his bloody hand holding a shimmering blade. In a swift motion, he cut their bindings. He turned to leave and did not look back, leaving the bewildered girls behind.

Nick's wing of the house was cut off from the other side by a solid mahogany door, and he was alone as he walked down the curving hallway. The pathway made it appear that the hallway went on forever in a circular manner. When he reached the end, he stopped before the doorway leading to the attic apartment

Luckily, his keys were still jingling in the pocket of the pants he carried. He unlocked the door, but it only opened a quarter of an inch.

"Shit," he muttered and started banging on the door. "Steph, it's me. Open up."

A moment later, he heard her walking down the steps.

"Who is it?"

"It's me, Steph." *Hurry up, goddamn it.*

She unlocked the padlock Nick had forgotten he'd installed for her on the inside.

"Nick!" Her eyes went large. "Oh, my God, what happened to you? Are you all right?"

She grabbed at his hand, looking at the dried blood. He pulled himself away.

"I'm fine." He brushed past her up the steps. "Rough night is all."

"I'm sure. I saw the whole thing from the window." She followed behind him, tying her purple robe around her waist as she stepped into the open space of the apartment. He stopped only a few steps in, the upstairs being one large and open room, with only the bathroom and a closet behind closed doors. The sun shone bright through the floor-to-ceiling windows that overlooked the yard and river.

A feeling of guilt struck him, as if he might have done something shameful the previous night that he couldn't remember.

"My head is spinning. Do we have any aspirin?"

"Let me take a look at your hand."

"Aspirin first, please."

Stephanie sat him in the bathroom and gave him three aspirins and a glass of water.

"Jesus," she said, examining his palm. "How did you do this?"

Nick studied the deep horizontal slash. The water churned inside his stomach, and he thought he was going to vomit again. "A broken bottle. It was an accident." The wound was gaping, probably in need of stitches. He stared into the flap of skin covered in dried blood.

"Oh, God, I'm going to be sick." Nick fell on his knees before the toilet, heaving up the water and the bitter aspirin.

Stephanie rubbed his shoulders as he gagged on bile.

"I'm dying," he muttered.

"You're not dying," she told him, and turned to start up the shower.

***

Nick felt better, but his whole body was still trembling. At least the shower helped calm the pounding in his head, and now, clean and dressed, he was able to drink a full glass of water and sip at a bowl of soup. The warm broth both stung and soothed his raw throat.

There was a knock at the door.

He looked at Stephanie, not sure he could deal with talking to anyone right now.

"I'm not dressed," she told him.

You're never dressed, he wanted to say, but he got up from the table. Ever since they'd moved into the mansion, all Stephanie bothered wearing was her purple silk robe and pajamas.

The banging increased as Nick got to the landing.

"I'm coming; I'm coming," he said.

He unlocked the padlock and swung the door open.

Karl stood alone, smiling his toothy grin. "Ah, good morning, Sir General." His voice boomed.

"Karl, what's the matter?" Nick was shocked at Karl's clear eyes, as if the man had not touched a sip of alcohol last night, although he remembered Karl going drink-for-drink with him.

"We've had a busy morning," he said. "Come now. Time is of the essence."

Chapter 50
The Pit

"Simon Kalispell, I presume?" Mark Rothstein's words were as gruff as his weathered face.

"Yes. Mr. Rothstein, right? Can I help you?"

Two armed men stood behind Mark Rothstein, and several more were standing by the Jeeps.

"Call me Mark. Yes, as a matter of fact, you can help me. We require your assistance. Both you and Jeremy Winters."

"What's the matter?"

"Please, it's best if you come with us." Mark stared at Simon, unflinching. In their proximity, Simon could see old and faded tattoos on most of Mark's exposed skin, his knuckles, and jutting out from under his shirt collar.

At the waiting cars, Simon saw the other lieutenant, Sultan, leaning against the Jeep with his arms crossed, looking up at the sun with a pleasant grin.

Simon did not move from the doorway.

"There's been an incident," Mark went on, "outside of town. We've heard that you're the best scout in all of Alice, and Jeremy knows the lay of the land outside the gates better than anyone. We need your expertise. Is there a problem?"

Simon looked to Jeremy.

"No," Jeremy said. "Of course. We just have to put our shoes on."

"Good." Mark stepped inside the apartment. "And who is this?" He reached down to rub Winston's head.

"Winston."

"What a good-looking boy."

Winston's tail was wagging, his side leaning into Mark's leg.

"An old boy, huh?"

"He's got a few years on him. And a few still ahead." Simon finished lacing his boots and walked over to Bethany.

"Okay, be back soon." There were a million words that he wanted to say, but he couldn't say a thing, and neither could she. The looks on their faces as they made eye contact said it all. Bethany was on the verge of tears as Simon gave her a hug. He looked straight into her eyes.

"I hope you have a great day," he said and turned.

Simon knew that the convoy was expected soon. If she could get there, if he could break free … the plan might still work.

"We'll have the boys home in no time," Mark told Bethany. "I assure you." He smiled wide behind his beard.

Bethany offered a meager smile in return.

Simon grabbed his windbreaker, and the men stepped outside.

"Right this way." Mark led them to the rear Jeep, then walked to the lead car. Simon and Jeremy exchanged quick glances. Jeremy's face was pale.

Sultan stood, smiling. "You doing us a big favor, you know." He held the back door open for them to get in. A soldier sat beside them, and Sultan went to the front seat.

They drove north to Ridgeline Road, and then followed the road east.

Sultan spoke without turning around. "What you all do before this— before the war?"

Simon spoke first. "I was a student."

Jeremy answered. "I was a soldier. Still am a soldier."

"Ah, an army man," Sultan said, amused by something. "Ha! Be all you can be, or some shit, right?"

Jeremy didn't respond. Simon focused on the feeling of his pistols tucked in his pants.

"Me, I always been in sales, man. That was my shit, back in the day. Coke mostly, but pills too. Some heroin here and there, but that shit is nasty."

"What did Karl do before all this?" Simon asked.

"Karl?" Sultan laughed. "He done what he's always done—what he's doing now." Sultan seemed to dismiss his own thoughts. "Who knows? A gangster maybe, or some shit like that. Probably in jail when it all went down. That's what I heard anyway. But you can't always trust the beats you hears on the streets. Ha!"

Simon felt sweat droplets form on his face.

The Jeeps drove past the guard post and into the uninhabited and unprotected areas outside of Zone Blue.

Jeremy asked, "What exactly do you need us to do?"

"Hold on," Sultan said. "We're almost there."

They headed farther north and parked on the side of the road adjacent to a large open field beside three other Jeeps, and a small crowd of soldiers.

"Here we go," Sultan said, as their car came to a stop. He got out from the front seat and opened the back door for Simon and Jeremy.

Outside, Simon made eye contact with Martin Howard, Frank Morrow, and Chris Lockton, who were standing in the field by the side of the road. There were a dozen well-armed Red Hands and Dragoons forming a semicircle around them. Simon swallowed. Martin was sweating and his eyes looked glazed over. No one spoke.

Mark Rothstein walked over from his parked Jeep. "Now that we're all gathered together, let's get this show on the road."

The soldiers began walking forward, forcing everyone to move.

Martin spoke. "Where are we going?"

"My man," Sultan said. "Why you so worried? Look right up there." He pointed in the near distance where they could see a few Red Hands standing about. "This will all be over lickety-split."

Simon felt his pistol rubbing against his skin as he debated all of the possible scenarios that could unfold.

Should I turn and shoot Mark and Sultan? Make a run for it?

They would kill him no more than a few steps out. It was pointless. They were outnumbered and outgunned.

Mark Rothstein spoke from behind them, "So, here we are, gentlemen, at a crossroads of your own creation."

Martin Howard looked like he might throw up.

"We've heard some troubling news recently," Mark went on. "We heard that a group of citizens were conducting private meetings. At first we weren't sure what the group was meeting about, but we had some assumptions. As it turns out, our beliefs were correct. Isn't that right, Mr. Lockton?"

Chris Lockton cleared his throat. "As a matter of fact … yes. The group in question was involved in treason of the highest order."

Everyone turned to Chris.

"You!" Martin looked incredulous. "Chris—you son of a bitch!"

Chris ducked to the side behind several of the Red Hands, as Martin leaped toward him.

"How could you, Chris? After all this time together! You've been working with them all along, haven't you? You double-crossing sack of sh—"

Martin's words were cut short by a swift fist in his stomach from one of the Red Hands. He doubled over, but was grabbed by his shoulders and set back up on his feet. In the confusion, Simon exchanged glances with Jeremy.

It's now or never.

"I wouldn't do that if I were you, gentlemen," Mark Rothstein said.

Simon turned to see Mark's dark eyes glaring at him. Several of the guards had their rifles aimed point-blank at the square of his back.

"We wanted you to pull them out back in town," Mark said, "to make a public example of what we do to aggressors. Hand them over. Slowly."

Jeremy looked at the soldiers and then at Simon. "Do as he says."

They lifted their jackets and let the soldiers take the pistols tucked into their pants. Right after, a fist struck Jeremy hard in the face. Blood poured out of his nose, but he did not fall.

"Tough one we got here," the soldier said, shaking his hand. He rubbed his knuckles and stepped forward to continue the beating, but Sultan put a hand on his shoulder.

"No point, man," he said. "Just wait."

They pushed the group onward toward the soldiers in the field, who, they could now see, were leaning on shovels and smoking cigarettes. One was dangling a baseball bat loosely at his knees.

Mark continued. "The people of Alice will rejoice at us having found the party responsible for supplying our enemy with information, causing the death of their beloved leader, Tom Byrnes."

Frank Morrow shook his head. "You sons of bitches. You'll all get yours. Every single last one of you."

"That is," Mark Rothstein said, "if we decide to tell them. We now have enough of our men in Alice to no longer care what you peasants think. And without their leaders, the people will fall."

Jeremy spoke. "They'll fight back, you know. They'll fight you tooth and nail. You might win in the end, but they'll rip the hearts out of half of you."

"Oh, Mr. Winters … I do not think so. We will soon be implementing our new town-wide security system. When the foghorn blares and an attack is imminent, the people of Alice will be made to gather in the gymnasium at Alice Elementary, which will act as a bomb shelter. The memory of your fearless leader being blown to pieces in a bombing is still fresh in everyone's mind. When that happens, and the people are huddled together in that dark, cavernous room, do you know what we'll do? I'll give you a hint. What's the best course of action to take when you find your foes hiding in a cave? Why, you simply seal the entrance and walk away. Let the course of events unfold as they will. The windows and back doors have been barricaded. Saves ammunition, that way. When the Priest gets back to town we'll use some gas on them, if he has enough left. Ease their suffering."

"You're a sick bastard, you know that?" Jeremy said.

The group stopped before a pit, over ten feet wide. They were prodded forward until they were only a foot away from the ledge. The stench and the flies were awful. The bloated and decomposing bodies of Alice's missing citizens lay before them in a mass grave, arms and legs in dramatic poses, overcome by rigor mortis.

Frank shook his head. "You'll never get away with this. You'll rot in hell—" A fist struck the back of his head, and Frank fell to his knees, his hands flailing to his side to stop him from falling face-first into the grave. A slight landfall of dirt cascaded into the open hole.

Then the soldiers kicked at all of their knees until the whole group was kneeling, skirting the edge of the wretched pit that opened like the doorway to damnation. Simon felt faint from the stench and the dozens of flies that were tickling his skin. Martin Howard was at the head of the line, his body trembling, and when Mark Rothstein walked up behind him, Martin began to vomit. Mark gripped the rosewood handle of his machete and unsheathed the cruel blade, gleaming in the sunlight.

"All right, Martin. So much for your little solar project, huh? Any last words?"

337

Simon was kneeling beside Martin and saw the man's eyes flutter on the brink of passing out. "Fuck them, Martin," Simon said in a hiss. "Fuck them all."

He said it louder. "Fuck you all!" He heard laughter from some of the soldiers and Sultan's chuckles the loudest. He half-turned to see Mark Rothstein from the corner of his eye.

"Keep your chin up high, Martin."

Martin turned, facing Simon with tears rolling down the sides of his cheeks, and he opened his mouth to speak.

"Oh, God—" he let out, as Mark Rothstein brought the blade down in a swift motion. The blade passed clean, cutting halfway through Martin's neck. A hot mist sprayed over Simon and up into Mark Rothstein's unflinching face.

Before Martin Howard could die, Mark kicked him square in the back with the heel of his boot, throwing the man forward to bleed out amongst the dead.

Mark wiped the blood off his face with his palm and licked his lips. Simon was next in line.

A soldier called out, "Let me try my pistol."

It was the man dangling the battered baseball bat in his hand. The soldier patted the handle of the gleaming revolver strapped over his chest.

Mark shook his head. "Save your bullets. Now, Mr. Kalispell," he continued. "What did you say the name of your dog was?"

Simon looked straight ahead. He could feel the recorder tucked in the liner of his jacket against his stomach.

"Don't matter." Mark shrugged. "I'll find a name that suits him."

Simon felt his vision throb with the pounding of his heart. The guard leaning on a shovel flicked his cigarette butt into the pit and onto Martin's back, where it smoldered.

Mark continued. "Your friend, Will Holbrook told us all sorts of things this morning, only an hour or so ago. We can be very persuasive when we want to be. Especially when we have a person strapped to a gurney. He screamed out Bethany's name during a fascinating routine involving a razor blade and his fingernails. Bethany is someone important, we gather. Will seemed to have regretted having said anything at all, because he grew quiet—

even under the most excruciating of circumstances.

"The boy was strong, I'll give him that, but I'm afraid he reached the end of his rope. There's only so much blood a man can lose. We would have offered you the same treatment if we thought it might have done any good. But you don't seem the type to crack under interrogation. So, I'll skip the foreplay and give you one last chance to tell me who she is, redeem yourself."

Mark leaned in close, seeing the stony redness in Simon's face as he muttered, "If you so much as touch her … I swear to God … you have no idea what you're unleashing."

"Oh, is that so?" Mark looked to Sultan, and they both let out a laugh. "I'm quaking in my boots. Just shivering. Will told us all sort of things, even about you, Mr. Kalispell, and your journey. When this is all over and Hightown is ours, we'll have you to thank."

Me to thank?

Mark Rothstein raised the blade of his rosewood machete, still wet with Martin's blood. "Stand back boys, this one's ripe to pop."

The events that followed were difficult for Simon to comprehend. His pulse was beating rapidly and his vision was a blur. He was about to turn, jump, beat at the face of Mark Rothstein, when shots rang out in the distance.

He flinched low.

There was a popping sound, followed by more, and then something extraordinarily heavy whacked into his chest. His body flew backward, sending his back crashing against Mark Rothstein's shins. The air was forced out of Simon's lungs, and he tried to gasp. The group of Red Hands and Dragoons began shouting, jumping to the ground, and firing their weapons. Mark kicked Simon forward and shouted to the Dragoons beside him.

Simon saw a flash and felt a jolt of pain. All turned to black as he fell face-first into the open grave.

Chapter 51

Migration

There was commotion on Brian and Carolanne's journey when the supply column was forced to halt. Carolanne looked at Brian with large eyes.

"I'm sure everything's fine," he told her, unable to see anything in the rear of the covered supply truck.

They held hands, and soon the column began moving again toward Alice. Brian peeked out from the cloth door covering the back of the truck, and saw the forwarding guards were remaining behind. Before long, they were safely behind Alice's front line, and parking on the supply grounds.

"Something's strange here, right?" Carolanne asked, as they jumped down from the back of the truck.

"Reckon so."

Brian looked at the soldiers walking around the blacktop—men with red handprints painted over their hearts. Other soldiers holstered huge steel pistols over their chests. Everyone's expression was blank, stern.

"It's not usually like this," Brian told her. "They're always happy to see us. We trade cigarettes and knives and whatnot."

The gasoline trucks began pumping their fuel into the underground storage containers while the cargo was unloaded onto pickup trucks.

"Come on, let's get to work," Brian said, pulling Carolanne's gaze away from the soldiers. "Keep your head down, and don't look at anyone crosswise."

They helped unload the few crates of goods that Zone Red supplied other than the gasoline and oil. A few of the craftier soldiers in Hightown had begun work on a small mushroom farm early on in the Zone's establishment, and with its success, the indoor growing room now took up three times the amount of space and grew a variety of edible fungi.

Today, Brian and Carolanne were unloading a box of chanterelle mushrooms, two boxes of shiitake, and several smaller crates containing herbs, such as wild sage and thyme, all headed for the kitchen, where Brian was expected to work.

When the cargo was unloaded, they stood in line with the small procession heading into Alice, holding a single suitcase.

As the line inched forward, Carolanne said, "Brian, I'm not sure I can do this."

"There's nothing to be scared of."

She whispered, "What if they turn us away?"

"They won't."

A tall guard beside the gate looked at Brian and Carolanne as they stepped forward, reading from a clipboard.

"Names?"

"Brian and Carolanne Rhodes," Brian said.

The guard scanned the list.

"You were approved by Tom Byrnes." He looked at them through narrow eyes. "Why'd it take so long for you to arrive?"

Brian swallowed back a lump in his throat. "I was still needed in the kitchen."

The guard looked back to the papers. "I see you're a chef."

"Yes, sir."

"And you, girl? What's your reason for being here?"

Carolanne looked ready to crack. "I—um, we're married. I work in laundry. I do laundry."

The guard stared at her. Carolanne's cheeks flushed red, and Brian could feel her trembling beside him. If the guard asked her another question—anything—he didn't think she would be able to answer.

The guard looked at his clipboard.

"Hope you can cook worth a damn." His eyes flicked up at Brian.

Brian let out a breath. "Yes, sir, I can."

"You're going to have to surrender your firearms, and I'll have to inspect your bag."

"That's fine." Brian put his suitcase on a folding table. "We're not armed."

The guard paused, looking at him. "You came in with cargo, unarmed?" He shook his head.

"Yes, sir. I reckon it wasn't the smartest idea."

They held their breaths as the guard stuck his dirty hands into their clothing and meager belongings, tossing everything about. He pushed the open suitcase toward Brian.

"Pack it up and be on your way."

They walked off fast. Bethany was supposed to meet them at the gate, but she was nowhere to be seen.

"Where is she?" Carolanne looked around. "Where are we supposed to go?"

"I haven't a clue. None of the normal faces are here, not even Pat O'Hern, and he's always at the trade grounds. Just follow along with the group."

They followed the flow of people to the heart of town and found the supply office. A soldier sat behind a desk, and when they gave him their names, he checked some papers and produced an apartment key on a numbered key ring.

"You're to report to the kitchen ASAP," he told Brian.

"Yes, sir."

They walked away. Foul-looking soldiers littered the streets and smelled something fierce. Many of them were drunk and working on getting drunker.

"I don't want to wash their clothes." Carolanne looked at them, repulsed. "I don't want to go near their clothing."

"By the look of it, most of 'em don't ever wash their clothes, so you might get off lucky."

When they got inside their small apartment, they closed and locked the door.

"I'll ask around about Bethany," Brian said. "Remember what Uncle Al told us. We can't appear desperate or off-kilter. We gotta go about our day like it's any other."

Carolanne nodded.

"Brian," she said, "I'm scared."

"I know you are. I know. I am too. But we got to follow the plan. First, we get Bethany out of here. Next, when Uncle Al sends word, we begin the operation. Let's get cracking."

Brian put the suitcase on the kitchen table and began handing the clothing to Carolanne, who folded each item in turn and placed them aside. When the suitcase was empty, he cut away the liner and unscrewed a piece of material at the bottom with a Swiss army knife. Brian reached in and removed a small bundle, wrapped in cloth.

Carolanne moved the suitcase off the table, and Brian placed the item down.

"You sure you know how to use this thing?" Carolanne asked.

"Steven and I used to talk to the truckers on the interstate all the time. There wasn't much else to do in Nelson. I still got my ham radio license back at home or maybe down in the bunker."

Brian unwrapped the small radio made for a truck or a car along with a folding solar charger, a handheld microphone, and a Morse code telegraph key.

"I meant that thing—the Morse code thingy. You actually know Morse code?"

"You have to learn it to get your ham radio license. It's been a while, but I remember it plenty."

Carolanne watched as Brian went to work connecting the wires.

"I got to leave for the kitchen in a minute," he said. "The rest of our stuff is in the produce boxes. I'll bring the weapons back tonight."

Chapter 52
Puzzle Pieces

Sunlight flickered in through Simon's twitching eyelids.

Consciousness was hazy. It took a moment to focus on the blue sky and silky, white clouds overhead.

Then reality came rushing back.

"Bethany!" Simon shouted, attempting to sit up. Arms held him back, grabbing at his shoulders, and for a moment he thought the pile of corpses had come alive, pulling him down into the bowels of hell. Then he realized he was not lying in the pit at all, but rather on a hospital gurney. The arms grabbing him belonged to a clean-shaven man wearing camouflaged fatigues.

"Mr. Kalispell—*Simon*—lie down, please!"

His head was throbbing and his chest was on fire. Each movement sent spikes of pain throughout his body. Simon relented and let his muscles relax.

"What happened? Where's Beth? Is she safe?"

The man didn't answer. Fingers were holding his eyelids open; a penlight shined straight into his pupils.

"I'm not sure who Beth is," the man said. "Now, Simon, tell me what you remember. What's your last memory?"

"I was ... I thought I was dead ... I was about to be killed, and then, I don't know. There was gunfire, and everything went black."

The clean-shaven man nodded. "Do you know what day of the week it is?"

"How long was I out?"

"A few hours."

"Wednesday. Where are Jeremy and Frank?"

"They're here. They stepped away a moment ago." The doctor took a seat beside the gurney. "My name is Mark Buckley; I'm a hospital corpsman first class. You're in the care of General Albert Driscoll. What you remember is correct. You sustained a ricocheted bullet shot to the chest and blunt trauma to the back of your head."

"Oh, Jesus." Simon's hands fluttered over his torso, scanning his body. His chest felt like it was on fire, and touching it made the flames grow wild.

"Relax, please," the corpsman said. "You're a lucky man. The bullet didn't penetrate the bulletproof vest you were wearing, but your chest is going to ache for some time. The blow to the back of your head concerns me the most, but I don't see any indication of a concussion, and your skull isn't broken or fractured. You're going to have a *bad* headache."

All at once, Simon remembered the tape recorder and started patting for the pocket in the jacket he was not wearing.

"My coat—*where's my coat?*"

"On the chair." The doctor pointed to a chair next to the bed where the jacket was placed after being cut off his body.

Simon leaned from the gurney, stretching to reach it.

"Stop—stay right there. I'll get it."

The corpsman handed Simon the jacket, and an emptiness filled Simon's chest as he felt the void where the recorder should be.

"Oh no, oh no, no, no … it must have fallen out in the pit. Where are Jeremy and Frank? I need to talk to them."

"They're speaking to the officers. They should be back any minute." The doctor looked over his shoulder to a guard standing beside a white tent only a few feet away. "Parker, go see if you can find the two sergeants. Tell them that Mr. Kalispell is awake."

"Yes, sir." The guard took off.

Simon relaxed back on the gurney. All around him, men in camouflage were walking around with purpose. The doctor continued inspecting Simon's injuries, but Simon's mind was elsewhere. He gazed over the field, inspecting the tents and mobile offices, looking for the familiar features of his two friends.

A few minutes later, he saw them. Jeremy, Frank, and a man wearing fatigues came walking out of a large camouflage tent erected in a clearing close to Simon's gurney. When they saw Simon looking at them, they smiled. "Simon," Jeremy said. "You're awake."

"Jeremy, the recorder—I don't have it!"

"It's okay, Simon. It's okay. We have it. It's being delivered to General Driscoll as we speak."

Simon let out a breath. "Oh, thank God. I need to speak to him, to General Driscoll."

"We'll be moving out shortly," said the tall, gray-haired man accompanying Jeremy and Frank. "I'm Lieutenant General Casey Edmonds, the ranking officer under General Driscoll. Your friends here have told me your story, and I've listened to the recording. You've been shot, I understand."

"Where are we?" Simon asked.

"We're right outside of Zone Red at a forward post," the doctor said. "I was with the cargo team delivering supplies when we spotted what appeared to be a group of people in the far distance across a field. We halted the procession, and two of our snipers went out to scout. They reported a gang of maybe a dozen armed men surrounding several others whom we recognized from their outfits as belonging to Alice. Through binoculars, we recognized the leader of Alice's Ranger battalion, Frank Morrow.

"As we were waiting for orders from HQ, we saw a man get nearly decapitated. When we saw the executioner get ready to kill the next in line, the commander on duty made the decision, and we opened fire. We moved in and rescued your two friends here, Jeremy Winters and Frank Morrow. We hauled you out of the pit unconscious, but alive. I'm afraid most of the men responsible for what happened have escaped."

"*It's … begun*," Simon whispered.

"What's that?"

"The first shots have been fired. Was Bethany on the return caravan?"

Jeremy shot Simon a fierce look. Apparently Bethany's identity was still a secret.

"Who's that?" the lieutenant general asked.

"It's just … was there a girl on the caravan, a Bethany Rose?"

The lieutenant general raised an eyebrow. "Why? If she was supposed to be there, I would imagine she was."

Simon took a deep breath, attempting to clear his rambling mind.

This is my home, he thought. *Alice is my home. It's too late to go back to the cabin. Winston. Oh, God. I can't just walk away. I have nowhere left to go.*

He pictured his dog, his tail wagging wide, his happy, brown eyes … What were they doing to him?

"What now?" Simon said in a huff. "What are we going to do? You've shot and killed several of Karl's men and discovered their pit of bodies—residents of Alice who were ruthlessly massacred."

The lieutenant general spoke. "As of right now, we don't do a thing."

"But—how can we not?"

"We've sent an envoy to Zone Blue, and peace has been made. The entire situation was an accident. We didn't know that the men we opened fire on were soldiers of Alice and that they were executing those responsible for Tom Byrnes's death. We have left the pit as it was without further investigation."

"What!" Simon shouted. A spike of pain jolted from his ribs. "How can you believe that? They're going to attack Zone Red, you know—the Red Hands are going to attack you!"

"I *don't* believe that we made peace—and neither do they. Nobody does. This is politics, my boy: handshakes one minute and hand grenades the next. One of the executed residents we found in the pit, Margaret Alton, worked for us. She was supplying information on Karl and his men when she went missing. We know fighting is inevitable, but waging war is a delicate procedure. However, if the Red Hands think that they can attack Hightown and win, they are greatly mistaken. Their men aren't real soldiers; they're a bunch of hooligans. We have them outnumbered and outgunned. They won't stand a chance."

Simon shook his head. "You won't have them outnumbered for long. They have an army marching toward Alice as we speak. Hundreds of men, maybe thousands. We don't know their numbers. Nick Byrnes' personal guard, Will Holbrook, informed us just last night. Then this morning, they killed him, tortured him for information."

Lieutenant General Casey Edmonds grew quiet. Then he said dismissively, "Still, they no longer have the element of surprise. We'll fully man the line and add additional machine gun nests. Our walls are strong, and we have hardened bunkers. We'll cut them down like ducks in a pond."

Mark Rothstein's gruff voice came flooding into Simon's memory: *When this is all over and Hightown is ours, we'll have you to thank.*

Oh, Christ …

"What if they have tanks?" Simon said. "Mobile rocket launchers and helicopters? Dozens of them."

"But they don't—do they?"

Simon sat up in the bed, holding his aching head. A knot the size of a golf ball had formed under his hair.

"Hey," the corpsman said. "You need to relax."

Simon shook his head. "I have to see General Driscoll."

"Like I mentioned earlier," the Lieutenant General reiterated, "that's not possible."

The doctor ran to a small table. "You need painkillers, at least."

Simon put his hand up to stop the man. "No, I need to keep my head clear."

"You nearly had your head taken off."

"Just some ice and aspirin. I'm fine."

The group looked at Simon, his exposed chest black and blue.

Jeremy handed Simon a new and folded T-shirt from the chair, and pulled from his belt Simon's Colt .45.

"Found it on one of the dead Red Hands." Jeremy held the pistol for Simon to take.

Simon took hold of the handle, feeling the cool and familiar metal in his palm. He nodded to Jeremy, and then turned to the lieutenant general.

"Listen to me, please. I'm going to lay it all on you. At home in Alice is General Driscoll's niece. She's under suspicion by the Red Hands, and when they find out who she is—if they haven't found out already—they'll use her largely to their advantage. She'll become a bargaining chip."

Lieutenant General Edmonds looked incredulous. "Is this true? Why haven't any of you informed me of this? If it is true, why wouldn't the general mention something sooner?"

"Because we couldn't tell you," Simon continued, buttoning his shirt. "She was ordered by General Driscoll, her uncle, to never tell a soul. The general wanted it to be kept as secret as possible. She broke that promise when she told us, and now we're breaking it once again."

"But this is different."

"I know, and that's why I just told you. Not only that, but I believe the Red Hands have discovered the whereabouts of a large cache of weapons—tanks, helicopters, vehicles—dozens, all brand new, with enough ammunition to wage a devastating war."

"What makes you believe that?"

"Because *I know* the location, and I shared this information with several people—Jeremy, Bethany, and Will Holbrook. Will might have told his interrogators the location of the weapons and vehicles. Mark Rothstein implied as much. If the Red Hands get ahold of the cache, you'll have a much bloodier war coming your way."

"And you know where these weapons are?"

Simon nodded. "By memory. Take me to General Driscoll."

The painful throbbing in Simon's head was still ever-present. Yet, all at once, clarity overtook him, and a map-like chain of events began to unfold in his thoughts.

"I have a plan, and not just about the weapons—I have an idea. I might know how to win this war."

The lieutenant general looked dismissive. "We have high-ranking officers orchestrating our strategy. What makes you think you can come up with a better plan?"

Simon asked him, "What happens when you remove the head from a snake? The body twitches and kicks but can no longer function. Soon, it lies dead, the poison still inside. Like you said, the Red Hands are *not* soldiers, and I think I know how to cripple them. Please—I have to see the general right now."

Lieutenant General Casey Edmonds stayed quiet for a moment.

Then he turned, facing two soldiers standing nearby.

"Private Long, Private Richards," he shouted. "Get a transport ready ASAP. And send a wire to General Driscoll to expect my arrival."

"Yes, sir," they said, and took off running.

Chapter 53
Cinderblock Walls

Karl led Nick down the long, winding hallway of his wing, past the mahogany doors, and into the shared portion of the house.

"Jesus Christ," Nick muttered. "What the hell?"

"The men took to revelry last night. Perhaps not in the most civil of manners."

The entry room was destroyed, the furniture missing—dragged outside to be burned—and anything that might have been on top of the furniture had been tossed aside and broken.

"This is my house," Nick said. "You need to get your men under control." His head was pounding, throbbing against his skull.

"My apologies, Sir General." Karl bowed his head. "I'll see to it that the men clean up proper. Presently, we are needed in the basement."

"The basement?"

"Follow me."

The rest of the house looked much the same. Men were still sleeping on couches or where they had collapsed on the floor, drunk, and some half-naked. A few had vomited where they lay, and their faces were plastered to the ground.

Nick's hangover came back strong.

"Here, Nick. I had a pot of coffee made." Karl poured them each a cup of coffee in the kitchen, and they walked to the doorway leading to the basement. Two guards saluted as they passed.

At the bottom of the landing, the basement opened up to a carpeted and well-furnished room. Two Red Hands stood at attention at the bottom, shouldering rifles. The previous owner had installed a bar along the far wall, a pool table in the middle of the room, and a dartboard in the corner. The room was untouched by the previous night's celebration.

"Want a drink?" Karl laughed, nodding to the bar.

Nick soured his face. "That's not funny."

Karl led him to a hallway extending to the unfinished portion of the basement, with doors on either side to the boiler room, storage area, laundry facility, and a workshop. The floor here was concrete, and the walls were cinderblock. In the far rear, behind a closed door, were the staff quarters.

"Right this way, General."

Karl opened a side door.

Nick walked in.

"Oh, fuck …"

They had entered the laundry room. On the far wall stood a line of washers and dryers. Tables for folding laundry had been moved aside and piled on top of each other. In the center of the room lay Will Holbrook, strapped to a surgical gurney over a drain in the floor. The life had been taken from him. Blood still dripped to the drain in slow, sticky intervals from where it had pooled beneath him.

"What did you do?" Nick was bewildered. Will's body was barely recognizable; whole pieces of him had been removed and placed on a stainless steel table. A single bulb hung from a cord over the body, casting strange shadows over the cinderblock walls.

"This man committed treason," Karl said, "defiling your very name. He and his band of mutineers have been rounded up and eliminated."

"Who else?"

"Frank Morrow, Jeremy Winters, Simon Kalispell, Pat O'Hern, Martin Howard, and lastly, Bethany Rose."

"They're all dead?" Nick's hangover went from bad to worse. "Martin Howard … is he dead?"

"Yes, Martin is dead at long last. Chris Lockton proved himself to be a worthy comrade. His outburst during your speech played into the right ears. We've brought Pat O'Hern and Bethany Rose in for additional questioning."

"Questioning? For what?" Nick looked at the form of his former guard on the table, naked to his exposed viscera. "Are you going to question them like this?"

"I don't inquire as to the good doctor's methods. He's a master at his craft."

"And what, exactly, *is* his craft?"

"You see it before your eyes—a work of art."

Nick shook his head.

"William gave us a good deal of information before he expired. He informed us of the location of an abundance of weaponry—vehicles, tanks, and helicopters. He gave us this information in exchange for his life. A promise we kept. We only did one thing first, which was to remove his genitalia, and then we opened the door for him to leave. In the end, he decided to take the honorable way out and beg for our mercy, which we showed him by ending his suffering."

Nick's ears picked up. "Weapons? Where are these weapons?"

Karl laughed. "I knew that would wake you up, old sport. Not far. We've sent a scout to check the legitimacy of the claim. In two days' time, Priest Dietrich will arrive in Alice. But first, his men will arm themselves with whatever vehicles and ammunition there is to take. We will signal the horns, eliminate the peasants here in Alice, and ride into Zone Red and to victory beyond."

Nick envisioned himself on horseback, leading a charge with his Dragoons. Maybe now, though, he would be riding on the back of a tank rather than a horse.

"What about the others?" Nick asked. "Pat and Beth? What information do they possess?"

"Pat knows the layout of Hightown better than anyone in Alice. He's been a lifelong friend of General Driscoll. Bethany must know the layout as well, being that she recently arrived. Not only that, but her name came up during our interrogation with Mr. Holbrook. However, we couldn't get much out of him. The boy was strong, I'll give him that."

Nick stood motionless. He was in the presence of a true psychopath.

"If we're going to do this, let's get it over with," Nick said, his face sour. "Interrogate them both at once."

"Oh, come on now." Karl clapped the back of Nick's shoulder. "Lighten up; you're too serious. Try to enjoy life. They need to be interrogated separately, and this is the only room with a drain. Besides, it is up to the good doctor to decide the methods."

Too serious? Nick could not imagine a more serious scene than the one he was witnessing. The sound of Karl's laughter combined with the pools of blood, the lifeless body, the table of entrails, and the smell of musky death in the air made his head spin.

"Let's get out of here. No need for a second interrogator. Go on as planned."

Just then, a short man with dark, beady eyes hidden behind wire-rimmed glasses entered the room. The man paused before Karl and Nick, a sense of agitation across his face. He was carrying two leather satchel bags.

"Ah, Doctor Arthur Freeman. Please, let me introduce you to General Nicholas Byrnes."

"Oh, yes," the doctor said.

Dr. Freeman walked around them, eyeing Will Holbrook for any changes made by Nick or Karl. He scratched the bald spot on the top of his head, as if deciphering some great divination.

Karl leaned to Nick's ear as the doctor removed a portable stereo from one of his bags. "Let's leave the good doctor to his work."

Karl left, and Nick followed, looking over his shoulder to see the doctor remove gleaming tools—scalpels, forceps, dissection scissors, even a chef's knife—from his bag, one at a time, and place them on the stainless steel table. Each move the doctor made was precise. Nick shut the door as the doctor was polishing a fillet blade.

Outside the door, Nick asked, "He's … crazy?"

"The man is an artist, and the world is his canvas. Perhaps he is a bit of an eccentric, but the good doctor is the best field surgeon you will ever have the pleasure of meeting. He can put things back together just as easily as he can take them apart."

"He seems to enjoy his work a bit too much."

"Ha!" Karl bellowed. "In more ways than you could imagine."

"What's that supposed to mean?"

"The man"—Karl raised his fingers like a Boy Scout giving an oath, his other hand over his heart—"is an honest-to-God cannibal. Swear on my mother's grave. Even before the war he was a wanted fugitive. Rumor has it that he enjoys his meals fresh and still wriggling. You see, this end-of-times business has benefited him greatly."

They walked up the hallway as classical music floated from behind the closed door.

"Schubert," Karl said. "The man has impeccable taste." And then he started to laugh. "In more ways than one."

Nick shook his head, looking over his shoulder to the private chamber.

Walking back into the game room, they were met by Mark Rothstein, Sultan, and the young sergeant, Ryan Pechman.

Karl stopped short before his injured and frazzled officers. "Nicholas," he said. "Go on upstairs. I'll be right behind you."

Nick passed the officers, noticing that Mark was limping with a bandage tied around his thigh, and Sergeant Pechman was clutching a bloody cloth over his stomach.

"What happened?" Nick insisted.

Mark opened his mouth to speak, but Karl spoke up. "I will give you a full report in a moment. Leave me to confer with my men." His looked straight at Nick, the lines in his face unflinching. "Now, Sir General."

Nick was going to insist he stay, but his stomach was churning and he needed another aspirin—desperately. He went upstairs without further hesitation.

The men stood before Karl Metzger.

"What happened?" Karl asked.

"They were out there, in the field."

"*Who* was out there in the field, Mr. Rothstein?"

"Men from Zone Red. They had scouts hiding, snipers."

"Jesus …" Karl shook his head. "Incompetent fools! Are they dead? The ones you had rounded up?"

"Um …" Mark looked to Sultan. "Martin is for sure, and Simon. I saw him take a bullet to his chest, and I walloped his head with the butt of my rifle. He's in the pit. I don't know about the rest."

"You left them there? Alive?"

"It's just that … we were under fire," Sergeant Pechman said. Karl stared at the sergeant, making the young man fidget. "They—they killed four of us before we knew they was coming."

"And how many of them did you kill in return? Hmm? Was it all of them, the entire group of scouts? Because if you did not, then it is certain that Zone Red has saved those men that you failed to kill and has now discovered our intent."

"I don't think so," Sergeant Pechman said. Mark and Sultan exchanged glances and inched away from the injured man.

"No?" Karl turned to him, amused. "You don't think so, do you? And why is that?"

"They sent an envoy with the cargo team. They've apologized. They didn't know it was us out there and the men we was executing were prisoners. They've fallen back, left the grave untouched."

"Oh." Karl's eyebrows rose. "Well, maybe we got off lucky then."

"Um, yes, sir, I think—"

Karl Metzger stepped toward him, bumping into Sergeant Pechman's chest, making the injured man wince. He loomed tall over the young sergeant, casting his face in shadow.

"Who … the fuck … asked for your opinion?"

"I-I, um," he swallowed, "sir—"

Karl reached out and grabbed Sergeant Pechman by the throat. His eyes seemed to throb as Karl's grip tightened, and he dropped the bloody rags clutched to his wound, grabbing at Karl's wrists.

His feet lifted off the ground for the last conscious moment of his life as something audibly snapped. When Karl let go, Sergeant Pechman fell to the ground, his eyes staring up at the ceiling, eyelids twitching.

Karl unholstered his pistol, shot the man in the head, and re-holstered his pistol. Mark Rothstein and Sultan did not budge. The smell of cordite loomed thick in the air.

Karl sighed and rubbed the bridge of his nose. He turned toward the staircase.

"Find out who was killed out there and who was not," Karl shouted behind him. "And bury that hole in the field before Zone Red goes snooping through the bodies—if they haven't already."

Karl gestured to the body of Sergeant Pechman.

"Get someone to clean up this mess."

"Yes, sir," Sultan said, watching as the pool of blood spread from the young sergeant's head, inching toward the toe of his boot as it soaked into the rich carpet.

Chapter 54
Shadows

Simon Kalispell and Frank Morrow stood atop a tall wooded hill overlooking the entrance to Zone Red. They watched as the massive gates leading into Hightown opened for the column of supply vehicles, Hummers, and flatbed trucks all departing to the town of Sullivan and Livingston Park.

The plans were a go.

Simon had stripped down to a pair of shorts and was armed with only a knife and his father's Colt .45 holstered to his side. Frank was dressed much the same, but wore a thin camouflage jacket.

The campfire before them had dwindled down, and they were using the cool charcoals to darken their skin. When mixed with the mud and the grass they had smeared on their bodies, the men melded into the rocks and the trees and the earth below their feet.

Conversation was minimal, as they each turned inward to personal thoughts.

I am the wind. I am the rock. I am the tree, and my roots grow deep.

In the distance, the line of supply vehicles disappeared into the wilderness, and the gates to Zone Red were fastened shut.

Simon sat with his back straight, his eyes closed. Images of his best friend Winston along with awful pangs of worry and doubt fluttered through his thoughts, but he chased them away to the best of his ability. His mind must be kept clear and open. Yet, it was the images of Bethany that were the hardest to suppress. The smell of her clean hair—botanical, like sweet thyme—still stung at his nostrils.

I am the wind. I am the rock. I am the tree, and my roots grow deep …

Simon inhaled deeply. Exhaled, and opened his eyes.

"You ready?" Frank asked.

"Yes." Simon stood. He had never been so ready in his life.

Frank picked up the scoped, silenced assault rifle with the collapsible stock and grabbed the satchel they kept around the base of a tree, away from the fire, and swung them both over his shoulder.

The men walked into the woods and disappeared like trails of smoke.

***

The guard post was visible despite the darkness of the night.

Simon and Frank were watching the guards in the trenches go about their scheduled routines. It had taken over an hour of crawling against the cold ground beside bushes or rocks and shadowy crevices to get within a few yards of the front line. Slowly, the two men crawled close enough that they could hear guards talking.

Two men passed the trench in a loop every five minutes, without any disruption or irregularity. Simon and Frank waited and counted the laps until they were certain of the timing.

Their bodies were pressed against the dirt, their camouflaged flesh looking akin to the earth and rocks. The voices of the two guards grew louder until they were directly in line with them. Simon was close enough to reach out and touch the face of the nearest man as they passed.

It was at this moment that Simon's thoughts became inexplicably sharp. All formations of Bethany and Winston were gone, and his head was so clear that his mind and body seemed capable of moving quicker than the world around him. It was as if he could see a split-second into the future.

He was the wind, the rock, and the tree.

Simon and Frank used their calm breaths to guide them like a metronome as they counted to one and a half minutes. Then they moved.

In a single motion, they dropped into the trench, looked in either direction down the dark cavernous lanes, and with a fluid bounce, they leaped onto the opposite side. They crawled fast on their forearms and knees, and continued counting to four minutes. Then they stopped, flattening themselves down against the earth.

They waited until the voices of the next patrol passed and then moved on, all the while keeping an eye on the watchtower to their side, but the spotlight remained dark.

They crawled until the trenches were well behind them, and then they got to their feet. Running was risky, so they prowled from one tree to the next and from rock to rock, leapfrogging until they made it in complete silence to Ridgeline Road.

The road was deserted.

Simon took the lead as they headed now to chop the head off the serpent.

Chapter 55
Silver Thermos

Mark Rothstein sent six men to the site of the open grave. They scouted the area first to be sure no soldiers from Hightown were staking them out. It was nearing evening as they approached the pit, so they used the headlights of their trucks to illuminate the field around the corpses. Inside, a faceless body wearing a uniform from Alice lay sprawled on top.

"That one's Simon Kalispell. Got to be," one of the guards said to the ranking officer.

The officer nodded. "Find out, then get on with it."

The men started dragging the scattered corpses from the firefight into the pit, taking inventory and then pushing them over the ledge.

"Hey, look here," the guard said, pulling out IDs from several of the bodies. "This one is Jeremy Winters, and this other is Frank Morrow. We got them sons a bitches all accounted for." He compared the images on the IDs to the bodies, but their faces were bloated, and some were shot or bludgeoned beyond recognition.

The officer came over. Something caught his attention. Frank Morrow's pants cuff was pulled up to shin height, and something long and silver was attached to his ankle.

"What's that?" the ranking officer asked, as a soldier unstrapped the cylindrical device from Frank's ankle. It was over an inch in diameter and about a foot in length.

"I don't know, sir. Looks like a thermos."

"That's not a thermos, you idiot. Weren't these men patted down?"

The man shrugged. "Should have been. Maybe just scanned for a weapon. They was coming here to die, after all."

The officer shook his head and grabbed the gleaming metal tube out of the soldier's hand. He unscrewed the top, and removed several large pieces of coiled paper. He knelt down, flattening the corners against the grass. In the light from the trucks he studied them as best as he could.

The men gathered, staring over his shoulder.

"Get back. I can't see worth a damn."

The writing was done in fine blue ink with detailed mechanical drawings. "Oh my," the officer said. "Do you know what we're looking at here?"

Underneath the blueprints were pages detailing an operation titled "Blue Rapture."

The officer skimmed through each page, then coiled them back up and put them in the tube. He pressed them into the arms of the man kneeling beside him. "Take these straight to Karl Metzger. Now!"

"Yes, sir." The man got to his feet.

"Better yet, I'll go myself. You stay here. Peters, come with me. Johnson, you're in command. Bury these men."

"Yes, sir," Johnson said.

The ranking officer ran to one of the trucks and peeled away from the gravesite.

"If this is what I think it is," he patted the silver tube, "we'll win this war without a single shot fired."

Chapter 56
Blue Thunder

Being a chef gave Brian Rhodes some privileges, such as being allowed outside past curfew to go back and forth between his apartment and the kitchen for meal prep. During dinner service, Brian left to check on Carolanne and see if there had been any further broadcasts. But there was nothing new. Not since earlier that afternoon when a message had come beeping through the headphones.

PHASE I OPERATION BLUE THUNDER TO COMMENCE.
WAIT FURTHER INSTRUCTION REGARDING PHASE II.

Following that afternoon broadcast, Carolanne went to work in the laundry room and had only just returned a few minutes before Brian.

"How'd it go?" Brian asked.

"Good," she replied. "I think it went fine."

"I sure as hell hope it did." They talked for a little while longer, then he kissed her goodbye and walked outside into the cool evening air, heading back to the kitchen for cleanup. It was a short walk down the road to the volunteer fire department, and as Brian was reaching for the handle of the glass door, he heard a voice hiss out in a whisper.

"*Flowing?*"

Without thinking, Brian answered. "Water—*water.*" It was the code Uncle Al had made him memorize.

"*Brian Rhodes?*" the voice said.

Brian turned.

"Who's there?"

"Quiet," the voice whispered. Two human forms stepped out from around the side of the building. They looked like ritualistic gods—effigies of humans made out of mud and earth.

"My name is Simon Kalispell," Simon introduced himself. "This is Frank Morrow. General Driscoll sent us. We have new orders for you. We need somewhere safe to hide. Not your apartment."

Brian nodded. "I scouted a place earlier."

He led Simon and Frank to a side door, and up a staircase leading to the second floor. They were quiet, trying not to rouse the attention of the kitchen staff.

"I know this place," Simon said, stepping into the small, stuffy room. "Nick was going to use it as an office before he moved into his mansion with the rest of the Red Hands. It doesn't look like he ever finished settling in." Simon nodded to a pine desk in the corner. There wasn't a single pen or piece of paper on it.

"From what I gathered from the kitchen staff," Brian said, "Nick hasn't set foot in the firehouse in weeks. Takes all his meals at home, too. No one will come looking in Nick's own office. No one has reason to come to the second floor at all, it's all storage."

"I'm sure you're aware," Frank said, "the operation has begun."

Brian nodded. "We got the message today. Carolanne's back at the apartment; I'm going to go get her now. From here on out, we gotta stay hidden."

"All right," Simon said. "Hurry."

Brian left, walking swiftly to the apartment.

Carolanne jumped at hearing the door open, and stood looking at him worriedly.

"Jesus," she said. "You scared the hell out of me. Why are you back?"

"Gather everything; it's time to go."

She swallowed. "Go where?"

"Into hiding. Two men are here to help, back at the firehouse. Come on, I'll explain on the way. Get the radio."

Brian watched the road for several minutes, making sure no one was around, and then he led Carolanne down the street, holding the suitcase tight against his chest.

The road was deserted in the late hour, but by the time they arrived at the firehouse, Brian saw Carolanne was covered in sweat.

"Don't be nervous," he whispered to her. "We're safer here than back at the apartment."

They walked up the stairs, and to the door to the office.

"Carolanne," Brian said, entering, "meet Simon Kalispell and Frank Morrow."

Carolanne nodded. "Hello," she whispered. They shut the door, keeping the lights off. Using a penlight, Brian set up the radio from his apartment.

"I've heard a lot about you—about you both," Simon said. "Bethany has become a good friend of mine. Any word on her? Hear anything about a dog?"

Brian and Carolanne exchanged glances in the darkness.

"We're … not sure," Brian said. "Don't know anything about a dog, but we've heard rumor that Bethany was taken to Nick's mansion. We also heard rumor that you're dead. Both of you."

Simon looked grim and shook his head.

"That son of a bitch. That son of a bitch—I'll kill him. If he's so much as laid a finger on her, I'll chop off his hands."

Everyone looked at him. Frank had never heard Simon so worked up.

"If that asshole did take her," Brian said, "I'll help you tear him to shreds."

"As far as you hearing that we're both dead," Frank said, motioning to himself and Simon. "That's good news. That is exactly what we want them to think."

On the floor of the office, Brian unloaded his assault rifle, smuggled in the bottom of a crate of mushrooms, and a few pistols. Simon laid out his two newly acquired shotguns, one pump-action and the other a double-action.

"Won't the other chefs know you're missing? Don't you have to go down there?"

Brian shook his head. "No one's keeping track of who's doing what in the kitchen, especially not for the night shift. The guards don't think of the chefs as much of a threat. Usually they're drunk or passed out when they're supposed to be watching the staff."

They sat in a circle for what seemed like hours. When the chefs downstairs left for the night, Brian slipped out and returned with a sack of food—bread and nuts.

They ate with relish, especially Simon and Frank, who had draped blankets over their shoulders.

A light blinked on the radio as it picked up a transmission. Brian leaned over, holding the headphones to his ear, writing as the ticks played out:

INITIATE PHASE II BLUE THUNDER

Brian read the command out loud to the room.

"That's all that it says?" Simon asked.

"That's it."

They were silent.

Simon spoke in a whisper, "It begins …."

Chapter 57
Toxicodendron Radicans

Earlier that day, when Carolanne heard the orders for Phase I to commence, she had left for her work detail at the large laundry facility near the firehouse, and begun the operation.

She would be the first to strike at the Red Hands without firing a single shot.

Many of Alice's older or disabled residents were given the job of washing and folding laundry, and they were surprised to see a young girl when she first arrived.

Carolanne had entered the laundry room wearing her backpack, which normally contained a light jacket, and greeted the fellow workers she had only recently begun working with. There was old Bobby, who was missing a leg, and Sylvia, the elderly lady who was losing her eyesight.

It was Sylvia who was washing the piles of dark brown uniforms, those of Nick Byrnes's Dragoons, who were ordered to wash their uniforms frequently and appear crisp and tidy. The same order had been issued to the Red Hands, yet they were less willing to oblige.

"Sylvia," Carolanne had said, nodding to the pile of dark uniforms, "why don't I give you a hand?"

Sylvia gave Carolanne a look. Everyone did their own task at the laundry, but Carolanne had been the helpful type ever since she'd arrived.

Sylvia smiled. "Sure. There's plenty over there, if you want to get a jump on them."

Carolanne smiled back. "I'll give you a hand here first. I don't mind."

"Suits me, I guess."

Carolanne wheeled the carts full of wet laundry—uniforms, socks, T-shirts, and underwear—to the dryers on the other side.

Bobby gave her a brief smile as he folded laundry from a giant heap before him, his brown eyes glazed with cataracts.

It's now or never, Carolanne, she told herself.

Her hands fluttered and she felt dizzy as she unzipped her backpack, looking between Bobby and Sylvia. She pulled out a towel folded around something the size of a small pillow and tossed it in with the wet laundry.

Wrapped in the towel was a bale of plant leaves tied in a mesh laundry bag, which Brian had snuck in with a crate of sage and wild herbs from Hightown. As the dryer started up, the bag containing a large quantity of *toxicodendron radicans*—commonly known as poison ivy—spun around and around with all of the clothing.

Carolanne repeated this process with each load as the day wore on, using a fresh bag of poison ivy after the third cycle.

At the end of the shift, after folding a large quantity of the laundry herself while wearing plastic gloves—after telling Bobby and Sylvia her hands had gotten irritated from the detergent—she picked up her backpack with the used poison ivy and left for home. Along the way, she dropped the bag in a pre-dug hole by the side of a house surrounded by trees and kicked dirt over it. Her knees were shaking and she looked over her shoulders, expecting to see figures emerge from the shadows at any given moment.

Hours had passed since then, and she sat now on the carpeted floor of the firehouse room telling Frank and Simon her story.

"Do you think it's going to work?" Simon asked.

Carolanne shrugged. "I don't know, but look at this."

She pulled up her sleeve and shone a penlight on her forearm where a spotty red rash had developed. "I guess I wasn't as careful as I thought."

Chapter 58
King of the East

Karl Metzger and his officers had gotten little sleep, if any, the previous night. A sergeant had arrived late at night and out of breath. The man clutched a long, thin silver document tube in his hands. Karl removed the papers and unraveled them on the billiard table in the basement.

"Tell me again where you found these?" Karl's eyes did not look up from the blueprints.

"Attached to the corpse of Frank Morrow," the man responded.

"So, Frank Morrow, Jeremy Winters, and Simon Kalispell—they're all dead?"

"Yes, sir."

"You're sure of it?"

"Yes, sir. They were wearing their uniforms and had IDs in their pockets."

"But was it them? You saw their faces?"

"I … their faces were beat up pretty bad, I—"

"Sergeant." Karl's baritone voice loomed in the room. "Was it them or not?"

"Y-yes, sir, it was them all right."

Karl studied the papers one by one.

"That will be all, Sergeant," he said. "Please call Sultan and Mr. Rothstein down here."

"Yes, sir."

A moment later, Karl was showing his officers the papers.

"If what we got here is true," Sultan said, scanning the mechanical drawings, "there's no way we're gonna lose this war."

"That may be true, Sultan. What are your thoughts, Mr. Rothstein?"

"My thoughts?" Mark pointed to the papers. "No thoughts. We should have left already."

Karl remained quiet. Mark and Sultan knew better than to interrupt him when he was contemplating.

"All right." Karl spoke up. "Don't talk to anybody about this without my authorization. Get that sergeant back here, the one who found these papers. He's coming with us. And get the best engineers you can muster. Don't tell Nick a thing, not yet. Understood? We leave at dawn. Dismissed."

Karl stood, rolling the papers back into the tube as Sultan and Mark Rothstein took their leave.

Karl went upstairs, making his way to Nick's wing of the house. He walked through the mahogany doors and down the hallway, where he noticed the entrance to the library open. Music could be heard inside. He knocked on the doorframe.

"Come in," Nick shouted.

"General," Karl said. "What's that you're listening to? Beethoven?"

"No. Saint something or other. I don't know anything about classical, but that's all there is in this house."

Karl listened for a moment. "Ah, the *Introduction and Rondo Capriccioso*. Camille Saint-Saëns. I should have known."

"Yeah. Great." Nick was sitting deep in a plush leather couch, a tumbler of bourbon in his hand. He was wearing a clean uniform, his pants creased and his shirt pressed.

"I'll be stepping out in the morning," Karl explained.

Nick sat upright. "What? Where are you going?"

"Nowhere important, I assure you. Just some business I must attend to. I should be back before evening, but if I'm not, make sure the foghorn is sounded during dinner when the townspeople are gathered together at the firehouse. Herd them like cattle."

"Are you sure our army is on schedule? I don't want to keep my people locked up any longer than necessary."

Your people will never see the light of day again.

Karl smiled and continued. "It's for their own good, General. Dietrich and his men will be arriving at dawn in two days' time. They will take the weapons from the park and march to Alice. We are to feed them proper, let them rest, and then … we will march to Zone Red, to its imminent demise. The people of Alice will thank you for keeping them safe, even if they grumble at first at being locked up in the gymnasium. They will forgive you and love you all the more for having their best of interests at heart. Soon, Nicholas, you will be the king of the East Coast—in charge of water, food, and fuel."

Nick's eyes glazed over.

"Check on the men while I'm gone," Karl said. "Make sure the soldiers are well fed."

"Where are you going?"

"I will be back before you know it."

Nick slumped back down on the plush couch.

Karl scanned the dark wood interior of the room and the gigantic marble fireplace blazing fire.

"Have another drink; relax. I'll have my men bring you more firewood. Tomorrow there is much to do, and the morning after, we ride to war. Get some rest."

Nick turned to respond, but Karl was already backing away from the door.

***

Upstairs, Stephanie was watching the sky outside the wall-length windows and gazing at the river, twinkling in the moonlight. Lately, she was spending more of her days sleeping and her nights awake. It helped keep her migraines under control.

She moved to the front window, gazing out over the lawn as the sun began to rise. The front lawn had been carved out like a maze, with trenches zigzagging back and forth and machine gun nests constructed in concrete bunkers.

She blew back steam from her cup of tea and sipped gingerly.

A Hummer and a pickup truck rolled down the driveway, past the checkpoints, and parked in front of the house. Karl Metzger, Mark Rothstein, Sultan, and a few men that Stephanie did not recognize walked out of the house and entered the waiting cars.

She watched Karl and his officers drive off out of sight.

Chapter 59
Omphalotus Olearius

Brian left for the kitchen before dawn.

He was the first of the chefs to arrive, and soon, several line cooks came in. A young man with a lazy eye approached him.

"Brian," he said, "where'd you go last night? You never came back to clean and prep."

Actually, I was upstairs the whole time.

"Fell asleep," Brian told him. The boy shook his head and laughed.

"You're lucky nobody noticed."

Brian shrugged.

The head chef came into the kitchen while breakfast was being put in chafing dishes, tying an apron over his chef's whites.

"Okay, listen up," he called out. "We've been issued commands for a big meal tonight. Half of the livestock is to be butchered, and over half of the produce is going to be needed. We're going to make a simple stew with some fresh bread. The food is to be delivered along the entire line, and all of the Red Hands and Dragoons are being issued double rations, so let's get to work. We have plenty to do."

They're sucking Alice dry. Brian looked down at his cutting board. *They're getting ready for a fight.*

The butchers left for the slaughter field outside and came back later with grim expressions on their faces and aprons stained in gore. They smoked cigarettes by the back door, and were numbly silent.

Karl Metzger's and Nick Byrnes's men no longer ate with the rest of Alice's

370

residents, but rather had their meals put in large vats and storage containers to be picked up on the backs of Jeeps and served on the lawn of Nick's mansion, and various spots along the front line.

Brian began removing the crates of fresh mushrooms and onions, prepping only the food headed out for transport.

Another chef across the way walked over to him. "You take all the mushrooms?" he asked.

Brian didn't look up from his station. "Here, take the buttons."

"What you got there?" The chef leaned over the station, picking up a light brown, broad-headed mushroom with long strips of gills on the bottom. He put the mushroom to his nose, sniffed, and then popped it into his mouth. "They're good," he said.

Brian swallowed.

"Chanterelles," he answered, and then added, "Heard Karl asked for them himself. He's keen on them."

Brian waited, cutting through the mushrooms with his heart pounding, afraid the chef might know that chanterelles are hard to cultivate in growing rooms and are rarely domesticated.

But the chef just took the crate of button mushrooms and left.

Brian let out a silent sigh and continued dicing.

When he got to the bottom of the crate, he removed the bags of fresh herbs and began dicing them up. By the time he got through the sage, his wrist was growing tired, but he kept at it.

He looked around the room at the other chefs, all bent over their stations, and slipped on a pair of latex gloves, which was not an uncommon practice in the kitchen. He rolled the leaves of basil in tubes before slicing them in strips and tried to keep his head down as he cut through the remaining poison ivy that was tucked in the bag. Sweat stung at his eyes when he looked up at the guards, but they all looked bored, smoking cigarettes, and playing cards.

The meat was brought in by the slab and chopped down into smaller pieces. The pieces were seared in the pots, and then the vegetables were added along with the herbs, water, and even some red wine. Then the tops of the pots were sealed so the stew could simmer.

Brian helped the staff load the food containers as lunch was served. The Red Hands arrived with their flatbed trucks and loaded the large containers of stew to be delivered to all points along the line. They did not thank the kitchen staff, but grumbled at having to carry the heavy buckets.

"They should be doing this," a rotten-toothed soldier muttered.

"Soon 'nuf," the other man replied.

There was much debate as to why such a large meal had been prepared, and some speculated that it was because the Red Hands were leaving and wanted to take with them as much food as possible. At least, that was what everyone hoped for, but in the back of their minds, everyone knew that the soldiers were being well fed because war was on the horizon.

Brian walked back into the kitchen with a huge weight off his chest.

I did it. I got away with it.

Nobody in the kitchen had noticed, but Hightown had never in the past supplied chanterelle mushrooms to Zone Blue. Chanterelles were difficult to propagate, and the men who worked in the growing room had never bothered to try. The mushrooms that Brian diced up in the stew were called *omphalotus olearius*, commonly referred to as jack-o'-lantern mushrooms due to the fact that the mushrooms glowed a bioluminescent bluish-green color in low-light conditions. In daylight, the mushrooms resembled chanterelles to the point that they smelled and tasted appealing—much like chanterelles.

Jack-o'-lantern mushrooms are toxic to humans and easily harvested throughout the Northeast, growing in large clusters on trees and their roots—both living and dead. Although they don't cause death, they do cause severe cramping, diarrhea, and vomiting. Adding to this effect were the dozens of psychoactive mushrooms that were mixed in with Brian's crate, handpicked from Zone Red's own small cattle farm. The poison ivy, if digested, can cause serious swelling in the mouth and throat, along with moderate to severe respiratory problems.

These ingredients were simmered in the great vats of stew and passed out to the Red Hands and Dragoons all along the front line.

Chapter 60
Head of the Serpent

"Are we gonna blow 'em all up?" Mark Rothstein leaned over the wide space between the two backseats in the Hummer, trying to glance at the papers in Karl's lap. He envisioned the enormous cloud that such an explosion would produce. The thought gave him chills of excitement.

"Oh, Mr. Rothstein, no. We're not going to blow them up. We are, after all, here to claim the gasoline, not blow it all to smithereens. Not to mention what the radiation would do to the water supply here in Alice."

"Right."

Karl spoke over his shoulder to the two engineers hunched over in the cargo area, clutching their canvas toolboxes.

"What we have here," Karl explained, "are plans for an operation called *Blue Rapture*. The plans originated back when the Zones were first established as a failsafe for General Driscoll and his band of loathsome cretins. We are under the impression that the operation was recently put into effect by several of Alice's men who failed and died before they could reach their directive. Their failure has given us a strong advantage, as the plans include instructions for arming and handling a one-point-two megaton nuclear explosive package from a B-eighty-three nuclear bomb. The operations manual and technical schematics are now in our possession."

Karl passed the papers to an engineer in the back named Tyson, who had once worked in a nuclear plant and had some knowledge of how to handle a nuclear device.

Karl continued. "The weapon itself is three and a half feet long with an eighteen-inch diameter. It has been removed from its bomb casing and made operational by either a trigger or time delay. It's all there in the manual and blueprints. The bomb is being kept in a steel drum in the basement of a house down the road. *Operation Blue Rapture* calls for the total obliteration of Alice as a last resort."

"Jesus," Tyson muttered, looking over the papers. "This is no joke."

Karl smirked. "No, sir. It is no joke at all."

The Hummer and pickup truck stopped before a house on Ridgeline Road and turned down the long driveway only a few blocks away from Nick's mansion, not far from the front line. It was quiet in this part of town, uninhabited.

"All right," Karl said, opening his door. "Let's get to work."

The men jumped out of the car and walked toward the back of the house. The two drivers went inside the entrance to make a sweep, and after several minutes, they unlocked the glass door to the greenhouse in the rear of the home.

"All clear, sir."

Karl walked past his men, to a cinderblock toolshed built against the house.

"This is it," Karl said, studying the blueprints. He opened the shed door and looked at the pavers under his feet. He knelt, feeling along the crevices between the slabs, then went to a rack of tools and removed a pry bar. The concrete paver came up easily, revealing a door underneath.

"Have at it, boys."

Karl smiled, tossing the stone paver to the side.

The men cleared the room and removed the floor under their feet. When they finished, they circled a metal trap door in the center of the small toolshed.

"Open it," Karl said.

Tyson put his toolbox on the ground, removed a pair of bolt cutters, and cut through the padlock with ease. He swung the doors open, and the men looked upon a staircase descending into darkness. Tyson removed a flashlight from his bag and went down first, followed by the other engineer.

"Go with them, Sultan," Karl commanded.

Sultan nodded, and walked down the steps.

After a moment Karl yelled, "What do you see, Sultan?"

"There's a whole mess of supplies down here."

"The steel drum, Sultan. Do you see a steel drum?"

"Yeah, we got a steel drum all right. Smack in the center of the room."

The two engineers pulled away a thick canvas sheet from a cylindrical, thirty-gallon steel drum, with a radiation warning symbol painted on the side. The metal was pure black, and a cap was fastened to the top. There were two openings on the lid, secured with rubber stoppers. One was used for filling and dispersing of fluid and a smaller one for ventilation. The larger lid was open a crack.

Mark Rothstein began walking down the stairs with Karl following behind.

Karl turned to the two drivers and the sergeant standing behind him. "Stay here. Keep your eyes open."

Just then, Tyson pulled at the two-inch diameter rubber stopper to get a look inside. If he had been properly trained in explosives and not a former engineer from a nuclear plant, he would have inspected the barrel thoroughly before touching it.

But Tyson was not trained in explosive ordinance disposal.

Sultan said, "Smells like gasoline down here."

Karl called down from the top step, "Don't touch a thing."

Tyson grasped the plug.

The plug snagged a cord, setting off the small bundle of C4 secured to the underside of the lid hanging above the full tank of gasoline. It also traveled to the secondary small bundle of C4 overhead, fastened to a dummy battery operated electrical box and lightbulb, with a pull-down wire switch. That switch, too, would have detonated the bomb.

The room seemed to contract and then exhale a sudden large and violent breath. Tyson, Sultan, and the second engineer vanished. The floor exploded to the greenhouse ceiling, rocketing the two drivers and the sergeant into the air, where they were lost in a blazing sea of fire. Smoke, rocks, and debris burst up the stairway, shooting Mark Rothstein and Karl Metzger backward like corks whacked out of champagne bottles.

The glass walls of the room exploded outward all at once, releasing a plume of fire and smoke in the air. Then the room breathed in, and everything came crashing down. Half the floor disappeared into the open cavity of the hidden basement, and a downpour of glass shards clattered to the ground.

Karl Metzger saw none of this. The gust of hot smoke and rocks shot him backward like a bullet, and all went black before he hit the ground.

***

Smoke was visible high in the air, but much of the sound of the explosion was contained, muffled by the ground. Officers from the front line sent two men to investigate, and their Jeep came to a halt beside Karl Metzger's Hummer.

As they were opening their car doors, a person came stumbling from the side of the house.

"Lieutenant Rothstein, is that you?" one of them asked, running to the man.

Mark collapsed in their arms. He was bleeding from his mouth and from a serious wound to his chest. Both of his legs were injured, his face had numerous lacerations and twinkled with glass shards, and one eye was swollen shut.

"They're all dead," he said, his body limp and trembling.

"What? Who?"

"Karl … Sultan …" Mark coughed, spitting blood over his lips. "They're all dead. Get me outta here."

"Karl's dead?" The stunned guards looked at each other. "Who's in charge?"

"I-I am. Now, get me out of here. We're under a-attack."

The two guards remained motionless.

"They killed Karl?"

Mark spat. "I told you, h-he's dead; now get—"

The men dropped him in the grass and ran to the Jeep.

"Wait … wait!" Mark screamed back. "We haven't lost—you fools! You fucking—" His words were cut short in a fit of wet coughs.

The men got in their Jeep and drove toward the front line, where they told the officer in charge that an old gas boiler has exploded in one of the houses and it was of no concern. The men gathered as much food and water as they could and left Alice under the pretense of a patrol. They did not return.

Deep in the brush of the neighboring lawn, Simon Kalispell and Frank Morrow secured their binoculars and began backtracking toward the firehouse. A terrible weight had lifted from their chests as they witnessed the explosions. They knew that Frank's rushed work setting up the bomb and detonator, as Simon secured the remainder of his family's photo albums, painted the radiation symbol, and removed his father's two shotguns, had been successful.

Chapter 61
It Begins

When the foghorn blared during lunch service, a force of Dragoons and Red Hands surrounded the townspeople, informing them to leave their food trays on the tables and file into the large gymnasium at Alice Elementary. A credible threat was received, they said, a bombing was possible. The doors were locked behind them, the handles strung with thick chains, and boards were nailed across the frames. The only windows in the gymnasium were high, near the ceiling, and steel bars had been welded vertically just in the case the townspeople became crafty.

Brian backed out of the kitchen during food service, disappearing up the stairway to join the others. Outside, the occasional popping of gunfire could be heard as any stragglers were discovered and dealt with.

Carolanne had not left the room since the previous night.

"This is almost over, sweetie," Brian told her.

She nodded. "I know, it's just ... Bethany. I'm so worried."

Simon looked stung. "The thought that she could be all alone, held captive by those repugnant men while I'm helpless to do anything until the plans are well under way ... it's maddening."

"I couldn't agree with you more," Brian said. "Here, I got some dinner." He opened the cloth sack he took from the kitchen, placing everything on Nick's desk. There were some apples, half a loaf of bread, and dried jerky.

The night could not arrive soon enough.

Carolanne sat with the radio headphones over her ears, listening to the silent channel as the men inspected their weapons. They cleaned the gears and barrels until the guns sparkled with grease and applied camouflage to their faces and skin.

Brian looked at Simon, almost naked, with an old Colt .45 and a few spare magazines holstered to his belt, and said, "You sure you don't want some clothing? A shirt, long pants?"

"I'm fine."

Frank looked up from assembling his rifle. "I would not mock his methods if I were you. There is not a finer scout in all of Alice—or Hightown, for that matter. The man has a way of disappearing in the wilderness that surprises even me."

"Of course," Brian said, knowing full well that Frank Morrow had years of Special Forces training. "I'll follow your lead. The both of you."

Nothing new came over the radio, which meant the operation was a go. Brian armed himself in the same fashion as he had for his previous journeys, which felt like ages ago. He wore a tactical jumpsuit and vest with spare clips for his assault rifle and pistol on his belt and clipped to his chest.

Frank carried the silenced scoped rifle with the double gauge shotgun slung over his shoulder. Simon took the pump action shotgun with a pouch full of shells, along with his pistol. They shared among them a limited amount of TNT, some explosives, and several hand grenades in satchel bags.

What they could scrounge up of medical supplies—gauze, bandages, IV drips—was set in boxes by the door. Carolanne would be needed before the night was over.

It was one thirty in the morning.

They stood to leave.

Brian looked at Carolanne sitting on the floor with a blanket over her shoulders, her eyes huge.

"We'll be in the hallway," Simon said, and he looked at Frank, silently indicating they should take their leave.

"Carolanne …" Brian walked to her.

"No," she said. "Don't—don't say anything."

He squeezed her tight as she wrapped her arms around his chest. He felt the warmth of her tears and her hot breath on his neck.

"I'm going to end this," he said. "It's just … not fair. It's not fair for us to have to go on living this way. I'm going to end this war. I'm going to bring peace to Alice—peace to us."

"Just come home safe, please. I can't … lose you. I can't lose both you and Bethany in the same week. Please, be safe."

Brian wanted to scream, punch the ground, shout to the heavens, hear thunder crash, tear houses down with his own hands, destroy cities. But he did not say a word, only held Carolanne tight, breathing in her beach-like scent as they kissed.

"Go. You have to go." She parted from him, wiping a tear.

Brian walked to the door, looked back at Carolanne standing alone in the dark room … and left.

Outside, he walked past Simon and Frank in the hallway.

"You okay?" Simon asked.

Brian kept walking. "Let's get on with it."

***

The night was dark and still, but faint voices could be heard in the distance. The small infirmary was overflowing. Earlier that night, many of the Red Hands had begun feeling a bit strange. Their stomachs were ill with pangs of abdominal cramping, and many of their throats felt restricted and raw. A few began throwing up. Bright lights looked odd, and their thoughts were becoming erratic. Explosive diarrhea followed, and soon many were doubled over in pain.

This was all to be expected.

Frank led the group onward with his silenced rifle from shadow to shadow toward Alice Elementary. No enemy movement could be seen until they neared the side door of the school. Two men were stationed outside, and one was doubled over and gagging.

"Jesus Christ," they heard the sick man say. "What the fuck is going on?"

"*You?*" said the other, crouched several feet away in bushes. "I'm shitting my brains out here. We gotta get to the doctor."

"No, man." The first guard paused, gagging. "Karl will kill us if we leave our post. Kenny and Sam already left for the doctor; we can't leave the school unguarded."

"I ain't seen Karl all day, and those fuckers inside ain't going nowhere. Jesus, my head is throbbing. I'm feverish, like I'm hallucinating and sweating or something."

"I know." The other man paused to dry heave. "I feel the same." A whooshing sound cut through the air like quick wind and the man turned to his friend in the bushes. "Jim—"

Jim had been shot with his pants around his ankles and was lying dead. Frank fired a second bullet from his silenced rifle, striking the standing guard in the shoulder, whacking him up against the brick wall. Another bullet struck his chest. The man slid down the wall, his heart beating the last few pumps of blood out of the open wound, and before he could scream, they were upon him—demonic-looking men with black muddy faces—pressing a palm against his mouth as his last few breaths of air escaped.

"It looks like your stew did the trick," Frank whispered to Brian.

"I reckon so."

Frank checked the dead soldier's pockets for keys and was happy to find a set, so no one would have to check the guard who had been crouched in the bushes at the time of his demise. Frank unlocked the doors as Brian gathered the soldiers' weapons and dragged their corpses far into the brush.

He led the way down the hall toward the gymnasium.

The school was so quiet, that as they neared the shuttered doors, they feared that it might be too late and the townspeople had been killed.

They removed the barricade, and Frank found the key to the padlock and chain.

He opened the door, and they entered the pitch-black room.

Hundreds of silent eyes stared back at them. Then someone produced a flashlight, and then another.

"*Turn it off. Turn it off,*" Frank said in a hiss. It was possible that more Dragoons or Red Hands were wandering the halls.

The lights were extinguished, and Frank Morrow addressed the crowd.

"As you are well aware, war has been declared against us by both the Red Hands and by Nicholas Byrnes. For too long, we the people have been forced to keep our eyes shut at the proceedings going on all around us. Not any longer. It's time to remove the veil held in place by the villains who were blatantly invited into Alice by Nicholas Byrnes. With the aid of General Driscoll, we are fighting back—all who are willing—tonight."

There was noticeable excitement in the crowd.

Frank continued. "Everyone in this room knows who I am. My name is

Frank Morrow, the ranking officer of Alice's Ranger division. To my side is Simon Kalispell, the second in command of the Rangers, and Brian Rhodes, a most welcome friend from Hightown and now third in command. I have met with General Driscoll in the North and have been given the authority as general in charge of Alice. Nicholas Byrnes's authority and title are null and void, and his leadership will be destroyed. Nicholas Byrnes is no longer our leader or a welcome friend and is in direct violation of our laws and ways. He will be exiled or killed, God willing. His authority is, from this point forward, irreversibly revoked."

The crowd stirred, and many had to be hushed down.

"I will not lie or give you false hope; this is not going to be easy. We're up against a hardened and ruthless enemy, but we have the support of Zone Red. Before the sun rises, we will reclaim Alice as our home and stomp away the vermin who have infested it. Karl Metzger is dead, praise God, and so are his lieutenants, Mark Rothstein and the man named Sultan. Nick Byrnes will have his hour tonight, and we will all bear witness to his demise as we tear down his gates."

At the news of Karl Metzger's downfall the people again had to be hushed. Frank explained the plan and the part that the residents of Alice were expected to play to see victory carried out.

"All in favor—all who will stand and fight, knowing full well the capabilities of the enemy that we face, and who will not give in to the ruthless oppression that will see us all dead—will you not follow me at this hour?"

The people all raised their hands despite knowing full well that it meant certain death for many in the room.

"That settles it," Frank continued. "Tonight we go to battle. Not later, but now, we free our hands from the binds that hold them in oppression. We will march against Nick and his Dragoons and hold them accountable for their crimes against humanity. First, I am going to need a few volunteers."

Frank picked from the crowd twenty trusted officers and hardened soldiers. Brian handed the men the few weapons they had taken from the slain guards.

"We are leaving now to raid the Alice Police Department to free the storerooms of their weapons and ammunition. Prepare yourselves to depart upon our return. Anyone unable or unwilling to fight should remain behind.

Anyone with medical training, or who is already injured, you are to report to the firehouse before dawn, where some medical supplies have been stockpiled. We will need more, so gather what you can."

With those words, the twenty men turned and left Alice Elementary.

For an hour, the people waited in the dark as Frank led his team to the police department. With the townspeople locked away, the center of Alice was deserted. Frank's men overwhelmed the two Dragoons guarding the police station—one rushing out of the bathroom with his pants clutched in on hand, a rifle in the other. Brian's wild mushrooms were having a devastating effect.

The armory was in the basement behind a solid metal door. They used a swipe-card found on one of the dead guards and rushed inside.

Rows upon rows of assault rifles of all variety along with pistols, knives, and grenades lined the walls. The men filled duffel bags to near bursting and then swung even more assault rifles over their shoulders.

Back in the dark gymnasium, the crowd grew boisterous as the twenty soldiers returned, dispensing the arms amongst the crowd. Frank held a quick counsel with his senior officers, discussing logistics.

The sound of approaching vehicles could be heard, but several men had already placed explosives in the streets and set themselves up to ambush any oncoming vehicles.

Alice's army was ready to storm the gates of Nick Byrnes's castle faster than the Red Hands could take men off the front line to counter the resistance … not that they would be able to take any men off the front line, if the plan was successful.

"This is it, people," Frank shouted. "Follow your orders and stick to the plan! Remember, we fight together as a team, as a town—as a family! Kill anyone who stands in our way! We march now to the death of our enemy! We march to victory! We march to war!"

The people shouted and cheered.

"Move out!" Frank commanded.

He turned with Simon Kalispell and Brian Rhodes at his side, and the three men led the people of Alice to battle.

***

Miles away on the front line, Karl's sick men stirred. In the far distance overhead, lost in the sky, was the gentle sound of something humming. The sick and wretched soldiers manning the line did not know it yet, but that strangely familiar sound meant death approaching.

Chapter 62

Ghost Army

Lieutenant General Dietrich, "the Priest," stood tall on a massive boulder, turning to face his army in the flat gully below.

"Rise now," he said, with his hands in the air. "Rise now, for the end is near. Our journey is almost complete. We march to Alice where General Metzger awaits, and by God's good grace, to victory beyond."

The bandage circling the top of his head was itchy and in need of a change, but Dietrich maintained an air of composure before his band of soldiers, many of whom had sustained injuries far worse than his own. The fighting in Masterson had proved more ferocious than anticipated, and his men were weary from war and from the constant marching that followed.

The aid who patched up the Priest's head had said it would heal fine as long as Doctor Freeman could stitch it up proper.

But the Priest proclaimed, "It is up to God to decide one's fate. If the hands of our Lord work within the good doctor, then so shall it be."

"You're a crazy one, Dietrich, thinking God's got something to do with this," the aid had told him.

Standing tall upon the rock, the Priest gave the command: "Rise now, men. Rise now, and face the road ahead," and a sea of men rose like apparitions birthed from the carnage and wreckage all around, claimed from the desolate earth on which they trod.

No further camouflage was needed of Dietrich's men, for the soldiers resembled the gray and dusty rocks of the earth itself, so soiled were they in mud and gore and as twisted as their surroundings.

The tall, gray-haired priest led the men upon horseback, sitting straight as an arrow in the saddle, his head up. His baritone voice bellowed, echoing out over his men in gospel song.

"Mine eyes have seen the glory of the coming of the lord:
He is trampling out the vintage where the grapes of wrath are stored:
He hath loosed the fateful lightning of His terrible swift sword:
His truth is marching on!"

Some men sang and mumbled along, not knowing or caring about the words.

The hours passed, and Dietrich could feel dampness in the late night air as he sang aloud.

"Glory, glory, hallelujah!"

They were close to the ammunition stockpile, and he could feel the excitement through the singing of his men, whose voices grew louder as their pace quickened. With the aid of the vehicles in Sullivan Park, they would be in Alice in no time at all. They would be sleeping on beds and eating real food, at long last.

He glanced back at his men. His army appeared like a rambling horde dispatched straight from the depths of hell, adorned in an assortment of dark, leathery necklaces made of dried human ears and jewelry crudely constructed of white and gold teeth. They carried an assortment of weapons, from high-tech machinery to scraps of sharpened metal and hammered spears.

The men trampled through the woods in the darkness of night, keeping a vigilant eye for the tall barn in the middle of the park.

Any minute now. Dietrich smiled.

"His truth is marching on!"

The barn appeared, and the woods opened up to a massive paved lot before three buildings.

"Give me some light," the Priest ordered, and flashlights as well as floodlights were brought forward. The army moved into the clearing. Officers ordered men to open the barn doors, and trucks were driven forward to gather the supplies.

"Where are the guards?" Dietrich looked about. Four men sent from General Metzger were supposed to be guarding the lot, but they were nowhere to be seen.

A sergeant galloped his horse to the Priest's side. "There's hardly nothing here."

Dietrich didn't answer. In the paved lot sat a solitary tank, the treads in need of repair, two transport vehicles, and several flatbed trucks. The Priest squinted through his one good eye and scratched at the bandage around his head. He looked to the barns and at the men walking back and forth. They were carrying boxes of ammunition, rockets, and the like, but the officers were muttering that there were only a dozen or so crates.

Then it hit him.

At the same time, two of his men came running forward.

"Dietrich, sir! The guards—they're dead! Been shot, off in the woods!"

The Priest turned to his officers. "Galloping speed—now! Fan out!"

The war begins with me ...

The command was spread throughout the men; the soldiers dropped boxes, munitions spilling to the ground. Far off, in a crate full of tank shells in the back of the barn, sat a satchel full of plastic explosives. A wire went from the satchel, around the barn's molding, and traveled outside, forming a circle around the large lot. The wire was buried several inches below the sandy soil, and it attached to additional satchel bags and explosive ordnances hidden underground.

The other end of the wire traveled far, trailing off into the woods, where a dozen snipers lay perched high up in the trees, their eyes pressed to the lenses of their thermal scopes. One of the men spoke into a radio and was issued back a command. He pulled a small switch out of his pocket, coiled the end of the wire around a pin, and pulled the trigger.

"Fall back!" the Priest ordered, hunched over his steed, heeling the warhorse to a full gallop.

All at once, the ground beneath the army exploded, sending colossal drifts of dirt and slabs of pavement high in the air. Dietrich pulled on the reins of his horse, coming to a stop before a smoking pillar. The explosions rippled over the ground from satchel bag to satchel bag, igniting the ammunition left in the barns and dug underground, as well as several barrels of fuel. The Priest watched his men evaporate in walls of fire.

His horse reared then buckled, and Dietrich fell to his side, but was fast on his feet. The horse got back up and pulled away, speeding off into the dark woods. The Priest was alone in the blazing inferno with his dying and maimed soldiers all around.

The men of Hightown, along with a team of Alice's elite soldiers from Zone Green—recalled from the far south on General Driscoll's orders—appeared all at once out of the shadowy woods and unleashed such a barrage on Dietrich's men that half of his remaining party was cut down within the first minutes of the battle.

An endless supply of rockets, machine gun fire, tank shells, and missiles crashed down upon his men in a torrential rain, turning the expansive dirt ground into a frothing sea caught in a storm.

"My God," the Priest whispered.

Chapter 63
War

A soldier named Peter Hasting doubled over in the trenches, heaving and gagging with nothing left in his stomach to vomit up. His sweat-soaked jacket lay flopped on the ground like something dead, the old red handprint smeared with mud.

"Oh, Christ almighty," he mumbled. "Oh, Lord in heaven, what the hell is the matter with me?"

What's the matter with everyone?

Half of the line was experiencing stomach ailments and feverish conditions to varying degrees. His commanding officer had called for a medic over an hour ago, but no medic had arrived. It was the same all over Alice; some men were completely immobilized and others were experiencing respiratory ailments with rasping breathing, their lips blistering and swollen.

Food poisoning was suspected and the chefs were all woken and rounded up, but many of them were sick too.

Peter picked his head up out of his lap. He thought he heard a noise, something faint. Wind perhaps, maybe a swarm of insects. Sweat stung at his eyes.

That ain't no wind.

He stood. A spectacular array of twinkling stars, so bright that they burned his retinas, pixelated before him in a full spectrum of prism-like colors. He gazed at the dark sky, searching for the invisible sound as it grew louder. A strange feeling pitted deep in his chest. His thoughts were becoming abnormal and unstable. His vision was hallucinatory and his body felt as if it were spinning around in a circle, spinning and spinning …

"Ohhhh, sweet Jesus, no … oh, Lord in heaven, what have you done to me? I'm gonna be sick."

The sound in the sky grew louder, almost deafening, piercing and vibrating his eardrums to the point of pain. Now it was right overhead. The sound beat down upon his frazzled mind, making him cower and shake in paranoia, imagining an army of demons in the night ready to pounce.

In the center of Alice, far from the line, the foghorns blared.

War, he realized. *War is coming … War is here.*

A terrible crash pierced the night. A fireball licked up to the heavens, filling the horizon with a blaze of orange and red. The spectacle of the event made Peter's lips quiver as a tear streamed down his cheek.

The blast was followed by another blast, and then another. At first, the explosions were distant, somewhere in the town, but soon places along the line close to his position erupted into flame. The vivid intensity of bright fire imprinted afterimages on his retinas. Machine gun fire and tracer rounds were illuminated in the air, but whatever they were shooting at, Peter could not see, and his perception of the unfolding events could not be trusted.

His body shook to the core, and his carbine felt slippery in his hands.

"What demon are you?" he yelled to the heavens, his rattled mind frantic with delusion and despair. Down the line, other soldiers were shouting and panicking in the same fashion, the explosions devastating their poisoned minds and bodies into alarm as the toxic and psychoactive ingredients swirled throughout their bloodstreams. Some ran over the trench line in either direction, crying, trembling, screaming.

"Karl! Where's Karl?"

The sober-minded individuals, the unaffected or those who had not eaten the poisoned stew, grabbed at the fleeing men, attempting to beat reason into them with fists and boots.

Something cracked far off in the woods, across the rolling, shadowy field separating the trench line from the forest and wilderness beyond. The noise steered Peter's attention away from the fires burning all around. The crackling grew louder. The tops of the trees in the forest swayed and shook, and some toppled over.

Peter's eyes grew large.

What demon …?

The roar of engines preceded the line of tanks that stormed out into the open field, their massive treads, like metal teeth, toppling the thin trees and cutting away at the earth. Gunfire and tank shells struck the line, falling like raindrops from a hellish sky.

"Christ in heaven!" Peter ducked down.

Bullet fire erupted from everywhere, mixing with the slurred shouting of men. Off to Peter's side, a guard tower exploded in a terrible combustion, sending splintering fragments of burning wood to rain down on the scrambling soldiers.

There was a man standing in front of Peter, speaking, but Peter could not hear the words coming from his mouth. Hands grabbed his collar, and his body was shaken, slammed hard against the trench wall.

"Get up! Get the fuck up! Fire your weapon!" The mouth belonged to a sergeant, and for a moment, Peter felt fine—his mind sharp, his body calm.

He stood, turned with his rifle, and looked out over the trench wall. And what he saw caused his poisoned fears to return like a tsunami. Both sides were launching star shells—flares that slowly descended to the earth on little parachutes like glowing stars, illuminating the approaching army and the trenches with bright burning light. A sea of soldiers and armored vehicles were advancing toward him—fast.

In the distance, behind the approaching wall of men, a steady wave of smoke trails shot into the sky from the mobile rocket launchers in the rear.

The trench line exploded to shreds, the cement and wooden walls splintering. Peter was blown off his feet in a wave of rubble.

"Where is our artillery? Where are our mortars?" shouted the sergeant beside him, gripping a wound on his arm.

Peter tried to speak, but dirt in his mouth caused him to sputter and cough.

The mortar battalions were the first to get rocketed by the helicopters, along with the infirmary, which was overflowing with men. In minutes, a small number of rockets had wiped them all out. The helicopters were now strafing the front line, the heavy machine gun fire and missiles raining down hellfire upon the scrambling soldiers.

General Driscoll's soldiers crossed the field, and Peter wet his pants as the monstrous treads of a tank glided directly overhead, from one side of the trench to the other, dirt cascading upon his face. Men poured in the dugout on either side of him, and a fist struck him so hard that a strobe of white light consumed his vision.

Peter fell, and did not stand back up again.

***

Jeremy Winters marched behind a fast-moving tank, leading a column of men who had been ordered to follow his lead. When they exited the woods into the open field, he shouted, "Stay in formation! Stay in formation!"

His battle-hardened infantrymen looked back at him with stony eyes, listening to his words through the hail of machine gun fire plunking against the row of armored vehicles leading the advance. But bullets found their way around the tanks, and men began to fall. Explosions from short-range mortars and RPGs pockmarked the ground, sending geysers of dirt into the air and rocketing screaming soldiers to their sides.

The field before Jeremy resembled the torrent of a raging sea, the lights from the towers and trenches before him like a burning city on the horizon.

Something large struck the ground behind him, and the rumbling surged through his feet. He turned to see a rock the size of a small car bounce and tumble over the earth, just missing him and his men, and leaving a gash as it rolled. When he turned forward, another rock crashed down beside him, crushing the leg and torso of one of his men, who hollered and roared. The rock rolled further, crushing the leg of another man before coming to a standstill.

They're using those stupid fucking catapults. Chris Lockton, you son of a bitch!

"Fan out!" Jeremy yelled. "Fan out!"

Rocks, bricks, and debris of all kind struck the earth. Rusted and twisted metal from lampposts, squared landscaping rocks, and hundreds of smaller pebbles and stones rained down from the dark sky, crushing and maiming men in a macabre scene straight from the Middle Ages.

Something stung Jeremy's cheek, causing him to momentarily reel. He felt at the pain on his face and then looked to the ground, where a dismembered hand had fallen. Panicked, he then saw an entire bare arm crash to the dirt, mixed in with broken glass from an exploding lamppost, followed by feet, viscera, severed heads, and bare bones.

We're fighting the devil.

The catapults achieved their intended effect—to strike fear into the hearts of the soldiers—but Jeremy only felt angered at seeing the dismembered body parts of allies rain down upon him.

"They're trying to scare us!" he shouted to his men. "These men, they're only throwing stones! Pebbles! Move on, show them how real soldiers fight—show them how real men kill!"

It seemed to take a lifetime before Jeremy and his men crossed the no-man's-land and poured into the trenches. The reserves were fast approaching from the rear in transport vehicles and school buses with armor-plated windows and machine gun nests constructed on top of the roofs, the once bright yellow exteriors painted dark green. Explosions marked the land, and many men perished, unable to escape the fiery confines of their vehicles. But soon, the advancing soldiers tore apart the defensive line of the Red Hands and all who stood in their way.

Jeremy and his detachment had been ordered to proceed east to the reservoir and filtering plant as the bulk of General Driscoll's men followed the crescent-shaped trench line, flanking the defenses from the side rather than face them head-on. This initial charge against the Red Hands was taking place in the westernmost corner, farthest from Nick Byrnes's mansion on Ridgeline Road.

Jeremy's men diverted into the thicket of Alice Springs Park, and moved forward into the foreboding woods. Bullets whizzed by, smacking into the leaves and branches.

The soldiers fanned out, fighting the pockets of fleeing Red Hands who scattered behind trees and improvised defenses.

In the darkness, the terrain was difficult to navigate, and Jeremy tripped over roots and slipped on wet grass until he and his men arrived at the small stream that led to the reservoir.

The Red Hands were retreating to the fortification surrounding the water plant in haste, and the fighting became short range.

Jeremy was stuck behind a tree with bullets ripping at the bark as he watched a man from his detachment named Reynolds jump through a thicket of brush to find an old, bearded enemy soldier skirting along the bank of the stream.

The bearded man dropped his rifle.

"Don't shoot! Don't shoot!" he called out.

The old man fell to his knees, his quivering hands high in the air. Reynolds had his rifle trained on the man, his own hands trembling on the trigger, as bullets whizzed by and plucked at the water like skipping stones.

"Get down—facedown!" Jeremy heard Reynolds shout.

Before the surrendering man had time to do as commanded, a bullet struck him in his chest, toppling him over into the stream.

Reynolds's eyes went large, and the sergeant who had shot the man ran up.

"No prisoners, Reynolds! Don't waste your time! Keep moving!"

"He was surrendering!" Reynolds protested.

"No prison—"

A barrage of bullet fire walloped the sergeant and Reynolds at once, splintering the nearby trees and peppering the water behind them in plunks. The two men splashed in the stream, and their bodies were swept off in the current. Several Red Hands stamped out of the brush and continued toward the reservoir.

Jeremy fired at the fleeing men, but they were soon lost in the brambles. He jumped out from behind the tree, calling the soldiers behind him to advance.

"Let's go!" he shouted. "Move! Move!"

The army crashed through the woods, coming to a steep incline over an earthen embankment. At the top of the incline, machine gun fire pelted the ground from well-fortified bunkers before the water plant.

Jeremy and his men crept to the edge, only daring to look up at intervals. The bullet fire was so intense that a few men were shot through the tops of their helmets while looking up for only fractions of a second.

"Stay down!" Jeremy commanded. "Keep your heads down!"

He turned to the men who were huddled all around him and those still running through the woods to catch up. "Davidson, get over here!"

Davidson ran to Jeremy, keeping his back against the steep incline as dirt rained down from the bullet fire only inches above him.

Jeremy took out a pocket map. "Call it in."

He pointed to the coordinates, and Davidson spoke into his microphone. It seemed like eternity before the helicopters arrived, spraying the bunkers with large caliber ammunition, turning the cement and stone to rubble.

Jeremy and his lieutenants threw smoke grenades over the hill as the helicopters flew back to the front. The men who had night vision goggles adjusted them over their eyes.

Jeremy stood tall, looking out over the crowd of soldiers awaiting his command.

"The reservoir is ours—move out!"

Jeremy turned and ran headfirst into the blinding smoke and sporadic gunfire that cut through the fog. The army followed, roaring a thunderous cry.

***

Over this fence is where I'll find Bethany, Simon thought in meditation. *Over this fence is where I'll find my best friend, Winston. Over this fence is pure evil— men who want to see humanity erased.*

Over this fence is freedom.

Over this fence is how I find home.

I am the wind. I am the rock. I am the tree, and my roots grow deep …

Simon, Frank, Brian, and a handful of hardened soldiers waited, crouching low behind a fence and a wall of bushes separating Nick's mansion from the neighboring yard, ready to flank the maze of trenches in Nick's front lawn. They were alone, with the rest of Alice's army fast approaching the front gates. The first explosion could be seen far away, rocketing a ball of fire into the air. The enemy was now on high alert, and the foghorn blared from across town.

Words came to him that were not his own. *Some of us are monks and some of us are warriors. You, Simon, come off as a teacher, but I see fierceness in you that you may not yet be aware of. You must be careful, because that fierceness can tip your own scale in either direction—the way of destruction, or the way of ceasing destruction. Something bright burns inside of you, and you must take good care of that flame to see it grow into a blazing fire of your own choosing.*

Simon's mind dwelled in a deep layer of meditation as he studied the armored guard tower in the rear of the property.

I am the wind. I am the rock. I am the tree, and my roots grow deep.

I am the teacher, the student …

He repeated his mantras over and over, but the sentences were soon overtaken and replaced by simple names: *Winston, Winston, Winston … Bethany, Bethany, Bethany …*

Simon checked his watch. *Tick, tick …*

An hour earlier, a jet-black inflatable Zodiac raft had floated down the Ridgeline River, carrying a six-man Special Forces team, handpicked by General Driscoll. The men paddled against the steep, rocky shoreline, nearly as invisible as the fish swimming beneath the surface of the water.

They brought the boat ashore two properties away from Nick's mansion, and the men dispersed to their intended location—the roof of a tall and marvelous home at the end of an expansive backyard. Once in position, the three snipers and three spotters laid out their mats, and the gunners adjusted their eyes against the scopes of their .50 caliber anti-material sniper rifles. They took aim through the night vision and thermal processing scopes and waited for the clock to count down.

When a spotter said, "Ready in ten," they grew still, and the soldier continued counting down, "four, three, two—"

On one, they opened fire on the top tier of the tower in Nick's backyard. The .50 caliber ammunition penetrated the fortifications as if the wood, cinderblock, and sandbags were made of butter. After the three snipers had squeezed off a complete magazine each, there was nothing left to the top portion of the tower except splintered timber and pockets of flame. The snipers reloaded and took aim for the number of machine gun nests along the zigzag line of trenches in the front yard.

Simon witnessed the destruction of the tower and did not flinch. Never before had his mind been so clear.

This is my home … this is my home … Bethany …

His eyes flashed open.

I am the teacher. I am the warrior.

He jumped to his feet, pounced over the fence, and ran to the tree line bordering the broad side of the trenches circling Nick's property like a maze of moats.

Simon stopped with Frank, Brian, and the soldiers at his side, and they each lit a stick of TNT—the type Simon had only ever seen in Western movies.

As they threw the dynamite over the thicket of trees, they heard the drumming blades of a helicopter swoop down, and the sound of gunfire erupted like a volcano bursting forth lava into the sky from Nick's front lawn.

The soldiers of Alice were now knocking down the front gates of the house as the helicopter exchanged fire with the fortified emplacements and strafed pockets of men with barrages of large-caliber ammunition.

The TNT exploded, sending up a cloud of dirt taller than the trees bordering the two properties. Simon, Frank, and Brian each lit another stick and crashed forward out of the bushes.

They threw the TNT far off into the yard as they poured into the trench line.

A Dragoon who had been rocketed over by the first explosion was now getting back on his feet and unholstering his sidearm. Simon pulled the trigger of his shotgun, and the man flew backwards.

A great wave of fire and smoke erupted as the second sticks of TNT detonated, and Simon moved fast into the twisting maze of trenches.

Dazed and injured men stumbled forth, trying to find their footing, and they were mowed down before they had time to see the faces of their enemies.

When Simon had fired all five shells of his .12 gauge, he discarded the weapon and drew his pistol.

Bethany, Bethany, Bethany, he repeated. Then, the words were replaced by a new mantra, one soaked in the fighting of which Simon was now engaged: *Nick, Nick, Nick, Nick …*

Simon ran into the dizzying corridor of trenches, with Brian and Frank quick at his heels, throwing grenades toward the machine gun emplacements in the distance. His mind was processing his surroundings with such clarity that events seemed to unfold in slow motion, his body and consciousness moving at such speeds that his rational thoughts were left behind as if time did not pertain to his cognizance.

Around every turn, every corner, Dragoons in dark brown uniforms came before him with sinister expressions, the steel of their pistols gleaming from their chests like badges of hellish sheriffs, and each in turn was struck dead. The majority of Nick Byrnes's men had eaten dinner from the stores of food in the mansion and were largely unaffected by the poisonous stew. Their minds were sharp, undistracted.

Simon was reloading his pistol as a group of Dragoons came rushing from around the bend in a narrow lane. Simon snatched a thick-bladed machete from the hand of a lifeless soldier and sprinted over a mound of dead Dragoons, jumping into the air on nimble feet and cutting and hacking away, turning and twisting his body in such a way that it appeared unnatural and animalistic.

Blood soaked his hands and face, sprayed upon his chest, and coated his hair in a mat. His vision was a throbbing red, and his only thought was, *Nick, Nick, Nick.* He was not the wind, the rock, or the tree; he was the predator, the bear, the cheetah, the tiger, a wild animal, able to move with blinding grace and a mind free of congealed thoughts. Simon was the alpha beast, the apex predator, the fastest and deadliest animal among a sea of carnivores, all with their fangs gleaming in the flashing lights of the explosions all around.

Man upon man ran forward and faced their demise upon the roaring current that was Simon Kalispell. He could not be stopped or hindered, even when bullets grazed him or pierced the fleshy part of his thigh.

He moved through the twisting trenches, roaring with rage, hacking through arms, necks, sinew and flesh, dropping whole limbs to the blood-soaked earth, making streams of muddy ground from the dead and dying. The eyes of the doomed witnessed the wild effigy of a man turned war god, covered in the mud and gore of his slain, while awaiting their own turns to face his blade.

Brian and Frank could not keep up. They were barely at Simon's back as they shot and killed dozens, helping Simon slash his way across the line.

At the far end of the trench, in a stretch of level ground separating an entrance to the trenches from Nick's front door, a wide-bodied sergeant named August scratched at the blistering rash around his neck and gave his battle-hardened men a few fierce words: "By God, the hour is upon us. We go now to turn this tide of war in our favor or face ruin at the hands of our enemy!"

The men shouted a howling cry and went screaming and snarling into the narrow gully of the trench before them, their bodies and minds shaped for one thing: war.

Simon broke into these men as they turned a corner, moving like the wind and water, as fierce as fire, jumping over the stabbed and lacerated before they had time to fall, and taking on the next man in turn. He was a blur of red, a vision of hell. Sergeant August ran forward at the end of the procession, his rifle at the ready, and Simon crashed down upon him, whacking through the man's helmet before continuing across the dirty terrain without missing a step.

Turning the corner were four riders, their warhorses hammering the earth as their neighing mouths snarled whiffs of steam. Simon grabbed a pistol from a fallen man and squeezed off the rounds with a hunter's precision before leaping in the air and cutting the remaining men down from their saddles, sending the horses to trample the dead and dying in the narrow lane.

The air all around Simon seemed to expand and contract with his every breath. He did not stop. He did not falter.

Frank Morrow had been shot, and Brian had fallen behind, dragging the general along by his shirt collar. As the soldiers of Alice caught up, Brian released the dying Frank to his people's care and sprinted up the trench lane to catch up to Simon.

"Guard the general! Guard the general!" they cried.

The remaining Dragoons were retreating into the house, as the yard now belonged to the people of Alice. The enemy took up position in the windows or stopped as they ran across the open lawn to turn and fire their weapons, only to be mowed down without discrimination.

Alice's army swarmed through the trenches, pressing up against the dirt wall facing the mansion. The people of Alice and Nick's Dragoons were now eye-to-eye over the short distance between the trenches and the house … and then Simon marched out alone and stopped in the open yard, staring up at the mansion. The machete in his clenched fist dripped with the blood of his slain.

Nick, Nick, Nick …

Simon, adorned in his bloody robes, seemed to have emerged from the earth itself, from some dismal plane, a clay effigy of a madman before the gates of hell, causing the Dragoons in the house to stare wild-eyed, entranced at this terrible vision. The shooting slowed. In the sky above, the helicopter had taken heavy fire and was spiraling out of control with a trail of circling smoke following its twisted descent. It plummeted to the earth, producing a wall of fire in the distance behind Simon, draping his glistening form in blinding firelight.

Simon breathed through clenched teeth.

"… Nick … Nick … Nick, Nick, Nick!"

His voice grew in volume, louder and louder, until the words became guttural.

"Nick! Nick! NICK! NICK! *NICK!*"

His voice was not his, but that of some monster, a bringer of plagues, and he beat upon his chest with his fist, shouting, "Nick! Nick!" The army in the trenches behind Simon was mesmerized by this man, their fellow soldier, and they roared a cry of victory.

Simon sprang toward the house with blinding speed, and Brian—who had been crouching low at his heels—jumped to join his comrade in battle. The armies resumed shooting at each other, and the people of Alice rose up from the dirt and flooded into the mansion of Nicholas Byrnes, following Simon Kalispell and Brian Rhodes.

***

Something startled Nick Byrnes awake.

The empty glass tumbler in his hand seemed to vibrate. The fire had burned down to faint trails of smoke and cinder in the fireplace, and the classical music had played out. The room was silent.

When did I fall asleep? What the hell was that noise?

All the previous day, Nick had checked on the line, going from checkpoint to checkpoint on the back of his great stallion. The men on the line all had the same question for him: "Where's Karl Metzger?"

He did not have an answer.

There was movement again, a trembling. The whole house seemed to shake. The intricate chandelier swayed overhead, the little hanging crystals clinking, making a melodic sound.

Nick heard muffled shouts carry through the walls. He sprang to his feet, grabbed his holster and assault rifle, and ran down the hallway. He unlocked the mahogany door at the end and turned the handle.

Mother of God …

The room was crawling with his men, flooding through the doorway, shouting and screaming. Injured men were being brought in on stretchers or dragged in from the trenches, leaving red trails in their wake.

Nick's head swam, and his knees went weak.

Men rushed to circle him, barking at him with a barrage of words.

"We're under attack!"

"The front line has been breached!"

"Alice's soldiers are in the yard!"

"We're getting killed out there!"

"What do we do?"

"What do we do?"

"What do we do?"

Nick ran to a window and looked out over the trenches. A black helicopter was buzzing in the air, raining down a barrage of bullets and explosions, and the entire yard looked as if it were ablaze.

Oh, dear mother of God …

Nick recoiled. He could not speak. He could not process what he was seeing. Bullets began striking the window frame, and patches of drywall and wood exploded off the walls behind him.

Several officers grabbed his shoulders, pulling him down and out of the room. His rifle slipped to the floor.

Back in the hallway of Nick's private wing, with some of the noise of the gunfire suppressed, Nick was able to regain his composure.

"Jesus Christ! Why didn't someone get me sooner?"

"We tried," one of them said. "We were about to break your door down."

"Never mind. What the hell is going on?"

"We're under attack. The line's been breached, and they're gaining ground!"

"Can we push them back?"

The men looked at one another, exchanging pale expressions. "Sir, we're trying."

The color drained from Nick's face. All at once, he was aware that the alcohol he had drunk the previous evening was making his head spin.

Where the hell is Karl Metzger?

"All right," Nick said. "Radio for reinforcements—now! Flank the enemy off the yard. Have the men fall back to the house, and you all—defend every doorway in this hallway."

The room shook with another explosion somewhere close—in the house. Plaster rained down from the ceiling.

"Now, goddamn it!" Nick shouted, and the men dispersed. A sergeant opened the mahogany door leading to the house to get to a radio. He took several steps into the room and then vanished in a flash of bright, orange fire. The heat could be felt pouring through the doorway.

A man standing beside the doorframe toppled backward. "Fuck!" he shouted, patting at patches of fire on his chest and arm.

Nick turned and ran down the hallway as his few loyal officers took up position in the doorframes. He unlocked the door to the attic apartment, and ran up the stairs. Stephanie was standing at the top, wide-eyed with tears rolling down her cheeks. Her hands squeezed the cord of her purple silk robe.

"Nick …" Her voice wavered, her body trembling.

Nick stormed past her. The front and rear wall-length windows had been shattered and lay open to the outside, struck by bullets or rattled by explosions, and the wind was whipping the room into a frenzy.

Stephanie clung to Nick's arm as he marched toward the front window. Strangely, the noise of battle quieted. There was a voice. Someone was shouting his name, repeating it over and over, screaming it like an animal, a monster. Nick froze.

His feet skirted dangerously close to the jagged glass frame of the front window. As the wind blew his dark hair back, he stared in amazement at his lawn set ablaze. The people of Alice lined the trenches, running to the front, pressing their bodies against the trench wall, ready to pour into his house.

Standing in the yard was a man—barely a man, but a thing of war itself, shirtless, carrying a large blade and shouting Nick's name over and over, with the frame of a helicopter in the far back roaring with fire. The man began to run, sprinting toward the house, and the people of Alice hollered so loud that the gunfire could barely be heard. Bullets pelted the ceiling above him, and the edge of the window by his feet was splintering. Nick jumped away.

Oh, God … dear God. Oh, God in heaven. Where are my reinforcements? Are there any reinforcements? … Is the line destroyed? … Is all hope lost? … I'm not going to die like this. I'm not going to die like this! This is not the way things were supposed to happen!

The roar of the attack rattled the fibers of the house, the timbers and beams groaning from the onslaught. Stephanie huddled in a corner, crying and shaking. Nick stood in the center of the room, watching the open doorframe … waiting.

***

Brian chased after Simon as he crashed through the door to Nick's mansion. The people of Alice were fast at his heels and filtering in. Dead and dying Dragoons littered the floor, and pockets of fire burned all around. The air was thick and reaching boiling temperature.

Brian, along with several soldiers, followed Simon as he turned to the right and kicked in a solid mahogany door, charred black and still smoking from a recent explosion.

The hallway was long, and it turned in a circular bend.

Just a few steps in, and enemy soldiers opened fire, hidden behind a doorframe ahead. Brian ducked to his side, stuck in an exchange of gunfire. Simon and a group of Alice's soldiers had sprinted past the door, able to dodge the enemy before they had time to react. Simon paused, looking back.

"Go on!" Brian shouted. "We'll clear the room. Go!"

Simon turned, and sprinted forward.

During a momentary cease in the gunfire, two of Alice's men stormed into the enemy's room.

Brian was right behind them, but by the time he entered, the two men were already slain. A beast of a man stood before him, and the two limp bodies of the soldiers lay slumped at his feet.

The room was a library of sorts, the books and leather furniture strewn about, everything riddled with bullets. A blaze of twinkling sparks blew in from a half-open door in the back of the room, fluttering through the air like fireflies. Small fires burned among the books and debris.

The giant of a man turned to face Brian.

Brian's eyes shot large, and his mouth dropped open.

"You … you were dead."

Steven stood before him, his forehead furrowed by a scar. His torn military fatigues were ripped, displaying his muscular chest. His body was black with soot and stained and splattered with carnage.

"St-Steve?"

The eyes staring back at Brian seemed to register something, but it was hard to decipher an emotion of any kind.

Several more of Alice's men stormed through the doorway, crashing into Brian's back. They stopped short, staring at this giant before them.

Brian half-turned, lifting his arms horizontally. "I got this. Go on. *Go.*"

The men did not move. They were transfixed by Steven, who stood in the middle of the room, his eyes locked on Brian, like some Romanesque statue of a warrior deity.

"Go!" Brian shouted. "Go—*now*, goddamn it!"

The men scurried out, and Brian kicked the door shut.

"Steven ... is that ... *is that really you?*"

Steven's eyelids fluttered, and he started walking toward Brian.

Brian stepped backward, looking over his shoulder at the fireplace mantle.

"S-Stevie, I—"

"You ... left me."

"No, Stevie, I would never—"

"You ... tried to kill me. You left me for dead."

"Steven." Brian's back hit the cold marble, and Steven continued toward him. There was fire in Steven's eyes, a haze of madness.

"You son of a bitch."

Steven closed the last few steps, and Brian shoved his rifle at him in the open palms of his hands, his face aghast.

"I ain't gonna fight you, Steve. I don't want to do this."

Steven smacked the rifle out of Brian's open palms and his massive hands grabbed Brian by the collar, lifting him high in the air. Brian stared down at him: his cousin, his brother. He did not kick or throw a punch.

Steven turned and threw Brian across the room to crash and roll over the ground. Brian got to his knees, wheezing for air.

"Steven, I'm so sorry. I've missed you so much. You're my best friend."

Steven stopped short for a moment and then continued.

"No, no, no!" Steven said through clenched teeth. "You tried to kill me. You left me for dead. Everyone deserted me, even my own uncle. My family. *You*—they said that *you* were dead! They told me that they found your body!"

"Steven." Brian crouched on his knees, looking up at his cousin. "I came back for you, I swear it. Your uncle loves you—he was devastated when I showed up without you. We all love you. Everyone. You're my brother, Stevie. Listen, I got to Bethany. I got her to Uncle Al. But they have her. These guys that you're with, they have her prisoner. We gotta save her. We gotta get her out of here. They're torturing her, Steven. Your sister. They are *torturing* her."

Steven shook his head. "That ain't true. They told me she's dead, too. They told me you died trying to get to her. Sent scouts that saw it themselves; told me so."

"Well, I ain't dead."

Steven closed his eyes against the facts trickling into his ears.

"No, Brian—no!" He grabbed Brian by the collar and dragged him to stand, then punched him hard.

"Fight back, goddamn it! Fight back!" Tears began rolling down Steven's face as punches flew.

Brian dodged a few blows, but Steven's fists found their way through. He fell before his cousin, blood stringing from his nose.

"Fight back, Brian! Fight back!"

"I ain't gonna fight you … never again."

"No, Brian. No!" Steven hollered to the heavens. He stopped throwing punches and his hands went slack. Then he fell to his knees.

"Stevie." Brian reached out and squeezed his cousin's shoulder. "Whatever you're messed up with, it ain't too late to get out."

Steven shook his head. "No. I've … done things. Things that can't be made right."

"Steve. Stevie, it ain't—"

The door to the outside flew back on its hinges, kicked in by the heel of a boot, and three men stormed inside. A gale of fluttering sparks enveloped their bodies.

"What the hell is going on in here?" The voice bellowed from the badly injured Mark Rothstein. A soldier helped him through the door, and by his side stood Captain Black.

"Steven," the captain shouted, staring down at Brian on his knees. "This is him, isn't it? Your cousin. Go on then; this is your chance. Kill the son of a bitch. This is what you want, right? Vengeance. Kill this man who left you for dead—fulfill your destiny."

Steven stared at the ground.

The captain stepped forward, raising his rifle.

"Stand aside then, lad. I'll help you. It's okay."

Steven turned to Brian. "Run," he whispered, and then stood tall, facing the three men.

Captain Black stopped short.

"Now, Steven, son—"

Steven had the captain off the ground in a flash, held by his throat, and he threw the old man hard against Mark and the soldier. All three toppled over.

"Steven!" Brian shouted, getting to his feet.

Steven reached back and shoved Brian over.

"You lied to me!" Steven roared to the captain. "You all lied to me, you sons of bitches!"

The unnamed soldier got back on his feet, attempting to flee toward the outside door. Steven sprinted forward, punching the man hard in the square of his back. Something cracked, and the man fell.

Captain Black was still on the floor, and all the old man had a chance to say was, "Stev—" before Steven beat upon his head with both fists. The captain's ruffled hat fell to the side.

Mark Rothstein dragged his injured legs to stand. He had lost his firearm from the fall, and unsheathed his rosewood-handled machete, hobbling fast toward Steven, faster than his wounded legs should have allowed.

"Steven!" Brian shouted.

Steven stopped beating upon the captain's lifeless body, and rose to face Mark Rothstein. As Mark swung down, Steven grabbed his wrist tight below the machete, and they grappled momentarily. Then Steven's eyes went large and he let out a shriek. Mark's free hand held the handle of a small dagger, the blade sunk deep between two of Steven's ribs.

Steven gripped both of Mark's hands tight, and his wide-eyed stare turned to boiling anger. He squeezed with all of his might and the fingers of Mark Rothstein crunched and popped.

Mark screamed and stumbled backward as Steven let go of his mangled hands.

The sleek, rosewood handle of the machete was now in Steven's grasp, and he chopped the blade down onto the crown of Mark Rothstein's head in one fluid movement and let it go planted to the bridge of the lieutenant's nose.

Mark Rothstein fell, one eye still open wide.

"Jesus, Steven!" Brian grabbed his cousin's shoulders, helping him onto his back as blood sputtered over Steven's lips.

"Oh no, oh no, Steven, no."

Steven looked up at him, his body overtaken by uncontrollable spasms. "Th-th-this-this-this is it, B-Brian."

"I'll get a doctor." Brian tried to touch the knife handle protruding from his cousin's chest, but Steven clutched it tight. "I ain't gonna lose you again."

"N-no, Brian ... no." He held Brian's hand, pulling his arm in close, holding it under his chin. "I-it's okay," Steven said, his eyes clear and staring upward. "It's-it's okay, Brian. It's-it's okay, okay." His body was trembling and the blood around him was pooling fast. "It's okay, Brian, it's-it's ... okay."

The air in his lungs rasped and then he stopped talking. His body stopped shaking. His eyes hazed over.

Brian held his cousin's head in his arms, letting his tears fall freely.

***

The house became quiet, the gunfire sporadic. The minutes that passed could have been hours. Then Nick heard his soldiers downstairs, the shouting and gunfire nearby. A few sharp explosions like grenades echoed up the stairway, and after another brief period of silence, a faint creaking came from the stair treads.

Nick swallowed. His mouth was so dry. His teeth felt like sandpaper against his lips.

He could not think—could not process his thoughts. He would escape this, somehow. This was not the end, not yet ... it couldn't be.

His palm squeezed the cold handle of his .357 magnum, and he drew the dark and gleaming pistol. In a fluid motion, he grabbed Stephanie by her arm and yanked her away from the wall to stand before him.

"Nick!" she shrieked, sobbing and shaking.

Armed men came pouring into the room from the doorway, fanning out in either direction, their rifles pointed squarely at him.

"I'll shoot her!" Nick shouted, the pistol pressed at the base of her skull. "I'll shoot her—let me go!"

"N-Nick!" Stephanie tried to speak, but the words would not come out, jumbled up like chewing gum in her mouth.

A bright red light flickered in Nick's eyes. He looked down to see several laser targets dancing about his upper chest.

"I'll shoot—"

A crack filled the air, and Nick's leg gave out under him. He'd been shot above the kneecap, and the pain was electric. Stephanie toppled over, and as the men circled in, a beast entered the room—the man from outside who had clawed his way through the trenches, slashing and chopping at his men.

Nick groped for his revolver, found it, leveled it at his own temple, and cocked the hammer back.

His finger had just touched upon the trigger when a foot kicked the gun hard, and the shot went wild, just grazing his scalp. Yet he still held on to the handle, and as Nick looked up through foggy eyes, the wild man swung a machete down upon his hand, slicing through his finger and striking the blade into the wooden handle of his revolver, where it stuck. The wild man tossed the machete away, pistol, flesh, and all.

Nick howled, trying to pinpoint if—and how many—fingers might be missing. But before he could think, the wild man was on top of him, his fists crashing down, pounding into his face with unbridled fury. After about a dozen strikes, Nick's arms went slack and consciousness began to fade. The pain seemed to lessen and numbness, almost pleasant, overtook his body. Words registered in his ears, and Nick realized the man above him had been shouting the entire time.

"Where is she? Where is she?"

Nick coughed up broken teeth. "W-who?"

"Bethany! Where's Bethany Driscoll?"

The man held Nick by the collar, lifting his back off the ground, their faces inches apart, and Nick looked through his swollen eyes at a man in the throes of pure madness.

Bethany ... Driscoll? Nick thought. *Driscoll! That bitch in the cellar is a Driscoll?*

The entire time, a huge bargaining chip had been merely feet away. Nick had not given her a second thought since Karl took him down to the cellar. He never wanted to go back down there again, not after seeing what the doctor did to Will Holbrook.

"B-Bethany ..." Nick muttered, and the wild man's fists began pounding at him again.

"B-b-basement," Nick muttered through the blows. "Basement! Basement! *Basement!*"

The man stopped, his fist cocked in the air, his muscles taut like iron beneath his grime-soaked skin. "She's in the basement?"

"Y-yes … probably dead. I-I didn't know who she was."

Nick expected the man's fist to strike him again and again, to relentlessly batter his already fractured face until long after he was dead.

But the man released him, and Nick lay slack on the floor.

His vision was hazy as he saw the wild man run past the others, out of the room. A soldier was grabbing Stephanie by her arm. She was kicking and punching with her eyes closed, hollering and screaming.

Steph … What … have I done …

As consciousness faded and the men circling him held his limp arms, rummaging through his pockets, he saw Stephanie blindly leap back, breaking free from the soldier's grip. The soldier sprung forward to catch her, but only grasped onto the corner of her purple robe. The material ripped in his hand, and she stumbled, falling through the broken window facing the Ridgeline River.

"Holy hell!" he heard the soldier say as he ran toward the windowsill.

Nick shut his eyes tight, picturing Stephanie falling through the air, her ripped purple robe fluttering backward until she struck the earth. He opened his eyes, glaring at the man standing inches away from the window's ledge, looking down. The soldier still held the strip of silk robe in his fist, the purple material blowing back in the wind.

Nick Byrnes shut his eyes again, and embraced the pure darkness as the world faded away.

Chapter 64
The End of Chaos

Simon ran past the soldiers in the stairwell, and nearly collided into Brian as Brian stumbled into the hallway from a burning room, clutching his thigh above his kneecap.

"Simon," Brian said in a pant. "Simon, what happened? Where are you going?"

Simon looked at Brian. The man was injured, his face swollen and blood trailing onto his shirt. The room he had just emerged from was ablaze, and the smoke was flowing into the hallway. Soldiers had entered the rear door with a hose and were attempting to quell the flames.

"It's Bethany. She's in the basement."

Simon began running down the hallway again, and Brian hobbled to keep up.

"It's my knee," he called to Simon. "Twisted it fierce."

Simon stopped running and turned back, putting his arm under Brian's shoulder.

"I'm all right," Brian said. "I'm fine. I'll manage."

"I got you."

Simon and Brian emerged back into the main house, where the dead and dying were all around. The occasional popping of gunfire could still be heard as the soldiers of Alice dealt with the last few pockets of resistance, yet most of the men were now tending to the injured, putting out the fires, and securing the prisoners.

Simon and Brian continued across the once-majestic entry room, with the double staircase cascading to the second floor, when a sound made Simon stop as if hitting a wall.

Barking …

He looked up at the railing at the top of the stairs. Several soldiers surrounded a dog, their rifles up. The dog was glaring fangs and snapping his jaws.

A soldier was saying, "Hey, easy now. Easy boy."

"Winston!" Simon yelled. "Winston! He's not dangerous, put your guns down!" He almost dropped Brian as he ran to the staircase. Upon hearing his name, Winston's ears pointed up and his jaw snapped shut. He darted around the soldiers, and sprinted down the staircase into Simon's waiting arms.

In a flash, a series of images flickered through Simon's mind: Winston curled up on their bed in the cabin in British Columbia. Winston sitting in the sun as Simon meditated in the crook of the tree by the stream. He saw his dog's head out the van window with his big tongue panting as the terrain sped by. He saw him flee from the Mexicans in the town when they were ambushed and the van was taken away. He saw himself and Winston rolling around on the ground in his old house, in his old room, in another lifetime, when Winston's fur was only fuzz and they were both so young.

"Oh my buddy, my boy …" Simon buried his face in Winston's fur, letting Winston lick at his fingers and hands.

"He tried to bit me," a soldier called down.

Simon looked up at the soldier, but didn't answer. The air was thick with the cries of the dying and the wails of the maimed.

"You're scared, boy; I know. Come on," he said to his dog, and held Winston by his scruff. He turned back to Brian.

"I'm fine," Brian protested, but he took Simon's help anyway.

In the kitchen they found the stairway to the basement.

Simon shouted to a soldier at the bottom, "There's a girl down here, a girl. Have you seen her?"

The soldier shrugged.

Brian and Simon hurried to a hallway in the back just as a soldier stumbled out of a room, doubled over and trying not to vomit. He looked up at them.

"Don't go in there." He wiped his mouth on a sleeve. They ignored him and stepped inside. Pat O'Hern lay on a gurney in the center of the cement-walled room, dead and dismembered. Another body flayed of skin and ritualistically taken apart, some bones boiled white, lay upon a table in the far corner like a shrine.

Oh, my God …

The depth of the Red Hands' madness was beyond evident.

What if we had lost? Simon thought.

Winston made a low whimper. Simon whistled at him. "Come on boy, stay with me."

They went from room to room, brushing past soldiers, and then to the service quarters in the rear.

And that is where they found her.

She was alive, yet unconscious. IV tubes were connected to her arms, and a doctor was checking her vitals as they entered.

Simon rushed to the side of her bed, and Brian limped to a chair and collapsed.

"Beth—Bethany?"

Her eyes fluttered, the whites showing.

"What's wrong with her?" Simon asked the doctor. "Is she okay?"

"You guys shouldn't be in here; give her some space." He leaned forward to usher Simon away, but Brian reached out and touched the doctor's shoulder.

"I wouldn't," Brian said.

The doctor sighed. "She's fine. She's been drugged, but aside from that, she'll be all right. She needs food and water, but they had her connected to an IV, so she's not too badly dehydrated. They were keeping her alive."

"What drugs did they give her?"

"Sedatives. Sleeping pills. I'm guessing you guys know her?" He motioned to Simon, who was holding her hand.

"Give him a minute," Brian said. "Jesus, I thought she was dead."

"Our men captured and questioned the guards stationed down here," the doctor explained. "They were waiting on orders from Karl Metzger before beginning their interrogations. She was sedated all the while, but they kept her very much alive. She's lucky." He motioned in the direction of the laundry room. "That room there … I've never seen a more deplorable act."

"I want to talk to the guards." Simon turned to the doctor.

"I'm afraid that's not possible."

"Why not? I helped lead this attack, I—"

"The guards were taken outside and hanged."

Brian shook his head. "And so nothing changes."

"Listen," Simon said, "you need to get some protection on her and take her to the safest place possible—right away."

The doctor raised an eyebrow. "There are wounded soldiers everywhere who need urgent medical attention. She's perfectly healthy, considering."

"This girl … she's General Driscoll's niece. We need to get word to him that she's been found alive and safe."

Simon stared at the doctor, and after a brief pause the doctor said, "I see."

He turned and shouted to a soldier by the door. "Send word to the general that we're on our way, and that we have a certain young lady named Bethany in our care. Get a stretcher and have a transport ready."

"Yes, sir." The soldier turned to leave, but Brian called to him.

"Hey, I need to send word to the firehouse—can you send someone? Have them find a medic named Carolanne. She needs to know that we're alive, all of us; Bethany, Simon, and my name is Brian. She'll be minding the injured."

The soldier paused, looking at the doctor.

"Do as he says," the doctor commanded. "Send someone."

"Yes, sir." The soldier left.

The doctor studied Simon, the expression on his face earnest.

"My God, boy," he said, "you need a medic yourself." He looked at Brian, who was gripping his kneecap tight. "Both of you. At least clean yourselves up. You don't want your faces to be the first thing this girl sees. The two of you look in a mirror?"

"I'm fine," Simon said, and turned back to Bethany. Her eyes were closed. He stroked her hand, and found a tube of medicated ointment that the doctor had on the bed. He spread the oily solution to the raw skin around her wrists, where the ropes had kept her secure.

"Oh, Bethany, what did they do to you?"

The doctor turned his attention to Brian, unrolling his pants leg.

"I'm fine," Brian said. "Help her."

"Like hell you are. The girl is better off than the two of you," he said. "And look, she's coming around."

Simon leaned in close as her eyes fluttered and opened, taking a moment to focus on first the ceiling and then Simon's face. Her expression lightened from confusion to happiness as she saw through the gore and recognized the man hovering before her. Then tears came.

"S-*Simon*," her voice croaked.

"Shh, easy. Take it easy."

He wrapped his arms around her, and she cried into his shoulder.

"Get me out of here."

"I will. We are. They're bringing a stretcher. We're leaving. The war is over."

"I can walk. Just help me up."

"You've been drugged and tied down in bed. Wait for the stretcher."

They split apart, and Bethany studied Simon's face again, her trembling fingers touching the side of his cheek.

"What happened to you?"

Simon smiled. "I'm fine." He looked over at Brian, whose face was set in agony as the doctor touched and examined his damaged knee. Then he looked down at his feet, where Winston lay curled in a ball.

"I'm home," Simon said.

"What?"

"I've done it," he whispered. "I'm finally home."

Epilogue

His eyes twitched and then cracked open. Whatever dark crevice of his mind first became conscious was trying to rationalize his sudden reentry into the world, as he stared into an unknown void.

I'm home, under the covers, and I'm a child, his mind substantiated, then jumped, *I'm staring at the cement ceiling in my cell in Huntsville—or maybe Atlanta … No, I'm staring at the ceiling of the train car, and any minute now the door will slide open and the conductor will find me lying here using my stained, orange jumpsuit as a blanket.*

But …

… wait

I'm staring at the sky …

It was the smoke billowing out from the house that woke him from the depths of unconsciousness, causing him to cough himself awake. With each convulsion of his body, he remembered where he was and how much pain he was in.

Karl Metzger attempted to move, but the rushes of agony forced him to stop.

He lifted his right hand, flexing his fingers one at a time, and then he moved to his toes and began twitching each and every muscle in turn, seeing what was there and what was not.

A fire was raging in the house, and the flames were bellowing out through the doorway. The heat was so intense that he felt the hairs on his body singe. Drifting cinders floated through the air, some searing his skin where they landed. The room was sunken, with flames burning through the ground, and he saw the outline of a decapitated head mixed in with a pile of bricks and cement.

Smoke was pouring out like rapids on a river, escaping through the shattered glass frame of the greenhouse. Asphyxiation was close at hand if the flames did not reach him first. His arms reached out and his body twisted and turned over, shedding the blanket of thick dust, rocks, and glass shards off his chest. Gritting his teeth against the pain, Karl peeled his body off the ground, where dried blood had kept him stuck to the floor like glue.

As he crawled, his wounds reopened; yet onward he went, ignoring his suffering and the pangs of bright light and dark spots that at times consumed his vision.

Outside on the lawn, when the intense heat had dissipated, he turned, panting on his back, to see the flaming house that had almost become his pyre.

Karl stared in fascination, and then a funny feeling overtook him.

He began laughing. "You cannot kill me—no one can kill Karl Metzger, although they try!"

The laughing was uncontrollable, but the moving and twitching in his abdomen caused sharp discomfort.

He pushed himself up on his elbows and then his forearms. Dizziness gave him pause. A length of splintered wood lay in the lawn, mixed with other debris exploded from the house. Karl grabbed it and used it to pull himself to his feet. It was a slow and deliberate process, and twice he nearly passed out.

Where the hell are my men?

Before he could finish asking his own question, he knew the answer. He knew it as the sun was turning the early morning sky a paler form of black, the horizon filled with a burning orange tinge and clouds of gray smoke. Karl saw at that moment the blades of helicopters—one, two, maybe more—moving up and down along the front line, far off in the distance like malicious flies.

I've been defeated.

He stared a moment longer, and soon laughter returned despite his body's painful protests. "Burn it all down, then. Ha! Let it turn to ash! There is always another fire to start, another town to ignite! The inferno of the world, it will never be extinguished! The horizons will forever burn, and I will hold the torch!"

Karl Metzger turned toward the river to where a narrow gate led to a path down the steep embankment and to the Ridgeline River below. Moving was hard, and the bleeding from his open wounds was made worse with each step. But Karl Metzger made it to the gate and the steep staircase and ramp beyond, where a small dock bobbed up and down on the water.

On the platform beside the dock was a tall wooden rack, the pegs constructed to hold canoes and rafts. Two rowboats were tied there, and it took a considerable amount of strength to pull one down and drag it to the bobbing water. Blood made his grip slippery, and before he dropped the boat in the water, he had to sit and catch his breath. He tied a tourniquet made from a scrap of his tattered shirt around his kneecap, and then he pushed the boat into the water. He slid his ragged body into the hull and let the boat drift over the bounding swells.

After some time, Karl found an oar bungeed to the side and paddled his way toward the opposite shore.

You cannot kill me ...

His vision was grainy, with swells of bright lights. His strength was fading. The oar almost fell from his numb fingers.

"Easy does it, old man. Stay with it."

The opposite bank was steep, just as in the towns of Fairview and Alice, but Karl could see a natural, earthen ramp where several small docks jutted out among old half-sunken and lopsided yachts.

As Karl rowed closer to shore, he saw a fishing boat pulled up on the embankment, identical to his own. He followed its course, rowing until the bow of his small boat hit land. A man wearing a black trench coat stood watching him the entire time, not moving from his perch atop the hill. The man shifted his briefcase to the other hand and pushed his glasses up the bridge of his nose. Karl stood on shaking legs, careful not to slip on the blood pooled inside the hull. He swallowed, staring at the only man who could put fear in his heart.

"Hey!" Karl shouted. "Arthur, ol' pal. Be a sport, would you? Give me a hand here."

The beady eyes of Doctor Arthur Freeman stared down at Karl Metzger.

http://www.BrandonZenner.com
http://www.amazon.com/author/brandonzenner

Thank you for reading The After War. *Please read on past the Acknowledgments for a preview of Brandon Zenner's novel,* Whiskey Devils. *As always, the best way you can support an independent author is by leaving a review on Amazon. Each and every review is read and appreciated by the author, both good and bad. The Amazon link above will take you there. Sign up for his email list on his website to stay informed about a possible continuation of the series.*

From The Author

Back when I was sixteen, and some of my older friends were getting their driver's licenses, we used to drive out to a nearby park to spend our afternoons walking miles of trails and gazing at the large, calm reservoir smack in the center of the woods. Perhaps my teenage mind still clung to a portion of childhood creativity, but I soon began to envision the creations of a story that would take over a decade to develop into this novel. The distant hills were swarming with soldiers and the open fields were places of war. I knew back then that I wanted to be a writer, with much thanks to authors like Kurt Vonnegut, who showed me at a young age that fiction could truly be anything that the writer wanted it to be. A year later, when I was seventeen and had a driver's license of my own, I went to the park by myself day after day, walking the same trails and plotting out the story and characters. Originally, this novel was titled *Chaos*, but that name didn't seem to fit as the years went by. I did try to sit and write the novel in my early twenties, but two things happened: 1) I wasn't a good enough writer at twenty years of age. 2) The story wasn't there yet. Years passed, and when I was twenty-eight, I forced myself to hammer out the words. I didn't care how they came out; I just couldn't put it off any longer. So I finished the manuscript, and low and behold … it stunk. It was hard for me to swallow that it would have to be rewritten from scratch. To ease my mind, I started writing longhand an idea that had only come to me a few days previous. That idea would develop into my first novel, *The Experiment of Dreams*. Months passed, and when I had sent *The Experiment of Dreams* out to be edited, I decided to sit and give *The After War* another shot. I had dreaded the thought of having to start the novel all over again, thinking the task would be impossible. But once I began to type, and the words started flowing, I realized how much I missed the characters, and wanted to live in their shoes once more. I wanted to get Simon out of the cabin safely, and I wanted to witness again the struggle between Brian and Steven as it developed. I also included a new main character, and it seemed impossible that he wasn't there from the beginning: Winston. This time, the manuscript came out the way I had intended, and my writing was much more polished. It still took years to finish, and in the interim, as the manuscript was being edited and proofread, I finished another shorter novel, *Whiskey Devils*. It is strange to still be working on my first novel, despite having published two others. It brings me immense happiness to be done with *The After War*, but I'm also terribly sad to see these characters go. They came to be when I was sixteen, and now, twenty years later, it is like losing my best friends. I grew up and aged with them, and their characters developed much as my adolescent mind matured into adulthood. Goodbye Simon and Brian, you will always be with me. Winston, you're such a good boy.

There are many ways to connect with me, I will supply links to me Facebook page and Twitter bellow. However, the best way to learn about current and future projects is by joining my email list. As a thank you, you will be sent a short story, absolutely free. In the past, I offered every single person in my email list a copy of my novel, *Whiskey Devils*, for free when it launched. You can sign up on my website:

http://www.brandonzenner.com/contact.html.

While you're there, check out my blog, where I give some behind the scenes information on my novels and methods.

Okay, that's about it. Here are my Facebook and Twitter links. Remember to check out the preview of *Whiskey Devils* after the acknowledgments.

https://www.facebook.com/brandon.zenner
https://twitter.com/SlapstickII

All the best,
Brandon Zenner

Acknowledgments

In no particular order, the following people deserve my complete and utter gratitude for their contributions in helping me create and finish this novel: Nicole Gauge, Finnbar McCallion, John Graham, Hal Zenner, and Catherine York. As always, a special thanks goes out to my loving wife, Mallory Zenner, and my amazing daughter, Sadie-Mae Zenner.

Preview: Whiskey Devils

"From the very first page it is action packed ... I read it in one day."
   -Boundless Book Reviews

"This action-packed story just keeps on delivering ... Powers is a marvelous noir hero who you just can't help rooting for."
   -Readers' Favorite Book Review

Chapter 1

Spring, 2003

Weaving through the crowd, I passed my exhausted coworkers, their faces gaunt and ghostly pale in the fluorescent lighting. All of them were salivating before the punch-out clock like a pack of ravenous hounds eager to tear into the flesh of that Friday night. They leaned from one leg to the other, purses in hand, sunglasses dangling from open collars. The din of conversation lessened as I neared the clock, and all eyes were cast upon me.

They were thinking, *"Is he really going to do it? Is Powers leaving early?"*

The receptionist's sharp stare burned with scorn from behind her blond bangs, but I ignored her gaze and approached the clock. My time card was in my hand, 'Evan Powers' scribbled on top. The paper glided effortlessly through the punch-out machine, making a slight mechanical noise as it stamped out the time, 4:47. The clicking noise echoed in the now-silent room, and I hightailed it to the door, daring my eager coworkers to follow.

Warm air cloaked me in all of its glory as I flung the door open. My flesh tingled—honest to God, tingled—like the sun was drawing out some poison from the office's artificial cold air.

As I crossed the parking lot toward my car, I resisted turning to look through the wall-length window of the manager's office. Kim would be staring up from a stack of papers on her desk, watching me in disbelief as she checked the time on her watch. No one left before the clock struck five. No one.

Yeah, I did it. I left early. But fuck it—I quit. So there's that.

The well-traveled engine of my Buick rumbled to life, sputtering out clouds of grey exhaust. I backed out, put the car in drive, and sped the hell out of there.

A cigar was waiting for me in the glove box, and I clamped it between my teeth as I loosened the collar of my button-up shirt.

I laughed out loud, feeling a bit like a madman who laughs alone at the world, thinking, "I'm free, you fuckers—I'm free!" A cloud of cigar smoke was sucked out the window, replaced by the clean springtime breeze.

Traffic was already forming on the highway, but I had managed to beat the mass of cars that would stretch on for miles only minutes after five o'clock. The landscape gradually changed to an immense array of blossoming trees and flat wilderness as I distanced myself from town, driving deeper into the heart of the New Jersey Pine Barrens. My housemate Nick and I rented a nice piece of property: three acres of trees and land, with many more acres of wilderness in every direction. Our nearest neighbor was old Mr. Patrick, or Grandpa, but we didn't cross paths with the man too often. We invited him over whenever we had parties, but Grandpa rarely showed up and never stayed for long. He was cool with us, but when our parties got going, and a handful of ragged hippies turned into twenty, thirty, forty, sixty—whatever—he would take off. Not before schooling us all in a game of horseshoes, of course, and drinking about a six-pack of beer. The man could put them away.

I drove past Grandpa's mailbox and our driveway soon appeared. Nick's work truck came into view as I pulled in, and way out in the back of the yard I spotted him standing beside our massive garden. Nick had been living in the rental house for fifteen years. Our good friend, Darin Long, had been a housemate with us for the past five years, but due to his mother discovering that she has cancer, he had moved back home to Montana. Now it was only the two of us, all alone in that low ranch in the middle of the woods.

Hippie Nick, he was sometimes called, or more recently, The Old Man. It was a term of endearment. The guy had lived through the cultural revolution of the '60s and '70s, which meant that for most of our friends, myself included, Nick Grady was the closest thing to a legitimate hippie that we would ever encounter. The guy followed the Dead, marched at civil rights protests, and did all of that fun stuff that made him practically a sage in the eyes of my stoner friends.

I got out of the car and passed Nick's work van on the way to the house. The G and R in Grady Construction and Repair on the van's side were barely legible, faded with time.

Our front door was unlocked, and I went straight to the kitchen. We had a strict nonsmoking rule indoors, for everything other than herb, so I had to be quick with my still-burning cigar. I grabbed two beers from the fridge and went out the kitchen door to the backyard. Nick was under the apple tree next to the garden, swaying with a beer in hand. The Dead blared from his portable CD player, the extension cord trailing all the way back to the house, lost like a snake in the grass.

Water droplets rained down from the sprinkler over the budding tomato plants, zucchinis, peppers, and everything else we'd planted only a few weeks ago. The corn stalks were already about two feet tall.

Nick moved to the music, barefoot, with his wrapped hemp necklaces and beadwork bouncing on his grey-haired chest. The only article of clothing the guy ever wore at home was a pair of cutoff jean shorts. When he saw me approaching he nodded.

"Hey there," I said.

Nick smiled a crooked smile, a rubber band stuck between his lips as he pulled his long hair out of his face. A cooler was out there next to the few battered Adirondack chairs, and I could tell by the look in his eyes that he was already a few beers in. I handed him the beer I had brought from the kitchen anyway. Sierra Nevada, always Sierra Nevada. It was the only beer the guy would drink if given a choice. However, if he didn't have a choice, he'd drink most anything. Especially bourbon. We went through the stuff like it was water.

The song ended and he yelled out, "Yo, Powers! What's up man?" He was evidently in a great mood.

"Nothing, Nick." I tried to be nonchalant, but my lips cracked into a smile. "I did it."

His eyes lit up. "You quit?"

I nodded.

"Ha!" He bounced over on quick feet and hugged me with his strong, skinny arms. "I'm so happy for you, brother. I know that job was dragging you down."

"Thanks, man."

"Want to call some people up, get the bonfire going?"

I shrugged. "I wouldn't mind having a few beers."

His face was radiant, and I knew he was swallowing back the question he'd been asking me for years now. The words were trying to burst free from his mouth, but I was going to wait a little while longer before letting him know that I would work for him full time. And I'm not talking about his handyman service; as good as he was at repairing cabinets, replacing shingles, and even doing some landscaping for a handful of local Pineys. I'm talking about his *other* job. His real job.

"You doing some shooting?" I nodded towards the small arsenal on the coffee table: his old western style six-shooters. They were a hobby of sorts, first for him, and then for me. After all, we did live in the middle of the woods. Not to mention that the house one over from old Mr. Grandpa's was the fire chief's, and the man was a regular at our parties—as clean cut as he was—and he kept an eye on the police radio for call-ins about noise. I consider myself clean cut as well, in comparison to most of the transients who pass through our doors. My hair is short, I wear nice pants and shirts, and I keep myself in decent shape. Ever since I met Nick, I've been trying to get the guy to go running with me, or use the weight bench in the basement. But he always declines. "Look at me," he says. "I'm skinny enough. There won't be nothing left of me." It was true. The guy was a rail: skinny and strong. A lifetime's worth of hard labor made it impossible for him to ever be a pound over weight.

Nick looked to the black powder pistols. "Knock yourself out," he said, and went back to swaying with the music, mumbling along with the words while looking out over the sea of vegetables glistening from the sprinkler water.

As the sun began to set and the beer in the cooler dwindled, we loaded and fired the six shooters at a wide tree stump across the yard. The process of loading a black powder revolver is tedious, but that made shooting them all the more enjoyable. We had to work for our fun.

While we were shooting, the house phone rang several times, and soon our driveway became illuminated by headlights. A few people showed up with more beer, weed, and various low-grade narcotics and hallucinogens. Ritalin,

Adderall—that sort of thing. Most everyone, myself excepted, got stoned the minute they crossed onto our property. Weed was never my thing. I rarely smoked, which was in contrast to the company I kept.

This guy named Mario showed up tripping on mushrooms, sitting a foot away from the blazing flames in the fire pit, his bright orange hair seeming to glow in the flickering light. I thought about asking him for a few caps, but decided against it. Ever since Darin moved out, Nick and I had to be on the lookout for people fucked up on the more serious drugs, like cocaine, heroin, and even speed. That was a big no-no at our home. Darin used to be our enforcer of sorts. He was a strong guy, although his short and stout build made him appear youthful, especially with his long dark hair kept up in a ponytail. Ex Army, believe it or not. But that life wasn't for him. Darin was a feel-good stoner who liked lounging around the house shirtless, just like Nick.

But Darin was gone, so it was up to Nick and I to watch over our guests. Just last party I found a guy taking a line of coke in our bathroom. He was so strung out that he forgot to lock the handle, and when I told him to get rid of the shit or leave, he started spewing vulgarities at me through his clattering jaw. Before his erratic mind thought it was a good idea to throw a swing, Nick and I had his arms behind his back, and we did the old heave-ho out the door, holding the back of his belt and his collar. I learned long ago in my bartending days to never let the other guy swing first. Unless of course the other guy was so fucked up that he couldn't hit the side of a wall. Or if the guy was a lawyer. Never hit a lawyer first. But back at my old bar, the local clientele were far from lawyers.

Lucky for us, the crowd was mellow as the alcohol and marijuana flowed. At some point the fire chief showed up, wearing a big grin. He disappeared with Nick inside the house, and when he came back out, he was baked out of his mind.

"Hey, Powers," he said, his red eyes sparkling.

"What's up?"

"Check this out."

The fire chief swung a canvas duffel bag around from his shoulder and opened the zipper. A copious amount of fireworks lay inside.

"Cool, huh?"

"Yeah," I smiled. "Cool."

The night wore on and the fireworks were ignited to thunderous ovation from the enamored crowd. The fire chief kept his radio turned up in case the noise got called into the cops.

Maybe fifteen people were gathered in the backyard when I saw headlights approach from down the driveway and stop short of the house. I checked the time on my watch. It was impossible to see in the darkness, but I knew the headlights belonged to the black Plymouth Fury Gran Coupe that had been arriving at our house at that same time every week, for years now. I looked for Nick in the crowd and spotted him by the fire.

"Hey," I said, approaching.

When Nick looked at me, I tapped my watch and nodded toward the car. His face soured.

"Motherfucker," he muttered, and swilled back his beer.

Nick went to the house, and a moment later he emerged from the front, walking toward the car. He opened the passenger door, illuminating the car's interior while stepping inside.

It wasn't long until the passenger door opened again and Nick got out. The Plymouth reversed out of the driveway, not bothering to swing around the circle. Nick had told me in the past that the man didn't like it when strangers were at our house during his stops. But then he had gone on, "If he makes his stops on a Friday, it can't be avoided. Fuck him."

When Nick got close, I handed him a beer. His face was set in the same crazed anger that always overtook him after leaving the man in the Plymouth. I silently prayed that he wouldn't start hitting the bottle hard, like he often did after the man's visits, and go off on one of his insane rambles. Not now, not tonight. Tonight, I was celebrating my new life. My new path, as twisted as it might become.

"You okay?" I asked.

Nick took the beer and our eyes met. His face softened. "Yeah, man." He patted me on the shoulder, and we walked into the yard to join the circle of people watching the fire chief light off the last of his fireworks.

And there was Becka. Her fair complexion illuminated in bouncing shadows from the fire; her dark, somewhat curly hair pure black in the night.

"Hey," I said, walking up to her. "When'd you get here?"

She turned and smiled at the sound of my voice. "Hey, Powers. Just a minute ago. I was looking for you."

She patted the grass beside her and I took a seat, making it a point for our thighs to touch.

"I did it," I told her. "I quit."

"The office?"

"The office."

"Powers," she exclaimed. "That's wonderful, man!"

She reached over and wrapped her arms around me, burying her face in my chest.

This was good. This is what I needed. I needed Becka, her arms holding me tight all night long. When was the last time we'd hooked up? A week ago? Maybe more. Nick jokingly referred to Becka as my girlfriend, but we were nothing like that. Just friends. Two people in their mid-thirties who had been in terrible relationships, much like all the other loners out there who find themselves still single past their twenties. We just wanted to keep things cool. Sure, we liked each other, but we didn't want to make our relationship something more than it needed to be. For her birthday last year I bought her a small oval locket. Nothing fancy or expensive. I regretted giving it to her the moment I saw the surprise and uncertainty on her face. She did wear it, though, up until recently. She said she misplaced it, put it down somewhere, and that it's got to be around. Probably at home. Probably fell from the kitchen sink. She'd find it, she told me.

But who knows.

Becka had been friends with Nick for years longer than I'd known either of them. I once thought that Nick and Becka had a romantic past, but Darin later set me straight. Besides, their ages are decades apart … not like that would stop either of them.

As the last explosion filled the air, the fire chief turned to the crowd. "That's it," he said, displaying his empty duffel bag. "That's all she wrote."

Nick stood a few feet away from the crowd and we caught each other's eyes.

"Hey, Becka, you gonna be here for a few minutes?"

She looked up at me with a smile and then turned to the fire. "I'm not going anywhere."

I hugged her shoulder and stood. "Be right back."

"Hey, grab me a beer while you're at it?" She displayed her near-empty bottle, the light from the fire making it transparent.

"Of course." I smiled, walking towards Nick. "Be right back."

Nick and I stood apart from the group as the fire chief shook out a few stray firecrackers into the fire, turning the duffel bag upside down and shaking it out.

"Hey," Nick shouted over the roar of our friends laughing and jumping away from this madman dumping explosives over the open flame. "I got something serious I want to talk to you about."

"Yeah," I said. "I know."

"You give my proposition some thought?"

I nodded, not that he could see me with his eyes transfixed on the fire. With Darin gone, Nick was shorthanded. He'd been asking me to work full time at his operation for years, but I always declined. I was too clean-cut for that life, I used to think. I was better off as a part time employee. But after spending three years stuck at a cubicle in the stalest environment that I could imagine, wasting away the best and most productive time of the day— between nine and five, when the human mind and body is at its best—I was starting to see things in a different light. Plus, he was offering me more than just hours—he was offering me a management position. Small responsibilities at first, but they would grow over time. But the real benefit, I thought, was that Becka and I would be spending more time together.

"Yeah, Nick, I've given your proposition a lot of thought. I'm in. I'm all aboard."

He turned to me. "Seriously?"

"Seriously."

He extended a hand, smiling like a little boy. "Oh, brother, you are most needed!"

We shook, and then of course he hugged me.

"Man, this is going to be great!" he shouted, arms out in the air, holding his beer aloft to the night sky. The light from the fire flickered dancing shadows all over his body.

"We'll start tomorrow," he said, taking a swig of beer and bouncing on his toes.

I smiled.

He tossed the empty straight into the roaring flame, and grabbed two cold ones from the cooler. He popped the caps and handed me one.

"Cheers, brother," he said.

We clinked glasses.

"Cheers."

He took a long pull, and I again prayed to myself that he wouldn't get too fucked up. I didn't need him screaming crazy shit at our guests, crying, sobbing, and talking nonsense.

"I think it will be best if we start late," he said after a burp.

"Agreed."

Sipping my beer, I watched Becka transfixed on the fire, a smile on her radiant face as she swayed to the music. As much of a free spirit as she was, Becka had something about her. She had class, and an amazing mind that I wanted to keep discovering. She wasn't the type of person to lay her cards out on the table; I had to keep guessing what was in her hand. Her beauty was the type that tongue-tied men, but there was more between us than sheer attraction. We had a chemistry that couldn't be put into words, but only be felt as a throbbing heat in my chest. It was intrigue that kept me coming back for more; it was her quiet, pondering eyes that displayed indecipherable emotion. Simple words from her lips carried the weight of the world and affected me like I imagine poetry inspires minds greater than my own.

Her shadowy form beckoned me to approach and sit with her on that lush field of grass for as long as eternity would allow.

Turning, I grabbed two beers from the cooler. I was about to tell Nick that I would be back, but he had seen the rapture in my eyes and had begun to drift away, chatting with the fire chief.

"Welcome back," Becka said, looking up to me as I approached. There was longing in her stare.

Feeling a bit drunk, I smiled coolly and took a seat beside her to watch the roaring flames.

Tomorrow, my life would change—for the better, I thought. I would be managing a productive and quite illegal drug operation. But now, in the present moment, I didn't want to contemplate the future or lament the past. I wanted to stay stuck in time, right where I was.

Chapter 2

My head was spinning. The last time I looked at the clock it said 2:00 AM and Becka was giving me a goodbye kiss. Now, 10:45 AM blazed from the clock. I desperately wanted to sleep the day away, but there were two things that were driving me out of the bed:

1. I had to pee, bad.

2. I needed the largest and coldest glass of water that was possible.

Nick's room was on the way to the bathroom, and his door was cracked open. The bright sun shone through the American flag that he used as a curtain along with the dozen or so blue glass bottles that lined his windowsill, casting the room in varying shades of red and blue. Those colors in the morning had a strange effect on me that I wasn't sure if I liked. They were somehow both agitating and soothing.

After my morning pee that seemed to never end, I stuck my head into Nick's room, expecting to see him passed out on top of his blankets, still wearing his cutoff shorts.

But he wasn't there.

As I walked into the kitchen the back door flew open, and in came Nick bouncing on his toes, holding a tall glass of something red with a green sprout sticking out.

"Hey, Powers, you're up!"

He was wide wake, apparently.

I rubbed my eyes. "When'd you get up?"

He shrugged. "About an hour ago."

The kitchen smelled of coffee, which was most welcoming. I poured myself a tall glass of water and a mug full of hot, black coffee and sat at the table.

"This is what you need, man, if you want to fly right." Nick opened the refrigerator.

"A bloody Mary?" I was going to dismiss the idea of drinking anything alcoholic, but I had to admit, it sounded appealing.

Nick made a drink and put it on the table before me. He then went to the cabinet to remove two aspirin from the container, along with either a Ritalin or Adderall left over from a party, placing them all next to my drink. Then he went to the stove to scramble some eggs.

"You're in a good mood," I said, looking down at my variety of drinks and pills.

"Damn straight." He cracked eggs into a bowl.

Watching him at the stove, a flashback from last night passed through my memory: I saw Nick get in one of his dreaded drunken moods, crying while crawling across the grass in inebriated delirium. It was around the time everyone left and my memory was becoming fuzzy. He was shouting the same fragmented statements, things he only ever brought up at the tail end of a serious bender. But he always cut himself short of explaining what he was rambling about. He spoke as if battling some demon inside him, so all I would get is "It's—they … they's took me, man—it was *them*. I only, didn't want to do it, man," and he would be crying. "I-I was a just a k-kid, man, those fucking-fucks, they-they took me, man!" Whatever he was talking about, I wasn't sure that I wanted to know. Occasionally, he would shout the same jumbled utterances while sleeping. I was warned a long time ago to never wake him up if I heard screaming in the middle of the night. So I never did. Darin had known Nick way longer than I had, so he was able to wake him out of those episodes without getting himself killed.

Nick put a plate of eggs before me along with a bottle of hot sauce.

"Eat up," he said. "Then go take a shower. We're leaving in half an hour."

I nodded. I had made an agreement, but I'd been half expecting Nick to be just as hung over as myself. Unfortunately, he wasn't.

***

We took Nick's van to the highway, and then drove south for about twenty minutes. He was taking me to two locations, both of which I was already familiar with. The first was his office, since I was now expected to help keep tabs on the books. The building itself was tiny, an old one-car garage, the sliding door patched up with drywall and converted into a single office room with a bathroom in the back. A battered wooden sign read "Grady Construction and Repair" over the front door.

It was a *mess*.

Papers everywhere, filing cabinets overflowing with files, and Nick's blue glass jars and bottles bordering every spare inch around the room's two windows. On top of the cabinets was an assortment of rocks and crystals.

Nick read the expression on my face. "Don't worry about all this." His hands danced over the room. "We can clean up however you like. This," he said, pointing to the corner of the room, "is where we keep the important stuff." He grabbed the sides of a filing cabinet and slid it aside. Then he knelt down, feeling the edge of a strip of molding. He pulled, and the baseboard came free of the magnets keeping it in place. Nick put the molding aside, and reached into a cavity to remove several large ledgers, placing them each on the desk in turn.

"These are the books," he said. "Expense reports. Payroll. A section of the wall pops free too, with the safe behind it."

"How are the books standing?" The random slips of papers jutting out from the pages answered my question. A few even fell out and drifted to the floor.

"Well," Nick said, scratching the side of his face, "not as bad as they look, but I'm close to falling behind. I'm juggling too much at the moment."

I nodded.

"All right then." I started rolling up my sleeves. "Should we start?"

"Not yet." Nick shook his head. "We're going to the warehouse first. With Darin gone, I'm shorthanded at the operation. I want to show you a few things. That's where you'll be needed the most."

We had negotiated a salary on the way to the office, and had settled on a fair rate—more than fair. About twice of what cubicle-hell was paying me. I would do whatever was needed. There was no way I was going to fuck this up; it wasn't like I could bounce around from job to job forever. This was it.

Nick put the ledgers back in the hole in the wall, replaced the molding, and moved the cabinet in place. The little shiny rocks jittered on top.

Then he turned to the door, and I followed him out.

We drove to another part of town, closer to the shore. The area was industrial, with large warehouses belonging to FedEx, UPS, as well as about a dozen or so smaller companies. Nick drove across a vast and vacant paved lot, and parked around the corner of a windowless rectangular building, all steel and metal. The wall approaching had a large faded mural of graffiti, which must have been vibrant, perhaps even nice when it was first spray-painted by whatever talented kids vandalized it. The graffiti had been painted over with a nearly transparent coating of white paint, but the colors showed through. This was the first time I was seeing it this early in the day, and the rainbow, cartoonish mural of a girl's face along with some zigzag signatures were legible.

Nick parked next to a white sedan with several moving vans nearby. A dark blue Mercedes Benz sat a few spots down. The car was a little beat up, but still looked sharp.

My part time work for Nick had always been late at night when the other workers were long gone. It was Nick's design that not all of his employees should meet and know each other. A good business model when you're in his type of work. The only people I ever worked with in those long dark hours were Becka and a security guard named Jeff. But that guy didn't talk much, just drank coffee and watched old movies on his portable television. That's how I got to know Becka: at the warehouse. She'd been working for Nick … I don't know, maybe seven years longer than myself? Maybe more.

Nick got out, and I followed him to a side door. Earlier, he had given me his master code. I still had my own code, but along with my promotion came the responsibility of increased knowledge. Only myself, Nick, and one other employee had the master code. Nick entered it on a keypad and a little LED flashed from red to green. Inside, a large man stood up from a folding chair holding a crumpled crossword puzzle and a pencil.

"Nick," the man said, nodding. "Mark, brother, meet Powers."

The day shift guard named Mark reached out and shook my hand. He stood a foot taller than the both of us, and his palm looked like an elephant stump coming out of his black leather jacket.

"My pleasure," I said.

"Same."

"That your Benz out there?"

He nodded.

"Nice car."

"Thanks." He sat back down, his attention going to the folded newspaper. "I'm looking to trade it in. You in the market, let me know."

We walked directly across the hall, to a second door leading to a second warehouse. It was like those Russian Matryoshka dolls that get pulled apart to reveal smaller dolls nesting inside. A warehouse within a warehouse.

Nick took me to the door and knocked.

My previous work took place down the long hall to the left, in a room around the corner in the rear of the building, and I looked over my shoulder to where I normally worked with Becka. She was nowhere to be seen. Whatever Nick was about to show me was new, but I had a good idea of *exactly* what was behind that thick door.

A sliding viewing port opened, and a set of eyes looked out. The viewing port closed, and the sound of a heavy lock clacked from the hollows of the metal door. A moment later it opened and we stepped inside, shielding our eyes from the glaring light.

"Holy hell," I muttered, stepping into the room. The temperature was hot in there, muggy, and my eyes were practically blinded from the succession of thousand-watt high pressure sodium light bulbs lining the ceiling. A sea of tall marijuana plants filled the room, all set in arranged rows, some attached to an elaborate hydroponic system. The smell of fresh marijuana was as thick as soup.

Continue reading here: http://www.BrandonZenner.com
Or here: http://www.amazon.com/author/brandonzenner

RECEIVED APR 1 8 2019

DISCARD

CPSIA information can be obtained
at www.ICGtesting.com
Printed in the USA
LVHW041103140419
614129LV00003B/661